THE INNOCENT

THE INNOCENT

Richard E. Kim

THE INNOCENT

Houghton Mifflin Company
Boston

Second Printing c

Library of Congress Catalog Card Number: 68-31587
Printed in the United States of America

To Penelope, David, and Melissa,
in memory of First Lieutenant K., Republic of
Korea Army, d. April 13, 1955.

"In the dark of night I howl at the sky with all my sorrows . . . but there is nothing out there to listen to my story. Do you understand?"

Colonel Min

The author gratefully acknowledges the generous help given to him during the writing of this book by the John Simon Guggenheim Memorial Foundation.

THE INNOCENT

Chapter 1

The war came to an end late one evening in the summer of 1953, and before we could grow accustomed to the eerie stillness in the trenches and bunkers along the front line, I had already been relieved of my rifle company and was in Pusan, on my way to the United States, where I was to attend the Officers' Advanced Course at Fort Benning in Georgia. There were fifty-one of us in our group, young colonels and majors, fortunate survivors of the war, now waiting for a transport ship to sail for the Pacific. The mood of my fellow officers was expansive and their behavior exuberant; they had managed to live through the bloody war; they had done their share of work; and, having welcomed the opportunity to go abroad, to America, as if on a well-earned vacation, they gloried in their smart dress uniform in place of baggy fatigues, heavy boots, and steel helmets; and they dreamed of such exotic places as Hawaii, San Francisco, Chicago, and New York; but, above all, they indulged in the thrilling, seductive sensation of men who had not a care, not a worry in the world. They did not think about tomorrow and tomorrow, not for the moment anyway; like schoolchildren let out of the classroom, they were contented. The atmosphere was contagious, although I was able not to succumb to it. It was not because I did not approve of the euphoric state of mind my fellow officers seemed to float in, but because, at the time, I was deeply immersed in brooding speculation concerning the uncertain future of our country; I was trying to convince myself that the destiny of the nation was somehow inseparably bound up with what I was—or rather with what I became, as a result of the irrevocable, momentous decision I had made before I came down the battle-scarred mountains of the central front; I had decided to stay in the Army.

"Oh, but why, Major Lee?" Reverend Koh asked me. "Why, indeed? The war is over and done with and that's that. Your place from now on should be back in your university."

The way he said it startled me. For a moment, I was overcome with a certain shock of recognition that came from nostalgic remembrances of things past. I blurted out, "The late Colonel Chang used to say that to me. 'I hope the Army will let you go back to your university.' You know — that's what he used to say."

"Yes, I remember that," he said. "I remember that. It seems as though it was only yesterday when we . . ." His voice trailed off as he looked straight into my eyes.

It was in the winter of the first year of the war in Pyungyang that I had first met him, an Army chaplain; he had been out of the Army for a few years and was still working with the North Korean refugees on the Tent Island outside the harbor of Pusan. I had written him that I would be sailing from Pusan on my way to America, and he had come to see me off. He, too, had shed his steel helmet and fatigues for a straw hat, a faded blue denim shirt, and khaki trousers. In the shadow of his straw hat, his darkly tanned lean face twitched and he said quietly, "They are all dead now." He paused and touched my arm. "And here we are."

We were standing on the front deck of the transport ship, leaning against the rail, engulfed in the shimmering haze of a sizzling sun. It was hot. Under my shirt I could feel the sweat oozing down my chest and back and soddening my starched uniform; my chin felt the steamy heat through the collar whenever I tugged at the knot of my tie. I thought of the snow-covered Pyungyang, of the cold, frozen North Korea, and the chaplain announcing, "I am Chaplain Koh of the Third Brigade." The clean, crisp, wintry morning after the blizzard that had left behind it a thick, deep layer of dazzling white snow, and the . . .

"I think you are making a serious mistake," he was saying, "in staying in the Army. You are still young and you have a most rewarding career in teaching ahead of you. You've done your share in the war. What more could anyone expect you to sacrifice in the Army! The Army can get along without you now."

"Can it?" I said. The sweltering air choked my breath with a nauseating vapor of oil, grease, soot, and the rotten, polluted water thick with ugly scum. The stench that pervaded the humid air was intolerable and the deafening cacophony of noises from the piers and the nearby railroad yard unbearable. "Or, for that matter," I added, "can the country?"

He seemed jolted by my words. He gave me a penetrating look. "The country! Oh, this miserable country!" he cried out impatiently. "What is going to become of it! The country is staggering with hordes of hungry, weary refugees, the unemployed, the disabled, the homeless, and all that our politicians are doing is bickering, squabbling, cutting each other's throats. They are all rotten, I tell you, those politicians! They are nothing but a bunch of subservient, petty, greedy, inefficient nincompoops! My God, is this what we deserve after all these years of bloody fighting! The rich are getting richer, the poor are getting poorer. The police are nothing more than a one man's terrorist gang, spies are snooping around everywhere, extortions and tortures are rampant. Where is justice, where is democracy, where is freedom? Tell me, is this what the people have suffered through the war for? If our politicians couldn't care about the people during the war, I suppose they could care less about them now that the war is over. And what about the military? You know as well as I do about our generals! Those petty little ignorant men, pompous asses getting fatter and fatter from war-profiteering, scared to death of that one stubborn, blind, old fanatic locked up in the inner chamber of that idiotic palace of his in Seoul, surrounded by a gang of fawning little monkeys, running the country as if it were his private kingdom. Ah, your generals! What have we accomplished by all our suffering in the war? What have we gained? What have we saved and protected from the Communists!"

I had not expected this outburst from him. For a moment, I was overcome with his raw emotion. At last, I said, "Now you understand why I want to stay in the Army."

"No, I don't! I don't understand it at all. What do you expect from the Army? What do you think you can accomplish in the Army? Too many generals, and too many of them are beyond hope, and they have the power and they run the Army. You know that. It is hopeless!"

I could not restrain myself. "For a man of your calling, isn't that too despairing a thing to say!"

"Ah, but what can you do with them? Reform them? Make moral men out of them? If that's what you think you will be able to accomplish by staying in the Army, I am afraid you are being too idealistic."

His bitterness astonished me. I cried out without premeditation, "You disappoint me, Reverend! Considering that you are a man of God, the task of saving man can hardly be a venture too idealistic to be a pipe dream from your point of view!"

He glared at me with a flash of resentment. "Salvation of man through divine grace is one thing and . . ."

I did not let him finish. "And salvation of man through human endeavor, through man's sweat and blood, here and now, is another thing. Is that what you were going to say? My dear Reverend, forgive me for saying this, but, as I understand your faith . . ."

It was his turn to cut me short. "Am I not committing a sin of despair? Is that what you meant to say?"

I nodded.

He remained silent.

"Dear Reverend, do you remember having once said this to me in Pyungyang? You said, 'I hope the Army hasn't succeeded in corrupting you.' And you also said, 'I hope you are not yet capable of being too cynical or too blindly professional.' Do you remember?"

With a faint smile on his dark face, he said, "Did I say all that to you?"

"You know, your hope has not been in vain. But I want you to know that I am not alone in deciding to stay in the Army. There are many of us. Can you imagine? During the war, there was only one thought in our mind: to get it all over with so that we could return to wherever we came from. In my case, back to my teaching position at my university. Besides that thought, it seemed we had been too busy facing the enemy to think or worry about what was behind us. Then, one day, suddenly, we could turn around and sit down and look around; and what we saw was not pretty. So, what could we do? Close our eyes to shut off from our vision the ugly truth and realities that had existed behind our backs all along? My men were thinking and dreaming of nothing else but going home, going back to whatever they still had left. And what have they got left from the war? What sort of world will they be going back to? You know, we thought and thought about this, brooded about this, in the sudden silence on the mountains where there were no more enemies to fight and kill or be killed by, and we brooded and brooded about what we saw down the mountains and in our cities. My men, peasants and students, where will they find themselves and what will become of them? And what will become of me?"

"Were you afraid to return to the cities of man and to the ugly realities?"

"No, dear Reverend. It is precisely because I wanted to return to the ugly realities and do something about them that I decided to stay in the Army. And there is nothing idealistic about it. We realized that in a country like ours, an underdeveloped nation as Americans call it, a country that has just gone through a devastating war, the military has absorbed the elite of the nation, not by choice but through the practical necessities of the war. In a country like ours, where democratic institutions are still infantile and fragile and chaotic, where nearly a half century of foreign colonization has left it without sufficient administrative experiences and organizations, indeed, organizational abilities and technical skills necessary in a modern state, it is ironic and unfortunate in some ways but it is true that the military has emerged as the single largest, most efficiently organized and coherent establishment in the country. And it has the power. You must realize, Reverend, that as it stands now, our military has under its command nearly a million of our young men. And among these million young men is the best of the nation."

Reverend Koh stared hard at me. "If you are thinking of someday organizing a military coup d'état, you must be out of your mind!"

His remark, totally unexpected, shook me out of my theorizing. Taken aback, I said, "What gave you the idea that I was thinking of staging a coup d'état?"

"Good Lord, don't you realize where your train of thought is bound to lead you? Perhaps I am looking at it from the other side of the coin. The way I see it, our politicians are beyond hope of salvation. I must be very firm on that score. The same is true with our so-called generals. I must be adamant on that score, too. Now, then, as I see it, the combination, collaboration, and collusion of these two elements in our society is bound to bring about a worsening situation in the country, cancerous injustices, corruptions, asinine inefficiencies — in short, a chaotic, dog-eat-dog world. Then, someday, people like you, having stayed in the military, intelligent, hard-working, idealistic young people like you, will attain positions of some power and authority, influence, and decision-making in what you just said is the single largest, most efficiently organized institution in the nation which, it so happens, harbors the cream of the country, to say nothing of its awesome power. Well, then, when the country is about to go down the drain, and I think it will if things keep on going the way they are now, the only people who can save the country would be, well, people like you, and the only way you could accomplish that would be by taking over the country — in short, a military coup d'état. It all seems perfectly obvious to me. Only, I am a little surprised that I haven't really thought about it before."

"I have to confess, Reverend," I said, "that I haven't let my thoughts go that far before. All I knew when I was coming down from the mountains was that I had suddenly realized how important and significant an establishment the military was for the destiny and future of a nation such as ours. And I saw the corruption, stupidity, and ignorance of its leadership, and I wanted to stay right in the middle of this nation within the nation, so to speak, and . . ."

"And bring about its salvation!" he said. "Ah, you are an idealistic young man."

"If I am that, my dear Reverend, then you are . . ."

"An idealistic old man?" he said with a broad grin. "I am engaged in the divine salvation of man's soul and spirit, but what salvation, salvation of what are you engaged in? The evil in the world cannot be cured by human effort alone."

"No matter!" I said impatiently, and then with a sudden onrush of fierceness in my voice that shocked me, "We are engaged in the salvation of man by man, dear Reverend, salvation of man here and now, of what man has and knows he has, here and now, and to that end we are committed. Eternity is your affair, Reverend, but before the realm of eternity there is the realm of here and now, on earth, where I know I am breathing, living, living, Reverend, alive!"

He did not respond to the outburst which I could not control. He gazed at me for a long moment, then with an impatient gesture, he swung around, hands gripping the rail. He muttered in a whisper, "There, there, beyond those ships, on our island. The refugees and their hungry children. My God, oh, my God, how easy is it to tell *them* that man does not live by bread alone!"

Through the blinding haze I could see the Tent Island, forlorn outside the harbor, its silhouette wavering upon the dark, glistening water as if in a mirage.

He turned to me. There were tears in his eyes. "If people like you were ever to stage a coup d'état to save this unfortunate land," he said, "I wouldn't say you were all out of your mind."

I could not find words to reply.

"Well, Major Lee," he said gently, "bon voyage."

We shook hands. Little did we know, then, that in a year's time he, too, at the age of fifty, would be back in the Army as a chaplain once again.

I saw him again when I returned from Fort Benning, and again in Seoul when I left for America once more a few years later to attend the Command and General Staff College at Fort Leavenworth in Kansas. He was then chaplain of a combat team on the eastern front. Upon my graduation from the Command and General Staff College, I was first assigned to the staff of the Military Academy, then of the Defense College; and my duties later as a military attaché found me in Southeast Asia and in Europe. It was in Turkey where I was sent to observe a field exercise of NATO units that I received orders to return home. Back in Seoul, I was to be assigned to the Joint Chiefs of Staff.

But all this is by the way.

I was very young when I took part in organizing a coup d'état.

Chapter 2

There was no time to think. Our work on recruitment, organization, operational procedures, mobilization schedules, and battle plans had all been completed, impeccably, inexorably. The machinery of our coup d'état was set in motion under the control and supervision of the Command Group composed of nine officers, including myself. Although the formal leadership of our coup was exercised by a group of general officers of the Army, the Air Force, and the Marine Corps, headed by Lieutenant General Hyun who commanded the 7th Army Corps, it was the Command Group that had been entrusted with the day-to-day task of organization and operations. The Command Group was led by Colonel Min — General Hyun's confidant and special assistant.

Colonel Min was a good friend of mine from our civilian days in Seoul, where we both had taught at a university. From the first moment our coup d'état was conceived, there was no question in our minds that Colonel Min was to be our leader — although I, for one, had occasions to wonder, in spite of and perhaps because of my friendship with Colonel Min, just how it was that he, rather than the respected and popular General Hyun, had come to command the personal allegiance and loyalty of so many of us who would gladly die for his cause, which, needless to say, was our cause.

Yet as the launching date of our coup came closer, nothing else mattered except to ensure that each step in the countdown was executed with maximum precision. It was not the time, then, to brood on the *raison d'être* of our coup d'état; it was not the time for me to indulge myself in the privilege and luxury of withdrawing, even for a moment, into the secluded, tranquil recess of my private thoughts. For, we had already gone past the point of no return. There was only time to act.

It was August 18, four days before the coup. I was still in Seoul, supervising the activities of our network in the capital area. For the past several weeks, I had been operating out of my office at the headquarters of the Joint Chiefs of Staff. The headquarters at the time was housed, temporarily, in a building which used to be a department store in the very heart of Seoul near the bustling market by the South Gate. My office was in the basement which, for some reason, was called the ground floor; directly under the sidewalk, it was small, surrounded by heavy, gray walls without a window; there were two skylights of a sort, thick, opaque panes of glass in the ceiling, through which I could see day after day a countless number of shuffling feet of dimly discernible figures of people going to and from the market. It was always shadowy in my office so that I had to have on an overhead fluorescent lamp whose pallid light I detested. It had taken me a long time to get used to the office's darkness in the winter, heat in the summer, and to the incessant rumbling and thudding of the streetcars, to say nothing of the spasmodic growling from the nearby boiler room accompanied by the rushing of hot and cold water through the clanking, crackling water pipes that clung to my walls and ceiling like some monstrous tentacles. It was time to leave this room; by nightfall, I would leave Seoul and join the Command Group of our inner council which had been set up at the 7th Corps headquarters on the central front; it was time to act.

At ten minutes past five o'clock in the afternoon, Brigadier General Ahn, chief of the Special Projects Section, came down to my office. I was — ostensibly — one of his special assistants. The elevators in the building were out of order, so he had to walk down four flights of stairs to my basement office. He was gasping and kept on mopping his face with his handkerchief. He sat on the edge of my desk and loosened his tie. I switched on an electric fan for him.

"It's raining outside," he said, still out of breath. "Well, you wouldn't know the difference in this room. How can you breathe in here? It's absolutely stifling. You could have used the room next to my office. It's air-conditioned, as you know. It's usually very comfortable, but today it has been simply crazy. Freezing cold, and the maintenance people couldn't do anything about it. Like the damned elevators. Nothing seems to be working right today. I can't stand the heat in here. I suppose it's on account of my having been tied to my desk all day in that icehouse up there."

"Have you arranged for my leave?"

"Oh, yes. Your leave. I had a better idea, Major Lee, so I managed to have orders cut for you to go on an inspection and consultation tour. Of course, you don't have to explain to anyone what you are supposed to be doing. Security reasons, you understand. And, naturally, with this arrangement goes a top security clearance for you. The papers are all in order and my aide will bring them down to you shortly. Now, this way, you can be anywhere in the country at any time, and besides, you can be in a position to request official cooperation from any unit commander for transportation and such."

"Thank you, that sounds fine. How long may I be gone from here?"

"Two weeks," he said, getting off my desk. He offered me a cigarette, which I declined. "Two weeks. Will that be time enough for you?"

"Yes, I think so."

He puffed on his cigarette. "Two weeks is a long time."

I did not respond.

"I am becoming a little tense, to tell you the truth. Two weeks is a long time. Anything can happen in two weeks. Anything unpredictable, you understand. There was a talk this morning that the Defense Minister was planning a trip to Taipei and might ask me to come along. Some wild ideas of his about a joint sabotage operation. You know, their agents posing as Chinese officers in North Korea and so on. Well, of course, all this is rather vague at the moment."

"I understand, General," I said. "I won't be gone for two weeks. In fact, I shall be back in Seoul soon."

"I am glad to hear that. I will be ready."

"Yes."

"Look, Major. I suppose you are not in a position to tell me when . . . ah, never mind about that."

"I am sorry. You will hear from General Hyun in due course."

"Yes, of course. Do give him my regards, will you? And please do assure him of my loyalty."

"Yes."

"Who will be in charge here while you're gone?"

"Lieutenant Colonel Hwang of the Airborne Brigade. He will be in touch with you."

"Yes. I know him personally."

"I will be in touch with you, too."

"Yes. Do keep me posted, will you? General Hyun has the personal loyalty of all the Special Projects personnel, including our Commando Groups."

"Thank you."

"Oh, I almost forgot. What about your transportation? Would you like to fly out? I can arrange that if you wish."

"No, thank you. That might be a little too conspicuous."

"Well, it's raining hard, anyway. I'll have my aide get you a jeep, then."

"That will be fine."

"Well, good luck."

We shook hands.

"Do give my best regards to the general."

I nodded.

He was about to go out of my office, when he turned around and came back to me.

"Please pass this on to General Hyun," he said. "I have a report that General Mah has been to see the President quite frequently in the last three days. And today he's spent the entire morning inside the headquarters of the American Command, holed up with their Intelligence people."

I had that information already through my own sources. "Yes. I'll report it to the general."

"Do that, will you? I don't like the way Mah's been bustling around these days, whatever he may be up to. He is a dangerous man."

Major General Mah, forty-three-year-old former sergeant major in the Japanese Army, was the head of the special branch of the Armed Forces Intelligence, a position which, through an anomalous Presidential order, gave him absolute control not only of the Secret Police but also of the elite Presidential Brigade stationed in Seoul, as well as the Metropolitan Police.

"Yes," I said. "He is a man we have to watch closely."

"He is an evil man," said General Ahn, "as you know."

"There is no question about that."

"Well, what are you going to do with him?"

I met his challenging eyes with silence.

"What is the decision of the Command Group on him? Shouldn't I know?"

He was going a little too far. "What is your suggestion, sir?"

"Kill him."

I stared at him.

"I say we kill him before he gets us all," he said. "Don't you agree, Major?"

There was something peculiar in the tone of his voice which unnerved me, its chilling, matter-of-fact bluntness tempered, however, at the same time, with creepy solicitousness. "That will be up to the Command Group," I said. "Don't you agree, sir?" He had pledged himself to the decisions of the Command Group, of which I was a member, as he knew, while he was not. With a deliberate casualness, I added, "I am sure the Command Group will come up with a recommendation for General Hyun."

"If General Mah starts sniffing around," he said, "and I can bet my life that he already has, then we are in trouble. There is bound to be a security leak sooner or later, and if Mah catches on to it, you know we've had it. We'll all be shot. There'll be no question about that. So I say again we kill him soon, now."

I watched him, this thirty-eight-year-old veteran of innumerable Commando raids and clandestine operations in North Korea, this brutally efficient, one of the most decorated young heroes of the war, this professional soldier with a blood-reeking service record. His darkly handsome face, its roughly textured profile accentuated by an inch-long scar on his left chin, was topped with short, cropped hair; he carried his head slightly tilted to the right, thanks, he would say, to his right leg on which he limped as a result of a bayonet wound. He was sinewy and leaned on a straight, black cane with a silver top. A year before, I had seen him (he was a colonel then) at the Military Academy when he lectured the cadets on one of his Commando operations; in front of a large map he retraced his tactical movements using his cane as a pointer, but it was not long enough when he had to reach the top of the map; with a click and a swish the top of his cane shot out a needle-sharp dart which, flashing in the light over his head, tore into the map; and the cadets, with a roaring cheer, adored their hero . . .

"Major, did I say something wrong?"

I shook my head. "No, no."

"I seem to have shocked your sensibility," he said almost in a whisper, "but you can't expect to reform an evil man like Mah with the loving logic of a heart as humane as yours."

I felt my face flush, with what I did not know.

He drew himself up to me. "Think of what Mah stands for in this country. The very symbol of evil, corruption, and injustice. Think of those hundreds of people, innocent people, he's assassinated, thrown in jail, and tortured. This little dictator catering to the whims of his boss. Think of our colleagues he's broken and exiled."

"I am fully aware of his crimes, General," I said, suddenly overcome with a profound, disturbing sense of anger and frustration, "and the punishment he deserves."

"Ah, then, you do agree with me, don't you, Major," he said triumphantly, "that we can't cure evil by simply locking it up in a jail!"

A strange, undefinable rage seized me, but I did not speak.

His hand slashed the thick, gray, smoke-filled air. "Evil must be wiped out, Major!" he said; then, again in a whisper, "I still think General Mah, the little caesar, should be liquidated, don't you?"

I retorted, "The evil in the world cannot be cured by . . ." But I could not finish my sentence: I did not know how, and then his jeering voice stopped me short mercifully, "Idealistic, aren't you!"

Chapter 3

The moment I drove through the East Gate and into the suburbs of Seoul, I knew I had made a mistake by not taking along a driver with me as General Ahn's aide had advised. After my talk with General Ahn, I had wanted to be alone; I had not relished the thought of either making small talk or not speaking at all with another human being who was traveling with me. But I had underestimated the weather. The rain was not falling hard when I left Seoul, but it became heavier and heavier. By the time I had driven barely one third of the way from Seoul to Chunchun the rain turned into a torrential downpour. The canvas top and side curtains of the jeep were utterly useless. I was drenched from top to bottom. The rain hit the windshield so hard and in such a heavy volume that the windshield wipers hardly moved. The unpaved road became thick with slimy mud. The jeep, of World War II vintage, a hand-me-down from the Americans, groaned and rattled and squeaked. I had a shivery feeling that its headlights were getting dimmer and dimmer, its windshield wipers were about to snap off, and it would suddenly whimper and tremble and come to a halt, leaving me alone in the darkness in the maddening rain. But it pulled through. I managed to drive into a small village along the road and scurry into a dingy little truck stop of a sort, where I waited exactly forty-five minutes for the rain to stop.

It was nearly ten o'clock. I was to meet Colonel Min by midnight. I drove on as fast as I could on the muddy, winding, mountain road. The mountain air after the rain was chilly. With my clothes still damp I was shivering. When I came down the last steep mountain before Chunchun, the air became warmer and heavier. I began to see and feel sticky, steamy vapor all around me. A little after half past ten, I drove into Chunchun. It was hot and humid. Fog was rising from the slough of the narrow main street. Lights wavered dimly from a few shops and restaurants and teahouses that were still open. At the end of the street, a convoy of seven Army trucks was parked along the road. Soldiers were climbing off the trucks out from under the canvas covers. "Twenty minutes' break!" someone was shouting. A dirty white Military Police jeep passed my jeep, splashing muddy water, and stopped alongside the convoy. I parked the jeep in front of a teahouse. Its neon sign flashed in green and red "Blue Bird" both in Korean and English. Inside, a phonograph was playing a chanson, a tremulous, nasal, French female voice whining "My little heart flutters like a little dove . . ." Debris-ridden slimy water was gurgling down the gutter, which I leaped over. I stood by the door under the neon sign. I checked my watch; it was five minutes to eleven; I was nearly an hour late. The door was pulled open from inside. Bluish light fell on me. I stepped back into the flashing neon light of green and red. Second Lieutenant Cho, Colonel Min's aide, came out.

"I saw your jeep just pulling up," he said. "How are you, sir?" We shook hands. "Sorry I am so late," I said.

"Oh, that's all right, sir. What matters is that you are here. Good to see you, sir. I can't tell you how glad and relieved I am to see you. Colonel Min will be very happy to see you. They are all waiting for you, sir."

I nodded.

"Have you had dinner, sir?"

"No, I haven't had time," I said. "Do you think I can get something to eat in there? I could certainly use some coffee."

"They have sandwiches, sir. And coffee, of course. Come on in, Major. We have to wait for my driver to come back here, sir. I've sent him for gasoline."

We walked inside. The room was small and square, with pinkish walls haphazardly covered with a few indistinct paintings and travel posters. Half a dozen or so paper lanterns, the middle one in the shape of a bird with wings outstretched, hung from the ceiling, swaying and revolving in the breeze stirred up by a large, tall, electric fan by the counter. There were four enlisted men at a corner table, the only other customers. We took a table near the door. A teen-age girl in a dark blue, polka-dotted dress came over to us, shuffling her rubber clogs, and took the order. A young woman behind the counter was changing the record on the phonograph. Another dreary chanson. The young girl came back, wiped the table with a sponge, and took the ashtray away. The table smelled sour. My clothes were still damp, and in the stale humid air my face was perspiring. One of the enlisted men walked over to the counter. "How about playing something a little more gay, eh?" he said to the young woman, who shrugged but said nothing and did nothing. The soldier looked back toward his comrades and wagged his head, grimacing. They all got up from the table and trooped out the door. The woman snorted.

"You see, sir," said Lieutenant Cho with a grin, "this is the quietest place in town."

The sandwiches and two cups of coffee came; a thin cut of Spam clamped between two slices of pasty bread. The coffee was good.

"I am sorry you had to come all the way down here to meet me," I said.

"It's my pleasure, sir. Besides, Colonel Min wanted to make sure you arrived safely, if you know what I mean, sir."

"He wasn't worried, was he?"

"Not really, sir. But when you called from Seoul, we were having a rainstorm out there and Colonel Min didn't like the idea of your driving all the way up there alone. The roads are pretty bad, sir, and it's foggy, too. So he asked me to come down here and meet you. I brought two MP's with me." He added, "Just in case, sir."

I smiled. "Two MP's to guide us through the fog?"

He was quite serious. "I meant, sir, just in case General Ham decided to pull a dirty trick."

Lieutenant General Ham commanded the 4th Army, to which the 7th Corps, our Corps, belonged. "What makes you think he might? Rather, what has made Colonel Min think that General Ham might do that?"

Lieutenant Cho lowered his voice. "As you know, sir, he called Colonel Min this morning and said he would come out to the Corps headquarters. Colonel Min said he would be glad to come to General Ham's headquarters, but General Ham insisted that he would rather not see him there."

"Well, is General Ham out there now?"

"He is out there all right, sir, but not at our place. He flew in this afternoon in his chopper, just before the rain started, said a few words to General Hyun, then went right on to the front to the 34th Division."

"That's our Division," I said. "I mean, the Division commander is our man."

"Well, sir, he is General Ham's cousin, on his maternal side, as you know."

"That shouldn't make much difference to us. We know where the Division commander stands. If General Ham counts on that cousin business, he is quite stupid, more so than I would have expected him to be."

Lieutenant Cho's young face looked angry. "I just don't like the way General Ham is playing his little game with us. That's what Colonel Min said to me, sir. 'Ham is playing his dirty little game and I don't like it!' Colonel Min was furious."

I finished my sandwiches. "I can't quite imagine what Colonel Min looks like when he is furious, as you say." I smiled. "I've never seen him scowling or heard him shouting in fury, have you?"

"I see what you mean, sir," he smiled, too. "But I know he was furious. It's the way he gets suddenly so quiet, without a word, then as suddenly he says things. So calmly, too, and you know he means every word of what he says. I should know him, sir, after all. I've known him for more than ten years. He has practically raised me, sir, since I lost my parents."

"I didn't know that." I finished my coffee. "So — how did the others take General Ham's behavior? Were they furious, too?"

"Of course, sir!" He pushed the empty plate and the cups to the side of the table. "First, General Ham wanted to see Colonel Min. Alone. Just the Colonel. Then, he called from the 34th and said he wanted Colonel Min *and* the Command Group to come out to the 34th."

"When?"

"Tonight, sir."

"When tonight? It's already past eleven."

"Actually, he said one o'clock."

"For heaven's sake."

"That's exactly it, sir. According to Colonel Min, General Ham said, 'I hope one o'clock is not too late for you all. I've been suffering from a severe case of insomnia lately worrying about you people, so I'll be fully awake.' Can you imagine, sir?"

"That's melodramatic!" I said. "What is he up to?"

"That's it, sir. He is up to no good. For one thing, he wants to see who is in the Command Group."

"That won't help his game," I said.

"Divide and conquer. Do you think that's what he is up to, sir? It won't work, of course."

"Of course not. We'll see what happens."

"I don't know what you think of him, sir, but I am convinced that he should be . . ."

I cut him short. "That's enough, Lieutenant."

"Yes, sir."

I tapped him on the shoulder. "Why don't we go outside?"

We got up. I paid for the sandwiches and coffee and we walked out. The fog had become thicker. I could barely make out the other side of the street. The convoy had left. I took the side curtains off the jeep and we climbed in.

"It's just that this business with General Ham is getting on my nerves, Major. I say this again, sir. I can't tell you how relieved I am to have you out there with Colonel Min."

"What are you talking about?"

"The Colonel's been a little strange lately. He has been listening to that music again."

"What?"

He shrugged. "That spooky music, sir. Oh, by the way, could you get that record I've asked you to get for Colonel Min?"

"Oh, yes, I almost forgot about it." I reached for my suitcase in the back seat and took out the record. I handed it to him. "Is that what you call spooky music?" I could not help chuckling.

"Not the first part of it, sir, the piece with chorus singing and drums banging away and trumpets and tubas and everything. I know the tune." He shrugged. "The first part is all right, sir. It is invigorating stuff. But the second part. That's positively spooky, like funeral music. Is that by the same composer, sir?"

I nodded. "Well, I see what you mean, although it is not funeral music and it does not really sound like it."

He was quiet for a moment; then, abruptly, "Well, anyway, thank you for getting it for him. The one he has has a couple of big scratches."

"Is that what worried you? Well, I brought you the new record."

"No, no, I didn't mean that, sir. What I meant was that he's been listening to this record again lately. For hours sometimes. That's not quite right, sir."

"Lieutenant, come out with it. What's on your mind?"

"Nothing really, sir. I am sorry I blabbed. I am a little worried about Colonel Min, that's all, sir. I know he's thinking something serious and deep and I know something is troubling him, because when he is like that, listening to that spooky music alone in the dark for hours, it means he doesn't want to be disturbed. And I know, too, sir, that something is going to happen, but when it comes to serious matters I am not much of a help to him. So you see, sir, why I am relieved to see you. Maybe he will talk with you about whatever he has on his mind." He gave me a sheepish smile. "You two are," he said, then in halting English, "birds of a feather." And, in Korean again, "If you don't mind my saying so, sir."

I laughed. "You mean, two blue birds!" I gave him a tap on the shoulder. "Don't worry. He will be all right. I'll keep an eye on him for you." We laughed loudly in warm comradeship, yet I could not help feeling a little disturbed deep within me, for I, too, had seen Colonel Min when I knew he was seething with a mute agony over things I could not fathom; and then, like a man possessed, he would wander out of our apartment and walk the silent, deserted streets of Seoul, sometimes till dawn; and the late Park — how I missed him! — he and I would follow him discreetly for some distance, then we would quietly come abreast of him and we would go to a shabby little cardboard hut near the Chungechun, where an old North Korean refugee couple would fry us buckwheat pancakes and give us the fire-breathing corn whisky of the northern plains. Min had only a month before come to the South from the Communist-dominated North. The three of us, all teaching at a university, shared a three-room apartment behind the Duksoo Palace; but Min did not stay with us too long: he accepted a position of schoolmaster in a small village in Chulla province in the far south and left Seoul, which he detested, where political turmoil was at an extreme, with intrigue, riots, assassinations, factional mass murders shrouding the lives of the people. That was in the fall of nineteen-forty-seven. Then in the winter of forty-eight, in the middle of the Communist-led Yusoo Mutiny of a regiment of the recently created Army, Min appeared in Seoul and told us that he had joined the Army but he would not explain to us why. We kept in touch with one another through the years before and after the war. I saw him once in Pyungyang and later on the western front where he commanded a Ranger Brigade. Our friendship continued and when he first conceived of plans for our coup d'état I was one of the few he confided in. That was in Paris, nearly a year before, at a sidewalk café not far from the Arch of Triumph, two forlorn Orientals in a European city sitting next to a boisterous group of young American tourists, boys and girls; immersed in our shared, private world of frustrated nostalgia for our war-torn country, our country, for better or worse, with its corrupt society, its inefficient, dishonest politicians, and its chaotic, degenerating, despairing day-to-day existence, all tottering under a ruthless dictatorship that was inexorably leading the people of the land to the brink of ruin — all this in the face of an equally ruthless dictatorship in the North, against which they had fought in the war to save the . . . but to save what? The next morning when I saw him off to the lands of Scandinavia at Orly Airport, we knew that our minds had met and that we would prevail.

Lieutenant Cho's driver and the two MP's returned. It was close to midnight.

"All right," I said, to no one in particular. "Let's get started."

The MP's went with Lieutenant Cho's driver, ahead of us, and Lieutenant Cho drove my jeep. The fog had become so thick and heavy that we nearly had to grope our way out of the town as if blindfolded. When we reached the end of the main street, where at a dimly lit rotary three roads met and parted, I looked back toward the now deserted town. I could not see it any more. It was as though the impenetrable fog had waited for me to leave, then swiftly, silently smothered it out of my sight.

Chapter 4

Outside Chunchun, the fog became somewhat whiter than it was back in town and the air less humid and stifling as we labored higher and higher up the slippery, winding, mountain road toward the north. Though barely visible, I knew there was a deep ravine that dropped abruptly from the left shoulder of the snaky road that crept along the sharply cut side of steep, rocky mountains. The cloudlike fluffy fog swayed like a floating ceiling over the ravine between the mountains. Gazing hard ahead, trying to see through the wall of blinding fog, I could not help feeling that, at any moment, we might crash into an unseen, unseeable bluff, or miss a turn and plunge into the unfathomable ravine. But Lieutenant Cho was a good driver and I soon put the dismal thought out of my mind. The taillights of the jeep ahead of us, though dim and blurry and intermittently out of sight, gave us a bearing of a sort. Thus reassured, I suddenly felt drowsy and inert; I stretched myself, leaning my head against the back of my seat.

Without taking his eyes off the road, Lieutenant Cho said, "You must be tired, sir, having driven in that rain. We'll be there in about half an hour and once we get there I am afraid you may not have time for sleep. So, how about taking a quick nap, sir?"

I pulled myself up. "I guess I am tired, but I don't think I could sleep even if I wanted to. I seem to have too much on my mind."

With a nod, he said, "I see what you mean, sir."

We drove on in silence.

Then, abruptly, he said, with a quick glance my way, "Colonel Min isn't really my uncle, sir. Did you know that, sir?"

"How on earth did you know I've been thinking about him? No, I didn't know." I looked at him as if I saw him for the first time. He was twenty-five or -six, big and muscular with heavy shoulders and long arms. He wore his cap deep onto his face, so that the visor almost hid his big, round, gentle eyes; a pug nose, full lips, a square jaw that always made me think of a bulldog; he was fanatically loyal to Colonel Min. They were from the same town north of Pyungyang.

"Colonel Min was a very close friend of my father's, sir. My father was several years older but they were good friends. We lived practically next door back in the North. His father was very old and Colonel Min was the only child, so I think his parents really did everything for him. Not that they were rich or well-to-do, sir; as a matter of fact, they weren't. Oh, they had some land but it wasn't much, but his father, who was one of the most respected men in town on account of his revolutionary activities against the Japanese when he was young and so the Japanese cops really gave him a hard time — anyway, sir, his father saved up all the money he could so his son could get an education. I guess our family did have some money and when my father went to Tokyo to go to a college there, Colonel Min's father sent his son, too. My father and he went to the same college. That was in nineteen-forty-one. But they had to come home in a couple of years because the Japanese were pressuring them to volunteer for their army. Well, that's what I learned from my father."

"Yes, the Japanese were quite hard-pressed then. At first they wouldn't even think of drafting us because they didn't trust us. But they became really desperate later on."

"Then they started drafting us, do you remember, sir?"

"I barely missed being drafted myself."

"All that business made Colonel Min the hero of our town."

"Oh?"

"Colonel Min would chew me out if he finds out I've told anyone about it, sir, but I guess you are all right to let in on it. Hasn't he ever told you about it, sir?"

I shook my head.

"That's more like him, sir, as you know. Anyway, when the Japs came around to draft him, he refused to go. Naturally, they threw him in jail and beat him up. Then they took him out a week or so later to send him down to Pyungyang, I guess, to put him in a concentration camp or something like that for people like him. Well, he managed to escape on the way and disappeared. My father didn't have to worry about the draft because he had three children, my big brother and sister and myself. And my father was sick, I think he had tuberculosis, so they let him be. Then, the Japs got hold of Colonel Min's father, who was almost seventy then, and threw him in jail and beat him up. I was only a kid at that time but I still remember Colonel Min's father when he was finally let out of the police station, I mean, the way he had been tortured by the Japs, or to be more exact, sir, though this really makes me feel ashamed, he was tortured by Korean detectives working for the Japs. Colonel Min's father died a few days after he came home, and his mother, the poor old lady, she died, too, a few weeks after that. I went to both funerals and I still remember my mother crying and crying, and my grandfather, too, the first time I ever saw him cry. Then, after the funeral of Colonel Min's father, my father went out of town for a few days, presumably to go to Pyungyang to see a specialist at a hospital; but he was trying to get in touch with Colonel Min, who was hiding in some mountain. My father finally found him and told him about his father's death and the circumstances. His mother was still alive then."

"Did he come back to the town?"

"Yes, he did, long enough to see his mother. I guess my father arranged it somehow. Yes, he did see his mother, sir, but that was the trouble."

"What do you mean?"

"After seeing his mother, Colonel Min took off once more and there was no trace of him. But I think the Japs smelled something and there was this one particular Korean detective who was hated by everyone in town and he came to the house, the Colonel's house, sir, and interrogated the old woman. I am sure he beat her up because I could hear her wailing even from our house and my mother was cursing this detective and the Japs all in one breath. But, apparently, the damned detective couldn't get anything out of her, so he took one of the maids, a teen-age girl, to the police station and beat her up. The poor girl spilled everything and I think she had brought food and clothes to Colonel Min once or twice before, so she knew where he was. Anyway, sir, the detective went after the Colonel but that's the last thing anybody ever saw of that bastard again. He never came back." He turned his face to me as if to solicit my reaction.

I remained silent.

"The son of a bitch just disappeared, sir," he said. "But we all knew what happened to him."

"Did you?"

"Of course, sir. Not that anyone ever found his body, but the whole town knew he was dead. Somewhere."

We had by then left the mountains behind us and were driving on a straight road, the main route of supply, that was in the bottom of the valley. Here and there, lights began to flicker in the damp, misty, night air. We were passing an American depot, with rows of Quonset huts and tents, oil drums, and trucks and tanks, all lit up by floodlights.

"Then, a few months before the Japs surrendered, Colonel Min showed up in town and that was really something. My father must have known that he was coming, so he took me with him to the railway station, and would you believe it, sir, he had become a second lieutenant in the Japanese Army!"

"I knew that part."

"He looked really good, sir, I must say. In uniform and riding boots and a saber and a pistol and everything. I still remember that there was a group of Japanese soldiers and sailors at the station and they all saluted him and the cops in town couldn't lay a finger on him. The whole town simply adored him. He was our hero. Not because he became an officer in the Jap Army, of course not, sir, but because, well, you know what I mean, sir."

"Should I?"

"Sir?"

"Never mind."

The jeep ahead of us came into full view, though blurred by the fog, for a moment as it crossed a pontoon bridge. To our left, a mountain brook roared by, its swollen water thrashing against invisible rocks. Lieutenant Cho shifted the jeep down into a lower gear and, turning left, steered it onto the bridge which, undulating and swaying in the turbulent foamy eddies, squeaked and groaned. Beyond the bridge, we turned to the right.

"It won't be long, sir," he said. "Colonel Min will be really happy to see you."

I nodded. "When did you see him again?"

"Beg your pardon, sir?"

"Colonel Min came home as a Japanese officer. When did you see him again?"

"Well, sir, I forgot to mention that he had brought a Japanese officer with him. A real Japanese, I mean, sir. I don't know much about that, sir. What this Japanese officer was doing with the Colonel or what the Colonel was doing with him in our town, well, no one explained to me. But it appeared as though they were good friends, because they both stayed in the Colonel's house and they were both invited to our house for dinner and all. I am sure lots of people in town were puzzled by all that. My mother, I remember, was a little wary of having the Japanese officer, I think he was a captain, in the house but she didn't say anything when my father simply said that this Japanese officer was Colonel Min's guest and so he was our guest, too; it was all a little mysterious, particularly when the three of them, my father and the Colonel and this Japanese captain, went into my father's study after dinner and talked all night. Then, four days later, Colonel Min and his Japanese guest left the town and I guess they went back to their post somewhere in Manchuria or near the Mongolian border."

"That must have been not too long before the Liberation. Did you see the Colonel after the 15th of August? I mean, in North Korea?"

"Yes, sir. Just once." He looked my way with a grin. "It's a funny thing, sir. I saw him just once before I would see him again in the South and it was in a public bathhouse."

"In your hometown?"

"No, sir. In Pyungyang. It was purely accidental, sir. I was visiting my grandparents there and one morning I went to a bathhouse nearby. It was very early in the morning and I was the only one in the big tub. Very steamy and vapory, almost like being in this fog."

The fog was getting thick again as we continued to descend into a lower, flatter region of the valley.

"I was having a good time, swimming and splashing around in that big tub, all by myself for a while, then someone stepped inside. I remember all this vividly because it was in the winter, sometime in January of forty-six, and very cold outside, and when he opened the door I could feel the cold air rushing in with him. The door to the tub room had to be banged shut and he apparently didn't give the door a kick, so the door swung open again letting the cold air in. I remember I shivered, although I was in the hot water up to my chest, and asked the man to please close the door. 'You got to give it a good kick.' Something like that, sir. Well, it was so steamy inside that in spite of the cold air this man just brought in

with him, I couldn't make him out too well, that is, until he quietly
slid into the tub, and it was him."

I could not help laughing. "A naked confrontation, wouldn't you
say?"

He did not laugh with me.

"Did he recognize you?"

"Of course, sir," he said quietly. "We recognized each other instantly, that is, sir, while we were in the tub."

"What do you mean by that?"

"I mean, sir, that *I* couldn't recognize him once we were out of the
tub and got into our clothes. I just couldn't believe my eyes."

"I don't quite follow you."

"I got out of the tub first and went out of the room, dried myself
and put my clothes on, my school uniform. I waited for him. Well,
he came out, as skinny as he is today, and got the key from the at-
tendant for his locker and took his clothes out and they were the
uniform of an officer in the Communist Army, which was called by
no particular name at the time. I couldn't believe it."

"Why not?"

"I don't really know, sir. I just couldn't believe that he would
ever become a Communist."

"Well, he was not and he is not a Communist. You know that."

"I know that, sir. But when I saw him in that uniform, I couldn't
say a word to him. I think I just froze. You see, sir, my father at
the time was having troubles with the local Communists in our
town and with the Russians, and the Red Guard troops and all the
Communists were having a field day. Do you know what I mean,
sir? Taking over everything and terrorizing and throwing people in
jail. My father was involved in the local government, actually a self-
rule committee of a sort, which the Communists were trying to take
over, and they had the support of the Russian troops stationed in
town and, well, my father was kind of expecting to be arrested or
assassinated almost any day. Oh, yes, sir, there were lots of assassinations those days. So, when I saw Colonel Min like that in the

bathhouse, I got sort of frightened of him. I couldn't believe that he was one of them."

"He had just arrived in the country from China," I said. "He told me a little bit about that. He was in China just before the Japanese surrendered and he was with the Korean Brigade, I think, of the Chinese Red Army. Then, he came back to Korea with the brigade. He must have just arrived in Pyungyang when you saw him."

"That's how it all turned out to be, sir. Do you know what he did after that?"

I shook my head. "No. He never told me. All I know is that he crossed the border in the spring of forty-seven and came to Seoul, where I met him. We both taught at a university for a while and roomed together. Well, you know that part."

"Yes, sir. Well, soon after I saw him at the bathhouse, about a month or so later I believe, sir, he came home."

"Still as a Red Army officer?"

"No, sir. He was out of it."

"Did he work with your father, I mean, in politics?"

"No, sir. He wouldn't have anything to do with it. I know my father and others tried to persuade him to join their party and be in the local government. Take charge of the police, something like that, sir. But, no, he wouldn't hear of it. He simply went out of town and settled right into a little house on the small farm his family owned. 'I want to be a farmer.' That's what he's supposed to have said to my father and the others."

I smiled. "Colonel Min, a farmer?"

"Oh, he was quite serious about it, sir. He worked hard on the farm, too. We used to see him once in a while in town, on market days, selling the vegetables and fruits from his farm. Can you believe that, sir? But that didn't last long. One day, some Communist big shot from Pyungyang came into our town with a detachment of Red Guard troops and drove out to his farm and took him with them outside the town where the Russians were."

"Under arrest?"

"I imagine so, sir, though I don't know the details. Anyway, the next night, a little past midnight, he staggered into our house, all bloody and his clothes torn, and he had a Russian submachine gun in his hand. I didn't know what was going on and before I knew what was what, my father and my brother took him out of the house and that's the last thing I saw of him until we came to the South. I imagine my father helped him get in touch with a border smuggler and got him across the border to the South. After that, there was a rumor in town that Colonel Min had been taken into the Russian garrison and tortured there but he managed to escape, and that he shot the Russian garrison commander and the Korean from Pyungyang, whoever that was."

I kept silent. I tried to visualize the scene of the escape, the scene of the battle inside the Russian garrison, in full detail, in flesh and blood, but I could not. All I could see in my mind's eye was the flashing image of Colonel Min with his lean body and austere face, his clothes torn and spattered with blood, his and others', clutching a Russian submachine gun in both hands and firing it away in his peculiarly quiet way as though possessed by — but by what?

"We came to the South in forty-eight, sir, in the spring. By then the Communists had completely taken over the North and what little land and property we had was confiscated by the Communists. My father was branded as a bloodsucking landlord and so on and tried by the so-called people's court. Well, they kicked us out of our house and we were forbidden to live in our town. So, we lived like beggars for a while because no town or village would have us and I think the idea was that we would eventually surrender ourselves to the concentration camp or labor camp. So, we crossed the border, giving everything we had to a border smuggler. Those were the border smugglers' heydays, as you must know."

"Did all your family come?"

"No, sir. Just my parents and my sister and myself. My grand-parents died soon after we were forced out of the house by the Communists. They were almost seventy years old then and I think they simply couldn't take it any longer. You see, sir, we nearly starved to death, all of us, and my grandparents couldn't make it through. And then my big brother, who was a high school student in Pyungyang, became involved with an anti-Communist underground organization and took part in demonstrations and raids and was shot to death in one of the street demonstrations staged by students in Pyungyang. He was big like me, sir, and he was a good brother. He went to the Second Public High School in Pyungyang, a damn good school which I always hoped to go to someday."

"I was in Pyungyang during the war," I said. "I've seen the school, beautiful buildings and a pretty view of the city."

He was silent.

I felt uncomfortable. "I knew your parents were dead but I didn't know they had made it to the South."

He maintained his silence, then broke it quietly. "It seems to have made no difference, sir. In the end, the Communists got them anyway."

"Did they die during the war?" I said. "I lost mine in Seoul."

"My parents were killed by the Communists before the war, sir. Long before the war. They were murdered."

To my surprise and relief, there was not a trace of bitterness in his voice. He went on, not giving me a chance to say words of comfort.

"I should have said they were butchered, sir. Because that's what the Communists did to them. We, the four of us, were living in a small village in the South at the time. With Colonel Min. You didn't know that, did you, sir?"

"No. Was that when he was a schoolmaster down there?"

"Yes, sir. After we escaped from the North, we lived in Seoul for a month or so with our relatives; then, somehow, my father got in touch with Colonel Min, who asked him to bring everyone down to where he was. My father didn't have a job and he was sick and there wasn't much he could do in Seoul. Colonel Min said he had a

patch of farmland in the South which he got from the village in lieu
of a salary as the schoolmaster. Did you know that the village was
so poor it couldn't pay him much in money? The school was a
three-room affair and although he was called the schoolmaster, actually there were only two other teachers. Anyway, he said we could
all come and live with him for a while until we knew more about
what we could or should do. In the meantime, he had a small house
for all of us and we could all work on the land and get enough to
eat. So we all got together. The house and the farmland were just
outside the village. He got me into a local high school in a nearby
town but my sister stayed home to help the parents. We did all
right, sir. Oh, we weren't exactly well off, but at least we didn't
starve. My father's health got better, too, and he was also thinking
of getting a teaching job, maybe, at a local high school in town."

"What did your father study in the university?"

"Philosophy and literature, sir, the same subjects as Colonel
Min's. So, you see, sir, my father could have taught at school. Then
the Yusoo Mutiny of the Communists broke out, and, although we
were quite a distance away from the areas occupied by the Communists, there were lots of disturbances and activities by the Communist guerrillas in our area. And, one day, Colonel Min, who had
come into town on errands and met me there, and I went home together on his bicycle. There were villagers milling around the
house, all suddenly quiet on seeing the two of us. Then, as suddenly, everyone started talking, saying something to us, shouting,
and all I could make out was that six Communist guerrillas had
come down to the village from the surrounding mountains and
raided the police station and killed the three-man force and, then
. . . Colonel Min and I rushed into the house — and they were
there, lying in blood, my father, mother, and my little sister, their
clothes stripped off and . . . and hacked to death. All I could see
at first was the color of red, red everywhere, and I remember saying to myself — the Reds have done it, the Reds, the Reds have
done it . . . And a man came in and said somebody had gone into
town to alert the police. The guerrillas had just left the village and

headed back up into the mountains. Colonel Min ran out of the house, with me following him, and we went to the police station. The three policemen were all dead, shot and hacked. Colonel Min went inside the station. 'See if you can find guns, anything,' he said to me. But there wasn't a gun to be found. Nothing. Then Colonel Min ran to the house of one of the policemen who was from the village and practically ripped the house apart. There, we found a carbine, a pistol, and a case of grenades. Unlike the others, this policeman slept in his own house and, so, he had a private arsenal just in case. So began the three-day hunt for the Communist guerrillas, just Colonel Min and I going after them. It took us three days to catch up with them. The Colonel knew mountains. Oh, he sure knew mountains. He knew how to track them down! One night we finally spotted their hideout, a little cave. We threw grenades in. None of them came out. Colonel Min wanted me to stay outside with grenades, just in case there were other guerrillas nearby who might appear. He took the carbine and was about to go into the cave when two guerrillas came out of it firing their guns. Colonel Min got them both with his carbine. Then he went in and I heard three shots and Colonel Min came out with a guerrilla. It was dawn by then and we tied the guerrilla up and started down the mountain. This guerrilla was about fortyish, a grubby-looking Northerner from Hamkyung province, and he kept abusing us, knowing that we had escaped from the North. I would have liked to kill him and, indeed, I tried to, sir, but the Colonel stopped me, of course. But then, halfway down the mountain, the guerrilla was told that I was one of the family he and his gang had murdered, and, instead of showing remorse, he began abusing me again, and using obscenities he boasted, yes, sir, he boasted, in that filthy language of his, that he had raped my mother and sister and that they had all done it in front of my father. He knew he was going to be shot, so he couldn't care less how we felt about him. I was raving mad. I was really going to let him have it, when Colonel Min just stopped and said to me in his sudden, quiet way to stay right where I was. Before I knew what was happening, he took the guerrilla by the arm and dragged him back up the trail and disappeared from my sight. I was about to rush up to them when I heard a shot, one, single shot, which echoed and reechoed in the early morning mountain air. Then, Colonel Min appeared alone. We went down the mountain in silence, and it was only much later that I realized he didn't have his carbine with him. We buried my family, and for several days Colonel Min shut himself up in the house. Then he resigned from the job and took me up to Seoul, where I was to live with my relatives until he sent for me. Then he signed up for the Army."

"I saw him when he came up to Seoul and he told me he had volunteered for the Army but he would not explain why."

"He never told me why either, sir. But I think I know why, don't you, sir?"

I did not reply. I did not know what to say.

We drove in silence the rest of the way. Under the dark heavens where not a star could be seen through the rain clouds, the misty, damp air became chilly. In the wavering haze, lights began to appear here and there, on the ground, in the hills, pale and flickering like will-o'-the-wisps.

"Here we are, sir."

We turned to the left. An archway stretched before us. In the shadows of the brightly lit arch, near the sentry boxes on both sides of the driveway, two Sherman tanks squatted like ponderous monumental beasts, with their cannons and the heavy, turret-mounted machine guns pointing at the sky.

"Just in case, sir," said Lieutenant Cho, "just in case."

We drove in. There were more tanks, darkly looming in the thin fog along the driveway.

"We've moved an entire tank battalion right in here, Major," said Lieutenant Cho in a cheery voice; and, his left hand making a sweeping motion, "All approaches to the headquarters are covered by tanks. You can't see them, sir, but they are all there."

The plazalike open field of the headquarters was bristling with tanks, armored cars, half-tracks with anti-aircraft guns; in the middle of them two medium-sized helicopters sat like giant dragonflies with their blades drooping. Puddles of water glimmered dimly here and there. Save for the footsteps of the guards making their rounds and the distant droning of a generator somewhere, it was all very quiet. The headquarters buildings fringed the plaza which was like a bowl surrounded by hills. Quonset quarters and tents were on the hillsides, rising in tiers from the edges of the arena.

In front of the general's office building, someone stood alone in the shadowy light and waved at us.

"There's Chaplain Koh," said the lieutenant.

"When did he arrive here?"

"Yesterday morning, sir."

Lieutenant Cho stopped the jeep. Chaplain Koh came over.

"Good to see you, Major Lee," he said. "Welcome to the front."

We shook hands. "Where's Colonel Min?" I said. "Is he up?"

"Oh, yes. He's waiting for you," said the chaplain.

"Where?"

"In the auditorium. Between the chapel and the war room."

Lieutenant Cho came around the jeep.

"Did you say he is in the auditorium?" Lieutenant Cho said to the chaplain.

Chaplain Koh nodded.

Lieutenant Cho said to me, "See what I mean, sir?"

"What?" I said.

"He is there listening to that spooky music. All by himself, too. He is alone now, isn't he, Chaplain?"

"He is alone."

"Well, let's go and see him," I said.

"No, you go by yourself," said the chaplain.

"Go ahead, sir," said the lieutenant. "I'll tell the others you are here. Where are they now, Chaplain?"

"All in the war room."

"I'll see you later, Major," said Lieutenant Cho. "I'll have your quarters ready for you."

I started toward the auditorium. Chaplain Koh followed me. "I'll walk with you part of the way," he said.

"Lieutenant Cho seems worried about Colonel Min," I said. "How is he?"

The chaplain smiled. "He is all right. The man wants to be by himself, that's all. He can think better that way. Well, we should give him that privilege, shouldn't we? Except —"

"Yes?" We went around a tank.

"Well, it has become a nightly ritual for him, I am afraid."

"What do you mean?"

"Well, you go and see for yourself," he said with a grin. "I'll see you later with the others."

I nodded and went ahead toward the auditorium. The chaplain walked into the small chapel. It was dark and silent inside the large auditorium. I held the door open for a moment, not knowing whether to go in or not.

A voice sounded within in the dark. "Is that you? Major Lee?"

"Yes. I've just arrived."

"Come in."

"It's dark in there. I can't see my way."

There was a brief silence. "Yes. Wait. I'll get the light for you."

I heard squeaks and metallic scrapings of a chair on the concrete floor. The powerful beam of a flashlight shot out of the darkness toward me. "Come on in," he said. I closed the door and groped my way toward him. Suddenly, the air in the auditorium, empty save for the two of us, was filled with low, murmuring, melancholy sounds of strings, the wistful, lyrical melody of an English horn gliding pensively, quietly among them. I stopped halfway down the aisle. Shadowy and blurred behind the light, Colonel Min came toward me from the foot of the rostrum. We met in the oval rings of light and shook hands.

"I hope you had an uneventful journey?"

"Well, yes," I began; then, blurting out like an amateur actor who, in confusion and panic onstage, could not remember his lines which he had rehearsed for so long, "Have you ever killed anyone?" I thought his eyes glinted in the dark.

"Haven't you?" he said.

"I meant to say — have you ever murdered anyone? You know — in cold blood?"

He stood immobile without a word.

I heard a click, then another click on the record.

"Have you?" he said quietly and, I thought, coldly; then he answered himself quickly, holding my arm, "No, no, of course, you haven't!"

"I've been thinking about it all day," I confessed.

His grip on my arm tightened. "What is it? What's on your mind?"

I told him a half-lie and a half-truth. "I haven't been thinking about it exactly for myself."

He let go of my arm. "Then — for me?"

"Yes."

"Why?"

I did not answer.

He gave me a shadowy smile. "I feel as though I were being interrogated."

His calm words startled me. In confusion, I mumbled, "I am sorry. I didn't mean to sound that way."

"Will you judge me?"

In greater confusion, I said what I did not intend to say: "I shan't judge you!"

"Oh, but you will, don't you know?" he exclaimed in a whisper, taking a quick step past me. The circle of light went with him up the aisle toward the door. His voice, a little louder, echoed in the dark. "You will judge me, don't you know?"

I followed him hastily. He opened the door. There was a jeep just coming to a halt in front of the door. Its headlights illuminated

Colonel Min. His thin, long shadow fell on the aisle at my feet. With an involuntary jerk I stopped. Lieutenant Cho came bounding out of the jeep. The headlights dimmed and died. In the sepulchral darkness of the auditorium behind me, somewhere near the rostrum, the phonograph was still grinding out the dreadful music with appalling insolence, as though it would go on for all eternity.

F

Chapter 5

or some reason I could not help feeling a little bewildered, when I was out of the darkness of the auditorium, to find myself once again shrouded in the gray fog that showed no sign of lifting and to realize anew the blurry, ominous presence of tanks, armored cars, and guns. I had been with Colonel Min inside the auditorium for only a few minutes, but it seemed as though I had spent a good part of my life with him there.

Lieutenant Cho had come with Captain Yang, an aide-de-camp to Lieutenant General Hyun, the commanding general of the 7th Corps — our general. We all gathered around in front of the jeep.

"The general sent me down to see you, sir," said the young captain. "He would like to know what your decision is, Colonel. About negotiating with General Ham, sir."

"Is he alone?" I said.

"No, sir. General Shin and General Chung are with him." They were the Deputy Corps Commander and the Corps Chief of Staff, respectively. "They have been with him all evening, sir, as a matter of fact."

Colonel Min remained quiet.

"What have they been talking about, do you know?" I said.

"About General Ham, sir."

Lieutenant Cho snorted.

"Anything specific?" I said.

"I wouldn't really know, Major. I gather that they are a little worried in case General Ham and — I don't know if I should say this, sir, but they seemed to be concerned about the possibility that you, sir, Colonel Min, and General Ham might have an open break."

"I think it's about time," said Lieutenant Cho.

"You stay out of it," I said.

"Sorry, sir," he mumbled.

I thought Colonel Min smiled. "Well, what gave them the notion that I and General Ham might have it out?"

Captain Yang said, "They seem to be convinced that what General Ham wants now is to run the show himself. In short, sir, replace General Hyun and have us all accept him as the leader. It is quite outrageous."

"I'll kill him for that presumption!" hissed Lieutenant Cho. "I do really mean that, Colonel!"

"Count me in on that, too," said the captain.

"Calm down, calm down!" said Colonel Min. "Well, Captain, what's General Hyun's view on that?"

"Oh, you know him, Colonel. He would be happy to step down if only to save our cause."

"I see," said Colonel Min.

"He must be out of his mind even to think that we will risk our lives just to hand the whole country over to a man like General Ham," I said.

Colonel Min said, "Captain, you go back and tell General Hyun and the others that I am going out to the 34th alone."

I volunteered to come along.

"I want you to stay here."

"I can't let you go there alone. Besides, I may be able to say things to him which you may not want to."

"All right."

I said, "Well, Captain, you tell them I am going with Colonel Min, and if anything happens to us . . ."

"We know what to do, sir. Don't worry!" said Lieutenant Cho.

Colonel Min said, "Tell General Hyun that we are not going out there to negotiate with General Ham. We are going to tell him what to do, is that clear?"

"Yes, sir!"

"All right. Get going now, Captain," said Colonel Min. "And tell the generals to get some sleep. This is nothing to lose our sleep over. We will be all right."

"Good luck, Colonel, and you, too, Major." He leaped into his jeep and roared off.

"Now, let's get started," said Colonel Min. "Lieutenant, I don't want to see the others now. They may all want to come along and I don't want that. So, you go tell them that we've already left. And — I want the alert signal out. Tell that to Colonel Park. He'll know what to do. And tell Colonel Song to get in touch with our people in General Ham's headquarters. I want Colonel Kim to put surveillance on all approaches to the 34th, in and out, and also on all airstrips. And you, I want you to stay by the phone in the general's office. And where is Chaplain Koh?"

"He's gone to bed, Colonel."

Colonel Min laughed aloud. "That's more like him! Well, you go and wake him up and tell him to get ready to go down to Seoul in the morning. He can fly down, but I'll see him before he takes off." He turned to me. "I can't tell you how helpful he has been to our cause. He has recruited half a dozen generals single-handedly, as you know. And, of course, his contact with our civilian comrades has been invaluable. I think it is about time he should set up a base of operations in Seoul. You can help him on that, can't you?"

I nodded. "I am counting on his influence on the North Korean refugee groups, too. Has he been able to recruit chaplains?"

"Not all of them, but enough. At least we now have on our side all the chaplains of the units we will be sending into Seoul. Once we launch the coup, they will do the explaining of our position to the American advisers."

"Right. And my group in Seoul will deal with the foreign embassies and residents."

"Your diplomatic service experiences should be helpful there, I am sure. And that reminds me of my plan for you. Of course, I want you to be in charge of the foreign ministry once we take over. But before that, I want you to go to Japan."

"To Japan?"

"Yes. To Tokyo, to be precise. I'll tell you about it on our way. Well, Major Lee, let's get going."

The headquarters of the 34th Division, which was the 7th Corps' reserve division at the time, was about fifteen miles northeast from the Corps headquarters. I drove Colonel Min's jeep. Half a mile from the Corps headquarters, we crossed a small bridge over a mountain rapids, turned to the left and came out onto the main route of supply. Colonel Min was quiet, as though deeply asleep, except for the imperceptible stirrings he made when he puffed on his pipe. The sweet aroma of the tobacco drifted toward me like a thin fog. I glanced at him. I could not see his face too clearly. He wore his cap down over his face, the visor nearly hiding his eyes. As Lieutenant Cho would say, Colonel Min was a skinny man; but there was nothing fragile about him. He was indeed lean and short, but the austere features of his face and the erect carriage he always maintained gave one the impression that beneath the facade of a small build, clothed in an impeccably tailored and starched uniform, there was a body shielded by an impenetrable armored plate of resilient steel. His face was deeply tanned and the bronze tan made his skin look leathery, almost coarse. Yet, in spite of his surface austerity and somber carriage, I could not help feeling that there was within him an inner man, so to speak, of a genial nature and with a gentle face that would, given a chance, quietly beam at the world around him, radiating the warmth of his compassion for others and, perhaps, for himself, too. For, if one overlooked the severity and toughness of his features, one could, on rare occasions, catch a glimpse of a certain imperceptible delicateness of his countenance, of a finely etched, gently molded aspect which had been there all along. But something had rubbed it out, and, now, what the world saw was nothing but the toughness. I thought I knew better.

He pulled himself up in his seat and relit his pipe with a match. He looked up at the black sky. "Our weather people say we might have rain for the next few days," he said.

"That shouldn't affect our plans."

"Of course not," he said looking at me. "So much the better, don't you think?"

"Yes, I think so."

"Is everything going all right in Seoul?"

"Yes."

"That's good."

There was a sharp bend ahead and I slowed down.

"Look," I said, "you were going to tell me about sending me to Tokyo."

"Yes."

I looked at him. "Had this been planned before? I mean — had you planned it before I came out here?"

"Oh, yes."

"Well?"

"Can you be ready to leave at a moment's notice?"

"What do you mean?"

"Do you think Lieutenant Colonel Hwang of the Airborne Brigade can handle the situation in Seoul while you are gone?"

"Yes, I think so."

"You trust him, don't you?"

"Yes, absolutely. Why?"

"Oh, I don't doubt his loyalty. I meant his ability to take charge of your post."

"He can do it."

"I thought so."

"You seem to think that I may be gone for quite a while."

"What gave you that idea?"

"Oh, I don't know. I feel as though I am being sent away."

"Nonsense."

"In any case, you haven't yet told me what this is all about."

"The truth is that I don't know what this is all about. You have met Colonel McKay, haven't you?"

"Yes, I think so. He is the Corps' senior adviser, isn't he?"

"No, not that one. That's Colonel McCarthy. Colonel McKay is the second in command."

"Oh, yes. Medium height, blond, crew cut, a moustache."

"Yes, that's the one."

"So?"

"He is an American Intelligence agent."

"I am not really surprised."

"I've known that for a long time. He went to the Command and General Staff College with me in Kansas. Actually, I roomed with him there."

"Accidentally? Or coincidentally?"

"I would say, deliberately, from their point of view. I seemed to have been singled out. I was his assignment, you see. He was a major then. We were in Washington, D.C., a few times, where his family lives — according to him, that is — and I was introduced to a lot of people at several parties he gave in my honor. I knew I was being looked over, so to speak, if you know what I mean."

"It sounds fascinating."

"Oh, yes. They are very thorough. He knows, for instance, that I met you in Paris. They've been keeping an eye on you, too."

The thought of being spied upon by an American CIA agent was rather amusing. I laughed. "Now I remember meeting this Colonel McKay at a party in Seoul. He speaks Korean fairly well, doesn't he?"

"He is well trained. He went to their language school to study Korean."

"The one at Monterey, California?"

He nodded. "Actually, one of the Korean instructors there who was in my command during the war tipped me off on McKay. I had his background investigated, you see, when McKay turned up in Korea soon after I came back and, moreover, was assigned to my unit, the Ranger Brigade, remember? Then he followed me out here."

"For friendship's sake!" I laughed.

"Well, that's it. Believe it or not, we are good friends. He knows what I am up to and I know what he is up to."

"Well, what is he up to? How much does he know?"

"Not very much, but enough to hang me if he spills, but he hasn't yet, naturally. He is not sure how strong we really are and that's the catch. I know the U.S. is disgusted with the present regime, though they wouldn't throw it out on their own initiative. That wouldn't look good. Anyway, it's a damn good thing McKay hates General Mah's guts. He simply loathes Mah, who he thinks is an abominable criminal, and I can't say we disagree with him on that."

"Speaking of General Mah, what are we going to do about him?"

He brushed off my question. "Too early for that problem. Now, Colonel McKay wants me to go to Tokyo, and I can't leave, obviously, so I want you to go instead."

"Why does he want you to go to Tokyo in the first place?"

"I think he thinks he now has enough on us, though, of course, he has no idea when we'll start. That he will never know. My guess is that his superiors want to have a showdown of a sort."

"If they know that much about us and yet they haven't done anything to stop us, then they want something from us."

"Precisely."

"Just what?"

"A deal, I would think."

"What sort of a deal?"

"Obviously, they aren't going to stop us now, although Colonel McKay made it quite clear to me that they could whenever they wanted. I didn't tell him they couldn't stop us, not at this stage, anyway. We are too strong. But, they could cause a lot of trouble. That's their bargaining position."

"They could cut down on our supplies or even freeze them, although that wouldn't affect us too much."

"They could do more than that, of course. They do have their stooges, like General Mah used to be until he got out of everyone's hand. They could use them against us."

"General Ham?"

"Exactly. And a few other megalomaniacs among our generals. But I am convinced that they have given up on General Ham. Colonel McKay has actually dropped a hint or two to me quite recently."

"Then, what is this deal they have in mind? To make us their stooges?"

"I think they are smarter than that, don't you?"

"I am not too convinced."

"Well, this time around, they will simply have to be smart, and I think they are being realistically intelligent about the whole thing. They seem to be convinced that a coup is not only imminent but necessary and that our group is the best hope there is for that. They have offered to help us, in a manner of speaking."

"And what do they want in return?"

"A status quo, simply speaking. A national policy based on anti-Communism within the framework of a mutual defense treaty. That's the general guideline. We can't disagree on that as a matter of principle. We've got to be more flexible in our foreign policy, but that's a problem we can deal with later. And this may amuse you. Colonel McKay wants a clean, honest, democratic government — no corruption, that is."

I laughed. "What does he think we are!"

"And no secret police, no kangaroo courts, no firing squads. In spite of his profession, there is a streak of commendable romanticism in him and I must say I like him the more for that. And, of course, no dictatorial, totalitarian, authoritarian, anti-democratic, militaristic regime."

"And what did you say to that?"

"I said he should know us better by now."

"Certainly, he should know you better by now."

"He said he did, but he insisted on quoting Lord Acton. Power corrupts and absolute power corrupts absolutely."

"He should have said that to General Mah."

"As far as he is concerned, General Mah is beyond redemption."

"What are we going to do with him?"

"Who?"

"Mah."

He was silent for a while. "The Americans want him out of the picture. He has become too embarrassing to them."

"How do they propose to eliminate him?"

"Fire him and retire him from the Army."

I could not help snorting at the naïveté of the idea. "Mah is a criminal!"

He looked at me. "What, then, do you suggest?"

"Court-martial him."

"We will find him guilty, no doubt."

"No question about that."

"Then what?"

"He deserves whatever punishment his guilt will bring to him."

He replied instantly. "In short, you suggest we kill him."

"I said nothing of the sort!"

"Nonsense! You know the military court will sentence him to death. The Army is packed with people who would do anything to hang him, you know that. You simply want your killing him legalized."

"You make me out to be a civilized brute!" I said. "General Ahn wants to kill him. Now."

"I know he does."

"Will you kill him?"

"Why do you ask?"

"Will you kill him?"

"Would you kill him?"

"I don't know."

"In that case, someone will have to kill him for you."

In confusion, frustration, and anger, I cried out, "I would kill him if I had to!"

Abruptly, he swung around in the seat to face me. I felt his eyes boring into me. But he did not speak. It was only when I drove our jeep into the headquarters of the 34th Division that he said, matter-of-factly, "When we go back to the Corps, I want you to get ready to go to Tokyo. I'll have Colonel McKay arrange for the trip. Is that clear?"

H *Chapter 6*

alfway up the driveway toward a cluster of buildings which comprised the headquarters of the 34th Division, headlights shone suddenly out of foggy darkness ahead and a jeep came toward us splashing muddy water. I stopped our jeep by the side of the driveway. We both got out. The other jeep came to a halt next to ours. Brigadier General Yoon, the Division commander, leaped out. He was alone.

"Good to see you both," he said. "The sentry at the gate reported you just passed through." The thirty-six-year-old general, an old friend of Colonel Min's from their days in Tokyo, had been the chief of staff at the Corps until the month before. Stocky and rather jovial, he sported an American-style crew cut. "I am glad you didn't bring the others. It wouldn't have done any good. Only would have gotten them all raving mad."

"Where is he now?" said Colonel Min.

"Would you believe it! He's at the firing range, target practicing!"

I could not help swearing under my breath.

"I've had enough of him," said General Yoon; then in English, "Goddamn!"

"So — that's where he wants to see me," said Colonel Min, "at the firing range? Is he drunk?"

"Wouldn't you know! Look, I am getting tired of babying him. Cousin or no cousin, just give me the word and I'll break his bullying guts. I can keep him here under guard till we are through with the coup. As far as his headquarters are concerned, he has gone fishing in the mountains, ha, ha, ha! Goddamn it, we don't need him around messing up our work."

"That won't be necessary," said Colonel Min. "Besides, we do need him on our side or at least we have to neutralize him. As you know, he has cronies in key positions around Seoul and until we can replace them with our people, we have to go softly. We don't want a senseless civil war on our hands, do we?"

"Well, I see what you mean," said General Yoon. "How about the Marines and the Air Force, Major?"

"All set, General. As far as the Marines are concerned, we can count on the entire Corps. The Air Force, according to my latest count, can give us four fighter squadrons at Kimpo, one bomber wing at Suwon, and enough transport planes from Taegue to airlift one of your regiments from Chunchun. But you've got to make it to Chunchun without resistance on the way."

"No trouble about that. The Chunchun garrison commander is on our side. Have we been able to swing the artillery people?"

Colonel Min said, "Five artillery battalions altogether."

I said, "Three from the 22nd Division and two from the 17th Division."

"That's near Panmunjom, isn't it. The Americans aren't going to like it," said the general.

"Can't be helped," said Colonel Min.

"What about the Presidential Brigade? Any luck?"

"We can count on its armored units. They are solidly behind us."

"Good! I know the commander personally."

"He was one of my students at my university, believe it or not," I said.

"Well, so much the better," said the general. "How's Colonel Son doing?" Colonel Son, our man, was General Mah's deputy.

"Excellent, General. He's keeping an eye on General Mah."

"Has that son of a bitch made any move yet?"

"Nothing significant so far. We are watching him closely," I said.

General Yoon turned to Colonel Min. "We've got to get rid of him."

"How?" I said.

"Assassinate him."

Colonel Min did not stir.

"Just give me the word, and I will do it myself," said General Yoon. "He is a vicious, ruthless man and he can ruin us all unless we eliminate him soon."

I ventured timidly, "Don't you think there will be a proper time for that?"

The general blew up. "A proper time! What the hell are you talking about! A proper time is now! Before the coup, before he smells out what's going on."

My voice rose. "Assassinating him now isn't going to solve anything. As far as I am concerned, murdering him in cold blood or, for that matter, killing anyone in cold blood merely for the sake of ensuring our own safety will simply stain our cause with blood from the start. We will be resorting to the same methods General Mah has been using to eliminate his opponents and that will ultimately sabotage our own motivation and our own cause, which is to free the nation from the terrors and tyrannies of injustice with which evil men like General Mah have enslaved our people. We can't afford to descend to his level — no matter for what reason."

"You didn't know that General Mah tortured General Yoon's father-in-law to death, did you?" said Colonel Min to me. "General Yoon's father-in-law was one of the most respected journalists who was brave enough to criticize Mah in public. It happened while you were in Europe."

"Well, he is dead and that's that. There's nothing I can do about that," said General Yoon. "But you know, surely you must know

as well as the whole country does, that that bastard has taken as
hostages nearly all of those he considers potential threats to him.
One of my maternal uncles, the only brother of my mother's who is
in the south, is in his jail on some trumped-up charge of being a
North Korean agent. Even General Ham is no exception. Not that
anyone is in jail, but Mah has had General Ham's son, a second lieutenant in the Engineer Corps, assigned to his headquarters, just
to have him around as a hostage."

"I know all that, General," I said.

"Well, then, don't you see what can happen once the son of a
bitch uncovers our plans? He won't even have to roll out his troops.
All he has to do is round up the hostages whom he already has in
Seoul and tell our generals, including me, naturally, to do what he
tells us or else."

"Major Lee is aware of that, I am sure," said Colonel Min.

"Yes," I said.

"Well, then, let's do something," said the general.

"I have a plan," said Colonel Min to both of us. "But I think it
is a little premature to discuss it now. I will let you know about it
when the time comes. So, will you both agree to leave the matter
to me for the time being?"

"All right," said the general. "Whatever you say. I am aware
that you have to take other things into consideration, such as public and foreign opinion and so on. But from my vantage point up
here in the mountains, well, you understand my feelings."

Colonel Min nodded. He turned to me. "Well?"

"All right. I give you my word that I'll abide by the decision of
the Command Group."

"That's fair enough," said General Yoon with a grin. "I won't be
able to be with you much of the time but if and when the question
of Mah comes up, you have my proxy vote for assassinating him in
advance of our coup."

"Very well," said Colonel Min. "Let's get down to the more immediate business. Shall we go?"

We climbed into General Yoon's jeep and drove in the wavering fog on the muddy trail that led us to the firing range on a small hill behind the Division headquarters complex. The moment we drove around the last bend on the trail, we heard a burst of submachine-gun fire.

"What in the hell!" said the general. The jeep roared up the last stretch of the trail and onto the firing range. The general stopped the jeep and cut the engine. Another jeep, with its engine going, was ahead of us, its headlights illuminating the targets — bottles and beer cans lined up on a ledge. Standing next to the jeep, his back to us, General Ham, in T-shirt, fatigue trousers, and rubber shower clogs, was reloading his submachine gun. General Yoon switched off the headlights of our jeep. We remained in our seats. A young officer strode over to us. It was Captain Kang, General Ham's aide-de-camp. He saluted us. Colonel Min shook hands with him. The young captain let out a sigh. "Sir, I've just about had it," he said to Colonel Min.

"You aren't the only one," said General Yoon.

"I understand, Captain," said Colonel Min. "Patience. It won't be long now. How drunk is he?"

"Pretty bad, sir, as usual. Be careful, Colonel."

We got out of the jeep.

"Please, be careful, Colonel," whispered the captain.

Colonel Min nodded. We walked over to General Ham. We gave him a salute. He did not turn around to look at us.

"Just the two of you, eh?" he said. His high-pitched voice was unmistakably angry. "Where are the others?"

Colonel Min did not reply.

General Yoon said, "What the hell do you want to see them for? You can say anything you want to us."

"You keep out of it," General Ham said, swiveling around. He raised his submachine gun in one hand and pointed it at Colonel Min. "I am speaking to your boss here!"

Captain Kang stepped up and stood behind General Ham.

"Well, where are the others, Colonel?"

"Considering the time of the day," said Colonel Min quietly, "I would assume that they are all sound asleep."

Brandishing the submachine gun, General Ham laughed out. "Ha, ha, ha, that's a good one. I hope they have peaceful dreams, all of them." His tone changed. "What are you trying to do to me! Are you trying to insult me, Colonel!"

"Will you cut that out!" said General Yoon. "You wanted to see him, so he is here, at this crazy hour. Isn't that enough? Say your piece and get it over with. I've got to go to bed, too."

"I told you to stay out of it," said General Ham. "Cousin!"

General Yoon gave us a despairing look.

Colonel Min said, "General Ham, I didn't come all the way out here to quarrel with you. So, please tell us what you have on your mind."

"Are you all ganging up on me?"

"Please, General," said Colonel Min. "I am afraid you are badly indisposed toward us, and if you wish, General, we will be glad to come back and see you in the morning."

There was a moment of silence.

Abruptly, General Ham said, "Well, I want to know what you think of me."

"I beg your pardon, sir?" said the Colonel.

"You heard me. I want to know what you think of me."

"What do I think of you?"

"That's right."

Colonel Min glanced at us. "You are a lieutenant general of our Army, sir, and you command one of the most powerful and important field armies we have." In a quiet voice, Colonel Min continued, "And, as an Army commander, you are responsible for the welfare and interest of nearly two hundred thousand young men of our country in uniform. Shall I go on, sir?"

I saw Captain Kang grin behind General Ham.

General Ham did not respond.

"Come on," said General Yoon. "Let's get out of here."

Colonel Min said, "The general has asked me to tell him what I think of him, and I am going to tell him. Well, General Ham, if I may continue, sir, I think, in all sincerity, that you are one of the ablest generals and field commanders we have in our Army, that is, sir, when you choose to be. In combat, you can be a brilliant tactician and I have seen you being one during the war. In short, sir, I think the country can count on you in time of war, on the field of battle. That is, you are a good soldier, sir, someone whom all conscientious professional soldiers can be proud of."

In a surprisingly sober tone of voice, General Ham said, "There — you are insulting me again. So, I am nothing but a good professional soldier, eh?"

"I fail to see how that could be construed as an insulting remark, General," said Colonel Min. "Yes, you are a good professional soldier, sir. And, I should say, the country needs more people like you in uniform."

"So — that's what you are going to do with me?"

"Sir?"

"When you are in power, Colonel, that's what you are going to do with me. Keep me in uniform?"

Colonel Min kept silent.

"Isn't that enough? Wouldn't you like to stay in uniform?" said General Yoon.

"I didn't ask for your opinion, cousin," said General Ham.

"Now, you listen to me," General Yoon went on. "Take you and me. What the hell do you think you and I are good for? Out of uniform, I mean. What do you think you can be? A prime minister? A cabinet minister? Or the president of a bank? Hell, no! You and I are going to stay right here in the Army, cousin. As Colonel Min said, you are a good general, rather, knowing you as I do, you can be a good one when you try to be one. You are a commander of an army, and, who knows, maybe someday you may even get to be the chief of staff."

General Ham said, "I take it that you are either trying to insult me further or trying to bribe me." He stared at Colonel Min. "Is that what you all have figured out? To bribe me with the promise of making me the chief of staff of the Army when you take over the country?"

"You seem to think that we are going to occupy the country as if we were at war with an enemy in a foreign land. No, General, no one is trying to bribe you with anything. I am afraid you have failed to understand my position."

"I am so stupid, Colonel. You'll have to tell me again just what your position is."

"All right, sir. If our coup is successful and we have a chance to set the country straight, we would like you to continue to serve the country in the best way you can, the way you have served it so far, as one of the country's ablest generals. As to what your position will be, no one at this stage is prepared to say. And, in all sincerity, General, we must not think of such a thing."

" 'We must not think of such a thing,' " General Ham said. "Well, well, how noble of you — when you are dreaming of becoming the President."

"You are drunk!" shouted General Yoon.

"Shut up!" said General Ham.

"Gentlemen, we are not going to accomplish anything this way," said Colonel Min. "General Ham, if you please, I would be glad to see you in the morning."

"When I am sober?"

"If you like, sir."

"I am sober enough."

"Then behave yourself," said General Yoon, "cousin."

General Ham, his eyes glaring through his rimless glasses and his face perspiring, hissed at General Yoon. "I could kill you for that impudent remark. Be thankful that you are my cousin. I am sober enough. Captain!"

Captain Kang stepped up to General Ham.

"Captain, go get the carbine in the jeep."

"Sir?"

"I said, go get the goddamned carbine in the jeep!"

Captain Kang went over to the jeep and returned with a carbine. "Is it loaded?" General Ham said.

"Yes, sir."

"Give it to me."

General Ham turned to Colonel Min. "I am quite sober, Colonel, contrary to my dear cousin's low opinion of me. And I'll show you how sober I am." With a sudden jerk of his head, he flung the carbine to the Colonel.

"Now, Colonel, shall we find out who is more sober?"

General Ham clutched the submachine gun in his hands, facing Colonel Min, who stood with the carbine in one hand. General Ham raised the submachine gun, almost pointing it at Colonel Min's chest. I tried to step forward but was brushed aside by Colonel Min. General Yoon stood motionless.

I saw Captain Kang, a few steps behind General Ham, reach for his .45 pistol.

For one long moment, no one spoke or moved. The jeep engine, untended to, whined away. For the first time, I became aware of the thin fog all around us. General Ham tapped on the submachine gun.

"How about it, Colonel?" he said. He was sober enough and his voice was quite steady. "Shall we knock off some bottles?"

Colonel Min did not answer. He was holding the carbine in his hands, his head lowered, looking at the carbine.

"What's the matter, Colonel? Are you afraid I'll outshoot you?"

"This is ridiculous," said General Yoon.

"I order you to be quiet," said General Ham.

"You are in my territory, cousin," said General Yoon. "Don't you forget it."

Colonel Min said, quietly, "Captain Kang, take this thing back."

Captain Kang came forward and took the carbine from Colonel Min.

"Well, what's the matter, Colonel?" said General Ham.

"General Ham, if you don't mind, I would like to consider this meeting concluded."

"Just a minute, Colonel," said General Ham.

Colonel Min stood facing him. "Yes?"

General Ham grinned. "Would you rather chop those bottles with a sword, maybe, eh? But, I don't have any swords handy here; besides, we don't fight with swords nowadays, do we?"

"What the hell are you talking about?" said General Yoon. "Let's all get out of here and go to bed. You too, cousin!"

General Ham ignored him. "Well, Colonel, I am well aware of your violent temper and your great skill with a sword. Do you still practice it?"

Colonel Min kept silent.

"What is this?" said General Yoon.

"Ah — don't you know? Colonel Min is a great man with a sword. He can cut you in half with a sword before you can blink your eyes, isn't that right, Colonel? I know all about it. How do you do it? Like this?" General Ham, slashing at the foggy night air with one hand, yelled out at the top of his lungs: "Yaaaa!"

It gave me shivers. General Yoon drew himself up to General Ham. "Come on. This is enough."

General Ham pushed him away. "Colonel Min, you didn't know that I knew all about it, did you? That poor Japanese captain! Yaaaa! And there he was, chopped in half. Horrors! How did you do it? Anyway, you caused a great deal of trouble for me. You see, Colonel, I was a captain in your regiment and I knew who you were but, of course, you didn't know who I was. Thanks to your murdering your company commander, I came under the suspicion and mistrust of my Japanese fellow officers and missed my chance for a promotion. You didn't know that, did you? I was even denied permission to join the search party to track you down. Oh, I would have been glad to track you down. After all, a murder is a murder, whether or not it was committed by a fellow Korean, don't you agree?"

"What is all this about, General?" I said. "Are you accusing Colonel Min of having committed a murder?"

"Hacking a man in half . . . I don't know what else I could call it except a murder. Well, well, that's all in the sweet past, isn't it,

Colonel? And now, irony of ironies, you are in a position to track me down and tell me what to do. How ironical it all turned out to be, eh?"

"Is it true, Colonel?" I said. "About this Japanese captain?"

He did not speak.

"Was this Japanese officer — was he the one you brought home with you once?" I said.

He looked at me and then at General Yoon. He glared at General Ham; his face was seething with an almost savage fury. But, in a moment, I sensed his fury withdraw as if into and beneath the dark skin of his face and what I saw after that was nothing but a stony expression that was colder than indifference. He slowly moved up to General Ham. He pushed the submachine gun aside. "General Ham, you are right. Now I am in a position to tell you what to do, and I am going to tell you what to do. I am going to tell you, General Ham, that, from now on, you must stop dreaming a foolish dream, that you must stop overestimating yourself, that you must not interfere with our plans and work, and that you must abide by your original pledge to keep yourself neutral."

"Mind you," said General Yoon to General Ham, "Colonel Min's words are my words, too."

General Ham turned to me. "And you — are they yours, too?"

I nodded.

"So, I was right after all," said General Ham. "You are all ganging up on me. Very well. Captain Kang! Get ready. We are going back to the headquarters."

Captain Kang looked at Colonel Min.

"So — you are telling me what to do from now on," said General Ham to Colonel Min.

"Yes."

"We shall see, we shall see," he said. He handed the submachine gun to Captain Kang. "Well, let me tell you something before I go. Colonel Min, make no mistake about it. If I wanted to, I have all the power I need to crush you."

Colonel Min went closer to him. In a calm whisper, he said to the general, "General Ham, *we* have all the power we need to resist you — if necessary. Please, make no mistake about it, General."

"Yes, General Ham," I said. "We have all the power we need to resist you!"

General Ham stared at us. "Captain Kang! Bring the jeep around. We are going!"

Captain Kang did not move.

"Captain!"

General Yoon looked at Colonel Min, who nodded to him.

General Yoon said to General Ham, "Well, cousin, it looks as though you are going to be my guest for a few days."

In an oddly quiet voice, General Ham said, "Are you putting me under arrest?"

"I am merely stretching my hospitality, cousin."

Suddenly, General Ham laughed aloud. "I knew you were all stupid but I never realized you could be this stupid. Make no mistake about it, Colonel Min. I have all the power to crush you, every one of you, no matter where I am."

I thought Colonel Min smiled.

"Captain Kang! I said — bring the jeep around!"

Captain Kang, the submachine gun in his hand, did not stir.

Colonel Min said, "General Ham, if you are referring to your secret communication with General Mah and to your planned rendezvous with him at ten o'clock this evening, I suggest that you forget about keeping the appointment."

General Yoon nearly leaped at General Ham. "Why, you sneaky . . ."

Colonel Min restrained General Yoon. "No need to discuss the matter with him now." He turned to me and then to General Yoon. "I was hoping that, perhaps, some of us would accompany General Ham to his rendezvous with General Mah. That was the plan I referred to earlier. But, I am afraid the plan will have to be modified. General Ham, we will have to keep the appointment without you. I hope you don't mind. We will give him your regards."

General Ham stood motionless.

General Yoon said, "Captain Kang!"

The captain looked at us and nodded. He walked away from us into the fog beyond the jeep. We heard him call out into the darkness. "Captain Lee! Captain Lee! Bring the men up!"

In a minute, out of the fog came a squad of armed soldiers into our view. Quietly they came and stood by the jeep.

Captain Kang saluted General Ham. "Are you ready, sir?"

For a second, I could not help feeling an uncontrollable shock.

General Ham said to Colonel Min, "Are you going to murder me, too?"

In panic, I stepped up to Colonel Min, when he said quietly to General Ham, "No, General, we simply wish you to have a quiet rest here for a few days."

"We shall see who wins, Colonel," said General Ham. "I have the power to destroy you, all of you!"

Colonel Min said, turning away, "We have the power to resist you, General, as you see."

General Ham spat out, "You rotten murderer!"

Colonel Min swung around violently, facing the general, his face distorted and twitching with anger as if he were about to shriek out, but he did not speak. In a second, he composed himself, his face betraying not a trace of emotion, and he walked slowly toward General Yoon's jeep, alone.

I did not know what to think. I did not know what to say. It was only when the three of us — General Yoon, Colonel Min, and myself — came down from the firing range that I realized that I had not spoken more than a sentence or two during our confrontation with General Ham and that I had been paralyzed, for some reason, to my bitter chagrin, into a state of ludicrous panic. The fog was thicker and the air more oppressive down at the deadly quiet headquarters than it was up on the hill. I suddenly became aware of the fatigue from the long drive from Seoul through rain and fog; the sense of relief at the outcome of our confrontation (for, it was settled one way or the other without, thank heavens, bloody violence) ; and the physical exhaustion overwhelmed me, and I would have been glad to plunk myself down on any cot, then and there, and sink into an undisturbed, long sleep, without reflecting on that which had come to pass and without worrying about that which was to come. But there was no peace in my mind.

General Yoon drove us to where we had left our jeep. Until then, neither of us had spoken. When we got out of the general's jeep, Colonel Min held the general's arm.

"I am sorry we had to do this," said Colonel Min to General Yoon. "He is your cousin, after all."

"It was about time," said the general. "He has given me nothing but headaches."

"You'll make sure there won't be any security leak," said the Colonel.

"Don't worry about a thing at this end. Will you take care of his headquarters?"

"Of course. We will get in touch with our people at his headquarters as soon as we get back to the Corps. Would you call our headquarters and speak with Colonel Park? Where will you keep him?"

"There's a little cabin up in the mountains about two miles from here. Remember that one? Actually, it is a sort of hunting lodge he has used before to entertain American advisers. Well, he can now entertain himself for a few days. Speaking of American advisers, what do we do with his advisers at his headquarters?"

"I will have Colonel McKay take care of that."

"You trust him?"

"Yes."

"What do we do after that?"

"With General Ham?"

"Yes."

"Release him after our coup is well under way. I am sure he will come to his senses by then."

"There is one virtue in him. He knows when he is beaten."

"In spite of what happened, we do want him to be on our side. Besides, if we succeed, we will need him out here on the front, for a while at least."

"All right, then," said the general. "I'll give the instructions to Captain Kang and Captain Lee. Now, what about his rendezvous with General Mah?"

"To tell you the truth, I didn't know about it until he came out here. He was supposed to stop at the Corps. To see me, that is. That was the plan. He didn't stop and flew on to here. I thought there had to be some change in his plans. I was going to check with our people at his headquarters, but before I had a chance to do so, I had a call from his Intelligence chief, Colonel Bang. You know him, don't you?"

General Yoon nodded.

"Colonel Bang called me on the hot line and told me that he had been instructed by General Ham to make an arrangement for a secret meeting."

"Where?"

"Outside Seoul. There is a little village near the Military Academy. The rendezvous will take place about a mile north of the village."

"Did he tell General Mah why he wanted to meet him?"

"Nothing specific. He was playing a game, I am afraid. While Colonel Bang was on the line, a direct line, with General Mah at his house, General Ham came in and took it over from him. Colonel Bang told me that General Ham made it all sound rather mysterious. Something very urgent and important and so on, and that he wanted General Mah to keep it absolutely confidential. After I talked with Colonel Bang, I had Colonel Kim, our Intelligence chief, double-check it with Colonel Son in Seoul, and it was confirmed. General Mah has broken the confidence and informed Colonel Son about it. A piece of good luck for us. Colonel Son is making the arrangement for General Mah."

"Well, well, it's all working out fine!" said General Yoon. "What do you have in mind to do about it?"

"We will have to keep the appointment, don't you think?"

General Yoon grinned. "Naturally! We will have to show up at the rendezvous."

"Then what?" I said.

They both turned and looked at me as though they were surprised to see me there with them.

Colonel Min said quietly, "I don't know. I haven't thought about it that far ahead."

General Yoon said, "Bump him off. What else?"

I ventured, "I suggest we put the question to the Command Group."

Colonel Min nodded. "Of course."

General Yoon said, "Well, we know what the Group will decide to do, don't we? How about sending me down there? I would like to volunteer. After all, I am General Ham's cousin. If he can't keep the appointment, maybe his cousin can, ha, ha, ha!"

"I think it is not a matter to joke about, if you don't mind my saying so, General. I pledged myself to the decision of the Command Group and I shall do . . ."

General Yoon cut me short. "Do what?"

"Do whatever I can to settle this problem without resorting to bloodshed."

The general snorted. "What the hell do you expect? A lily-white revolution? Major, let me tell you something . . ."

Colonel Min interrupted. "That's enough."

"All right, all right," said the general. "Let me know how the Group decides on it. You know where I stand."

I felt I had to speak up. "I do not expect our coup to be a lily-white revolution, as you put it, General, but I do not want it to be an act of bloodstained vengeance."

General Yoon cried out, "Who is talking about bloodstained vengeance!"

"We are trying to create an opportunity for the country and the people to correct the past wrongs but not an opportunity to drink blood and dance to the tune of revenge."

"Oh, you and your fancy words, Major!" said the general. "You speak as though our coup were already successful and we had the upper hand. It is not revenge or bloody vengeance I am seeking, Major. I am talking about self-defense. Our self-defense! The success of our coup depends entirely on whether General Mah is going to strike us first or whether we are going to strike him first. That's how I see the whole situation from where I am. Don't you agree, Colonel Min?"

Colonel Min nodded. "There is no doubt about that."

"Then you have made up your mind to kill him," I said.

Colonel Min said, "I did not say that."

"Just why are you so upset about killing him?" said the general to me. "He will have to die sooner or later."

"Major Lee wants a court-martial for him," said the Colonel.

General Yoon sneered, "Well, it will all come out the same way; that is, Major, if we are lucky enough to live through this. Well, we want the same thing, don't we, Major? So, then, what's the difference?"

"I want to prevent our coup from being stained with unnecessary and wanton bloodshed, General. I want our coup to be an honorable one."

"And I want our coup to succeed, Major. It has to succeed first to find out if it was an honorable coup or not. I know, I know! I know what you think I am thinking. Means justify an end. Well, Major, I am not thinking about anything profound. I am thinking of survival, Major. My survival and yours, too. All of us. If we don't strike Mah now, he is going to strike us down. It is as simple as that. If you don't believe in what I am sure you think is my crude, barbaric way of thinking, you try, just try, to live through this world of men in some other way. I want to do some good things, Major, but if some bad man tries to chop my head off before I have a chance . . ."

"So you chop his head off first, General. We shall all end up becoming beasts."

"Hell! It is not a question of our becoming beasts. We are already beasts, don't you know? Only there are reasonably decent beasts and then there are evil beasts."

Abruptly, Colonel Min strode away from us. He flung himself into our jeep in the driver's seat and gripped the wheel.

"Get in," he said.

I did not stir. I thought his voice sounded harsh as though he were barking out a command. I felt bitter. I looked at General Yoon. He was shaking his head. He nodded to me, whispering, "Go on now!"

In that moment, I did not know what was happening.

Colonel Min said, "Come."

And only then did I realize that his voice was not commanding me at all, but pleading that I speak no more.

General Yoon tapped me on the shoulder. "We've got big mouths, you and I. Get going now. I'll see you around."

Suddenly, I felt choked by the dank, heavy, foggy darkness of the night that silently swallowed us. I gave a hasty salute to the general and crawled into the jeep. I felt very small.

Chapter 7

Colonel Min drove slowly out of the division headquarters. We did not speak for a long while. A ghostly veil of gray fog drifted in and out along the winding road, swaying up and down. A mile or so from the entrance to the division headquarters, we left the muddy road and drove onto the main route of supply. The sky was dark and the air chilly. I could not tell the time; the phosphorescent dial of my wristwatch dimly showed that the watch had stopped running somewhere around one o'clock. I glanced at Colonel Min. He had his unlit pipe clamped in his mouth.

"Can you tell me the time?" I said.

He did not look at me. "I don't have my watch with me," he said.

"Mine stopped," I said. "It must be nearly two o'clock."

"Must be," he said. "Tired?"

I sat up on the seat. "No."

"I am," he said.

"You have lots on your mind."

For the first time since we had left General Yoon's division, he looked at me. "I suppose I do," he said. "Don't you?"

"Yes."

"Are you still thinking about General Mah?"

"No," I confessed.

He looked at me again.

I said, "I have been thinking about what General Yoon said."

"About what?"

"That we are already beasts. Only there are reasonably decent beasts and then there are evil beasts."

"Does it bother you?"

"What?"

"That you are a beast?" he said quietly. "That we are all beasts?"

"Why should it bother me? I don't believe it. I refuse to think that way."

"Ah, but it *would* bother you, then, if you believed that we are all already beasts, is that it?"

"Even so, why should it bother me? If human nature is basically evil beyond redemption, then there isn't much hope for mankind, and there wouldn't be any sense in any of us trying to do good, would there?"

"That is quite silly and you know it. Besides, it is an easy way out, don't you think?"

"An easy way out of what?"

"Out of trying to do something good, trying to be a decent human being."

"Trying to be a decent beast?" My voice sounded bitter.

"Perhaps," he said calmly.

"Is that what you think of yourself, then? That you are a decent beast and those you destroy are evil beasts beyond redemption?"

He did not reply.

"Beasts devouring beasts. It's a pretty picture of humanity."

With a voice thoroughly devoid of any emotion, he said quite simply, "Yes, isn't it?"

Before I had a chance to refute his outrageous words, he assaulted me with: "There is more evil in the world, don't you know? And — evil must be destroyed."

I had had enough. The day had been a little too much to take. I shot back at him, "Who is going to destroy the evil? Chaplain Koh insists that the evil in the world cannot be cured by human effort alone."

He said, "And you insist that the evil in the world can be cured by human effort?"

"Yes!"

"I agree."

"What?"

"I said I agreed with you."

"Then you will agree with me that it is the good in man that will ultimately destroy the evil in the world."

"No."

"Then what?"

"Perhaps, the evil in man can be destroyed only by the evil in man. Who knows?"

"Well! There won't be anything left to salvage after that!" I had not suspected that my words would agitate him or infuriate him so much. He jammed on the brakes, grinding the gears. The jeep screeched to a wild stop, jerking and bouncing. He swung it around and whipped it roaring back toward the division.

Hanging onto my seat, I shouted, "What are you doing!"

His voice snapped, "We'll take a shortcut!"

I stared at him in the dark.

He slowed the jeep down. "Do you mind?"

"Go ahead."

He drove back about half a mile or so and stopped the jeep where, on the right side of the road, a narrow dirt road branched off into what seemed to me to be nowhere. Someone had put up a road sign once, but the letters on the makeshift sign were blurred and unintelligible. Colonel Min said, "This is it."

"Well, if you say so. I am not familiar with this region."

He let the engine idle and lit his pipe. "I am. I know this area inside and out, every inch of it. You were on the western front during the war, weren't you?"

"Yes."

"I passed through here when we began our counteroffensive and pushed the Communists back into North Korea. I had a battalion."

"Rangers?"

"No. Before that. Infantry. Right here."

He drove onto the road. The slushy mud on this road was thicker than it was on the main road. The jeep bounced and skidded on. "A horrible road. Do you think we can make it through?"

"We'll see," he said, quite unruffled.

The jeep slogged on, squishing muddy earth under its wheels. The hopping and bouncing headlights frantically thrust at the vapory wall of fog wavering above the slimy dirt. It was a rough, winding road that had not been much used by many. I could not see too far ahead, and had I been at the wheel I would have missed nearly all the sharp curves and bends which seemed to appear suddenly and from nowhere. Colonel Min did not miss any. It was as though he had been traveling on that road for years, back and forth, memorizing every single bump, dent, pothole, curve, and bend. He knew the road. In the dim glow of his pipe, I thought that I saw his taut, lean face break into a sardonic smile whenever he felt my tense reaction to a sudden, menacing curve, which he maneuvered with a deadly calmness.

He muttered something.

"What?"

"We'll make it through," he said. "Better hold on."

Until then, I had not fully realized that the road was gradually going downhill. The descent now became noticeably sharp and quick. Colonel Min shifted the jeep into a lower gear. The jeep slowed down with a groan and shudder. The fog became thicker and heavier. In a few minutes, the road leveled off and ran straight ahead. Colonel Min stopped the jeep and cut the engine. Silence rushed in and engulfed us.

"Where are we?" I said.

"We are at the bottom of a valley. The road cuts straight

through it. At the other end of the valley, it goes uphill and joins
the main route about two miles from our headquarters. Here." He
switched the headlights off. "Now you can see it better. Look up."
I could not make out much of the surroundings.
"Once your eyes get used to the darkness, you can see . . ."
"Yes."
I had not felt that the mountains were so close by. The bottom of
the valley was walled in everywhere by darkly looming, towering
precipices of the mountains. It was more of a gorge than a valley.
My eyes traced the silhouette of the crest of the mountain on my
right, following its jagged, undulating course. Clouds of fog swayed
up and down. Somewhere I heard a stream gurgling. Suddenly, I
felt as though we were completely sealed in by the dark mountains
which might come crashing down on us any moment. I thought I
heard a rock sliding down.
"Actually, these mountains are not that high. Steep and rocky
but not really high," he said. "Watch this." He reached into the
back seat and brought out a revolver. Before I could say a word, he
fired the gun into the dank air. The flash blinded me a moment,
then I heard the shot echoing off into the sky, against the mountains
which reverberated the sound one after another in an unending wave
of shuddering roars. I felt as though thousands of beasts, their
slumbers suddenly disturbed, crouching in fury somewhere in the
deep, dark caves of the convulsing mountains, began howling all
around me. Colonel Min put the revolver away into the back seat
and sat straight up in his seat. Then, taking me by surprise, he
turned on the ignition, and the engine came to life, shuddering,
trembling, and whining. A moment of shivery illusion overwhelmed
me; the sudden, frantic roar of the jeep and the sullen, growling, angry echoes of the gunshot seemed to clash against each other in the
ghostly, foggy, night air, swirling in the vortexes of sounds and fur-
ries; and the aroused mountains, black and brooding, massive and
menacing, now taking part in the eerie slaughter of sounds, seemed
to come closing in on us slowly and inexorably, nearer and nearer

from all sides, threatening to squeeze and crush us — Colonel Min switched the headlights on — the mountains rushed toward us from the right and from the left like a gigantic vise . . . Colonel Min drove ahead, stopped, and drove on a little farther, stopped again; then, he began rocking the jeep back and forth, each time changing the direction, swiveling, as it were, the jeep around. And only then it occurred to me that he was trying to find something out there in the dark, using the jeep's headlights as a searchlight.

"There!" he whispered. "There they are! Look!"

I squinted hard into the misty darkness. "What? Where?"

"There! There!" The stem of his pipe jabbed at the dark air.

Then I saw them, one, two, three, four, five . . . mound after mound of black earth.

Colonel Min whispered. "Graves. Mass graves."

"Graves?"

"Each one of them must have fifteen, twenty corpses rotted inside. More of them at the other end of the valley, with more skeletons inside."

Patches of gray fog wafted in over the mounds. I turned to him. "Your men," I said. "Are they your men's?"

He shook his head. "No. Communists and their prisoners. Political prisoners."

"Where were you?" I said. "Were you here when . . ."

"My men were up there," he said, looking up at the dark precipices. His hand swept the air. "I had them positioned up there, all around, all over. I was there." He pointed at an invisible crest of a mountain to our right. "Yes. I had my command post up there. From there, I had the full view of the valley, every inch of it, every corner of it. We had the whole valley sealed off. We had them trapped in here."

"The Communists?"

"And their political prisoners. None escaped. They were all massacred. We slaughtered them all. None of them got out of here alive. We killed them all."

"You killed them all." I realized I was whispering. "But — but why?"

He did not reply. He turned off the engine and the lights. The darkness blinded me for a moment, and the mounds, the mass graves, faded into the foggy air; then, as my vision became accustomed to the darkness all around us, I could feel their blurred, shadowy presence. I looked up toward the sky and saw that the black rain cloud had been shredded into hundreds of fluffy patches now aimlessly drifting amid the star-studded sky.

Colonel Min's hushed voice startled me.

"What?"

"The Japanese captain," he said. "Yes, I killed him, too."

It was like a *coup de main;* since we had left General Yoon's headquarters, I had been searching for an opening in the armor of his silence, as it were, through which I could assault him with questions on General Ham's accusation. Thoroughly taken by surprise, I blurted out, "Did he have to die? This — this Japanese officer?"

He said quickly, "Did he have to die? Did he have to die? I don't know. How would I know? All I know is that I killed him. Yes, I killed him! Did he have to die? No, that I don't know. I would never know. I was not a judge. I was only an executioner, don't you know?" His shadowy face turned to me and his voice slashed at me with a ferocious savageness. "I was only his executioner, don't you know? I was never his judge! Do you understand that? I never judged him. I never had a moment to judge him. I simply executed him. Did I have time to evaluate him, cross-examine him, judge him, and find him guilty of being an evil man who deserved to be executed? No, no, Major Lee. The evil in him manifested itself and it had to be destroyed."

"It had to be destroyed, you say," I said. "There — you did judge him!"

"Ah, you do not understand, Major. I did not set myself up as his judge, as the symbol of the good and the pure, handing down a fair, impartial, just verdict on the symbol of the evil and the corrupt in

man. No, no! It was a battle between the evils, don't you know!
His evil was executed by my evil. As you said, beasts devouring
beasts!"

He froze himself into a stony silence.

I dared not disturb him.

And he began, slowly, quietly, as if thawing himself out of the
mass of ice he had just been. "You asked me if this Japanese captain was the Japanese officer I had brought with me to my hometown. I suppose Lieutenant Cho has told you about that. No, that
was First Lieutenant Nomura. Nomura Tadashi. He was one of
my best friends. And Lieutenant Cho's father's, too. We all went to
a university together in Tokyo in nineteen-forty-one. And we
roomed together, too, in downtown Tokyo. We had a small apartment, Lieutenant Cho's father and I, and Nomura had one across
from ours. We became good friends. Nomura was the only son of an
impoverished Japanese noble family. His father had a title, baronet,
I think. Nomura never wanted to talk about that and about his family. At first, we were a little wary of him, I am afraid. In those
days, Japanese and Koreans seldom mixed. The first year there in
the apartment, we were polite to each other, met occasionally to
exchange our notebooks or to go over our examinations. That was
all. But three years of living together under the same roof, going
to the same classes, reading the same books, being interested in the
same subjects, well, all that enabled us to forget that he was Japanese and we were Koreans and whatever social and political implications our relationships entailed. We became fast friends. By the
third year, we practically lived together, sharing meals, books, and
nearly everything else. And only then did he reveal to us that he
thought Japan would be defeated in the war, that he hoped the defeat of Japan would bring an end to the sufferings of Koreans in-
flicted on them by the Japanese, that he hoped the end of the war
would bring a long-hoped-for liberation of the Korean people. He
believed that the system of emperors would come to an end and the
defeat of Japan would usher in an entirely new, purified society to

his country. He regarded the war as an act of purgation for Japanese people, the war they brought on themselves, a result of their hubris, their hamartia. A period of great atonement would follow the end of the war. He never lived to see that day. If he had, perhaps he would have been disappointed and disillusioned. He was a poet, a romanticist, a dreamy idealist who became a passionate Marxist in his second year at the university. Was I ever a Marxist? No — even in those days, I never seemed to have had what it takes to be an idealist. Lieutenant Cho's father was a Marxist, once, that is, until the Communists took over North Korea."

"I know how he died," I said. "Lieutenant Cho told me about it."

"Then you know. Yes, only to die at the hands of Communist-trained murderers. Yes, he was an idealist, too, just like Nomura. In fact, it now seems that they had more in common than I with either of them. Well, at the end of our third year at the university, Nomura had to go into the army. He had to volunteer, do you understand?"

"Yes. Then our turns came, too."

He nodded. "Yes. So — Nomura became a second lieutenant in the glorious, sacred army of the Sun-God, and he was sent to Manchuria. We gave him a farewell party just before he went to see his parents in Kyoto for the last time. We drank, we wept, and we promised to each other that someday, someday when the whole world recovered from its madness, perhaps we would meet again somewhere and help each other in building a new world, a sane world, a purified world, gathering up whatever was left from the ashes of the war. Perhaps I was an idealist, too, who knows? So he went off to a war that he hoped would defeat his country, yes, defeat his country for the sake of her ultimate salvation. And then, we, too, left the university and Japan and returned to Korea."

"Only to be drafted by the Japanese into their army, like Nomura."

"Yes. I tried to escape from them. Heaven knows I tried. But, in the end, I could not get away from them, and I decided that the best way I could escape from them was to join them. You see, I wanted to go to China, hoping that perhaps, once I was in China, I could run away from them and join up with the Koreans in exile who had combat units fighting alongside the Chinese against Japan."

"Some of them were with the Nationalist and some with the Chinese Communists. Which ones did you hope to find?"

"In those days, it didn't matter which side, did it? I managed to sneak myself out of Korea and go to Manchuria, near Mukden. Nomura was stationed there, you see. I knew that. He was a first lieutenant then, assigned to a makeshift officers training center set up by the Kanto Army. I hoped that he would and could help me to smuggle myself into China. It didn't turn out to be that way."

"He refused to help you?"

"No, no, that's not what I meant. I got in touch with him and told him my situation and my hopes and plans. Well, to make a long story short, he, in the end, convinced me that the best way, the best plan for both of us, was for me to become a Japanese officer. How? He had a plan. It so happened that the commandant of the training center was a young lieutenant colonel whose father was a vassal of a sort to Nomura's father. It seemed that Nomura's father had helped him through school before the Nomura family's fortune declined. This colonel was quite loyal to Nomura's father and to the Nomura family, and that was why Nomura was assigned to his training center as a favor. He had vowed to look after Nomura, you see. Nomura took me to see him. We planned this together, of course. I was to volunteer for the Army. I was to present myself and convince him I was a Korean loyal to the Japanese empire and its cause. And, naturally, being Nomura's friend didn't hurt our plan. Nomura asked him to make an extraordinary exception and take me into the training center as an officer candidate. Without checking me out with the Japanese authority in my hometown, or notifying them of my volunteering, said Nomura, because, as the colonel surely understands, there is a strong anti-Japanese sentiment among Koreans and if the fact of my having volunteered for the Japanese Army were to be publicly known in my hometown, no one could predict what might happen to my family, no one could imagine what sort of humiliation and abuse my family might become subjected to, although my family would be quite proud of my being in the emperor's army as an officer, and so on. The colonel never doubted Nomura's words. Besides, I think he was actually glad to take me in, if not as a great favor for Nomura, then just to have another potential officer to carry on the war. In any case, I became an officer in a month and a half."

"They were in a hurry to ship you out. I hadn't realized their training period was so short. Of course, as you know, I became an officer, formally, that is, in about three months."

"I became one in two months in this Army. Anyway, when I was duly commissioned, I stayed at the center for a while as an assistant of a sort to Nomura, another favor from the commandant. Then, finally, Nomura had to be shipped out as a company commander of a newly formed task force, and I volunteered to go along with him. The commandant made me a platoon leader under Nomura, an unheard-of thing for a Korean to take charge of a Japanese platoon, and we were to proceed to somewhere along the Mongolian border to guard against the Soviets and also to fight the Chinese Communists' Eighth Route Army. We had a week of leave before our departure and it was then that Nomura really took me into his confidence and revealed his plans to me. He wanted to escape. He wanted to desert, you see, to cross the Mongolian border into Russia and surrender himself and ask for political asylum in the Soviet Union. He wanted me to go with him. I wasn't about to give myself up to the Russians. I wanted to join up with the Korean exile groups. Of course, I couldn't quite convince him to surrender himself to the Korean units. In any case, we were of one mind on one thing, that we would escape at the first chance we could find. It was a stroke of fortune, you might say, that we were to be stationed so close to the Mongolian border. And then we decided to visit Lieutenant Cho's father. Mind you, it was not for any sentimental reason that we de-

cided to take a chance and go to my hometown to see him. Not to
see my family, either. I had already known that both my parents
had died. We wanted to see Cho because, you see, he was an underground agent for the Korean exile group with the Chinese Communist Eighth Route Army. He was the only one I knew who was
in constant contact with the exile group, who could help me to get
in touch with the group and to be trusted once I reached them. So,
Nomura volunteered to come along with me to my hometown, as an
added protection for me, just in case, although my being a Japanese
officer would undoubtedly prevent any kind of harassment from
the local Japanese police. Besides, he wanted to see Cho too, if it
ever turned out that he, too, had to join me and give himself up to
the Chinese Communists. Our plan was to have Cho send word to
his contacts so that if and when I, or both I and Nomura, made it to
the Chinese side, they would have had some sort of advance information on me or on us, however it was going to turn out."

"So — you went back to your hometown," I said, "and the whole
town adored you."

"Yes. They did. They didn't care about the fact that I was a
Japanese officer. The only thing they cared for was that I was still
alive. I think many of them instinctively knew what I was really
up to, although no one dared mention it. Yes, they were good to me."

I ventured, "Was it because . . . ? Could it have been because
of this thing about the Japanese detective? I mean, the Korean detective working for the Japanese police?"

"What Japanese detective?" His voice was calm.

I stared at his dark face.

"What Japanese detective?"

"Never mind," I said. "I didn't mean to interrupt you. I understand Lieutenant Cho's father was sick. Tuberculosis?"

"Yes, he had tuberculosis. He was a brave, kind man. He gave us
the names of some people in Manchuria, near the border, who might
be able to help us. Nomura and I stayed in town for a few days, I
paid my last respects to my parents' graves, then we came back to

Manchuria just in time for our departure to the Mongolian border. We arrived at our post sometime in the latter part of May. That was in nineteen-forty-five, and our first opportunity came in the second week of June."

"And you made it."

"No. We didn't make it. As I said, Nomura had wanted to go over to the Russian side, but he had to change his mind about it and had to decide to come with me. We had gotten in touch with a Chinese agent Lieutenant Cho's father had suggested that we see. This Chinese was an agent of the Chinese Communist Eighth Route Army, a Communist, that is. When Nomura told him of his intention of deserting to the Soviets, he advised Nomura against doing it. What he said to Nomura had a great emotional impact on him, I am afraid. The Chinese agent said that the Soviets were, at that time, not about to do anything to impair their relations with the Japanese. There had been cases of Japanese defectors crossing the border into the Soviet side and the Russians had simply arrested them and handed them back to the Japanese military authority. But I am a Marxist, said Nomura. The Chinese just snorted at him. It didn't make any difference to the Russians, he said. The Russians would surely invade Manchuria as soon as they could afford the effort, but, until then, such an act on their part as handing Japanese defectors back across the border was part of their grand deception. In the end, Nomura was convinced and decided to come over with me. As I said, we never made it. We almost made it through, but we were caught by the Japanese at the top of a mountain, which at the time more or less separated the Japanese-controlled sector and the Communist-controlled region. There had been a stalemate of a sort between them, and if we had made it over that mountain, we would have been in the Chinese sector. As it turned out, it was Nomura's orderly who had suspected us and when we rode out of the post that afternoon — yes, we went on horses — when we didn't come back to the post by the time we had said we would be back, the orderly reported to the battalion commander. We had planned it carefully, but we didn't know that a battalion adjacent to ours had just been moved out that afternoon. We didn't have that information, that the battalion was going to try to take the mountain and set up an artillery position. A search party was sent out and the battalion on the move was alerted. We didn't have a chance. Our battalion sent a captain out to Nomura's company to take over, and this captain, who had been a career non-commissioned officer, about thirty-five years old, joined the search with a platoon from Nomura's old company. Two days later, we were caught by the patrol from the other battalion; that was in the early afternoon, and by nightfall we were handed over to this captain who was given the job of escorting us back to our battalion, and then to the division. Only — he had no intention of taking us back all the way to the division. He meant to kill us on the way.

"We started around six o'clock in the evening, this captain with his platoon of men from Nomura's old company, some from my own platoon, too, all riding on horses. We came down the mountain and went about four miles, heading for the small village where we were supposed to spend the night, because traveling at night was dangerous. At night, there would be Chinese guerrillas swarming all over. And I am sure we had been spotted by the guerrillas already and I am equally sure that they had followed us, too. About a mile or so from the village, the captain stopped us. We dismounted. The captain called the sergeant in charge of the platoon, the same sergeant who had been Nomura's sergeant major. The captain ordered him to pick a squad of men out of the platoon and have the rest of the men proceed to the village. A squad stayed with us and the rest of them left. I think I knew then what the captain was up to. He was going to kill us. I am sure Nomura sensed that and the sergeant, too, because he began telling the captain that it was dangerous to break up the platoon there, at that time of the night, when the guerrillas might appear any moment, and so on. The captain wouldn't listen to that. Although it was in June, the night air was chilly. There was the moon, I remember, and I remember, too, that there was the dark, massive, silent mountain behind us and the endless, flat, great plains of Manchuria spread before us for miles and miles. And there we were, in the middle of nowhere, you might say, and the captain was getting ready for our execution. At first, I thought he was going to have us shot by the squad, a makeshift firing squad. But he had a more devilish plan in his mind."

"He was going to kill you himself?"

"No. He was going to have us kill each other. Not exactly, but it would have come out that way. He had me untied. We had been bound with ropes, you see, and now he commanded the sergeant to untie me. Nomura was still bound. The captain — I never knew his name — he had the squad surround us in a circle, in the middle of which he had Nomura kneel down on the earth. He had the sergeant hold onto me, and then he worked himself up into a savage tirade against Nomura. The point of his rage was that Nomura was a disgrace to the Imperial Army, to the Holy Emperor, indeed, to the Sun-God himself. He could understand why I would want to desert; a cheap, despicable Korean who could never be trusted. Yes, he could understand a Korean wanting to escape; he had never trusted, and he would never trust, Koreans even when they were in the uniform of the Imperial Army. But, Nomura, the son of a noble family, a volunteer, an officer, an officer of the invincible Kanto Army — that was a different story. In short, my act was a crime; I was like a thief or an embezzler, a small-time crook, you might say. I simply committed a petty crime, from his point of view. But, Nomura's act was treason; Nomura committed a sin. I was a mere criminal whereas Nomura was a sinner. So — the captain had decided that the most shameful punishment he could think of for Nomura was that he die at my hand."

"You — you kill Nomura!"

"Yes, I was to kill Nomura. Nomura was to die at the hand of a subhuman criminal, me."

"He wouldn't have had the authority to execute you and Nomura."

"Ah, did it matter?"

"And what about you? Were you to be shot? Or kill yourself?"

"Nothing of the sort. He would let me go when I killed Nomura. Yes, he would let me go. But, of course, the moment I took a step, he would have shot me. He wanted me to execute Nomura, in any case. He drew his sword. Nomura was blindfolded. He was on his knees. He was delirious, but he knew what was about to happen to him. He couldn't speak coherently but he was mumbling on, begging me to kill him. He would rather die at my hand than be hung by the neck at the division and have everyone see him die. First he begged the captain to let him commit hara-kiri. 'You aren't good enough to be a samurai,' sneered the captain. The soldiers were stone silent, as if mesmerized. The sergeant was shaking; I could feel his hand on my arm and, indeed, his whole body trembling. Nomura was hissing, 'Min, Min!' He was calling me by my Korean name, you see. 'Min, Min,' he was saying, 'please let me die at your hand! Remember our friendship and do me a last favor. Kill me! Kill me!'

"I stood there paralyzed, mesmerized as in a nightmare. Nomura's words still haunt me. As I said, he was delirious, and his maddening, high-pitched voice panting out, 'Kill me, Kill me!' The whole scene was like one on a slow-motion, hallucinatory screen. I felt as though I was both in and out of the scene at the same time. The soldiers, deathly silent, their grotesquely long shadows creeping on the earth. The sergeant's grip on my arm tightened and I smelled his rancid sweat and felt his body trembling. I heard Nomura gasping, his words no longer intelligible, just a faint whimpering. The captain whipped around to me and grabbed my arm and pushed me toward Nomura. Nomura looked so small. His head on the ground, his arms tied behind his back. 'Watch me!' hissed the captain. He raised his sword. It flashed in the moonlight, pale, deathly white. He slowly brought it down over Nomura's neck and then flipping the sword around, let the back of the blade touch the neck and Nomura screamed and shrieked and then he was silent. I

am sure he died then. 'Do it this way, hear!' barked the captain to
me. 'Now! Do it!' He thrust the sword to me. I was frozen still.
He slapped me on the cheek. My body was shaking and chattering
and cold. I was fighting myself against screaming out and fainting.
I was sick. My mouth was parched. And the captain slapped me
again. My mouth was filling up with rotten, sour saliva. And, like a
sleepwalker, I found myself taking the sword from the captain's
hand and taking a step toward Nomura, when the sergeant ran over
to the captain and began babbling, 'You can't do this! You can't
do this!' The captain slapped him away. And then I threw up and
collapsed on the ground, half fainted, my mouth dribbling and my
insides feeling as though they were tearing themselves up into
shreds. And I remember the captain kicking me in the side and I
doubling up. So there we were — Nomura kneeling down there
like a fetus, and I sprawled on the ground like a battered insect.
But I was still clutching at the sword, my hand gripping the hilt,
my half-dazed eyes seeing its steely white blade that seemed so long
on the earth. The sergeant pulled me up. The captain spat at me,
'Idiot!' Then, it happened. The captain took out his automatic
from the holster and bent over the back of Nomura. He pressed
the muzzle of the gun on the back of Nomura's head and shot him.
He shot him dead with one bullet. I remember the flash of the gun
and the black shadows of the soldiers all tangling up and the sergeant letting me go . . . and the captain slowly turning to me and
I was standing immobile and I saw him raise the gun and heard the
shot and I felt my left shoulder jerk; then I killed him. I felt the
earth was moving, the sky tumbling over my head; I did not think,
I forgot the soldiers, the sergeant, everything, and I was screaming,
roaring like a beast and I leaped at the captain with the sword. I
don't know what I did with the sword, how I used it — but I cut him
from his neck down to his chest. We fell together, I on top of him.
Then I fainted.

"I don't remember what happened immediately after that. When
I came to — I couldn't have been out for more than a few minutes,

I suppose — when I came to, I saw the soldiers mounted on the horses, rather, I saw the black shadows of the soldiers and the horses. The captain's body wasn't there, and I couldn't see Nomura's body, either. The shadows began moving. Then I heard a horse behind me. I tried to stand up. I couldn't. I twisted myself around to see what was behind me. The sergeant was there with his horse. He had a gun in his hand. I tried to shout, I tried to say something — I don't remember what. But my voice had left me. Only hoarse, unintelligible gasping. He bent down, I saw his eyes peering into mine. I was sprawled flat on my back, delirious but aware of the clear night sky with millions of stars. And the stars disappeared from my dazed vision and the shadowy, massive face of the sergeant slowly descended on mine. My body was twitching and convulsing. I thought he was going to kill me. I struggled to get up but he pushed me down and I ceased to struggle and let myself go and give in to an almost intoxicating sensation of leaden inertia. 'You aren't dead,' the sergeant whispered to me. 'You aren't dead yet. You aren't going to die, understand? Can you hear me?' I opened my eyes. His dark steel helmet was like an enormous mound of graves against the sky with stars twinkling around its silhouette. He whispered again, 'Wait till we are gone, then run. You run, understand?' He stood up, and his giant shadow leaped against me, and I saw him raise the gun in his hand. The flash and the explosion and the shower of dirt . . . and I fainted. I don't remember how long I was in that state of unconsciousness, but when I came to once more, they were all gone. I was there all alone, in the middle of nowhere, my shoulder on fire and bleeding, my face smeared with blood and slimy saliva, all my body splattered with the blood of the captain, all alone in the infinite expanse of the great plains of Manchuria, with only the cold, pale, blue moon and the wavering stars looking down on my battered, bleeding, aching body. I began crying. Then the Chinese guerrillas came.

"They had just ambushed the Japanese platoon in the village. There must have been more than fifty guerrillas, more like a cavalry detachment. It was a massacre. The Japanese were outnumbered and surprised. Only one third of them managed to get away. The guerrillas took me to the village and I saw bodies all over. Nomura's body, too. And the sergeant's, hacked to death. Those who got away must have taken the captain's body. I couldn't find it. You see, I told the guerrillas about what had happened, and they wanted the captain's body. But it was gone. Four Japanese had been captured, but the Chinese shot them all before we left the village. Yes — it was a slaughter.

"And — and it was a slaughter here, too," he said, raising his face toward the dark sky. "Here — all those graves out there. I killed them all. I slaughtered them all, don't you know! All those North Koreans and their political prisoners, our people . . . Our Intelligence had learned that a company of North Korean Security Police was heading this way with over fifty political prisoners. Remember, we were on the offensive and they were on the run; they had been routed out of Seoul. The American armor units were pushing so fast on the western front that they must have thought they had a better chance to escape through this mountainous sector. But they had been spotted by our reconnaissance patrol and my battalion was given the task of tracking them down. Why they had decided to spend the night here we would never know. They had been traveling at night and hiding out during the day. We caught up with them soon enough and trapped them here. We surrounded them in the middle of the night. They didn't know that by dawn I had already positioned my units all around them, all over, on the mountains. We had sealed them in. There was absolutely no way for them to escape from our net. The operation would have been simpler if I hadn't had the political prisoners to worry about. I didn't quite know what to do about them. But, first, I had to let them know that they hadn't a chance either to slip out from our trap or to fight their way out. It was a steel ring I had set around them. There was not one gap or crack. I wanted to convince them, I wanted to show them, that the only sensible thing they could do was to surrender. When the morning came, they knew they were trapped. By then, I had a loudspeaker set up at my command post up there, waiting, and, in addition, I had my regiment send a reconnaissance plane over and have it keep on circling. The bloody sun was rising higher and higher and we already began to feel the heat. We could see them all. Incredibly enough, they hadn't even dug themselves in. They had simply slept through the night in a huddle at the foot of a hill on that side across from where we are. It was unbelievable the way they were there completely exposed to our full view. They must have been out of their wits, having been chased and hunted for so long, and I suppose they were starving and exhausted. At least I thought so. I thought our tactics should be to convince them that they had now come to the end of their run, and to wait, rather than doing anything to provoke them to fight. There were those prisoners, you see. I was willing to wait as long as it took them to lay down their arms and give up. But my regimental commander couldn't wait; he didn't share my opinion. He wanted an immediate surrender. I had no choice. I spoke through the loudspeaker and demanded that they surrender. To show them that they were completely surrounded, I had my men fire into the sky, one position after another, all around them.

"It didn't work. The man in charge of them must have been a fanatic or a madman. He knew he didn't have a chance, but he wasn't about to give up. He was herding the prisoners into several small groups, in a circle, and it was obvious that he intended to use the prisoners as shields for his men. We watched and waited. Then someone shouted back to us. They wanted to make a deal. We would let them go and give them one hour and they would set the prisoners free after that. Or else, they would kill the prisoners and fight to the last man. Of course, I didn't believe that they would set the prisoners free, but, at the same time, I couldn't help believing that they would really kill the prisoners or use them as shields and try to fight their way out. Just to see what they would threaten to do, I replied there would be no such deal. Their commander responded by lining up a group of prisoners in our full view with his soldiers aiming at the prisoners with their burp guns. It was a nightmare. We could see each other clearly, though we had a better view of them. The yellow-green uniform with red shoulder patches . . . I can still picture them. The sun flashing off their guns. We were so close to each other in distance although, of course, we were high up there, and we could hear their footsteps and voices. I called the regiment. The colonel said we would not make any deal with them. We would catch up with them, no doubt, but we would have to go through it all over again. 'They are just bluffing,' the colonel said. 'I don't buy their bluffing! An unconditional surrender or else!' Or else what! I spoke through the loudspeaker again. They wouldn't surrender. The colonel called me and said I should tell them that I didn't believe those were really political prisoners at all but their own men disguised as prisoners to fool us. 'How do we know these are real prisoners?' said the colonel. 'You tell them that and see what happens. Maybe they are all Commies masquerading as prisoners just to insure their own protection.' I told the colonel that it was not likely. We saw them. I saw them through my binoculars, these skeletonlike men in rags! 'Tell them anyway,' said the colonel, 'and see what happens.' 'We mustn't push them too far,' I said. 'These are desperate men and they just might do anything. They might shoot some prisoners just to prove to us that they really are prisoners.' 'Then we will know for sure,' said the colonel. 'Well, what about the dead prisoners!' I said. 'If they really shoot the prisoners and if those prisoners turn out to be really prisoners, people on our side!' 'In that case, the Communists killed the prisoners, not us,' said the colonel. 'I can't take that chance,' I said. 'We can't sit there all day and let them stew us. We have to be on the move. We have to push up. That's an order.' A fool I was! I had no choice. I spoke through the loudspeaker again. No sooner had the echoes of my voice faded into the air than they pushed four prisoners out from their defense perimeter, those human shields. The prisoners tried to run. They knew what was happening. And the

Communists mowed them down with machine guns. I saw it all through my binoculars. The prisoners couldn't even run; they were just staggering away when they were gunned down. I called the colonel. 'Are you sure they are dead? Maybe they are faking, who knows?' he said. I was going out of my mind. I shouted back at the colonel, 'I saw it happen with my own eyes, Colonel! They are shot to death! Do I have to tell you that I can see their blood!' 'Well, don't get hysterical,' the colonel said. 'Did you really see the blood?' 'I am not playing a game here, Colonel,' I shouted, and hung up. He called me back instantly. 'Lob down a few mortar shells,' he said. 'That will tell them we intend to wipe them all out, prisoners or no prisoners. That's an order!' I didn't do it. I couldn't do it. The colonel called again. I told him I hadn't fired the mortars. A moment of silence and he asked me to give him the exact coordinates of the gorge. I gave them to him and then I knew what he was up to. I got panicky, I pleaded with him not to do it. You see, he was going to call for artillery barrage. He gave me ten minutes. I grabbed the loudspeaker and told them that in ten minutes they would all be blown up by our artillery unless they surrendered immediately. We were all going out of our minds. My operations officer kept on saying this was insane, insane, and we should let them all go. We could chase after them with patrols and sniper teams. But it was too late to do anything else. The Communists, too, had gone out of their minds. They began firing at us in all directions. I had no choice. I ordered a few mortar shells lobbed down without hitting them, to show them we really meant it about the artillery. Their firing stopped for a moment, and I called the regiment to hold the artillery barrage — and just then the first barrage of artillery whooshed in and that did it. A pandemonium broke out down here. I ordered my men to hold fire and I could see through the rising dirt and dust and smoke the prisoners running and crawling away in all directions and they were being mowed down by the Communists and the Communists were firing away at us, they too running in all directions. More artillery shells flew in. The air was filled with the explosions of machine-gun chatterings and the smell of powder. I had no choice. Some of them were digging in, some crawling up the mountains. I ordered my men to fire. It was as if my men were mesmerized in a bad dream and just waking up from it still in delirium. Perhaps they had been as frustrated and helpless as I had been, and now, giving in to their pent-up feelings, they poured out everything they had. They were blasting away at everything that moved down below here. Rifles, machine guns, grenades, rockets, mortars . . . it was now out of my hands. Down there, we could no longer tell who was what, the Communists and the prisoners, either blown up to pieces, sprawled dead, or still locked in a death struggle. A band of North Koreans somehow managed to hold on to a group of prisoners and they were edging toward the northern gap of the gorge. I shouted to my radioman to tell the unit on the hill commanding the northern exit to let them go, but it was too late. As I watched through my binoculars, the last surviving band of Communists and prisoners was pounded on by mortar shells and cut down by machine-gun cross fires. It was all over. We had slaughtered them all. Suddenly it was all very quiet, no one spoke, no one moved; there was the stinking smell of death all around us, the clouds of dust and hazy blue smoke of powder slowly rising from the bottom of the gorge in the blinding sun. It was all very hushed. Then we heard the drone of the reconnaissance plane that came diving out of the clear blue sky, circling and circling over our heads like an eagle, like a vulture — and the colonel called me to move my battalion to a new position. Yes — it was all over. We counted a hundred sixty-four bodies in all. We dug those graves, if you can call them graves, and buried them all together, the Communists and their prisoners alike. I did not go down the hill. I stayed up there, watching my men drag the bodies out and pile them up, then bury them away. My operations officer had ordered the bugler to sound taps, and I, engulfed in the waves of the bugle's echoes, I wept."

I muttered, feeling utterly helpless, "If the prisoners hadn't panicked you could still have had time to call off the artillery . . . But the Communist commander . . . surely he must have known he didn't have a chance . . ."

Colonel Min thrust his dark face up close to mine. He spoke in cold fury, "Do you know who my regimental commander was? It was a certain Lieutenant Colonel Mah."

I saw his eyes glisten in the shadow.

"Come! Let us go," he said quietly.

At the southern end of the gorge, we began climbing on a road that rose higher and higher in a spiral ascent, until at the halfway point of the steep mountain it joined the main route of supply a few miles from the Corps headquarters. On the main road, Colonel Min stopped the jeep. We looked back down toward the bottom of the valley. We could not see it anymore. Cloudlike gray fog, thick and heavy, sealed off the gorge like a ceiling.

I faced Colonel Min. "Captain Park . . . he had written me once when I was in Pyungyang . . . about the hand-to-hand combat he and his Marines had . . . in a valley like this."

He nodded. "I know of the battle. It was on the eastern front."

He was silent, brooding. "So, in the end, he went back to God, after all," he said.

"His last words were these: 'I have been clinging onto the precipice of History, but I give up. I am prepared to take leave of it.' "

"Ah, how like him! How like him!" he said. His voice rose. "How did I feel looking down at the bloody bottom of this valley? How did I feel? I'll tell you. I felt like a beast. I felt like a beast, don't you know?"

"That's enough. Don't say any more."

He looked up at the dark heavens. "In the dark of night I howl at the sky with all my sorrows," he said. Tears glistened in his eyes.

"But there is nothing out there to listen to my story. Do you understand?"

I gazed at his dark face. "No. There is nothing out there," I said.

"No," he said. His voice was defiant. "We have only ourselves."

Chapter 8

Lieutenant Cho was waiting for us when we returned to the Corps headquarters. He met us at the gate. I checked my watch with his; it was five minutes to three. He was on foot and climbed into the back seat of our jeep. We moved away from the glaring lights of the gate and stopped in the shadows.

"Is everything all right?" asked Colonel Min.

Lieutenant Cho shook his head. "I am afraid not, sir. You have an unexpected and, if I may say so, sir, an unwelcome visitor waiting to see you. General Ahn from Seoul, sir. He arrived about half an hour ago. He flew in."

I could not help swearing. "What is he up to? What is he doing here?"

Colonel Min did not stir.

Lieutenant Cho said, "At first, he wanted to see General Hyun. He called from the airstrip and talked with the general's aide, but Captain Yang told him General Hyun couldn't be disturbed and told him to see you instead. That was quick thinking on Captain Yang's part, sir. Anyway, I went down to the airstrip and picked up General Ahn."

"How is the situation otherwise?" said Colonel Min.

"Fine, sir. General Yoon had communicated with us about General Ham. We have been in touch with our people at General Ham's headquarters. Everything is under control there, sir."

"Has Colonel McKay wanted to see me?"

"No, sir."

"Have the members of the council been alerted?" '

"Yes, sir."

"Has General Ahn talked with anyone in the Command Group?"

"No, sir. I made sure of that."

"That was very wise," Colonel Min said with a grin. "Where are the Group members now?"

"They are waiting for you two, sir. Chaplain Koh, too."

"Where?"

"At Chaplain Koh's quarters, sir."

"Why there?" I said.

"You see, sir, General Ahn is waiting for Colonel Min in the general's aide's office and so they didn't want to go to the general's office and wait for you two. So they were going to the war room but Chaplain Koh said they should all come to his quarters and have some tea."

Colonel Min nodded. "Good."

I said, "Lieutenant Cho, has General Ahn said anything to you about why he came out here? Has he come alone?"

"Yes, sir. He is alone. No, he hasn't said much to me, except to say that it was very urgent for him to see General Hyun."

Colonel Min was quiet for a moment. "How much does General Ahn know about our Intelligence network and operations?" he asked me.

"Nothing, as far as I know."

"Are you sure?"

"Quite certain."

"Is there any chance that he might know about our connections with General Mah's deputy chief, Colonel Son?"

"I am absolutely certain that he doesn't know about it. Why do you ask?"

"Just a hunch, Major Lee. We'll soon find out how much he knows. I don't like his coming out here. It attracts attention."

"He could have talked it over with Colonel Hwang of the Airborne, who is looking after my assignments."

"Something's not right, sir," said Lieutenant Cho.

"What do you mean?" I said.

"General Ahn's still insisting on seeing General Hyun. I have a feeling he is not too anxious to see you; I mean, sir, he seems a little disappointed that General Hyun won't see him now."

"Major Lee, do you trust him?" said Colonel Min.

"Why do you ask that?"

"You know him better than I do, I suppose."

I hesitated a moment. "I think I'd trust him to do the job he's assigned to. For the coup, I mean."

"In short, you are not endorsing him completely, that is, without reservation. Am I correct?"

"Yes."

"Why? Why do you have reservations about him?"

I came out clean. "He is too bloodthirsty."

"Do you mean his eagerness to assassinate General Mah?"

"He calls it liquidation."

"Well, General Yoon wants the same thing. He is quite eager, too, as you know, to kill General Mah."

"There seems to be some difference between General Ahn and General Yoon," I said, "in the way they approach the question of what to do with General Mah."

"You'd better spell it out."

"All right. General Yoon is emotional and impulsive about it, whereas I am convinced that General Ahn seems quite deliberate, cold-bloodedly deliberate about it. It is as if he had it planned for a long time, even before the question ever came up in connection with our coup. Do you understand?"

Colonel Min nodded. "Yes. But, then, General Ahn isn't the only one who has thought of assassinating General Mah at one time or another."

"I am merely questioning his motivation."

He did not reply to that. After a moment of silence, he said, "I want you to come with me to see him, but I want you to make sure that you do nothing, say nothing, to let him know that we have infiltrated into General Mah's headquarters. Is that clear? I don't want him to know anything about Colonel Son. Also, not a word about General Ham. Lieutenant Cho, you haven't told him about General Ham, I trust?"

"No, sir. Not a word about that, sir."

"Good."

"Why all this precaution? You don't trust him either, do you?" I said.

"I don't know. Just being prudent, I suppose. Let him talk and we'll listen but we'll not take him into our confidence, for the time being. Lieutenant Cho, Major Lee and I will see him in the general's office and I want you to go to the chaplain's quarters and tell the others not to mention General Ham in case any of them happen to run into General Ahn later on. Not one word about it. All right. Let's get this over with."

"All right," I said.

"Remember this, Major Lee. Should General Ahn mention anything about or in connection with General Ham, we know nothing about him. Do you understand? Nothing whatsoever about where he is now, or nothing about his plans for a secret rendezvous with General Mah."

We drove on toward the general's office building. Then Colonel Min changed his mind. "I don't want to talk with him in there. Lieutenant Cho, you go in and tell him we are waiting for him outside." Colonel Min swung the jeep around and stopped it in the middle of the headquarters plaza. Lieutenant Cho hurried off to the general's office. We walked away from the jeep toward the tanks and the helicopter. Here and there, the shadowy, massive, squatting forms of tanks loomed in the misty night air. We stood under the drooping blades of the helicopter. We saw the door open at the general's office. In the hazy light of the lamp over the entrance, General Ahn paused for a moment, speaking to Lieutenant Cho. Lieutenant Cho was pointing his hand toward our direction. General Ahn came, limping. We gave him a salute.

"Let's cut out the formality, shall we?" he said cheerfully. "I didn't come all the way out here for that."

"General, it is a pleasant surprise," said Colonel Min.

"Well, I must say it is good to be out on the front. You know me. I feel much more at home out here than back in Seoul at my desk. Good to see you again, Major Lee."

"Surprised to see you, General," I said. "I left you only a short while ago."

"I know, I know," he said. "I tried to get hold of you back in Seoul but it was too late. You had already left. If I had been able to get in touch with you in time, I wouldn't have had to make this trip, which I am sure you, Colonel Min, think might be too conspicuous."

"I am afraid it is," said Colonel Min. "I understand you wish to see the general."

General Ahn tucked his cane under his arm. The silver tip of the cane gleamed faintly in the dark. "Colonel, let's be quite frank with each other, shall we? That's why I said we should cut out the formality. Of course, I didn't come out here to see the general. I came out to see you. I do mean that, Colonel, because, well, we shan't go into that now, shall we?"

"As you please, General," said Colonel Min.

General Ahn turned to me. "I do hope you won't be offended if I say this, but I should like to have a talk with Colonel Min in private. Do you mind?"

Colonel Min said, "I would like Major Lee to be present, sir, if you don't mind. And, if you don't mind, Major Lee."

"I don't mind," I said.

General Ahn said quickly, "If you say so, Colonel, of course I don't mind. After all, Major Lee here is my special assistant, too, not that I have seen much of him lately." He laughed.

"We are very grateful to you for your consideration, General," said Colonel Min.

"You are quite welcome, Colonel. Anything for our cause."

Colonel Min said, rather coldly, I thought, "What brings you out here, General?"

"Well, where shall I begin? The import of this information is so staggering that I hardly know where to begin. Have you seen or have you been in touch with General Ham recently?"

"No," said Colonel Min. "What about General Ham?"

"I am afraid we have a traitor on our hands. General Ham has been in cahoots with General Mah."

Colonel Min kept quiet for a while. "I don't believe it, General," he said. "I know I must believe your words, but I can't quite bring myself to believe that General Ham would sell us out. He has nothing to gain but everything to lose by going over to General Mah's side."

"Ah, but that we don't know," said General Ahn.

"How do you know about it? I mean, General, where and how did you get this fantastic information, if you don't mind my asking, sir?"

"In my position, I do have my own sources and resources of intelligence, as Major Lee well knows. But this one will surprise you. I was told about General Ham by General Mah in person."

"I beg your pardon, sir?" Colonel Min seemed genuinely surprised.

I, too, could not restrain my shock. "I don't understand this at all, General."

"I told you this is fantastic. Shortly after you left, Major Lee,

General Mah called me up and asked me if he could drop by my office."

"Just like that," said Colonel Min.

"Yes, just like that. I must confess I was frightened out of my wits. I was absolutely sure our plans had leaked and General Mah was rounding up every one of us. I wasn't about to be arrested sitting at my desk. So, to see what he was really up to, I suggested he come to my house. He said he would. As you know, I live out in the outskirts, rather isolated, and it is close to the camp of my Commando Groups. If General Mah is going to make a final move, I said to myself, I am going to put up a good fight. I had my Commando Groups alerted, naturally. I had defense plans, you might say. So, when he was agreeable to my suggestion, I was quite taken aback."

"So you two met at your house," I said.

"Yes. Looking back, I can't help laughing at myself, but, at the time, I was expecting a swarm of his agents charging in. Well, he came alone — that is, with his aide and the driver who did not come into the house with him."

Colonel Min said, "In what car, General?"

"What difference does that make?" said General Ahn.

"Just being curious, sir. Was it a black sedan, 1958 Plymouth?"

"No. It was his own jeep."

"Marked?"

"Yes."

"Was it a Headquarters jeep or a Presidential Brigade one?"

"I am puzzled by your curiosity. It was the one belonging to the Presidential Brigade."

"Thank you, General. Sorry I interrupted you."

"May I go on now?"

"Please."

"So General Mah told me about General Ham."

"Specifically about what, General?" I said.

"General Ham has contacted General Mah and has requested a secret meeting with him."

"When?" Colonel Min said.

"Tomorrow evening," he said. "I mean, this evening now that it is already morning."

"Do you know the details, sir?" Colonel Min said.

"That General Mah would not tell me about. I am sorry. He had good reasons not to tell me too much about what had gone on between them. He is bargaining. Colonel, he wants to make a deal with you."

"I beg your pardon, sir?" said Colonel Min. "Why with me? Does it mean that he knows of our plans?"

"What do you think? Of course he does. But I hasten to assure you, as he did me, that, at the moment, he is the only one who knows about our plans."

"There must have been someone who gathered the information for him." I said.

"Naturally," said General Ahn. "But General Mah would not reveal his source. Only to say that as long as he is alive, the secret is safe with him."

I snorted.

General Ahn said, "Consider this. I now have, rather, we now have information that General Mah wanted to defect to our side. That, I assure you, is serious business and we now have that advantage on him. If this piece of information ever leaks out, he is in for it as much as we are. What he wants is this. He knows all about our plans for the coup. Who we are, where we are, and so on. He claims he has gotten hold of our organizational secrets and to prove that he has, he cited several names at random. Yours, Major Lee's, and mine, of course; the general, and the members of the Command Group."

"What does he want, General?" Colonel Min said.

"Not so fast, Colonel. Before we know what he wants, we must understand why he wants what he wants. Here is the situation. He tells me that the Americans have been pressuring the President to fire him. Well, we do know that the Americans have become disenchanted with General Mah and have been trying to get rid of him. Of course, General Mah is the favorite of the President and the President has been resisting the Americans. Well, this time the President is giving in. That's what General Mah believes. In any case, he thinks he is about to be sacked, and you know what will happen to him once that comes through officially. Everyone will be out for his blood. Now, there are so many important people involved with him one way or the other that he can never be brought to a trial, which will spill all the dirt and filth, the goings-on among the higher circle of our government."

"So some people would try to get rid of him quietly," said Colonel Min.

"Precisely. Not so quietly, though. It will make lots of noises. He will be assassinated and the North Korean agents will be blamed for that, naturally."

"With the President's sanction?" I said.

"Naturally! What do you think?" said General Ahn.

"I am beginning to see a certain pattern in this," said Colonel Min. "It is beginning to be a little clear to me."

"I am glad you say that. I was terribly confused by all this, but then something happened. I am going too fast. So, General Mah's deal with you, Colonel Min, is this. He will release the hostages he now has in confinement, turn over to you all the documented results of his investigations of public and private lives of practically everyone who is somebody in this country. We are all included, of course. And he will quietly help our coup to a successful completion. He does not think he will participate openly in our coup and he does not think you will welcome his open participation either. He will understand your feelings about him, and, then, he still has a bit of conscience left in him not to turn against the President who, after all, is his benefactor. These are his words, not mine, mind you. That's what he said."

"And what does he want from us in return?" said Colonel Min.

"One of two things. Either a command suitable to his rank and experience on the front line, presumably a corps but he would settle for a division; or a safe-conduct and passport for him to go to Europe. He said nothing about money. I am sure he has taken care of that problem, and he knows he is not welcome in America. He wants to go to Europe. Switzerland, most likely."

"And if we refuse his deal?"

"Colonel Min, you keep saying we, we, but he wants to make this deal with you personally. And I am sure you understand why."

"No, sir, I don't. We all stand or fall collectively. We are all in it together, General. I am not running a private show."

"I understand what you say, of course. Well, if you, if we decline his deal, I am sure I don't have to explain to you what he will do."

"What will he do, General?" I said.

"Don't you know?"

"I thought, General, that you were quite willing to take care of him before he made his move," I said.

"You mean — kill him?"

"Yes, sir."

"What do you think, General?" said Colonel Min. "Do you think he is telling us the truth? And if so, do you think we should accept his deal?"

"I think he is telling us the truth. I have proof of that. And that's why I am having second thoughts about killing him. You see, now there are people other than us who would be glad to liquidate him. We may not have to do anything."

"You mentioned a proof?" said Colonel Min.

General Ahn looked at us both and dropped his voice; in a whisper, he said, "There was an assassination attempt on his life. He almost got killed."

Shocked, I was about to question him for details, when I became aware of Colonel Min's brooding silence; I did not speak.

"How did it happen, General?" said Colonel Min.

"How did it happen? How would I know? All I know is what did happen."

"What did happen, sir?"

"Just think. I could have been killed, too. You see, General Mah wanted me to come out here to see you about his proposals. I had no alternative. I agreed to do that. He was happy about it; he seemed tremendously relieved. He said he would buy me a drink, and take me out to dinner. He said he was a lonely man; he had no friends and so on. And I believe him. He is a lonely man."

"He is an evil man," I said. "You sound as if you have forgotten all about that, General, if I may remind you."

"There is no question about his being an evil man."

"Did you go out to the dinner?" said Colonel Min.

"I almost did. I said I would come with him. I wanted to go easy on him, you know. I wanted to tread softly. I felt as though I were holding a live bomb in my hands and it might, it could, go off any moment and blow all of us sky-high. You know what I mean. Then he changed his mind and said that for both of us to be seen together wouldn't be good. It would be too conspicuous, especially when he was being watched. I must say I was glad he said that and was glad to get out of the dinner. I didn't want to be seen with him."

"So he left your house without you," Colonel Min said.

"That's what happened. I saw him out of the door of my house and stood there for a moment to watch him go. Major Lee, you know my house. It's on a hill, Colonel, and a long driveway goes down the hill and joins the main street. From upstairs in my house, you can almost see the end of my driveway. It was raining still, rather hard, and I was standing there in an upstairs room, watching General Mah's jeep going down the driveway and onto the street, when I saw a dark brown sedan speeding up from behind General Mah's jeep. I saw it all. The splashing of rainwater all around the sedan as it rushed up and passed, rather, came parallel to the jeep; then I heard a burst of a submachine gun and the sedan sped off and disappeared from my sight. The jeep had crashed into bushes along the road by then. I ran downstairs and joined my aide who also heard the shots and we ran down the driveway — and there was the jeep, in the bushes, smoking away. I thought it might explode any moment. Then we saw General Mah staggering out of the jeep and the bushes. We ran to him and got hold of him. He was covered with blood, all over his uniform, hands, face. He had a .45 automatic in his hand which I hadn't seen before, but it belonged to his driver. My aide saw to that. The driver was dead. And his aide, a captain, he was dead, too. The driver, a sergeant, was shot in the back, twice, I think, and the captain was . . . well, you might say he was riddled by the submachine-gun bullets. It was a horrible sight. Just think. Only a moment before, General Mah had told me about some of the people he was suspicious of trying to kill him and there he was being machine-gunned at. A hair-breadth escape! And just to think that I could have been with him, sitting in the back seat of his jeep."

"Who was he suspicious of trying to kill him?" said the Colonel.

"Naturally, he didn't name them. Some people in the Army Intelligence, some in the National Police, some National Assemblymen, a few cabinet ministers, and then the American CIA."

"Why the American CIA?" said Colonel Min. "They would gain nothing by killing him."

"I don't know why he mentioned it. Perhaps he knows too much about their operations here."

"He couldn't be the only one who knows too much about the American operations in this country or in North Korea."

"Well, Colonel, I wouldn't know. That's what he seemed to imply."

"General Ahn," I said, "did you do it by any chance?"

"Do what?"

Colonel Min said, "Major Lee refers to this unsuccessful assassination attempt on General Mah's life."

General Ahn looked us over, then he laughed aloud. "I wish I had," he said. "And if I had tried it, I wouldn't have bungled it up like that!"

We were silent for a moment.

General Ahn said, "There is more to General Mah's proposal."

Colonel Min said, with what I thought was an undisguised sense of weariness in his voice, "Yes?"

"He told me that he had agreed to meet with General Ham this evening."

"You told me about that, General," said Colonel Min.

"Yes, so I did. But there's more. He proposes to arrest General Ham and his intimate associates, if you know what I mean. Arrest them and hold them in Seoul. For you, Colonel Min, that is. After the coup is successful, he will turn them over to you and you can do whatever you want to do with them."

I said, "In short, he wants to play a game with us with human lives."

General Ahn ignored me.

Colonel Min said, "And what do you say to that, General?"

"Well, since you are kind enough to ask my opinion on that, I suppose I should be frank with you and tell you precisely what I think you should do."

"You mean what we should do," said Colonel Min.

"All right. What we should do, then. I think we should kill them all."

"I beg your pardon, sir?" I exclaimed. "Do you mean to say that . . ."

General Ahn said, "Let me finish what I was saying, Major. This is what I think should and could work out. To our immense benefit and advantage, naturally. We should pretend that we would go along with General Mah's proposals and let him know that we are not wholeheartedly with him but that it is our *modus vivendi*, you might say, to cooperate with him at this time. He would understand that. After all, we shouldn't appear too eager to accept his deal. He might suspect us. We would tell him that we would like to see some concrete proof of the authenticity and genuineness of his intention to carry out his part of the deal."

"What sort of proof, for example, sir?" I said.

"Arrest General Ham and his cronies, as he says he would."

"Why not ask him to kill General Ham?" I said.

"That is perhaps a better idea, Major. It didn't occur to me. It didn't occur to me that you would be the one to suggest that, either."

Colonel Min said, "Now, this proof we are talking about. What does it really prove to us about General Mah?"

"Nothing," said General Ahn quickly. "Nothing at all."

"Then, why?" I said.

"Look! He is capable of committing every conceivable evil act without blinking an eye," General Ahn said impatiently. "He would kill General Ham for no other reason than to make him look good in our eyes. Don't you understand that?"

"Yes, I do, General," I said. "But if he really goes through with it, wouldn't that be a tangible proof that he would abide by his part of the bargain?"

"Are you willing to take him up on his deal?" said Colonel Min to me.

I paused for a second. "Yes," I said. "If his deal is genuine, I think we should accept it."

"Then what would you do with him?" said Colonel Min.

"Exile him," I said.

"That's better than spilling his blood, you mean," said Colonel Min.

"Yes," I said.

"Are you saying that we should exonerate him from all his crimes?" said Colonel Min.

"Perhaps after he goes into exile, we could try him *in absentia* and that would expose to the nation all of his crimes. And, perhaps, we could strip him of his citizenship."

"Heavens!" said General Ahn. "You are a cruel man, Major!"

I retorted, "I can't think of anything more cruel than killing him."

"You want him to have a slow death!" said General Ahn.

"If we should decide to accept his deal," I said, "I do not see any alternative."

"Who said we should accept his deal?" said General Ahn. "I said we should pretend to take him up on it."

"Then what?" said Colonel Min. "What, then, do you say we should do, having pretended, as you suggest, to accept his deal?"

"Listen! Nothing he would do will ever prove to us that he is sincere and honest about his deal. Nothing whatsoever! We don't really know why he is behaving this way. We shall never know. But that doesn't make any difference. What makes a difference to us is that he now has his fingers in our plans for the coup and he can explode us all to bits. It so happens that he is about to be sacked by his boss and he is full of vengeance. At least, that's what he says. But there is no reason on earth whatsoever that we should believe him. Is that clear to you? No reason whatsoever. The problem for us, I think, remains basically the same. General Mah simply has to be liquidated. He's got to be killed. And General Ham, too, that dirty, double-crossing betrayer."

"In that case, why did you suggest that we should ask General Mah to offer us an evidence of his good intention by arresting or killing General Ham?"

"To get them together," General Ahn said.

"I don't understand you, sir," I said.

"To get them together. Why?" said Colonel Min.

"We would kill them both at the same time," said General Ahn in a whisper, though there was no one around to hear us. "Don't you understand that? We can liquidate two birds with one stone, so to speak." He laughed again.

Colonel Min was silent.

"I am not sure if I like the direction our conversation is heading," I said, "if you allow me to say so. We are talking about human beings, General. Not some sort of lifeless objects that can be broken apart or put back together at our will."

"Here comes your idealism again!" General Ahn said. "But that will get you or us nowhere for our coup. Why don't you try to understand that? And why don't you agree with me that you'll leave all the dirty work of the coup to someone like me and Colonel Min here and . . ."

"That is enough, General!" said Colonel Min. "I am sure Major Lee did not mean anything personal about you."

"Of course, I understand that, Colonel. To tell you the sincere truth, I admire your idealism, Major. I do mean it, Colonel. Surely, after the fire and smoke and din of our coup are all cleared up, we do need people like Major Lee to get down to the real business of the coup, that is, the humane purpose and program of rebuilding and reshaping the country and the people."

"You want to kill both General Mah and General Ham," said Colonel Min. "What is your plan on that, General?"

"Simple. You people will trail General Ham from this end and I will trail General Mah from my end. That is, if we can't discover their plan in time. Or, I may even suggest to General Mah that he let me or you, Colonel, if you like, accompany him to witness his deed, so to speak, to confirm his good intentions. I can have the place, wherever it may turn out to be, ringed with my Commandos."

"Suppose General Mah brings his men with him? He could easily mobilize units from the Presidential Brigade," said Colonel Min.

"Ah, he won't do that. He can't! Remember, every one of his movements is constantly being watched. Whether or not that is true, we don't know. But, since that is what he told me, he couldn't possibly do a thing like that when he knows that we are also watching his movements."

"What is the rest of your plan, General?" said Colonel Min.

"We will kill them both as I said before. We will make it appear as an act of damned Communist agents from the North. Ah, some such thing. Simple enough. Or, it could be some sort of shooting it out, so to speak, between them. Everyone knows they never got along well with each other. We will have to play it by ear, I suppose. If General Mah's story about the assassination conspiracy against him is true, and I think it is true — after all, I saw one happen right before my own eyes today — as I was saying, if the story is true, then, we can assume that there won't be a thorough investigation from the government sources. As to what to do with General Ham, well, we can simply remove his body from the scene and dispose of it somehow. I can take care of that."

"Why not remove both bodies and dispose of them both, General?" I said.

"What is it? Am I running a funeral home? Ha, ha, ha! Well, I can do that, too, I suppose. Actually, that seems to be a better idea, Colonel. Major Lee, you surprise me. You are far, far ahead of me in thinking this thing out. But then, of course, you are an intellectual and I am not."

Colonel Min said, "After you dispose of the two bodies, what then?"

"Why, a green signal for our coup," General Ahn said. "There won't be anything standing in our way after that."

"It all sounds very simple," said Colonel Min.

"It is simple," said General Ahn.

"You've made it sound very simple, General," said Colonel Min.

"Ah! I am a man of simple nature, Colonel. At least, I would like to think I am. I value simplicity and incisiveness. Getting right down to the heart of the matter, you see. But, I am afraid it will have to be a little bit complicated this time."

"It is already quite complicated enough," I said. "I don't quite know where to begin and where to end in this matter."

"Anything else on your mind, General?" said Colonel Min.

"Yes, Colonel. I do hope you'll understand this and my position. I don't know how to put it to you in such a way that you'll not be offended."

"I can hardly imagine anything coming to me from you that could offend me," said Colonel Min. "I should appreciate every word you say to me in connection with our coup."

"All right, then, since you put it that way. Very gallant of you, Colonel. Well, here is a hitch, so to speak, to what we have been discussing. In spite of what I said to you, Colonel, General Mah wants to deal with you all collectively. That is, with you, Colonel, and with the rest of the Command Group."

Colonel Min gave me a quick look. He said, "General, that seems hardly surprising to me. In fact, I think that's the way it should be and it will be. I wouldn't have it any other way. If I were in General Mah's place, I would demand the same thing, wouldn't you, General?"

"I can't really blame him for insisting on that, to tell you the truth," said General Ahn. "You see, I told him that there was no need to make his deal collectively with everyone in the Command Group. I told him it would be more than sufficient and acceptable to everyone concerned if he and you two got together and worked this out. But, he wanted to be sure. Well, he is worried, to begin with, and then he isn't the kind of man who would trust others and I doubt if he trusts even himself."

I said, "Since we are supposed to kill him and General Ham anyway, I don't see why all this is necessary at all, General, this business of collective bargaining. What difference does it make, sir, if General Mah is going to be killed?"

Colonel Min said, "Major Lee, you don't understand. What General Ahn is saying is that General Mah wants really to trust us and wants us to trust him. Well, until General Mah settles his score with General Ham, I think we've got to show up as a group. And then we will take over from there. As a group. Am I right, General?"

"I am glad you said that, Colonel, I must confess that I do feel a little uneasy about assuming personal responsibility for liquidating them all by myself. I hope you understand my feeling. After all, I am not made of stone. I do have feelings. So, if we do this as a group, I think I would feel much better about the whole thing. Besides, the credit should go to us all as a group."

"We shall all be guilty, is that it, sir?" I said.

"I wasn't talking about any kind of guilt," General Ahn snapped. "What guilt? Quite the contrary, Major. We are going to make the entire country proud of us when it all comes out into the open after our coup."

Colonel Min said, "Nothing to get excited about. We will put this matter to the Command Group, and I am sure there won't be any objection to our accepting General Mah's proposals and request, as long as he keeps his part of the bargain."

"I have no doubt whatsoever that he won't," said General Ahn. "After all, from his point of view, his life depends on it."

"Either way he looks at it," I said.

General Ahn laughed. "Major Lee, you really are beginning to see it my way, aren't you? Unless, of course, you meant it as a sarcasm, the nuance of which I might have failed to catch on to, eh?"

"Enough, gentlemen," said Colonel Min. "No time for indulging in sentimentality. What we need now is daring and decisive action, don't you think so, General?"

"Naturally! That's the spirit, Colonel. That's why I always thought you were a man born to action. Oh, yes, I know lots about you. All about you, in fact. By the way, have I ever told you about this North Korean colonel, a security officer, who knew you? I am sure I haven't. Well, it was a pity because I had to have him shot later anyway, whether or not he knew you in the old days."

Colonel Min said, "I see."

General Ahn cluck-clucked. "Yes, he kept saying that if I checked with you about him he was sure you would try to help him. You see, he claimed that he had once saved your life. Before you came down to the South, that is. We captured him in one of our commando raids near Sariwon. Actually, he said you, too, saved his life. So it seems you two saved each other's life, so to speak. Does it ring any bells with you?"

Colonel Min said, "Yes, I knew him. In the old days, as you say."

"He told me you had shot your way out of the Russian garrison in your own hometown and he had helped you escape. Was he telling me the truth?"

"Why do you ask?"

"Well, if what he told me was true, I thought you should have put that in your service records. After all, you shot the Russian garrison commander and quite a few Russians and I would call that daring bravery, which should be recognized and properly rewarded. But you hadn't done that and I always admired you the more for that. So, although I've known about it all this time I haven't mentioned it to anyone out of my respect for your silence. Daring and decisiveness, Colonel, as you said. You are a born man of action and, if I may say so, a born leader. There's no denying that."

Colonel Min said, "I am sorry the North Korean colonel had to be shot. Indeed, I would have tried to help him."

"Well, I am sorry about that, too. But it was such a long time ago and the whole thing was very hectic those days, as you know."

"When did it happen, General?" said Colonel Min.

"Let me see now. That must have been shortly before we took Pyungyang. That makes it early part of October, nineteen-fifty. That's right. Now I remember it all clearly. Yes, that's it."

Colonel Min said, "I see."

"Well, I didn't mean to drag it out," said General Ahn, "but I just wanted you to know what I think of you."

Colonel Min did not respond to that.

General Ahn said, "Now, shall I wait around to see how the Command Group decides on General Mah's proposals or would you get in touch with me later?"

Colonel Min looked at me for a moment. He turned to General Ahn and said with a cheerful casualness that I hadn't thought he was capable of exhibiting, "Oh, well, General. Actually, there isn't any compelling reason for having to go through the formality of group discussion and voting on this matter with the Command Group. Do you understand what I am saying, General? I think the matter is as good as settled right here between us. No need to delay it, is there, General? I say this is settled and that should be quite enough."

General Ahn said, "I am relieved to hear that, Colonel. Time is of the essence. We've got to hurry now. You will lead the Command Group then?"

"Of course."

"I will fly back to Seoul right now," said General Ahn. "There are a lot of things to do. If either of us finds out anything more about General Mah and General Ham, we will be in touch. I am sure I'll have something to report to you once I am back in Seoul. General Mah will now have to tell me the details of his meeting with General Ham. I suppose you wouldn't want to approach General Ham from this end in any way?"

Colonel Min shook his head. "No. I think it best to let him think we are completely in the dark about his meeting with General Mah, don't you? Obviously."

"Obviously," said General Ahn.

I cut in. "I would like to protest this, Colonel Min. As a member of the Command Group, I would insist on bringing the matter to the Group. You two have decided to kill both General Mah and General Ham, but we don't know how the members of the Command Group would feel about that. I, for one, will not accept that extreme measure, and . . ."

"Shut up!" barked Colonel Min. "Stay out of this, Major!"

General Ahn grinned. "Now, now, gentlemen. No need to get all worked up."

Colonel Min said to me sharply, "I know how you feel about killing people and I am sorry you feel that way. But don't you realize you are outnumbered in this matter? The Command Group with the exception of you had already decided on this. You will have to accept the majority decision, Major."

I couldn't help shouting. "Or else!"

"Or else! Or else?" Colonel Min spoke in a mocking voice. "If you refuse to accept the majority decision, you will simply have to be removed from the Command Group."

I could not control my rage. "In that case, if that is your ultimatum, I resign from the Command Group!"

General Ahn stepped forward and put his arms around us; his cane touched my back. "Now, now, you two. What is this? Let's stop this quibbling, shall we? We've got far more important things, our coup and the destiny of our country, to worry about. This is no time for arguing among ourselves. Now, now. I will leave you two and I am sure you will come to a satisfactory understanding with each other. Remember, we are fighting against our common enemies and not among ourselves."

I disengaged myself from his theatrical embrace.

Colonel Min said quite viciously, "Major Lee, I want you to go to my quarters and wait for me. That's an order." He said to General Ahn, "I'll drive you out to the airstrip, General. We can settle on the details on our way."

Without a word to me, Colonel Min strode away toward the jeep between two tanks. General Ahn followed him, limping, squishing mud under his shoes. The thin fog still clung to the ground. The jeep's engine started with a roar. I suddenly felt desperate, confused, and forlorn. The headlights shot out of darkness. I was outraged. The world around me stank with evil and deception and murderous blood. I felt alone. The jeep drove away. Murderers — you murderers, I found myself hissing in a whisper charged with raging fury. Bloody murderers! Oh — you bloody murderers! What country, what people, what poor, innocent, suffering people are you trying to save from what — you blood-reeking, beastly murderers! I felt like weeping. I felt my heart ache with the pain of now realizing that I had naïvely let myself be tricked into undertaking the work of professional killers, extortionists, blackmailers, corrupt agents of evil, devils themselves on all sides. I was shaking with rage and guilt and remorse. I could not restrain myself from shedding burning tears, with frustration, indignation, and bitterness. I was there in the misty darkness all alone, surrounded by machines of death and evil men and the evil world. With a shudder, I knew that I was standing on the very threshold of unspeakable horrors of evil beyond redemption. I felt like shouting. I wanted to shout — to claim my innocence back, to proclaim to the world that there was still within me a spark of innocence and the throbbing of a wounded soul of the innocent. And, then, suddenly, I felt a soothing breeze of hope, a delicious, delirious hope for myself, and I deeply inhaled a comforting breath of hope and then — a brilliant epiphany — a thought flashed in my mind and stood before my vision like a beatific rainbow: Blessed are the pure and the innocent, for they shall inherit the earth. I smiled, in spite of myself, for I now knew what I had to do.

I Chapter 9

found my jeep in the parking lot next to the general's office building. There was not enough gasoline in the tank to make it back to Seoul, but I did not worry about it. I drove down the dark driveway lined with armored cars and medium tanks toward the main gate. The harsh, glaring light flooded the guardhouse and the two tanks. I slowed the jeep down and pressed the horn. I saw two MP's in the guardhouse, then saw four MP's lined up just beyond the guardrail, their figures in the shadows of the arch, their white helmets glistening from the floodlight. None of them made any move to lift the guardrail for me. I blew the horn again, and brought the jeep to a halt a few yards from the rail. I leaped out of the jeep. One of the MP's stepped forward to meet me across the rail. I did not have a chance to utter a word.

The sergeant saluted me, and said, "Sorry, sir. Colonel Min's orders, Major. We are not to let you pass."

I had not expected this. In confusion rather than in anger, I blurted out, "What is it? Am I under arrest?"

He said, "Oh, no, sir! We can't let you pass through here. That's all, sir! Colonel Min wants you to wait for him."

"Colonel Min said that to you?"

"Yes, sir. He gave me the orders on his way out to the airstrip. Just a few minutes ago, sir."

It was as though Colonel Min had been able to calculate precisely what my every move was going to be. I could not help feeling slightly peevish. I raised my voice. "Sergeant, you know who I am, don't you?"

"Yes, sir."

"In that case, you'd better let me pass."

"I am sorry, sir."

"I shall crash through." I made a move back to my jeep.

"Please, sir. I am just following my orders."

I went back to him. "Lift the rail."

"Please, sir!"

I ignored his plea. I tried to push the rail up. It would not budge. "Give me a hand, Sergeant!"

He did not stir.

I tried again, harder, and the rail, with a creak, lifted itself up. I went back to my jeep and flung myself into the seat. Then I saw the MP's, including the sergeant, barricading the way, raise their submachine guns. For a moment, I did not know what to do. I cut the engine off.

The sergeant came over to me. "Please, Major."

"Very well, Sergeant. I shall wait here until either you move your men away or Colonel Min gets here."

"If you promise, sir, to wait for Colonel Min, I'll be glad to move my men away."

I heard a telephone ring within the guardhouse. An MP called out to the sergeant. "It's Lieutenant Cho on the line." The sergeant excused himself and ran into the guardhouse.

I could not make out his voice on the telephone. I saw him nod a few times. He came back to me. The other MP's now lowered their submachine guns.

"Lieutenant Cho will be here in a minute, sir."

There wasn't much I could do. I nodded in silence.

The sergeant saluted me. "I am sorry, sir." He went back to his men, who now pulled the guardrail down.

I started the engine, backed the jeep up away from the light, and waited for Lieutenant Cho. There wasn't much else I could have done. I should have been angry and indignant at the way I had just been treated by the MP's — at Colonel Min's orders; but, strangely enough, I was not; I was more tired than anything else; a sheer physical exhaustion overpowered me and my mind felt a leaden inertia. By the time Lieutenant Cho drove down and stood before me, the only thing I wanted was to go to sleep.

"I am sorry about this, sir," said Lieutenant Cho in whispers, peering into the jeep. "Colonel Min called me from the airstrip and asked me to make sure that you wait for him. I don't know what has happened between you two, sir, but please, Major, I wish you wouldn't do anything rash, if you'll forgive me for saying that."

"I wasn't going to do anything rash," I snapped. "Am I under arrest?"

"I wish you wouldn't speak like that, sir. Of course not, sir. Who would think of putting you under arrest!"

"Do the others know about this?"

He shook his head. "Of course not, sir. They are now over at the general's office."

"Why?"

"Colonel Min wanted to call a meeting of the Command Group, sir. He wants you to be there."

"I didn't think he would want to call the meeting of the Command Group."

"I wouldn't know about that, sir."

"It seemed to me Colonel Min and the others had already decided what to do with General Mah."

"I beg your pardon, sir? I don't understand."

"Well, haven't they already decided to kill him?"

"You mean — formally, sir? Voting and all that?"

"Well, haven't they?"

"Not that I know of, sir. I know the feeling of the Group, but I know of no formal resolution. I should know about it, sir, after all — I am the secretary."

"Do you mean to tell me that there hasn't been a vote on this matter?"

"No, sir."

"How does Chaplain Koh feel about this?"

"I don't know, sir. He hasn't said anything about General Mah."

"Well, I am sure he feels the same way I do."

"What do you mean, sir? You are in favor of not killing him off?"

"Yes!"

"I really don't understand you, sir. I mean, sometimes."

"I am sure you don't understand me. Well, never mind."

"Yes, sir. In any case, would you please come and join the Group for the meeting?"

"I would rather wait for Colonel Min here, if you don't mind."

"All right, sir, if you wish. But, please, Major, wait for him."

I nodded.

"I will then see you there soon, Major."

I nodded again.

He drove back to the headquarters.

I woke with a start. Colonel Min was sitting next to me in the jeep. I found myself stretched against the seat. I sat up.

"Sorry to wake you up," he said. "I know you must be tired but we've got lots of work to do. Do you feel up to it?"

I rubbed my eyes and stared at him.

"The MP's told me what happened. I am sorry about that. I didn't think you would really try to leave."

"I was on my way back to Seoul."

"That was silly." He laughed.

"There's nothing amusing about that!"

"I am sorry," he said. "What did you have in mind?"

"Since I am outnumbered here, as you put it, I would call the meeting of delegates from other services to overrule the decision of the Command Group."

"And you think you would succeed?"

"I would do my best."

"Oh, come now. Let's stop this nonsense."

I flared up. "There's nothing nonsensical about my trying to stop needless bloodshed and murders!"

"Listen to me! And let me finish what I have to tell you before you interrupt me. I am sorry that I appeared to humiliate you in front of General Ahn and with the MP's, but I had to do that, don't you understand? I wanted to have General Ahn hear what I told the MP's to do about you. Of course, as I said, I didn't really think you would try to leave, let alone try to crash through the gate! I wanted to convince General Ahn that I believed every word of his. I am surprised you didn't catch on to that."

"Are you telling me that you were playing a game?"

"Yes."

"Why?"

"Why? I am really surprised that you still don't understand. We are all playing an elaborate game here. General Mah is playing a game, so is General Ahn, and so are we. For the time being, we have to play along. I wanted General Ahn to hear what he wanted to find out about our setup here, which I have no doubt he will report back to General Mah."

"I still don't quite understand."

"It is this way. We do not yet know whether or not General Mah's proposals and his motivation for making those proposals are genuine. That we will soon find out. Colonel Kim is checking it out with Colonel Son right now. We shall soon see about that. Now, I am not so certain as to why General Ahn wants to rule out categorically the possibility that General Mah may genuinely want to make a deal with us. As to his story of an unsuccessful assassina-

tion attempt on General Mah's life, Colonel Kim is also checking it
out with our people in Seoul, and I will see Colonel McKay about
that, too. The American CIA may have something on that. In any
event, I am a little uneasy about the way General Ahn has insisted
on killing both General Mah and General Ham, that is, before we
have a chance to find out just what General Mah may be up to. Do
you understand?"

"You are questioning General Ahn's motivation?"

"Yes. Just as you have said to me before about him."

"I told you he's too damn bloodthirsty!"

"I am not particularly worried about that part of it. I am more
interested in what I think is a slip of the tongue on his part."

"What do you mean?"

"What he said about the North Korean colonel."

"The security officer who knew you?"

"Yes."

"You see — this North Korean colonel — he was a major then, I
saw him die, before my very eyes. In North Korea. Near the thirty-
eighth parallel."

"Did you kill him?"

"You seem to have already judged me as a bloodthirsty murderer,
haven't you?"

I did not reply.

"And that's why you wanted to leave. What were you trying to
do? Wash your hands of me? Of us all?"

I kept silent.

"Do you really want to withdraw from the Group?"

I remained silent.

"Well, make up your mind!" he shouted in fury. "Do you want
to join our coup or not? Do you want to see your coup succeed or
not? Do you want to save the country or not? Do you want to save
our people or not? Answer me!"

"Save the country, save our poor, suffering people!" I shouted
back. "Save them from what? Don't you realize we are becoming

more and more like those we are against, those from whom we have pledged ourselves to save the country and the people! We are becoming just like General Mah and his cohorts!"

He shook his head with a sigh. "Good and pure do not necessarily and automatically come from good and pure. The world of man is not made that way. When will you ever see that horrible truth?"

"If it is not made that way, then we shall try to make it that way. We've got to begin somewhere."

He did not speak.

"We've got to begin somewhere!" I went on. "Don't you see that? Otherwise, it will be an unending circle of hell we will be helping to enlarge. The vicious circle has got to be broken somewhere. And we've got to take upon ourselves that task. We've got to make a clean break somewhere, sometime, now!"

With his eyes closed, he nodded his head. "Yes. Yes. You are right, of course. Who would, who could argue with that?"

"Then you will change your mind about killing General Mah and General Ham?"

He sat up straight. "I have not made up my mind about that!"

"Oh?"

"No, I haven't. And I didn't kill that North Korean major, either." His voice was weary. "Would you believe me?"

"Yes."

"Thanks. Now, would you come with me to the meeting? I shall put the matter of General Mah's proposals and also the question of what to do with him before the Group. We shall vote on these. Would you come and stop talking about withdrawing from the Group and all the rest of your nonsense?"

"On condition that you would try your best to influence the decision of the Group."

"How?"

"Obvious. We should not decide on a course of action which will force us to commit senseless crimes."

"Would you commit sensible crimes?"

"I resent that question!"

"Would you be prepared to commit a necessary murder?"

"You don't have to be so sarcastic. I don't like your mocking insinuation."

"I shan't force you to answer my questions. All right. You have my word that I will do my best to influence the Group to go along with your way of thinking. Just this once, mind you. Will you be prepared to accept the majority decision?"

"I would rather not commit myself to that at this time."

"Nonsense! I am giving in to your demand and I should have at least a promise from you that you will abide by the decision of the majority of the Group."

"Isn't it obvious that my motion will be outnumbered?"

"Don't be so sure of that."

"Is Chaplain Koh going to be there?"

"Yes."

"Would you be able to persuade General Yoon to side with us?"

"I suppose. He will do what I ask him to do."

"In that case, all right. I give you my word that I will abide by the Group's decision."

He nodded. "All right."

"Tell me before we go. About this North Korean major. You didn't kill him but you saw him die with your own eyes."

"Must you know?"

"Yes."

"He killed himself."

I could not help exclaiming. "I don't understand! Then why? Why? I mean, General Ahn's story?"

"That's what I want to find out about."

"I am confused. I mean, I can't quite grasp the meaning of this all. I can't begin to see the implications."

"There is always the possibility that the North Korean major might have lived, although even if he hadn't died as I believed he had he would not have had a chance to live. They would have shot him anyway."

"I am completely lost."

"You see — he killed a Russian major, the garrison commander in my hometown. He strangled him to death."

I said, "I thought you had killed the Russian!"

He glowered at me. Without a word, he left my jeep and strode over to his behind mine. He started up the engine and drove off. I thought I heard him as he passed me: "Come along!" I followed behind him.

The conference room adjoined General Hyun's office. It was a simple room, barely furnished except for a plain wooden table and a dozen or so steel folding chairs; a shaded lamp dangled from the low ceiling; that was all. We sat around the oblong table. Colonel Min sat at the head of the table, quietly smoking his pipe. Chaplain Koh was seated at the other end of the table directly across from Colonel Min. There was Colonel Song, in charge of Personnel; Lieutenant Colonel Kim, Intelligence; Colonel Park, Operations; Colonel Moon, Logistics. Lieutenant Cho sat behind Colonel Min. Captain Yang, General Hyun's aide-de-camp, sat behind Colonel Song. I sat next to Chaplain Koh. There was an empty chair next to Colonel Min, which would have been occupied by General Yoon of the 34th Division.

"All right, gentlemen," said Colonel Min, "let's get this over with. I think we all know why we are meeting here. I don't suppose I will have to explain any more about General Ham. We have arrested him, and General Yoon will keep him at a hideaway in the 34th Division sector until our coup is over. We will release him after that. That will be our policy on him for the time being. Colonel Kim, what is the situation at General Ham's headquarters?"

Colonel Kim said, "Fine. It couldn't be better. As you all know, General Ham's deputy commander is away in Japan at the moment. His chief of staff is on our side, and Colonel Bang, the Operations, is fully in charge of the situation. General Ham's staff, in short, is solidly behind us. In this particular circumstance, keeping General

Ham out of sight will pose little problem. Everyone, including General Mah, knows that General Ham pulls this sort of stunt rather regularly; I am referring, of course, to his unpredictable behavior, such as disappearing into the mountains for a few days of hunting and fishing. Especially, General Yoon's being his cousin helps. Colonel Min, you will take care of his American advisers?"

Colonel Min nodded. "Colonel McKay will see to that. It will be done discreetly, I assure you."

Colonel Kim said, "I have something rather important to report but I will wait." He spoke with a thick Northern accent; tall and muscular, he folded his arms over his chest, his eyebrows knit closely, his sharp eyes staring at his notes in front of him on the table; he had commanded a battalion in the war and had taught at the National Defense College. He looked up and gazed at Colonel Min. He said, "I'll wait till you are finished with the others."

"All right," said Colonel Min. "How about you, Colonel Song. Anything new?"

Colonel Song shook his head. "No. Nothing new to report." At the age of forty, Colonel Song was the oldest of the Group, except for Chaplain Koh; a sleepy-eyed, gentle man, he chain-smoked and was fond of quoting Confucius and boasting he was the only grandfather in the entire Corps, whipping out his wallet which contained, American-style as he put it, a folded packet of pictures of his granddaughters and his daughters; a lovable man, a graduate of Tokyo Imperial University with a degree in economics, he had commanded a regiment on the east coast in the war, twice wounded in action.

Colonel Park was saying, ". . . we now have three contingency plans, any one of which is highly desirable and flexible enough to meet our objective. The coordinations between the participating units from the other services have been excellent and have been checked down to the last detail, and I thank Major Lee for the operations plans to occupy Seoul. We can start anytime. As we stand now, we can mobilize one fourth of the entire armed forces. Otherwise, no change to report." Quiet, efficient, brilliant, few would have thought that his ambition had been to become a concert pianist; drafted by the Japanese in his third year at a conservatory in Tokyo, he had become a lieutenant in the Japanese Army; wounded in Burma, he was captured by the British and later was allowed to join the Korean unit in the Chinese Nationalist Forces; he had commanded a battalion in the war, taught at the Military Academy, and studied in America and observed the military establishment of Scandinavian countries and Israel; a reserved, a soft-spoken man, whose one luxury in the Army, in his words, was to have the Army ship his piano wherever he went, in peacetime, of course; he was fond of Chopin and, as Colonel Min would tell everyone, he was the only one, during the war, who played a duetto with a very eccentric British brigadier who had to have his piano even under enemy artillery fire. Now he sat brooding, silently puffing on his cigarette, doodling in the notebook in front of him.

"And how about you, Colonel Moon?" said Colonel Min.

"Not much change. We won't starve, I will guarantee that."

Colonel Song laughed. "Ah, that's the spirit!"

"But I can use more gasoline," said Colonel Moon, his dark face frowning. "We now have three days' supply of gasoline and fuel for armored units. I would be glad to scrounge up some more. At least five days' supply. Could you talk to Colonel McKay about that?"

Colonel Min nodded and looked back to Lieutenant Cho, who was making notes. "How about ammunition?"

"Plenty," said Colonel Moon. "Depends, naturally. But once the Marines take the depot in Seoul, we will have no problem." Colonel Moon, a former lawyer, a misfit in the Army as he would say, had joined the Army during the war as a specially commissioned major; he should have been a legal officer or a legislative liaison officer but the Army had turned him into an expert in logistics. He said, "Seriously now, I depend on Colonel Park to take the depot in Seoul as quickly as he can. Without having it all blown up. Otherwise, I can't guarantee that we will have enough supplies for every unit in action, just in case we might have to put up a hell of a fight — the contingency plan number three, that is. We will have to send in one of our divisions from here in that case and I won't have enough for an entire division. I've scalped them enough already out here."

Colonel Park said, "We will do. Don't worry."

Colonel Moon said, "Ah! I have to worry. It is in the nature of logistics officers. We never have enough."

"All right, we will go over this again with our people at General Ham's headquarters," said Colonel Min. "Chaplain Koh, sorry you didn't get much sleep tonight. Will you be ready to fly down to Seoul in the morning?"

"It is morning already!" Chaplain Koh laughed. "Of course, I am ready anytime."

"Major Lee reports that everything is under control in Seoul. You will get in touch with Colonel Hwang of the Airborne."

Chaplain Koh nodded.

Colonel Min said, "Captain Yang, how is General Hyun?"

Captain Yang smiled. "Sound asleep, sir. I did tell him that General Ahn was here. He wanted you to take care of him. He said General Ahn shouldn't have come out here."

"Well, Captain, General Ahn's gone back to Seoul now, so you can report to the general that everything is under control. You will not, however, report the decision of this meeting on General Mah and General Ham."

"No, sir."

"That I will do personally. Understood? Does the general know about General Ham?"

"Not yet, sir."

"Good. I will take care of that, too." Colonel Min turned to the Group. "Colonel Kim, would you rather I made my report first and then you would brief us on your latest intelligence?"

"Yes, I think so," said Colonel Kim. "Please go ahead."

Colonel Min nodded, putting his pipe down on the table. He leaned over the table, clasping his hands in front of him, surveying everyone, one at a time, his face revealing a faint trace of a smile.

He closed his eyes for a moment and when he had opened them his face had turned into a mask of impassivity. "Gentlemen, as you know, General Ahn has paid us an unexpected visit, and Major Lee and I have had an extremely interesting and significant conversation with him concerning General Mah," Colonel Min began in a subdued monotone. He did not take long to relay the substance of our conversation with General Ahn to the Group. "There are a few things we have to clear up before we can really understand the implications of the situation," he said. "And I think we are now ready to hear from Colonel Kim who had been in touch with Colonel Son and others in Seoul. I've also asked Colonel McKay to check with his people in Seoul to see if the American CIA and their other intelligence agencies know anything more than our people do. He will be here shortly. All right, Colonel Kim, make your report now."

Colonel Kim shuffled through his papers, numbering each sheet with a pen. "Here we are, gentlemen. This is as much as I can now report. More will come in later, I am sure. Now, let me begin chronologically. I have to explain that what I have tried to do, for the time being, was to double-check on what General Ahn has told Colonel Min and Major Lee. So, as I said, let me go through this in sequence. General Mah did have a telephone conversation with General Ahn. They have a direct line between them as we know. Now, we do not know as yet who called whom first. General Ahn has said that General Mah had called him first, so, for the time being, we will have to assume that that was the way it happened. Next, General Mah left his headquarters with his driver and his aide in a black sedan, 1958 Plymouth, with a civilian license plate. He went to the headquarters of the Presidential Brigade, where he left the Plymouth and changed into a jeep, covered. It was raining at the time. He proceeded to General Ahn's house in the outskirts. Oh, yes. He made a telephone call while he was at the Presidential Brigade, but we are unable to find out whom he talked with. Our agents followed General Mah's jeep and confirmed that General Mah had indeed gone out to General Ahn's house."

Colonel Min said, "Have the agents reported any sign of activity at General Ahn's house? For example, have they seen any of General Ahn's Commandos in or near the house?"

Colonel Kim shook his head. "No. No sign of activity. All very quiet. If General Ahn had expected any trouble with General Mah, well, he had kept it to himself."

"General Ahn told me he had alerted his Commandos," said Colonel Min. "Have you checked with our people there?"

Colonel Kim nodded, and said with a frown on his face, "We have failed to authenticate General Ahn's alert to his Commandos. Either he had forgotten to alert them or he is lying."

Colonel Moon said, "That is a very serious charge against General Ahn, Colonel Kim."

Colonel Kim said, "Yes, it is. Let me go on. Unfortunately, we are unable to check on what went on inside the house. If we had known of the meeting beforehand, I can assure you we would have had the house bugged. But it was too late."

Colonel Park said, "Perhaps somebody else has already bugged the house. Ask Colonel McKay about it, Colonel Min. I wouldn't be surprised if the American CIA has already bugged the house."

Colonel Min said, "Has Colonel Son had any information on that?"

Colonel Kim said, "I regret to say we haven't gone into that. I'll take care of that. Now, our agents confirmed the assassination attempt on General Mah. No, it wasn't General Ahn's doing, although I first suspected he might have done it himself. The description given by General Ahn checks out with that reported by our agents. A dark brown sedan, a 1957 Ford, with civilian license plate, which our agent was unsuccessful in identifying. It does not matter at this point, because the sedan was found later abandoned in an alley behind Duksoo Palace. This piece of information comes from our people in the Seoul Metropolitan Police. The sedan had been stolen; it belongs to a member of the National Assembly, who had reported to the police about the theft. He checks out all right. It was a genuine case of theft. But, here is an interesting item. The theft of the sedan was reported to the police approximately half an hour after the telephone conversation between General Mah and General Ahn had taken place, and we have tried to pinpoint the exact time of the theft and it comes out that the theft, according to our calculation, took place about the time General Mah was at the Presidential Brigade and made his telephone call."

Colonel Moon said, "Are you working on the assumption that the assassination attempt was faked by General Mah himself? Those coincidences and circumstantial evidences you seem to be accumulating . . ."

Colonel Kim nodded. "Yes. The fact is that there is nothing coincidental about it. The dark brown sedan was seen by our agents to rendezvous with General Mah's jeep near the Seoul National University Hospital. General Mah personally came out of the jeep, went over to the sedan which pulled up behind the jeep. The rendezvous lasted two minutes, then they parted."

"This is very serious!" said Colonel Song. "Not that I doubt General Mah can do this. But is there any possibility that General Ahn was in on it, too?"

Colonel Kim said, "We are not sure at this time, but, so far, there is no evidence that General Ahn was in cahoots with General Mah's diabolical scheme."

I said, "But how can we explain the deaths of General Mah's aide and his driver? They were gunned down while they were riding with General Mah, who himself was wounded."

"No! He was not wounded," snapped Colonel Kim.

"But General Ahn said he was," said Colonel Min.

Colonel Kim said, "Either he was lying or exaggerating."

Chaplain Koh said, "You don't like General Ahn, do you, Colonel Kim?"

"No, I don't," he said. "Don't ask me why. I just don't."

Chaplain Koh said, with a smile, "I hope your dislike of him does not color your judgment."

"I am aware of that, Chaplain. Believe me I am. I am going by the factual evidences here, and as far as I can evaluate the situation, General Ahn is either too dumb to see the truth or too shrewd to pretend that he doesn't."

Colonel Min said, "We will soon find that out. Do you have more to report?"

"Yes, sir. Gentlemen, we now come to the question of whether or not General Mah, as he is supposed to have told General Ahn, does indeed know of our plans for the coup. Has he really uncovered our organizational secrets? Has there been any security leak on our side? Has he really discovered our plans or is he merely playing a guessing game? If he does know of our plans and organizational setup, how much does he know at this stage?" Colonel Kim paused and quickly went through his papers. He held a small sheet of paper in his left hand and tapped on it with his pen. He went on, "Gentlemen, this is the report from Colonel Son. As far as Colonel Son knows, General Mah knows nothing about plans for the coup."

Colonel Min said, "Are you implying that General Ahn has deliberately lied to me?"

"If General Ahn has indeed told you that General Mah knew of our plans and organizations, then I am inclined to think that he was indeed deliberately lying. Why was he lying? That I wouldn't know. I am not denying that General Mah has no suspicion whatever of a coup. It is in his nature to suspect a coup at any time, always, but I am reporting here that, as far as Colonel Son is concerned, General Mah's suspicion has not yet reached a point where he could name names and pinpoint our organizations and so on."

Colonel Park said, "This is getting far more serious than I thought."

Colonel Moon said, "Colonel Kim, is there any way to find out if General Mah may really know of our plans and Colonel Son may not know about that?"

"Colonel Son is checking up on that right now. But I doubt very much that any information this important would have gone undetected by Colonel Son. To my way of thinking, the questions before us are, first, whether or not General Mah was simply playing his guessing game as I've just mentioned; second, whether or not General Ahn has deliberately lied to Colonel Min and Major Lee; third, whether or not General Ahn has indeed defected from us and told General Mah all he knows about our plans."

"And you suspect General Ahn's defection?" said Chaplain Koh.

Colonel Kim took his time; he glanced around the table, and said quite simply, "Yes."

"But why?" said Colonel Song.

"We shall soon find out," said Colonel Min.

I said, "Colonel Min, you too, then, suspect his defection?"

He said, "We now have a simple problem of whether we believe in Colonel Son or in General Ahn. Any opinions?"

"If I may paraphrase your statement, Colonel Min," said Colonel Moon, "the problem is whether we believe in Colonel Son, the deputy to General Mah, or in General Ahn, who has pledged his loyalty and support to our cause and, also, who has just as many reasons as any of us has for hating General Mah."

"There is no question about Colonel Son's loyalty," said Colonel Kim. "I'll stake my life on that."

"That's a pretty strong endorsement," said Chaplain Koh.

"If General Mah has indeed uncovered our plans," said Colonel Park, "would he have waited this long before he would take actions against us? Would he have gone through this elaborate game with General Ahn and with us, too?"

"And this fake assassination attempt, too?" said Colonel Song.

I began to lose my perspective of the whole situation; I did not know where it all had begun and where it would all end; it was all very confusing and bewildering. I could not help thinking, however, that there had to be a simple solution to all this, somewhere; and we had to find the solution, somehow, soon, before it all got out of control. I ventured, "There must be a simple explanation to this somewhere."

"No, there isn't," snapped Colonel Kim. "I wish there were."

"Ah, patience," said Colonel Min. "It will all come to light soon. I should like to repose my question. Do you believe in Colonel Son or do you believe more in General Ahn?"

Colonel Moon said, "I am afraid we will have to discredit General Ahn's words, some of them anyway. There was the question of whether or not he has really alerted his Commandos as he claimed to Colonel Min that he has. We can't find any evidence that he has. And then this question of whether or not the assassination attempt on General Mah's life was a fake one. General Ahn reported that it was a genuine attempt. He may not have known otherwise, but we know it was a fake one. Then we have this conflicting report as to whether or not General Mah knows of our plans. I am afraid General Ahn's case is not a very convincing one."

Colonel Park said, "Colonel Kim, does Colonel Son know about the meeting between General Mah and General Ahn?"

"Yes, of course."

Colonel Park said, "I meant to ask if General Mah has told Colonel Son about it."

Colonel Kim looked triumphant. "I am glad you brought that up. No. Not a word about that. Colonel Son is pretending that he knows nothing about it."

"Why shouldn't he have told Colonel Son about it?"

"I don't know."

Colonel Moon said, "Now, why should General Mah have picked out General Ahn and not someone else?" He paused to look around. "That is, if he had uncovered our plans and wanted to make a deal with us with that information as bargaining leverage?"

Colonel Kim said, "Yes. Why not directly with you, Colonel Min?" He answered his own question. "General Mah does not yet know of our plans or our organizational setup. Colonel Son's words check out on this point."

Colonel Song said, "If this is a case of General Ahn's defection, then why is General Ahn so insistent on killing General Mah?"

I said, "General Ham, too."

Colonel Moon said to Colonel Min, "You think General Ahn's insistence and plans for killing them are genuine?"

Colonel Min nodded. "He really wants to kill General Mah — and General Ham, too. Why General Ham, too, that I wouldn't know."

"Are you sure he is not simply pretending?" said Colonel Moon.

"I am quite sure."

"I am not sure if I understand all this," said Chaplain Koh. "I am racking my brains to see a pattern in this but I don't seem to be able to find one."

Colonel Min sat up straight in his chair. "Let me ask you this, gentlemen. Are we convinced that General Mah does really know of our plans and organizations?"

No one replied in words, but the general sentiment was apparent.

Colonel Min looked at everyone. "All right. In order to untangle this cobweb of a situation, we shall have to assume, for the time being, that General Mah knows nothing about our plans for the coup, beyond his suspicion. Now, then, I should like to pose my next question. Is General Mah about to be sacked from his position, as General Ahn had told us, that is, General Mah himself is supposed to have told General Ahn. Colonel Kim, do you have any information on that?"

Colonel Kim went through his papers again. "Colonel Son's report is that it is genuine. General Mah is indeed about to be fired from his position. General Mah has complained of this to Colonel Son on several occasions. He was quite bitter about it. Since it has been alleged by General Mah that the pressure from the Americans has been instrumental in persuading the President to decide on firing General Mah, I am wondering if Coloney McKay might have something to enlighten us with. Without some assurance from the Americans, I would think that the President would not quite dare even seriously consider firing General Mah casually. It takes one evil man to understand another evil man, and they are two of a kind. They understand each other all right."

Colonel Min said, "I'll check with Colonel McKay on this." He lit his pipe. "If the story about General Mah's impending dismissal is true, why would he go about faking his own assassination? Going to such an inhuman extreme as having his own aide and driver killed — just to make it look good? What is the motivation behind this?"

Colonel Kim said, "May I interrupt?"

Colonel Min nodded. "Go ahead."

Colonel Kim said, "According to Colonel Son, who examined the bodies of General Mah's aide and the driver, the bullets which killed them both were of .45 caliber, which makes it very hard to determine which bullets were fired by whom."

"Wait a second," said Colonel Park. "Are you saying that . . . This is horrible. Do I recall that, at the scene of the assassination attempt, according to General Ahn, General Mah was seen with a .45 pistol in his hand which belonged to his driver?"

"Right," said Colonel Kim. "The driver was shot in the back twice. Two .45-caliber bullets went through his body, shattering his back. The .45-caliber bullets could have been fired from any .45 pistol or from any .45 submachine gun. The aide was shot four times by .45-caliber bullets, two in the chest, one in the shoulder, and one in the head. He was riddled, completely blasted."

Captain Yang said, "I knew him. He was my classmate at the Academy. I've always told him to get away from General Mah."

"Too late now," said Colonel Song. "I am sorry for him."

Captain Yang said, "He — he did try to get himself transferred to . . ."

Colonel Min cut in. "That's enough."

"Yes, sir."

"You do understand me, don't you?" said Colonel Min.

"Yes, sir. I am sorry, sir."

"All right. Now, let's get back to the question of General Mah's motivation for staging this fake assassination attempt. Any opinions?"

Colonel Song said, "I can't quite fathom the depth of General

Mah's demoniac mind at this point, but whatever was his motivation for it, he must be in a desperate situation, and I can't really say I am saddened to know that. I think we will have to go cautiously on this. You do not push a desperate man too much. Yes, it seems he is faced with a desperate predicament, a last-ditch battle for his own survival, you might say."

Colonel Kim said, "If this report that he is about to be sacked is true, and it seems the report is true, then I agree with you, Colonel Song, that General Mah is in a desperate position and he will do anything under the sun to save his skin — murder, blackmail, defection — defection to us or to the Communists. I am not discounting that last possibility. He will do anything to save his neck and he is capable of doing what the Devil himself would not dare do."

Colonel Min said, "What makes you think of that possibility, Colonel Kim, that General Mah might even think of defecting to the Communists?"

Colonel Kim grinned. "Oh, I don't know. It just popped into my head."

Colonel Min frowned. "The Communists would simply shoot him, wouldn't they?"

Colonel Kim said, "He can always bargain with them."

Colonel Min said, "Yes, that's true. I suppose we can't dismiss that possibility. But, then, does this possibility have anything to do with General Ahn?" He did not wait for a reply. He went on quickly, "Colonel Kim, how much information do you have on General Ahn, besides his service records?"

"Not very much, sir. Why?"

"I want you to start working on him. Fast. Can you do it?"

"Yes, of course. But why?"

"I would rather not go into that at this time."

"Whatever you say."

Colonel Park looked up from his notebook, in which he had been writing with a pencil. "Well, here we are," he said almost in a whisper. "I have been working on a theory about General Mah's fake

assassination attempt and I think I am getting somewhere. Would
you like to hear about it?"

"By all means!" said Colonel Song. "You beat me to it!"

Colonel Min smiled. "Let's hear it."

Colonel Park gave Colonel Min a penetrating gaze, then looked
about him. His long dark hair fell over his large forehead. He
pursed his lips and rested his chin on his right hand which held the
pencil. "All right. Here it is. I have been going on the assumption
that General Mah does not know of our plans, but he is suspicious
of something brewing in the air. Everyone in the country is, as far
as I know. I have been also going on the assumption that General
Mah is indeed going to be dismissed from his position, which would
mean not only an end to his career but also a mortal danger to his
life. There will be so many people who would go out of their way to
skin him alive. He has made heaven knows how many political
enemies. I would hate to be in his shoes at a time like this. Anyway,
if we go on these two basic assumptions, I think we may begin to
see a certain pattern in all this tangled situation. I think what happened between General Mah and General Ahn may be this. When
General Mah received the message from General Ham who proposed a secret meeting, General Mah must have thought that something really big was in the making somewhere. His suspicion of a
possible coup was doubly strengthened and he began grinding out
his schemes. He starts casting his eyes about, trying to see who might
be hatching a plot against him and his beloved President. He thinks
about General Ham. No, he says to himself, General Ham is too
ambitious, too ambitious, mind you, not simply ambitious as any
man would be. No, General Ham is too ambitious to take a chance
to risk everything he has. He will bitch, pout, grumble, but an
either-or proposition, no, he won't take that risk. Now, who does
General Mah find in Seoul who has under his command a sufficient
number of combat troops who might be willing to challenge the
Presidential Brigade? General Ahn, the Commander of the Commandos, a young, ambitious, discontented hero who thinks he deserves much more than he's got. All right. So General Mah sets out

to build up an elaborate trap. I think General Mah baited General Ahn. Perhaps this is how it happened. General Mah tells General Ahn that General Ham has already spilled the secrets about an impending coup and has implicated General Ahn. General Ahn is baited and he swallows the bait. He is panicked, but he is shrewd enough to see that the reason General Mah came to him is that General Mah is willing to make some sort of a deal. That means although General Mah may know something about the coup plans he does not yet know the full details of the plans. So, General Ahn is willing to hear what General Mah has to say."

Colonel Min said, "May I interrupt you for a moment?"

Colonel Park said, "Of course."

Colonel Min said, "It seems to me that you are assuming that what General Ahn has told us is true, that is, General Mah, although he has latched onto our plans, is willing to make a deal with us. He might even cooperate with us and so on. Are you sure we can trust that?"

"I am sorry to say that there is no other way in trying to decipher this business. I have to go by that assumption."

Colonel Kim said, "I kick myself for not having bugged the goddamn house!"

"Well, we didn't know it would come to this," said Colonel Song. "Don't blame yourself."

"But still," said Colonel Kim. "Goddamn, I should have known better."

Colonel Min said, "All right. Let Colonel Park proceed."

"Colonel Min, may I ask you something?" said Colonel Moon.

Colonel Min nodded.

"I have a very strong feeling that you believe there is something fishy about General Ahn, am I right?"

Colonel Min did not reply.

Colonel Moon went on. "We have considered the possibility of General Ahn defecting from us. But your feeling toward him seems much more than that. Would you like to speak on that?"

"I would rather not go into that now, if you don't mind. Everything in proper time. I am more anxious to hear the rest of Colonel Park's theory, aren't you?"

Colonel Moon said, "Certainly."

Colonel Park was scribbling in his notebook. He looked up. "A new idea came to me," he said. "Well, let me continue. Now, where was I? Oh, yes. So — General Ahn is willing to hear what General Mah has in mind. Whatever General Mah might or might not have said to General Ahn — that we would probably never know. The truth, I mean. But I am tempted to think that they both played a very skillful game of charades with each other, each pretending to know enough about the other, and at the same time pretending to know nothing. General Mah isn't telling General Ahn all that he claims to know about the coup plans. General Ahn, on the other hand, isn't spilling it all to General Mah either. They are bargaining, bit by bit. I think this may be what happened. General Mah pretends that he knows the people involved in the coup plans but deals with General Ahn in such a way as to suggest that if General Ahn were to be spared, from General Mah's threat, that is, then General Ahn will have to prove himself to be in good faith with General Mah. How can he prove himself to be bargaining in good faith? General Mah suggests obliquely that General Ahn help him get in touch with the ringleaders of the coup plot. Then he will see what he can do for General Ahn. I am sure he offered a deal more concrete than that, of course, though we have no way of finding it out at the moment, short of interrogating General Ahn. I am sure General Mah put it all to General Ahn in such a way as to let his words appear to mean either of these: help me round up the ringleaders, or help me make a deal with them. But, of course, General Ahn thinks he is shrewd enough to have no delusion about what General Mah really means: help me round them up. But when General Ahn comes out here, for some reason, he conveniently forgets about that part of the game. So — General Ahn has agreed to the bargain, whatever it may be, and they set out to hatch a scheme, the substance of which has been related to us by General Ahn. This hocus-pocus about General Mah wanting to make a deal

with us and all that. Then General Mah pulls a brilliant though
diabolical stunt. I refer, of course, to the fake assassination attempt. Now, why this bloody melodrama? Let me line up a few
possible explanations. But, to begin with, let me also remind you
that General Mah has not confided in his trusted deputy, Colonel
Son, our trusted ally and confidant, about his secret meeting with
General Ahn or about the fake assassination melodrama, although
he did confide in him about General Ham's proposal for a secret
meeting. Why? That I don't know and I can't even begin to spec-
ulate on it. Now then, why this horrible melodrama? Number one:
It will provide General Ahn with a convincing and convenient piece
of information in trying to persuade us to believe that General
Mah's intended defection to our side is genuine, that General Mah
is, indeed, about to be fired and is in a mortal danger of his life itself. Number two: It will convince General Ahn himself that General Mah may be really bargaining in good faith, that he may indeed
want to defect to our side. This, I think, General Mah has succeeded in accomplishing, that is, sowing a seed of doubt in General
Ahn's mind. Number three: If the report about his impending dismissal is true, then we can assume that there may be some people
who would be anxious to kill him off before he may resort to a last-
minute, desperate, dirty trick. Perhaps the President himself may
be anxious to have him quietly put away. After all, doing away
with him may prevent possible political scandals and also provide
a good excuse to blame the Communists for the killing. In any
case, General Mah can either throw every one of his political enemies off his guard or confuse them all by plunging them into hush-
hush speculations as to who has done it, thereby buying time for
himself. Number four: General Mah can do either of the two; one,
he can build up a convincing case that the North Korean Communists are really out to get him — he is that valuable in our fight
against the Communists; it reminds everyone of the presence and
threat of Communist terrorism among us; and General Mah is
sorely needed to combat the Communists — an old story; two, General Mah can go to the President with an exaggerated story about

an impending coup d'état, stressing that both of them are in the same boat and the dear President needs him more than ever. You can almost hear General Mah saying to the President, 'Your Excellency, please give me time and I'll show you what I can do for you as I have always done. I'll crack down on the plotters and crush the plot. Your Excellency, sir, then you will know you just can't get along without me, you understand?' Number five: General Mah will go to the Americans. He knows they are ready to cash him in. He knows they have been pressuring the President to fire him. But he thinks he knows the Americans — ah — these childish, naïve, simpleminded Americans, he thinks, who would rather hang onto a status quo by hook or by crook than bravely and stoically face the challenges of uncertain, confusing, chaotic, unpredictable changes such as a coup d'état. In his wishful thinking and ignorance, he will conveniently forget all about the case history of the American policies behind those coups in Viet Nam. No doubt, he will tell them that a Communist-inspired and -led coup is in the making — another old story. Now, this is as far as I could go."

No one spoke for a while as though each of them had to take time to ruminate on Colonel Park's words. I felt helpless; I could not help feeling that way; the more I tried to see my way clear through the tangled mazes of the situation, the less articulate my reasoning became, and the more bewildered and impatient I became in my effort to find — rationally, logically, and sanely — a way out of this seamy, seedy, sordid, and evil scheme of things. I glanced over at Colonel Min, who seemed to be looking into the bowl of his pipe; a thin gray smoke was curling up from the pipe. He looked up.

"Colonel Park," he said, "you did say you had a new idea?"

Colonel Park nodded. "Yes. I was saving it. Now, gentlemen, having speculated on the possible motivations of General Mah's deliberately unsuccessful attempt to kill himself, let me tell you just one more thing which I think is more important and interesting than all the rest. The question simply is this. Why — just why — did General Mah feel confident enough to approach General Ahn, of all people, and why — just why — is General Ahn, of all people, undertaking this unsavory task of brokerage between General Mah and us?"

Colonel Min said quickly, "Precisely the point. Why indeed?" He jabbed the hazy, smoke-filled air with the stem of his pipe. "If you hadn't raised that question, Colonel Park, I would have brought that up myself."

Colonel Kim said, "I don't trust him."

"We've considered the fact that he commands the Commandos at a stone's throw from the Presidential residence," said Colonel Moon.

"Something is not quite right," said Chaplain Koh. "I am afraid there is something very seriously wrong and dangerous involved in this. What a mess!"

Colonel Min said, "Once more, I would like you to weigh the fact that General Ahn tried his best to persuade me, first, to bring you all to the rendezvous with General Mah and General Ham; second, he wants to kill them both. He wants that very badly. Major Lee here thinks he is too damn bloodthirsty. Well, I have no doubt about that. But, in this particular case, there is something a little more than his being simply bloodthirsty. Let me tell you what I think. From what we know and from what Colonel Park has just explicated for us, I think I will have to say, to my regret, that General Mah seems to have something big on General Ahn. What is it? What could it possibly be that is important and big enough to make General Ahn wriggle and dance to the tune of General Mah's flute?"

"The implications of your words are quite sinister, Colonel Min," said Chaplain Koh.

Colonel Min kept silent.

Colonel Kim said, "I am a little worried. Perhaps we shouldn't have let him go back to Seoul."

Colonel Min said, "I thought of that myself. I had a good mind to have him kept here, but that wouldn't have worked out. General Mah knows about the trip."

I said, "Obviously, General Mah knew and even approved General Ahn's trip out here, and if so, General Mah has not taken any action as yet. Does this mean that General Mah's deal or his intention for defection is genuine?"

"A good point," said Colonel Moon.

"We shall see. Very shortly," said Colonel Min. "Colonel Son has been instructed to keep his eyes open at his end. If, gentlemen, if General Mah should decide to act against us in any way before this evening's rendezvous, Colonel Son is ordered to execute his contingency plan number three: Kill him."

Colonel Kim nodded.

Colonel Park said, "And if not?"

Colonel Min said, "If not? That brings us back to the original purpose of this meeting: What do we do with General Mah?"

Colonel Kim said, "Kill him." He looked at everyone. "We've got to strike him first. The situation is getting out of hand. It is either him or us."

Colonel Min said, "Colonel Park?"

"Are we going to the rendezvous this evening?"

"No matter what we decide to do with General Mah," said Colonel Min, "we will have to keep the appointment, don't you think? Presumably, this is a rendezvous between General Mah and General Ham. We have been invited to join the party as an observer if I may put it that way. To witness, ostensibly, the good faith of General Mah in his proposition to us."

I spoke out, "I am willing, more than willing, in fact, to work this out on the assumption that General Mah's deal is genuine. I believe it is to our best interest and to the image of ourselves in carrying out our coup to avoid unnecessary bloodshed at any price. From what we know, General Mah's own position is being threatened by his own people, and that fact itself seems to confirm the authenticity if not sincerity of his expressed desire for defecting to our side. I think we should give him the benefit of the doubt."

"In short, you don't want to kill him," said Colonel Kim. "I am not worried about tainting the image of ourselves. The whole country is going to say, A good riddance!"

"It will still be on our conscience," I retorted. "This is a cold-blooded murder we are talking about, Colonel Kim!"

"Well, we are talking about a cold-blooded murderer himself!" said Colonel Moon.

Colonel Min said quietly, "All right. We are going to the rendez-vous this evening. Any objection?" He looked around the table. "All right. We shall go. But, we are not all of us going to be there. We are not ready to honor that part of the bargain, is that clear? I shall go there myself."

"I am coming with you, sir," said Lieutenant Cho.

Colonel Min nodded.

"I don't like the smell of it," Colonel Kim said. "Let me go instead."

"I can't spare you."

"We can't spare you, either," said Colonel Park. "You know that."

"If you don't mind my saying so, this is far too important a matter for me not to undertake myself. I am going to exercise the prerogative of the chairmanship. The coup can be carried out without me, but without any one of you, no. I shall go alone. If any of you is worried about my safety or security problem, don't. Colonel Son knows what he is supposed to do if it should come to a showdown. Besides, I don't believe General Ahn is going to desert us at this time. I believe he really wants to kill General Mah. I am sure he will come prepared for that. As I said before, General Ahn appears to have a very solid, urgent reason for killing General Mah — and General Ham, incidentally. Trust me on that. I repeat. General Ahn wants to kill General Mah. So — I shall go alone but I will not be alone. I will have Colonel Son and General Ahn."

I said, "I would like to volunteer to come along. After all, I am the special assistant to General Ahn."

Colonel Min gazed at me for a long moment. His eyes were cold. "All right," he said almost in a whisper.

"I would like to put this to a vote," said Colonel Moon.

"That won't be necessary," said Colonel Min.

"If you insist," said Colonel Kim. "I'll make sure you will be safe. Don't worry."

Colonel Min nodded. "Good. That is settled. I would like to see you later, Colonel Park, about the contingency plan number fourteen."

The contingency plan number fourteen was about the structure of the chain of command for the coup and the provisions for command take-over in case of emergencies.

Colonel Park said, "Yes."

"Good. Now, I should like to propose that we vote on the question of what to do with General Mah. Kill him tomorrow evening or accept his deal if it should prove to be genuine or kill him in any event."

I said, "I request that the last item be struck out. If his deal is genuine, there is no reason for us to kill him. Once we are certain it is genuine, we should accept it in good faith and carry out our part of the deal."

"General Mah wouldn't have any scruples about not carrying out his part of the bargain," said Colonel Kim.

"But, sir, we can't proceed with that assumption until it happens," I said.

Colonel Moon sneered, "It will be too late then."

Colonel Park said, "I don't think any more argument is necessary. So — let's vote."

Colonel Min looked at Chaplain Koh. "Allow me to say this, Chaplain, but you are free to abstain from the voting."

I spoke out quickly, "I don't think that is fair."

"Not fair to whom?" said Colonel Kim.

"To Chaplain Koh," I said.

"Ah — don't argue," said Chaplain Koh. "Thank you for your consideration, but I shall gladly participate in the voting."

"Good. All right. I think we've talked about this enough. Lieutenant Cho, are you ready for us?"

"Yes, sir." Lieutenant Cho stood up from his chair. He went

around the table, placing a small index card in front of everyone. The card contained two words: YES and NO. We would draw a circle around one.

"All right," said Colonel Min. "Let's get this over with."

Lieutenant Cho once again went around the table and collected the cards and placed them before Colonel Min. Colonel Min looked them over and gave them back to Lieutenant Cho.

Lieutenant Cho announced the result. The vote was five to two in favor of killing General Mah.

I was on the point of getting up from my chair when Colonel Min said sharply, "Not one more word from you, Major Lee. Is that clear? You've had your chance as everyone else here. Sit down!"

There was nothing I could do. I had no choice but to sit down and — oh, you cold-blooded murderers! Beasts! Beasts! We were all like beasts, like General Mah and his cohorts, like those we stood up against, in the name of justice and liberty and salvation — there was only one way to stop this cold, calculated, evil bloodshed; I would call for a meeting of the delegates from subcommand groups.

"There is one absentee vote I should like to put on record. General Yoon votes for killing General Mah."

I stared at Colonel Min.

He stared back at me coldly. He spoke matter-of-factly, "As the chairman, it is my duty to remind you that this meeting has now reached a decision concerning General Mah. The majority decision dictates that we shall do all in our power, take all the necessary actions, to execute General Mah. It is also my duty to remind you that should there be any member of the Command Group and the subcommand groups who ignores, disobeys, and sabotages the majority decision of this Command Group, I shall have him arrested and shot — including myself. Is that clearly understood?" He was looking at me as he spoke. Cold eyes, cold bloodshot eyes.

There was a knock on the door.

Lieutenant Cho went out of the room and came back in instantly. "It is Colonel McKay, sir. I had him wait for you in the general's office."

"Good," said Colonel Min. "Gentlemen, this meeting is now adjourned. Thank you all. Now — go get some sleep, if you can sleep at all." He turned to me. His face was impassive and his voice toneless. "Major Lee, I would like to see you when I am finished with Colonel McKay. Stay here. I shan't be long."

The others were getting up from their chairs and quietly shuffling out of the room. Colonel Kim stopped to whisper to Colonel Min, then joined Colonel Park and went out of the room. Lieutenant Cho was hovering behind Colonel Min.

Colonel Min said, "Lieutenant Cho, you may go."

Lieutenant Cho darted a quick look toward me and the chaplain, bowed slightly, and walked out.

Colonel Min was filling his pipe with fresh tobacco.

Chaplain Koh remained in his seat, looking down at his folded hands on the table. He did not look up.

Colonel Min lighted his pipe, gazing at the chaplain. His mouth belched out puffs of gray smoke which clouded his face for a moment. He leaned back against the chair. "Chaplain," he said in a whisper.

Chaplain Koh slowly raised his face and fixed his eyes on Colonel Min's. The chaplain's face looked old and weary, but his eyes were young and burning and defiant. "Yes, Colonel Min?"

Colonel Min's gaze did not waver. Without a word, he nodded slightly. He sat up. "Chaplain, I want you to see Lieutenant Cho before you leave. Would you go over your plans once more with him? He will take care of your transportation."

Chaplain Koh said, "Yes."

"Good luck in Seoul, Chaplain," said Colonel Min. "We shall see each other again very soon." He stood up.

I did not stir. He came toward me. I did not look up. He stopped and stood behind me. I did not budge from my chair.

"Will you wait for me here?" he said.

Chaplain Koh stared at me.

"You betrayed me," I said.

He was silent.

"And you betrayed yourself," I said. My voice shook with fury and shame.

"Major Lee!" Chaplain Koh said. "Hold your tongue and behave yourself!"

I heard behind me Colonel Min's quick footsteps. "Not one more word from you, Chaplain!" he spoke in whispers. "Not one more word!" He was at his side.

Chaplain Koh leaped to his feet.

"Chaplain, good luck!" said Colonel Min. "Take care of yourself."

Chaplain Koh nodded. They shook hands. Colonel Min stalked out of the room.

I stood up. Chaplain Koh charged up to me. His face was angry.

"I had to tell him," I said. "I had to tell him what I thought of him, don't you understand? He'd given me his word, don't you see? He'd given me his word!"

He glared at me.

I went on, "I had to try! And I would try again and again and again . . ."

"Shut up! That's enough!"

"Yes. Yes. What's the use of talking about it! I did my best." I stepped up to him and held his arm. "It was a lost cause, I know, but I thank you for your vote!"

He was shaking his head. "You are a fool," he whispered.

"I beg your pardon!"

Suddenly, his eyes were glistening with tears.

"What is it? What is it, Chaplain!"

He shook his arm out of my grip. "You are a fool, Major! Don't you see that?" His voice slashed at me.

I held my breath and stared at him.

Before I could utter a word, his voice, now weary and weak, whispered, "And perhaps I, too, am a fool?"

"You! You?" I could not help muttering. "You — of all people?"

His voice was once again charged with savage fury. "Why?

Why! Because I am a chaplain! Yes, yes! I have two cheeks to offer. Two cheeks to be slapped twice! And one life to be shot once! And do you think the evil in the world will disappear with that!"

"But you said . . ."

"Ah! That was my blasphemy, Major! Forgive me, oh Lord, for I knew not what I was saying! For we are not playing a nice, little, clean game by the heavenly rules of your book!" With that outburst, he left me alone, shocked and confused, in the bare, empty, deserted room.

Chapter 10

Although Colonel Min had ordered me to wait for him in the conference room, I did not relish the thought of being alone in the barren room dimly illuminated by one shaded lamp from the ceiling. The room had no windows. The stale smoke from cigarettes and pipes now hung low like a hazy mist. I got up from my chair and walked out of the room. But I had forgotten, momentarily, that Colonel Min and Colonel McKay were meeting in the adjoining general's office and that, in order to go outside the building, I would have to walk through the general's office. Only when I closed the door of the conference room behind me and stood in the dark did I realize that they were both there, near the window that faced outside, sitting side by side on a couch. At first, I did not make out their figures; then I saw the glow of Colonel Min's pipe in the shadowy dark. He stood up from the couch, his blurred figure framed by the window. It had become light outside though it was still dark gray and it was raining. I could now see the raindrops streaming down the window-panes. Colonel McKay, too, stood up from the couch. They both remained quiet, standing side by side, against the gray, rainy dawn outside the window. I had thought Colonel McKay was a tall man, but he turned out to be shorter, perhaps an inch or two, than Colonel Min.

"Major Lee," said Colonel Min, "come and meet Colonel McKay."

I had been on the point of tiptoeing out of the room. I went up to them.

"We've met before," said Colonel McKay, shaking my hand. "In Seoul."

"Yes," I said. "I didn't think you would remember me."

Colonel Min said, "Oh, don't worry. Colonel McKay remembers everything. He has — what do you say? — a photographic memory."

"I depend on our computerized filing system," said Colonel McKay, "if that's what you mean." He laughed.

"I was discussing with Colonel McKay your trip to Japan," said Colonel Min. "If all goes well, I would like you to be ready to leave tonight."

"Do you think the trip is really necessary?" I said.

"I do what Colonel Min here instructs me to do," said Colonel McKay.

"With your advice and cooperation," said Colonel Min.

I still could not make out Colonel McKay's face; a short, cropped haircut and a bushy moustache under his nose nearly hiding his mouth; the rest of his face remained in the shadow.

"If you both feel that the trip is absolutely essential, I am ready whenever you are," I said.

"Good," said Colonel Min.

"Fine," said Colonel McKay.

"Now, Major Lee," said Colonel Min, "you will excuse us. I shan't be long."

"I'll be outside," I said.

"Good. Get some fresh air," said Colonel Min.

"See you tonight, then," said Colonel McKay, "Major."

I walked out of the general's office and into the aide's room. Lieutenant Cho was there, sitting behind a desk. He stood up. "Major Lee."

"I didn't know you were here," I said.

"I've had your quarters ready, sir. The same ones you've had before, behind the general's mess. Your jeep's outside. I had it brought over." He handed me my raincoat. "This was in your jeep. Thought you would need it. It is going to rain all day."

I put the raincoat on. "What about tonight?"

"Rain, most likely, sir. That's what our weather people said."

I nodded. "I am waiting for Colonel Min," I said, moving toward the door. "I'll be outside." I changed my mind. "I am going over to the auditorium. Will you tell him I'll be there?"

"Yes, sir."

I opened the door. A cool wind gushed in. I shivered. The rain was pouring down, flooding the field with eddying pools of muddy water. Streams of water flowed down the round, transparent cockpit of the helicopter. The muzzles of the tanks' cannons, the heavy machine guns in the tanks' turrets, and the anti-aircraft guns mounted on half-tracks had been draped with canvas covers. Heavy raindrops were splashing down near the tanks' treads which had dug deep into the muddy earth. The sky was dirty gray.

Lieutenant Cho was standing beside me. "You'll be soaking wet, sir," he said.

"It's all right." I stepped out under the overhang.

"Major Lee."

"Yes?"

"You will have breakfast with Colonel Min, won't you, sir?"

I looked at him — at the face of a gentle bulldog. "Yes."

He smiled. "I'll have it sent over to Colonel Min's quarters."

"All right." I took a step out into the rain.

"Sir!"

"Yes, Lieutenant?" I did not turn around.

His voice followed me. "Thank you, Major."

I nodded and headed for the auditorium. By the time I reached the door, I was thoroughly drenched from top to bottom; my raincoat did not do me any good. The muddy water was ankle-deep.

The gray, rainy dawn had not yet fully dispelled the darkness within the auditorium. It was still shadowy and indistinct in there, but I could see rows and rows of steel folding chairs, the raised platform, the large movie screen on the wall behind the lectern. There was a table directly under the lectern down the center aisle, and Colonel Min's phonograph was still on it. I walked down the aisle. It was a portable, stereo phonograph with built-in speakers which Colonel Min had brought back from Germany. The lid was down. I lifted it up. There was only one record on the turntable. I picked it up. Sibelius. I put the record back on the turntable. I started the phonograph. When it began to play, I stepped back toward the half-way point up the aisle, took off my wet raincoat, sat down on a chair; then the door creaked open. I got up and turned around. It was Colonel Min. He came down the aisle toward me. He, too, was drenched with the rain. Water dripped from his cap. He took off his raincoat and cap and pulled out a chair in the middle of the aisle and sat down. He gave me a silent nod.

"I hope you don't mind my playing the record," I said.

"Do you like it?"

"It is too melancholy, too sad for my taste," I said.

As if he had not heard me, he whispered, "It is bitter music. Listen to the English horn! Singing its own elegy, its own dirge!"

We did not speak after that, until the record was over and the phonograph turned itself off with a click.

I watched him light his pipe. I waited till he had a few puffs. "I want to apologize — "

He did not let me finish. "Enough, enough."

"You did not betray me."

He did not speak; his shadowy face seemed to be brooding.

"You did not betray yourself either," I said.

He remained silent.

Awkward and uncomfortable, I was on the point of mentioning Colonel McKay to change the subject, when he looked at me fully and said, "I did not betray myself, did I?" Then, speaking as though to himself alone, "No, I did not betray myself." He turned to me again. "But not for you, do you understand? Not for you alone! For myself, for my sanity, for my salvation, do you understand that?"

I did not know what to say.

"Ah — enough is enough!" he said.

I nodded — rather mechanically, not fully comprehending his words.

To my relief, he began telling me about his meeting with Colonel McKay. That the Americans had been pressuring the President to fire General Mah was true; the President had at last given in to the pressure. Colonel McKay, too, had been able to establish that the assassination attempt on General Mah's life had been staged by General Mah himself.

I said, "And where does General Ahn come into the picture?"

He brooded on.

"You are convinced that something is not quite right with General Ahn," I said. "I know you believe that General Mah has something big on him, too. Do you think General Ahn has defected from us?"

He shook his head. "No. I don't think we have to worry about that. Not yet, anyway. Colonel McKay feels the same way."

"Does Colonel McKay, then, have something on General Ahn?"

"Yes, but he would not tell me at this time. He is not certain of what he has on him. No, he wouldn't give it to me until he is absolutely sure of his information. 'After all, he is a general of your army with which we have a friendly relationship and are most eager to maintain that relationship, and it will not behoove us to divulge information which we are, at this stage, unable to confirm.' That's what he said."

"I must say it is strange logic he is using. He is quite willing to help us overthrow our government!"

A faint smile appeared on his face. "Colonel McKay finally confessed to me that the Americans have bugged General Ahn's house. That, of course, is an admission that they have been suspecting him of something very serious. Needless to say, they have been bugging General Mah, too."

"Well, for that matter, I suppose they have bugged practically everyone in the country who is somebody. How about us?"

He laughed. "Not yet. But if our coup is successful and we are running the government, we will be. That's his joke."

"If they have bugged General Ahn's house, they must know the substance of the conversation between General Mah and General Ahn."

"They do."

"And he wouldn't tell you about it?"

"No. But he gave me his word that he would give me the information once it is confirmed. For the time being, all he would tell me is that General Mah has threatened General Ahn that he knew enough about the coup plans which implicated General Ahn and has asked him to help him get in touch with the ringleaders — us, that is. And General Ahn has agreed to it. Colonel McKay guarantees that General Ahn has no intention of defecting from us at this time and that General Ahn does indeed want to kill General Mah, no matter what. Soon. At his first chance."

"I think it is very unreasonable of Colonel McKay to withhold any information, whether or not it is confirmed, when he is supposedly helping our cause."

"It does not really matter," he said. "I am beginning to sense a certain pattern emerging from this situation involving General Ahn."

"Well?"

"I told Colonel McKay about the North Korean security colonel. Do you remember what General Ahn told us?"

"Yes."

"Well, to my surprise, Colonel McKay knew about that already."

"With the help of his computerized filing system!"

"Now, this is very serious, I think. When I mentioned this to him, he nearly jumped. You see, although he had known about this

North Korean colonel, he didn't know that I was somehow connected with it, that is, that I had known the North Korean officer years back. Of course, he thanked me for that piece of information."

"Well, what is he going to do with that?"

"That I wouldn't know."

"And what do you think it may all add up to?"

"I told you that I had seen this North Korean officer die before my own eyes."

"Yes."

"Well, General Ahn claimed that he had him shot. Either I am lying or he is. And I am not lying, of course. Naturally, there is always a chance, as I've said before, that I might have thought he was dead when actually he wasn't."

"But didn't you also say that even if he had lived, the Communists would have shot him anyway? He killed a Russian major, didn't he? That's what you said."

"That is true. That I saw happen."

"You were present?"

"Yes."

"In the Russian garrison in your town?"

"Yes."

"Was this North Korean officer — was he the one who had come from Pyungyang and arrested you?"

"Yes. You know that, don't you? Lieutenant Cho has told you?"

"Yes. You had come back to the town and settled out on your farm."

He nodded.

"You had come back to the country from Manchuria with the Korean units which had been with the Chinese Communist troops."

"I think I told you that myself years ago."

"Yes. Now, those units became the backbone of the North Korean Army and supplied its cadre. We know that. How did you leave

them? Were you demobilized? Discharged? Did you resign?
You came back to the country as one of their officers, after all."

"I simply left them and came home."

"And they wouldn't tolerate that. So they come looking for
you, a deserter. Am I correct?"

"Yes."

"So this North Korean colonel — wait, he was a major, then. He
comes to your town with his men and comes out to your farm. He
arrests you and takes you into the Russian garrison. Did you know
him before?"

"Yes. We were in the same unit in China and Manchuria. He
had just been made a major in the new army."

"And what happened in the Russian garrison?"

"Are you interrogating me?"

Though his voice carried no sting of accusation, I checked myself. "No, no, of course not! I would like to know. I would like
to try to piece things together."

He gazed at me. It had become a little lighter in the auditorium.
I could now almost see the color of his eyes. "Piece things together for what? To sketch in the rest of my past, my bloody past?"
His voice was calm and there was no hostility in the way he said
his words; it was, on the contrary, more like an amused grown-up
gently chiding the impetuous curiosity of a child.

He said, "Ah, never mind. It does not really matter now."

I went on, not without a certain degree of impudence, "Something happened inside the Russian garrison. You are supposed to
have killed the garrison commander — no, you didn't. You say
the North Korean major did. How odd, though. However, you somehow managed to break out of the garrison and made it to Lieutenant
Cho's father's house. There, his father and his brother helped
you out of the house and presumably they got you in contact with
some border smugglers who smuggled you across the border into
South Korea. Am I correct so far?"

"How odd, indeed. How odd, you say, that this North Korean
security officer should kill the Russian major — "

"You said you two were in the same unit. Were you friends?"

"Friends? No. Battlefield comrades, perhaps, with the same dreams and hopes for the liberation of their country — until the dreams and hopes came true and then they began to dream and hope for different things, so different that one of them could not tolerate the other or live with him."

"He could not tolerate you?"

"So much so that he volunteered to come after me. Yes, he, too, was once a university student in Tokyo, a student of politics at Waseda University. He was two, three years older than I was, and he had joined the Korean Brigade several months before I did. He was tough, already battle-hardened when I first met him. We were different in many ways, but there was one thing common between us. An almost shameless love of our country — ah — that's what we shared, do you understand? If a Communist can be a patriot, a nationalistic patriot, then he was one. To this day, I do not really believe that he ever was a true Communist and Marxist with an international allegiance and loyalty. Korea — Korea! That was all he could think of. His true loyalty and love were for his country and his people."

"Then — why? Why would he set out to destroy you?"

"You see, he also wanted to be a good Communist, a true international Communist whose allegiance and loyalty had to transcend the national boundaries and nationalistic consciousness of one's ethnic loyalty, although little did he know then that the only choice they would give him after the war was either for him to be a good Communist with his unconditional, unquestioned loyalty to the Soviet Russia or to the Chinese Communists and, of course, to their stooges. Perhaps he was born out of time. Perhaps his case is not unique when we consider the nature of the Second World War and what happened after the war to various Communist movements that had originated during the war. In any event, therein lay what in the end became the seed of his tragedy. He did not know which way to turn and he had to destroy himself."

"You say he killed himself?"

"Perhaps it was not tragic after all. Perhaps it was more pathetic than anything else. Yes — so he came to arrest me. No, that is not true. He came to persuade me to return to Pyungyang and work with him. I had joined them during the war, when it did not matter what you were, what ideology you embraced. Did it matter? We were all fighting against a common enemy and our common purpose then was to defeat this common enemy and liberate our country and return home. And that's precisely what I did. When our common enemy was defeated and the motherland liberated, it was time for me and them to part company. I thought nothing of it. I did not even think about it, to tell you the truth. Perhaps I was naïve? But I had too much blood on my hands, don't you see? I had too many things I now wanted to forget. I had done many a horrible, horrifying thing in those few, short years. And — all that at my age, too! I wanted nothing more than to come back to my hometown and settle on the farm near the graves of my parents, my poor parents for whom I had done nothing but bring suffering and misery and — well, the country was free now and there were more than enough people who wanted to run it. Let them, I said to myself, do you understand me? Let them! All I wanted was peace, a quiet peace and time, time to reflect on myself and on what I had done, time to turn back the clock, time to reclaim the lost innocence, if you like. I had grown up too quickly, too suddenly. I wanted the lost time back, back to myself and for myself. I craved peace and tranquillity and solitude for my life on the farm, far, far away from the hustle and bustle of crowds, soldiers and politicians, slogans and foreign ideologies, sensationalists and demagogues, true patriots and false prophets alike. I had heard them all. I had had enough of them all! Farewell to all that! I wanted to be a farmer. I wanted to be left alone and I would leave everyone alone. The world was full of people who wanted to do things for others, to others, who told you what was good for you and what was not good for you. Let them do what they wanted, but I wanted to be left alone. I had done my share of work, of sacrifice for the country and for the people. Let me just be. So I went out to the farm. Then he came.

"I said he came to persuade me. 'Leave me alone,' I said to him. 'Leave me alone. If you want power and glory, you can have them all. I don't want any part of your grand design, grandiloquent dream. Leave me alone!' Persuasion became insinuation, insinuation became intimidation, intimidation became threat, and threat became torture. No, there was no meeting of minds. 'Look around you,' I said, 'and see for yourself just where you stand and what you are. You are neither a good patriot, a good nationalist, a lover of one's country, nor are you a good Communist. Look at yourself,' I said, 'what has become of you? An instrument, a weapon, of those false prophets and false patriots, foreign lackeys, who are once more enslaving the people, who are corrupted by their own power, who are bent on setting up a totalitarian, dictatorial society in the name of justice, equality, and liberty. What has happened to your dreams and hopes?' I said. So he took me to the Russian garrison.

"We were to stay there overnight, then go on to Pyungyang the next morning. I shall never know why he decided to stay there for the night rather than go directly to Pyungyang the same day. After all, we were only a two hours' drive away from Pyungyang. It seemed he had known the Russian major, the garrison commander, personally. At any rate, it was still early in the afternoon when we drove into the Russian garrison. The garrison was then in a large apple orchard which had belonged to a Japanese. Needless to say, the Japanese was the wealthiest man in our town. He owned not only the orchard but a few rice plantations, as well as stores and a restaurant and a whorehouse. He had built a mansion in the middle of his orchard, and rows of tenant houses for the Korean laborers were about a mile or so from the mansion. The Russian commander and his staff were living in the mansion and their men in the tenant houses. They locked me up in one of the underground warehouses. I stayed there in a dark, damp cell of the warehouse all afternoon, in one of the many concrete cells where

the Japanese used to store his choicest apples, which, as rumors
would have it, were later wrapped in special papers embossed with
chrysanthemums and shipped to Japan for use in the Imperial house-
hold. It was late in the fall and it was cold in there. Then the night
came — not that I could tell the time — and a Russian soldier
came and dragged me out. The warehouse must have been nearly
two miles from the mansion. The Russian soldier, who I now saw
was a lieutenant, drove me in a jeep to the mansion. He took me
in and led me downstairs to the basement. There I found myself
face to face with the Russian major and the North Korean major,
my former comrade in arms and now my captor. The Russian lieutenant locked the door of the basement and stayed there with them."

"Interrogation?" I said.

"Torture, wouldn't you know? I remember there was a party
going on within the mansion, upstairs; when I was pushed into the
mansion, I heard singing and shouting and a phonograph going on
very loud somewhere upstairs. The officers were all there, I thought.
Yes — I remember the phonograph was blasting out some old Japanese war songs and the Russians were bellowing out, imitating the
songs, laughing and roaring, and I remember hearing glasses break-
ing and footsteps bouncing overhead. But, downstairs in the basement, behind its locked door, we were all quiet. The Russian major
was short and fat; his head was shaven smooth and his big, blue
eyes were darting from me to the North Korean major, back and
forth, back and forth; I don't remember his face too clearly now,
but it was a small face, somewhat out of proportion to his thick,
stubby figure. The Russian lieutenant was big and large, his head
also shaven and I remember how big and strong his hands were
when he dragged me out of the cell. The Russian major said something to the lieutenant and the big man pushed me forward to the
center of the room and, with one big hand, pressed me down on my
knees. I saw their boots; the three of them wore black boots and
I saw six boots before my eyes and they squeaked and squished.
I tried to raise my head and the lieutenant pushed it down. The

Russian major was speaking to the North Korean major, though I could not tell what he was saying. Then a pair of boots moved away — the lieutenant — and the next thing I knew, he began whipping me. I was whipped exactly nine times, on my back. I did not cry out, I did not budge, I did not even stir. The whipping stopped and the lieutenant pulled my hair, yanking my head up and back, so that I could see the Russian major and the North Korean major full in their faces. I remember the big, blue eyes of the Russian, expressionless, peering into mine. The North Korean major was quiet but his eyes were flaming and full of hatred. He hated me, understand? He was hating me with all his might. Such hate! Such vicious, violent, horrifying hate! And I said to him, 'Why do you do this to me? Why do you let them do this to me?' He spat in my face. The Russian major wanted to know what I said, I think. The North Korean major was shaking his head, furiously saying something in Russian. And the Russian major took out his revolver from the holster and handed it to the North Korean major, who had his own revolver strapped to his waist. He did not take the revolver and was shaking his head, staring, staring at me. 'Your master wants you to kill me,' I said to him. 'Why don't you kill me?' 'Shut your filthy mouth!' he screamed. The Russian major wanted to know what I said. His stubby fingers snapped, as if to say 'Finish him off! Let's get it over with!' And the Russian major hissed to the lieutenant — perhaps, to begin whipping me again. And the North Korean's boots stomped on the concrete floor and leaped over to the lieutenant. He snatched the whip, a long whip, from the lieutenant. I saw the tail of the whip slither on the floor after him. He said something in Russian to the two of them. The Russian major shrugged his shoulders and backed off a few paces and sat down on a chair. The lieutenant stood beside the major. Then the North Korean major started whipping me. He did not say a word. He was simply hissing with his violent breathing. He whipped and whipped, on my back, on my shoulders, on my arms, and — and on my face and that was enough for me and I couldn't take it any longer, I couldn't bear the humiliation any longer. Mind you, it was not the physical pain, not the bleeding pain that forced me to stand up, to stagger up, understand! I couldn't take it any longer, this insult and humiliation, this beastly humiliation! I stumbled on my knees and I staggered up. I collapsed. He whipped me hard across my chest and the tail of his whip slashed into my face, into my eyes, and I knew my face was bleeding, my eyes were bleeding, and I was screaming, 'What have I done to you! What have I done to you! What harm have I done to you! You hate me! Why do you hate me! What have I done to you! I have done nothing to harm you, to hurt you, to destroy you and your cause! What have I done to you!' He whipped and whipped me. What hate, what vicious, violent hate! What sadistic hate! And then — in one blinding, bleeding, aching moment, it flashed across my seething, boiling, burning mind that, that perhaps, perhaps, whipping me in his sadistic, demoniac hate and fury, perhaps it was he himself, not me, but he himself that was being whipped. But all this is perhaps my afterthought, looking back on it as I am now. Who knows? All I know is that, the next moment, I raised myself fully, spreading my arms, while his whip kept on lashing me, and I caught the tail of his whip and I hung onto it and pulled it with all my might in all my blinding rage and the whip came flying at me, coiling up in the air garishly lighted with red and blue lamps. The whip had jerked out of his hand and now it was in my hand and I began whipping him, half mad, screaming and screaming — 'What have I done to you!' I whipped and whipped him, not thinking for one moment that the Russians were there, not thinking that they could shoot me dead. The North Korean major raised his arms, and his elbows were bent, his hands covering his face, and the whip slashed and slashed at him and he was backing away inch by inch and I whipped and whipped him to the wall near where the two Russians were. And it was then that I realized I was the one whipping, and I staggered on my feet, vaguely aware that the whip now rested, coiled, beside my feet, and the North Korean major lowered his arms and looked at me and around him with his bloodshot, dazed eyes, and it was then that we, both of us, saw that the Russians, the Russian major, the garrison commander, and the big lieutenant — they were laughing and laughing and laughing. Their roaring laughter bounced and danced in the room, echoing and echoing, shaking the room, so it seemed to me, and, suddenly, I thought I could hear the roaring laughter and the old Japanese war songs and the tinkling and shattering of glasses upstairs and I felt my body freeze up for a second, then — then, I looked at the North Korean major, looked at his bloody face, bleeding face, looked into his bleeding eyes and he looked at me, at my bloody face, my bleeding face, looked into my bleeding eyes, and I was standing there still clutching the whip and the Russians were looking at us laughing and laughing and laughing. Suddenly the North Korean major flung himself at the Russian major, his body nearly flying in the air, his arms outstretched, his bloody hands and fingers outstretched and spread wide. The chair the Russian major was sitting on fell crashing onto the floor and both of them tumbled down, together, the North Korean major on top of the Russian major, and I saw his hands were around the other's neck, the open neck that the Russian's unbuttoned jacket had bared. I felt as though the room was whirling around and around and I felt dizzy and sick; then I saw the Russian lieutenant, who was suddenly jerking up as though waking from a bad dream, mumbling and stuttering. Then I saw him reach for his revolver and I slashed at him with the whip and he charged at me, and I whipped him hard with all my strength and I saw him getting the gun out of the holster and I whipped him and whipped him and the gun went flying from his hand and bouncing on the floor. I whipped and whipped him and saw him doubling up, his big hairy hands covering his face and I ran after the gun and he came after the gun, too, and I whipped him again and again and he was roaring like a beast, getting up from the floor, raising his arms over his head, and he grabbed the hissing tail of the whip and I let it go before he could snatch it from my hands and he fell backward on the floor, his black boots scraping against the concrete floor. Then I had the revolver in my hand and I instinctively clicked the bullet chamber around twice, cocking the hammer at the same time and when the big beast, now half standing, on his knees, raised the whip ready to lash at me, I shot him. I shot him twice.

"He was dead instantly. I knew he was dead. I didn't have to make sure. The memories and experiences of the battles all came rushing back to me. My face was bleeding and sweating and I was breathing hard but I was now calm and strangely composed. I was standing firm and quiet. It was as though a great tide of anger and battle had washed me clean and left me peaceful. I went over to the others. The Russian major was dead, strangled to death. He was sprawled flat on the floor, his arms stretched out, and his face now seemed to have shrunk into the open neck of his jacket. The North Korean major was sitting next to him, his knees drawn up, his arms dangling limp at his side. He looked up. I stood before him. He looked up at me, squinting his bloody eyes. One of his eyes was swollen, bleeding. He staggered up to his feet. I still had the Russian's revolver in my hand. His was in the holster. We stared at each other for a moment. Then he reached for his gun. He took it out of the holster. We were still staring at each other. He slowly turned his head and looked at the body of the Russian major. He looked back at me. Then he looked at the body again. We didn't have to speak. I knew what he was thinking. He raised his revolver and shot the Russian major's body, once, in the neck. Then we left. Still we did not speak. Not one word, do you understand? We unlocked the door and stepped out of the basement. There was no one in sight. There was no sound, no noise from upstairs. It was very quiet and hushed. We didn't run. We simply walked across the large hallway and out of the mansion. Still not one word had passed between us. The jeep was still there outside. We got in. He drove. We drove in silence down the graveled driveway which was about half a mile long to the entrance of the garrison. There were two Russian guards at the gate. Once again, we didn't have to speak. We knew what we had to do. He slowed the jeep down as the two guards came out of the sentry box; he stopped the jeep when they came close enough and shouted something in Russian and the guards, one on each side of the jeep, raised their hands as if to salute, then we shot them. He jumped out of the jeep, picked up the German submachine gun the Russian guard on his side had dropped on the ground, leaped back into the jeep and handed me the submachine gun. Then we drove out of the gate. He did not know our town and I had to direct him. About two miles from the garrison, I had him drive off the main road and onto a dirt road that was a shortcut to where Lieutenant Cho's family lived. I didn't really know why I directed him toward that way, except that the dirt road went along the side of a mountain and, in case we were followed, we could always abandon the jeep and start climbing up the mountain. The mountain road went winding for three or four miles and came out behind the town. There he stopped. We could look down on the town, quiet and dark. It must have been after midnight. The moon was up, half hidden in black clouds, cold and silent. He turned off the engine and looked at me fully, then he began crying. He wept without sound, leaning his head back against the seat, letting his tears bathe his face, as though abandoning himself to the whirlpool of his tangled emotions. I spoke to him for the first time. 'What will you do now?' He did not respond to my words. I said, 'I'm going to try to cross the border to the South. Will you come with me?' He sat up slowly and looked at me. He nodded, without a word. 'Wait here,' I said. 'I know someone who will help us find people who can get us across the border. Stay here. I'll be back soon.' 'I'll wait for you here,' he said. His voice was calm. 'All right,' I said. I got out of the jeep and started down the hill, at the foot of which was Lieutenant Cho's father's house. Halfway down the hill, it struck me that I still had the German submachine gun in my hand. I thought of hiding it there and picking it up on my way back. But I didn't let it go and carried it all the way down the hill. Lieutenant Cho's father and his brother came out with me. I told them what happened as we climbed up the hill. 'We've got to get you across the border,' said Lieutenant Cho's father. 'Yes,'

I said. 'Can you help me?' Without replying to me, he turned to his son and told him to run back to the house and come back with some money, clothes, and food. The boy ran down the hill. We climbed up the hill to where I had left the North Korean major.

"A few more steps and we would be on the dirt road, and I held Lieutenant Cho's father back. I wanted to be sure. We could see the jeep, shadowy in the moonlight, and I whispered, 'Chung! Chung!' That was his name — Major Chung, Comrade Chung! He did not respond. There was no sound. We waited for a few moments and I called again. Not a sound came from the jeep. I told Lieutenant Cho's father to wait for me there. I checked the submachine gun, loaded it, and crawled up the remaining few paces. I had to be sure. I lay flat on the dirt, pressing my ears to the ground. I could not hear a sound except the pounding of my own heart. I got up and went over to the jeep, a step at a time, the submachine gun at ready. I approached the jeep from behind, then I saw him, still in his seat. I went around the jeep, whispering, 'Chung! Major Chung!' I found him — his body — halfway out of the jeep on his side, his left shoulder leaning against the back of his seat. He was dead — or so I thought. The moonlight was bright enough in the jeep and I saw that his face was covered with dark blood, then I smelled the pungent odor of gunpowder and I looked for his gun. I found it on the floor at the foot of the other seat. I knew he had shot himself but I had to be sure. With the submachine gun in my right hand and his revolver in the other hand, I laid myself flat on the dirt in the shadow of the jeep, listening for sound, and checked his revolver. The barrel was still warm and the bullet chamber showed two empty holes. Yes — he had shot himself. I was now sure of that.

"There was no time to lose. I threw the revolver away down the hill as far as I could and called out to Lieutenant Cho's father to come up. Then, instinctively, I suppose, I searched for Major Chung's wallet and found it in a pocket inside his jacket. I wanted his papers, you see? I took his papers and whatever money there was in the wallet and threw away the rest of the contents, still in the wallet. Lieutenant Cho's father came up, with his son beside him, and they both stood next to me without a word. 'He's dead,' I said. 'He killed himself.' The boy — I think he was about sixteen — he just stood there, looking at the body. His father said to me, 'Come! Let's get away quickly!' He sent his son back to the house. The boy gave me a bow and quietly walked down the hill. That was the last time I saw him. You know — he was shot to death only two months later in Pyungyang during a student demonstration against the Communists.

"The boy had brought clothes for me and I changed my clothes right there, then we started on our way. I never had to use Major Chung's papers. Lieutenant Cho's father knew the border smugglers' route, you might say their underground organization. Before long he had me in the hands of my first contact, a farmer, who handed me over to a local fishmonger. Then I parted with Lieutenant Cho's father. The fishmonger had an old truck and he put me in a fish barrel and drove me to a fishing village about ten miles or so from our town. We got to the village before the sunrise and I was hidden in a cave on a cliff on the beach. When the night came at last, a boy of about fifteen appeared and led me down the cliff to a waiting boat. Two men rowed me out; I can't remember how far they rowed out, but we rendezvoused with what looked to me like a torpedo boat. Soon we were out in the open sea, heading for another rendezvous with a large cargo ship. There were nearly two hundred or more escapees like me on board. It was a South Korean ship and I learned that she was manned and operated by the members of the Northwest Youth Association, you know, the organization of anti-Communist North Korean refugees in the South. The ship picked up more refugees on the way to the South and at dawn we were at the other side of the thirty-eighth parallel. I had escaped from the North; I had left my hometown; and my exile had just begun."

He sat brooding, his dark face lowered, his arms crossed over his chest.

"I am sorry," I said.

"Sorry for what?" he said quietly without looking up.

"I am sorry I thought you'd killed the Russian major," I said, "and I am sorry, too, that you had to go through all that!"

"Now you know that I didn't kill the Russian major," he said. His voice was cold and steady. "But now you know that I did kill the Russian lieutenant."

"I didn't mean it to sound that way," I said. "Please!"

"Does it make any difference to you whom I killed?"

I did not know what to say.

"Are you relieved that I killed the Russian lieutenant instead of the Russian major?"

"I wish you didn't speak that way to me!"

He closed his eyes. "Sorry," he whispered.

"I am glad you told me about the circumstances," I said, "because now I know that, well, you know, you didn't have any other choice."

"Are you exonerating me from being a cold-blooded murderer," he said with a sharp bitterness in his voice, "now that you know I had no other choice?"

I stared at him, not knowing what to say.

"If there had been other choices," he assaulted me relentlessly, "would you have judged me a cold-blooded murderer?"

"Please!" I said helplessly. "Please! That's enough! We've said enough!"

"Yes, we've said enough!" He stood up from his chair. He looked weary. "Come! Let's go."

I got up and followed him up the aisle.

Suddenly, he stopped and turned around to me. "Listen! Listen to me!" he shouted in fury. His face was flushed with fierce anger, and his voice — at once defiant and pleading — burst out, "You — all you do-gooders, the noble-minded, the pure, the innocent — you — you — do you know with what anguish, with what agony, with what nightmarish human horror I have to say I did not have a choice?"

"Please! Please!"

"Don't you understand? Don't you know?"

"Please!"

And — as suddenly as his anger had exploded — he looked into my eyes with a somber, brooding, dark calm, and his voice whispered, as if to himself, "I am neither a saint, nor an angel, nor a god, don't you know? I had no other choice, you see, because I am a mortal man."

Chapter 11

In spite of the weather report that the rain would continue throughout the night, it began lifting shortly after four in the afternoon. By seven, when we were preparing ourselves to leave for our rendezvous with General Mah, the rain stopped. The sky began to clear up. The air became humid and warm. Thick fog began rising from the earth.

We had gone over our plans with the members of the Command Group, especially with Colonel Kim who had been in constant contact not only with Colonel Son in Seoul but with every single source of intelligence that was available to him. It was our good fortune to have Colonel Son where he was — in the heart of General Mah's headquarters as his deputy. We had learned that Colonel Son had been instructed by General Mah to take charge of the details of the rendezvous, which General Mah still believed was to be between himself and General Ham. Another piece of luck for us was that General Mah had also instructed Colonel Son to place General Ahn under surveillance, although General Mah had not yet confided in Colonel Son about his secret meeting with General Ahn.

When we met later once more for the final briefing, Colonel Kim said with a triumphant grin, "So — you see, we are now in a position not only of telling General Mah what to do and what to expect for the rendezvous but also of keeping an eye on General Ahn's every movement. General Mah wanted Colonel Son to tell General Ahn to be present at the rendezvous. Colonel Son is to give the details of the rendezvous to General Ahn at the last minute. And, Colonel Min, thanks to you, General Mah has been kept busy and incommunicado all day."

"Thanks to Colonel McKay, you mean," said Colonel Min. General Mah had been requested to appear for a series of private conferences and briefings with American Intelligence people. He had to leave Colonel Son in charge of the planning for the rendezvous. "He couldn't afford to turn down the American request," said Colonel Min. "Not at this time when his career and life may depend on winning back the Americans' good grace — from his point of view, that is."

"Colonel Son has reported to General Mah that he has been able to trace General Ahn to General Ham's headquarters. As far as General Mah is concerned, General Ahn flew out to see General Ham and flew back to Seoul. Colonel Son is certain that there has been no communication between General Ahn and General Mah since General Ahn returned to Seoul from here," said Colonel Kim. "Colonel Son will tell General Mah that as a result of his communication with General Ham there is to be a last-minute change of location for the rendezvous. As you suggested, Colonel Min, we changed it to an emergency airstrip about twelve miles from the village which as you know, gentlemen, was the original location proposed by General Mah."

Colonel Moon said, "What about General Ahn? Is he going to be allowed to bring out his Commandos?"

Colonel Kim said, "Colonel Park has taken care of that."

Colonel Park said, "This is the way it will be operated. Colonel Son is keeping an eye on General Ahn's movements. We have our people with General Ahn's Commando Groups and we will find out, when Colonel Son tells him to appear at the rendezvous, what General Ahn is going to do. Most likely, he will alert his Commandos and try to sneak them out of Seoul — some of them anyway. As soon as Colonel Son gets that information, he will contact Lieutenant Colonel Hwang of the Airborne, who had orders from me to intercept General Ahn's Commandos — in the name of General Mah, if you know what I mean. Colonel Son will see to that. So — Colonel Hwang will have no problem getting his Paratroopers out of Seoul. It will be done all properly and with authorization from General Mah himself."

Colonel Song said, frowning, "What if the Paratroopers fail to intercept the Commandos? I mean, what if the Commandos do actually appear at the rendezvous? We might have a bloody mess on our hands."

Colonel Kim said, "Ah! You worry too much, Colonel Song. That has been also taken care of. You tell him, Colonel Park."

Colonel Park said, "As you know, Colonel Son will be giving General Ahn the details of the rendezvous at the last minute, but he will not tell General Ahn that the location has been changed. General Ahn and his Commandos will proceed to the village, where Colonel Hwang's Paratroopers will intercept them. By interception, I mean that Colonel Hwang will tell General Ahn that he is to proceed to the airstrip, alone, and send the Commandos back to Seoul. This part of the operation, by the way, will be done in the name of this Command Group."

"If General Ahn refuses?" said Colonel Moon. "If he refuses to obey our orders?"

Colonel Kim said, "The Paratroopers will have to take care of the Commandos. Since the Paratroopers will be operating under General Mah's orders, thanks to Colonel Son, they will be properly armed. If it comes to that, the Paratroopers will have everything they need to knock out General Ahn's Commandos."

Colonel Song cluck-clucked, shaking his head.

"Can't be helped if it comes to that," said Colonel Kim.

"I think General Ahn will be smart enough not to risk everything there," said Colonel Min. "I am counting on his cleverness."

"Another part of this operation," said Colonel Park, "is to secure the airstrip with our men. And that will be taken care of by Colonel Jung of the Presidential Brigade. Colonel Son has been in touch with Colonel Jung. An amusing aspect of this is that this will be also carried out by orders of General Mah. General Mah has instructed Colonel Son to secretly deploy men from the Presidential Brigade around the village. Well, Colonel Son will simply have Colonel Jung's men from his armored units deployed at the airstrip."

"Thank you for all that trouble," said Colonel Min with a faint smile, "to make sure that we come back alive."

"I still don't like your going there," said Colonel Song. "Anything can go wrong."

"General Yoon was furious," said Colonel Moon. "He wants to go there himself. Understandable, of course."

"The matter has been settled," said Colonel Min.

"You will be going in two jeeps," said Colonel Kim. "I am assigning five of my special agents to you, so don't object. Besides, it would look better, you know, as though we were all there with you."

Colonel Min nodded.

"You, Major Lee, and Lieutenant Cho will ride with one of the agents in the forward jeep, and the other four agents will be behind you. They will be well armed. The four of them behind you will be riding in a jeep with a .50-caliber machine gun mounted on it. In addition, they will be carrying rocket launchers and grenades. I put a box of grenades in your jeep, Lieutenant Cho. Remember that."

"Yes, sir," said Lieutenant Cho. "What kind are they, Colonel?"

"Not fragmentation type. They are anti-tank grenades. I put a rifle with the attachment there, too. You know how to use it?"

"Of course, sir."

"Are you expecting tanks?" said Colonel Song, frowning. "It sounds as though you expect them to have a real combat!"

"I am simply expecting the worst," said Colonel Kim. "We aren't playing a game, you know. As you said, anything can go wrong. Seriously, I am not expecting that General Mah will come riding in in a tank, but I am expecting that he might come in one of his sedans and you know they are armor-plated. I guess you could call them tanks if you like. The bastard can pull more dirty tricks than you can count. Naturally, I hope they won't have to go through the trouble of using anything they are going to take with them. Incidentally, Colonel Min, I want you all to carry a couple of hand grenades. You'll see to that, Lieutenant Cho. I'd better give you a couple of submachine guns, too, come to think of it."

"Do we really need all those?" said Colonel Min.

Colonel Kim said, "By all means. You never know. Just take them. You will make us feel better here."

"All right, if you insist," said Colonel Min. "Anything else?"

Colonel Park said, "You will arrive at the airstrip by 2230, at the latest. The rendezvous is to take place at 2300 sharp. You know that. Colonel Jung will have completed deploying his men at the airstrip by 2200. Colonel Son is to go ahead of General Mah and you should expect to see Colonel Son at the airstrip when you arrive. You will enter the airstrip from the eastern end of it and when you enter, you will stop, turn off all the lights, then exactly ten seconds later, turn the lights on. Repeat this twice. Colonel Son, if he is already there, and if he isn't, then Colonel Jung, will follow the same procedure, after you finish. Then you will proceed to the center of the airstrip on the northern side, which will be on your right as you go. Colonel Son, or Colonel Jung, will take care of the rest from that point on. Any questions?"

Colonel Min said, "Are we sure that this emergency airstrip is not in use at the moment?"

"I've checked it out. It is not in use," said Colonel Park.

"What if someone in emergency wants to land?" said Colonel Moon.

"I am glad you brought it up, Colonel Min," said Colonel Park, "because I have thought of the problem. This is my solution which

I think serves two purposes. I am having an L-17 fly over the airstrip just about the time you will be arriving. It will buzz the airstrip once and leave you for the time being. It will then continue to fly over you in a circle, more or less, sending any light aircraft in emergency away from the area and, at the same time, keeping an eye on any unusual night traffic toward the airstrip. It will naturally warn you if it spots any heavy traffic heading for the airstrip; that is, General Mah might, just might do something unpredictable. For all we know, he might mobilize the entire Presidential Brigade."

"How would the L-17 warn us in such an event?" said Colonel Min. "By radio?"

"I ruled out the use of radio communication. It will buzz you. Twice. Remember. Twice. It will then go, and radio us. It looks better that way; it might pass for someone who wanted to land and couldn't. Of course, you are on your own after that."

"All right," said Colonel Min. "Anything else?"

"That is all from me," said Colonel Park.

"Same here," said Colonel Kim, "except to wish you all good luck."

Colonel Min looked at each one of us. "In that case, I have something rather important to report and to ask for your advice and cooperation. But, first, would anyone like some tea or coffee? I would like some tea. Will you join me?"

We had been sitting in Colonel Min's quarters. Colonel Min sat on his cot between Colonel Park and Colonel Kim. Colonel Song sat on a chair at Colonel Min's desk; Colonel Moon and I sat on a low wooden bench against the wall; Lieutenant Cho was sitting on the floor, in the center of which Colonel Park had spread a large sketch of the airstrip and its surroundings, including the network of roads. Lieutenant Cho stood up and went out of the room. The tin-roofed hut had two small rooms; Colonel Min used the other room as his office rather than the one adjoining the general's office. The room we were in had only one window. The sky was getting dark outside. It was dark inside the room, too, but no one had bothered to turn on the lamp on the table. Lieutenant Cho returned with a pot of tea, a teakettle with hot water, a jar of American instant coffee, sugar, spoons, cups, and a can of evaporated milk. It was as if he had them all neatly placed on a tray, which he now carried into the room at a cue from Colonel Min. Lieutenant Cho's big, stubby hands began serving us tea and coffee. I took tea.

"Well, well," said Colonel Song, clearing his throat. "This is a surprise!"

The others were quiet.

"This couldn't be a farewell party?" said Colonel Kim, laughing.

"Ah, nonsense!" said Colonel Moon.

I did not know what to say.

Colonel Park said, "Well, now, let's hear it." He bent over and picked up the sketch of the airstrip from the floor. The paper crackled as he folded it and put it in his breast pocket.

"I saw General Hyun just before we met here," said Colonel Min. "And Colonel McKay was with me when I saw the general. I had already seen the general in the morning as you know and I had made my report on General Mah. Gentlemen, I am going to exercise my prerogative as the chairman of the Command Group, with the advice and consent of General Hyun and upon recommendation of Colonel McKay, and ask you to reconsider our decision on General Mah."

No one spoke for a while.

At last, Colonel Park said, "Colonel McKay had been to see General Hyun?"

Colonel Min nodded. "Yes."

"And Colonel McKay told him that it was a bad policy to kill General Mah?" Colonel Park went on.

"Yes."

"And he agrees with Colonel McKay?"

"Yes."

"And, now, do you agree with them?"

Colonel Min did not reply immediately. He took time to look at each of us in the shadowy darkness. He said, "Yes."

"I see," said Colonel Park. "In that case, let's hear your alternative."

"Keep General Mah alive," said Colonel Min, "and bring him here. He can afford to disappear from Seoul for a few days, especially after the assassination attempt on his life."

"Bring him here," said Colonel Kim. "Then what?"

Colonel Min said, "Keep him here until our coup is over."

Colonel Song said, "Does this mean that we no longer consider him to be our major threat?"

"He still is," said Colonel Kim. "I don't like this."

"This alternative — is it based on the assumption that General Mah does indeed want to make a deal with us or defect to us and that we accept him?" said Colonel Moon.

"The alternate plan is not based on any assumption," said Colonel Min. "It simply recognizes the fact that, in view of the situation and of our own strength as you have just been briefed on by Colonel Kim and Colonel Park, there is no compelling need to execute General Mah at this stage of our plans. It is also in recognition of Colonel McKay's wish and advice that our execution of General Mah at this time will not be viewed favorably by the Americans, particularly by their State Department. Colonel McKay cited what he called a melancholy precedent in Viet Nam, if you know what I mean. And I don't have to remind you all that, for the time being, we need the assistance of Colonel McKay's people. And, also, the general's wish is involved here."

"What I want to know is what your wish is," said Colonel Park.

"I agree. What matters is what you personally feel about this," said Colonel Song.

"All right. Consider our plans for our rendezvous with General Mah," said Colonel Min. "We have trapped General Mah, we will shortly, that is. This is our first test of our real strength, gentlemen, and what we can see for ourselves is quite reassuring. In short, General Mah as a major, prime threat to our cause does not exist any longer. I think both the general and Colonel McKay are not asking us to alter an irrevocable course of action. We can now afford to accommodate their wishes. I propose, therefore, that we proceed in this order. First, our primary objective shall be to persuade, by force or otherwise, General Mah to come with us, whether there is a deal to be made or not. In short, we shall kidnap him. If this plan succeeds as I think it will, we shall have Colonel Son, who will take full charge of General Mah's headquarters in his absence, summon and arrest if necessary those on our list who are in command positions in and near Seoul, those who are not desirable from our point of view. Colonel Son will have an excellent, ready-made excuse for it: that is, General Mah has been gunned down and nearly killed and has now disappeared; it will be his duty to open an investigation, a quiet inquiry if you like. No one will stop him. Second, if the first plan does not work, then we shall proceed in accordance with our original plan. Any opinions?"

"Would you like to put this to a vote?" said Colonel Park.

"If you all want to," said Colonel Min.

I wanted to say something, but I did not know what. I merely watched the shadowy, dark face of Colonel Min who sat on the cot, immobile, impassive, and — inscrutable.

"Well, I don't think we have to vote on this," said Colonel Park. "What do you say?" He looked at the others.

"For you, Colonel Min," said Colonel Kim, shaking his head, "I will shut up just this once."

Colonel Song and Colonel Moon both nodded.

"And you? Major Lee?" said Colonel Park.

"You must be happy about this, Major," said Colonel Kim.

"Now, now," said Colonel Song.

I wanted to say something meaningful, something appropriate; I wanted to say something desperately. But I only managed to blurt out, "I must thank you all."

Colonel Park's sharp words cut into me. "Thank Colonel Min!"

"All right," said Colonel Min, standing up. "I want to thank you all, and I assure you we won't fail you."

Colonel Kim said, "Let's synchronize our watches."

We did and all stood up. Lieutenant Cho collected the cups and saucers. Everyone filed out of the room. Colonel Min walked past me without a word, without a look my way. Lieutenant Cho whispered to me, "We'll be all right, sir. Don't worry about a thing."

I stepped out of the room into the dark outside. We all shook hands silently.

Colonel Park came up to me. "Sorry," he said and tapped me on the shoulder. "Good luck."

"All right," said Colonel Min to everyone. "Let's get this over with."

"Lieutenant Cho, don't forget to pick up the submachine guns," said Colonel Kim. "I'll give the word to my agents."

Chapter 12

Twenty minutes past ten o'clock. In another five minutes, we would get off the main road and onto a dirt road going north, when the jeep behind us blew its horn three times, flashing its headlights on and off. The special agent who had been riding with us, sitting in the back with me, said to Lieutenant Cho at the wheel, "Slow down, Lieutenant. They want to pass us."

"What's up?" said Lieutenant Cho.

"Just a routine precaution, sir," said the agent. "We'll let them go ahead of us."

The jeep passed us at a high speed I had never thought a jeep was capable of doing; none of the four agents even looked in our direction. Lieutenant Cho accelerated our jeep. It jerked over a bump on the road. The submachine guns at our feet clanged against each other.

"Almost there, sir," said the agent to Colonel Min, who checked his watch and nodded.

We drove off the main road and turned to the right. The jeep ahead of us had now slowed down. The land was flat on both sides, but ahead of us I could see the dark hills rising. The fog became

thicker. The dirt road was muddy and bumpy. I saw the taillights
of the forward jeep dimly through the fog as they bounced up
and down, intermittently illuminated by the headlights of our jeep,
which also bounced on.

"Slow down, Lieutenant," said the agent, leaning slightly forward as he peered out through the windshield. "I think they want
to stop."

The dirt road turned to the left, to the west; the forward jeep
stopped; an agent was getting out of the jeep. Lieutenant Cho
slowed down and brought the jeep to a halt a few yards behind the
other jeep.

"What is it now?" said Lieutenant Cho, racing the engine in idle.

"He will explain it, sir," said the agent. "May I get out?"

Lieutenant Cho got out of the jeep. The agent bent over and leaped
out as Lieutenant Cho held his seat up for him.

The senior agent came to Colonel Min's side. "We are going to
wait here, Colonel, until we sight the L-17."

"All right," said Colonel Min, checking his watch again. "It should
be here any minute."

"Yes, sir," said the agent. "Would you mind stepping out, Colonel Min, and Major Lee, you too, sir? I want my men to put the
top down and also the windshield."

"Go ahead," said Colonel Min. "Lieutenant Cho, give them a
hand, will you?" We got out of the jeep.

The agents began working on the jeeps. The windshield was
down and the top folded down. Two agents were mounting the .50-
caliber machine gun on the forward jeep. The agent who had been
riding with us was checking the rocket launcher on our jeep. He
spoke to the senior agent. "Do you want me to load this thing?"

"Yes."

The two agents in the other jeep finished mounting the heavy
machine gun and were checking it, tapping on it, and swiveling it
around. Then they fed it with a cartridge belt; the long, sleek bullets gleamed in the dimmed headlights. The senior agent looked

over the rocket launcher on our jeep and checked the submachine guns. He called to the agents on the other jeep. "Bring the hand grenades over here, will you?" An agent brought a boxful of them; we each took two grenades; we put them into the side pockets of our fatigue trousers.

"Anything else?" said Colonel Min.

"Yes, sir," said the senior agent. "I hope we won't have to use all these, but if you decide we are going to have to shoot it out, we'll be ready. The only thing I want to make sure of, sir, is who is going to give the firing order."

Colonel Min said, "Major Lee will do it."

"Why me?" I did not mean to protest but I was taken by surprise.

Colonel Min said, "I want you to ride in the other jeep."

"Why?"

"When General Mah appears, I will see him alone. I want to see him alone. Remember this, all of you." The other agents had gathered around us. "When I talk with General Mah, I'll stand between the headlights from our jeeps. I want the jeeps standing twenty paces apart from one another and have them placed so that the headlights will cross each other, is that clear? In case we have to shoot it out, you will give a cross fire, understood? I don't think it will happen but if it does, and if I want you to start firing, I'll clasp my hands behind my back. Give me three seconds before firing. Three seconds after my hands are clasped behind my back — and you should be able to see me doing that — I will drop down on the ground and you will start firing. Any questions?"

The senior agent said, "I'll count on Major Lee to give me the firing order, then." He turned to an agent who stood next to him. "You take charge of this jeep and I want you to keep an eye on me. When Major Lee gives me the firing order I'll drop my arm and you can give them all you've got."

The agent nodded. "Sure."

We heard the sounds of a plane. We looked up at the sky. Though the moon was hidden by black rain clouds, stars were out.

We saw red and green lights blink over us and I could make out the L-17.

"All right," said Colonel Min. "Let's get it over with."

"Take care," I said to him.

"I will see you when we get to the airstrip," he said.

"All right." I walked over to the forward jeep.

As Colonel Park had briefed us, we entered the airstrip from the eastern end of it. There we stopped and turned off the lights. I began counting. Ten seconds later I ordered the agent at the wheel to turn on the lights. I had it repeated.

At the other end of the airstrip, headlights shone, then went off. Ten seconds. The lights came on again and off again. "All right," I said, "let's go." We drove slowly toward the center of the airstrip, driving along the northern side of it. Two agents in the back of our jeep were standing up, clutching at the machine gun. The runway was bumpy and uneven though it was surfaced with what felt like concrete. From the other end of the runway, a jeep came toward us, its headlights on fully. Colonel Min's jeep, behind us, had its headlights off. The other jeep stopped. Someone bounded out of it. We stopped. It was Colonel Jung of the Presidential Brigade Armored Regiment. I got out of the jeep. Colonel Min came out and stood beside me. Colonel Jung saluted Colonel Min. Just then the L-17 boomed down low from the western end of the airstrip and flew off toward the east and banked away to the north.

"Colonel Min," said Colonel Jung. "And you too, sir, Major Lee."

We shook hands. He was one of the youngest lieutenant colonels in the Army; bright and serious, he was an articulate honor student at my university before the war; tall, trim, and handsome and impeccable in his military bearing, fluent in English and French, he was a favorite of the American advisers and an idol of the cadets at the Military Academy.

"I take it that Colonel Son isn't here yet?" said Colonel Min.

"Not yet, sir. He should be here any minute. Shall I brief you in the deployment of my men, sir?"

Colonel Min said, "Please."

Colonel Jung said to the senior agent, who was directly behind Colonel Min, "Have all the lights off, will you? We can see better."

With the lights off, I saw that it was not as foggy as I had thought it was, though it was misty enough; in the dim starlight and the moonlight that filtered through the rain clouds the wet surface of the runway glimmered here and there. I could see the straight line of the runway and at the end of it the undulating silhouettes of the dark hills that surrounded the airstrip, running from the west to the north.

"I have three platoons out there, Colonel Min," said Colonel Jung. "All heavily armed. I thought of bringing out armored cars but decided against it. They would have been too conspicuous. I have one platoon deployed on that foothill at the other end of the runway. Another platoon where we are. You can't see them, sir, but they are out there, and they can see us. I have deployed the third platoon along the dirt road between two miles from the main road and the entrance to the airstrip."

Colonel Min said, "What about the southern side of the runway? It is wide open as it is."

"I am afraid we don't have enough men to cover that sector, sir. We will have to count on a cross fire." He said to the senior agent, "I have a machine gun set up at the western end of the runway. If we ever need to have a cross fire, will you cover this half of the southern sector with your .50 caliber? I put a marker up out there for your line of sight. It's white, so you should be able to see it."

Colonel Min said, "What is your signal setup?"

"I will have to depend on my flashlight here, Colonel," said Colonel Jung. "Two blinks and my men will emerge from their positions and surround the runway or us all if necessary. Three blinks and my men will commence firing. When I give three blinks, will you all please run to those bushes there and take cover? I have sandbags piled up there behind the bushes. You can't see them from here but they are there. Of course, this action will be taken only when I think what we have out here in the open is not enough. If the

L-17 up there buzzes us twice, as Colonel Park has arranged, that is, before General Mah shows up, we will have to withdraw to the foothills on the north; my platoon on the west will try to join us there; my executive will fire a green flare — a green flare, remember everyone — and my platoon out there on the road will retreat to the south. If anyone comes onto the runway we will have him trapped, but we will have the eastern sector open for us to withdraw if necessary."

Colonel Min told him of his own signal. "Major Lee, I've just changed my plan. I want you to stay here with me when I see General Mah." He turned to the senior agent. "You will take charge and give the firing order."

We saw lights on the dirt road that led to the western entrance to the airstrip. It was an open jeep — or so I thought — its headlight beams swaying up and down. It stopped about fifty yards from the entrance. The lights went off. They came back on. Colonel Jung counted quetly. Ten seconds. The lights were on again, then off again.

"Colonel Son, I think, sir," said Colonel Jung. He held his flashlight. He turned it on. Ten seconds. He turned it off. Another ten seconds. He turned it on. Ten seconds. He turned it off. The headlights of the open jeep came back on and it drove onto the runway, then dimmed its lights. Colonel Jung turned the flashlight on and held it. The jeep stopped about ten yards from us. Colonel Son jumped out of it. He came toward us, his heels clicking on the concrete runway.

I checked my watch. It was fourteen minutes to eleven.

We shook hands. The senior agent led his men away from us. They started the jeeps and deployed them in the middle of the runway, facing the western entrance.

"I can't tell you enough how good it is to see you here at a time like this," said Colonel Min to Colonel Son.

"Same here," he said. "Good to see you, Major Lee."

All the lights were off by then. The misty darkness enveloped us.

I could not see the face of Colonel Son too well though I was standing close to him. He was short and lean and his head came barely
up to Colonel Min's shoulders. Shadowy faces and shadowy figures
— I realized that the moon was emerging from black rain clouds
into scattered thin clouds. I looked about me. The long barrel of
the .50-caliber machine gun on one of our jeeps gleamed. I could
make out the dim reflection of the glimmering light of the moon on
the bullets in the cartridge belt that drooped from the barrel. I
caught a quick glint of the moon on the folded-down windshield on
the jeep. The special agents, two of them standing up in the back
seat hovering over the machine gun, were still and dark, looking in
our direction.

"We are ready, sir," said Colonel Jung to Colonel Son.

"Yes. This is what I have to do," said Colonel Son, speaking
slowly, enunciating each word carefully and precisely with a clipped
accent. "I have a radio in my jeep. I am to radio General Mah at
eleven o'clock sharp. I am to say — 'Have you caught the rat?'
Then he will say — 'No, but I have caught the fox.' If all is clear,
I am to reply — 'Bring the fox.' And if not — and this I will not
say — 'No, we want the rat.' "

Colonel Jung burst out laughing. "What the hell is all that
about!"

Colonel Son laughed, too. "Your guess is as good as mine. He
insisted on it. Apparently, he has spent a great deal of time thinking this up. When he was telling me about it, he was giggling and
rather silly, obviously having a good time and I am sure congratulating himself on what a clever and amusing fellow he was." He
tut-tutted. "I pulled a straight face and he said, 'You don't think it
is funny, eh?' I thought it was funny enough the way he was gab-
bing about it, so I said, 'It was very funny, sir.' 'Ah, I can see you
don't think it is funny. But you will see, you will see!' 'Yes, sir,
I will see, General, I will see.' He gave me a dirty look. Now, he
will get here exactly ten minutes after eleven, that is, if all is clear.
When he approaches the entrance to the runway, he wants me to

have all the lights on here and stand alone in the light, but he also
wants everyone in the light, too. So we will stand apart but will all
be in the light. I want someone to stand behind me when he comes
close."

"Why?" said Colonel Jung.

"Until the proper time comes, I want to have a ready alibi for his
sake and for my sake, too. I want someone pointing a gun at me
behind my back. He thinks General Ham is going to be here and I
will have to explain to him that General Ham is not here but why
I had to radio him that all was clear."

"All right," said Colonel Min. "How far is he behind you?"

"Twenty minutes. But he is out there, right now, on the main
road."

"What car is he coming in?" said Colonel Min.

"When we left the headquarters together, he was in his sedan,
the black one."

"That's the one with armor plate?" said Colonel Jung.

"Yes, and with a radio."

"Are you sure that's the one he will be coming in?" said Colonel
Min.

"I see what you are getting at," said Colonel Son. "He might have
changed cars, for all I know. No, I can't be too sure about that."

"So, then, you left together but were separated later on," said
Colonel Min. "Where?"

"Just before we got to the East Gate."

Colonel Min seemed to brood on it. "I don't quite like it," he said
after a while. "What about General Ahn?"

"I was coming around to that," said Colonel Son. "There is a
slight hitch to our plan."

"Yes?"

"As you know, our plan, which General Mah had approved, was
for me to instruct General Ahn to proceed to the village, the original meeting place proposed by General Ham. When General Mah
came back to our headquarters from the American Command, he

wanted to revise the plan and now wanted me not to contact General Ahn, that is, he didn't want General Ahn to be at the rendezvous. He would not explain why and he is not accustomed to having his subordinates question his motives."

Colonel Jung said, "Then, does this mean you haven't alerted Colonel Hwang of the Airborne? His Paratroopers — where are they now?"

"As far as General Ahn is concerned, he does not know where and when the rendezvous will take place. He knows that it will take place sometime tonight, of course. From my point of view, since he will not have time to move his Commandos out of Seoul even if he found out about the rendezvous now and even if he did he wouldn't know where to have them go, I thought it unnecessary to mobilize the Paratroopers. We have enough men out here as it is."

"You may be sure of that," said Colonel Jung. "So you are not expecting General Ahn?"

"I wouldn't be too sure of that," said Colonel Min.

"No, you are right," said Colonel Son. "You can never be sure of anything with General Mah. Don't forget. He still has a hatful of tricks left. One thing we can be sure of, though, is that General Ahn's Commandos are not going to show up anywhere tonight. Actually, it saves much time and trouble for us."

Colonel Min was silent.

Colonel Son said, "Now, after I talk with him on radio, he will arrive here — let us say — in ten minutes. He should if he is going to appear at all. When he comes, he will ask to see General Ham. Well, he will know he is not here. I will have to say something to him about that. Now, then what? What do we do after that?"

"You'd better leave it to me from that point on," said Colonel Min. "I'll do the talking."

"All right. Just give us the word," said Colonel Son.

I checked my watch again; one minute to eleven. "It's time," I said.

"All right," said Colonel Min. "Let's get this over with."

We all walked over to Colonel Son's jeep; there was no driver — he had driven out himself.

Colonel Son radioed. "Have you caught the rat? Have you caught the rat?"

The reply came instantly. "No, but I have caught the fox. No, but I have caught the fox."

"Is that his voice?" said Colonel Jung.

Colonel Min nodded. "It is."

Colonel Son turned his shadowy face to Colonel Min.

Colonel Min whispered, "All right. Go ahead."

Colonel Son radioed back, "Bring the fox. Bring the fox." He waited for a few moments, then switched off the radio.

Colonel Jung said, "I'd better go and stay with my men. I will be over there behind the bushes. I've piled sandbags there, Colonel Son, so if you need a cover, just run for it. I'll move your jeep." He started the jeep. "Good luck." He drove the jeep to the northern edge of the runway, in the center of it, reversed the jeep so that it faced the western entrance to the airstrip.

"Turn all the lights on!" said Colonel Son.

Colonel Jung came back running toward us. "Sorry, Colonel Min. I forgot all about the searchlights. I have two searchlights set up and ready. How could I have forgotten about that! One is halfway up the hill beyond the western entrance and the other one is up there beyond the bush. So if the searchlights go on, don't be alarmed. They are ours."

The special agents had been gathered by Colonel Min. He said to everyone, "We have a change of plan. When I want you to fire, I'll do what I told you before. I'll clasp my hands behind my back. Three seconds. I'll drop down to the ground. We will turn off all the lights out here and, Colonel Jung, you'll have your searchlights turned on. Is that clear?"

Colonel Jung said to the senior agent, "I want one of your jeeps moved to that end of the runway. Not the one with the .50 caliber. What do you have on the other one?"

"A rocket launcher, sir, and submachine guns."

"Good. Have the rocket launcher ready, will you? Let's have three of you stay with the .50 caliber. How many submachine guns?"

"Enough for everyone here, sir."

"All right, then. Have two of you in the other jeep. And now, Major Lee and Lieutenant Cho."

"Major Lee will stay in the jeep," said Colonel Min, "until I call him. You, too, Lieutenant Cho."

"Yes, sir," said Lieutenant Cho.

Colonel Jung said to the senior agent, "Give them the submachine guns."

"They are in the jeep already."

"All right. Good luck." Colonel Jung went back to his position behind the bushes.

"I don't see the L-17," said Colonel Son.

"It's up there, somewhere," said Colonel Min.

It was suddenly still and hushed. The moon had gone behind the rain clouds. I could see only the dim shreds of light through the clouds. The air was warm and damp. Colonel Min said quietly to me, "When General Mah's sedan — or whatever he is going to be in — appears, Colonel Son will wait till he comes close enough. Colonel Son will then move toward General Mah and at that point I want you to get off the jeep and come slowly and with a submachine gun. Try to walk behind Colonel Son in the shadow if at all possible. Stay close behind him and when you two get close to General Mah Colonel Son will start talking and you will then cover him."

"Just don't overdo it," said Colonel Son. "I have a sensitive back." He laughed.

I blurted out, "I can't see how you can be so cheerful at a time like this!"

Colonel Son shrugged his shoulders. "What else can I do?" He laughed again, giving me a pat on the back. "Come now!" he said. "Don't look so morbid."

Colonel Min said, "All right, that's enough now."

One of the jeeps quietly slid down the runway to the western end of it.

Colonel Min said, "Get going now, you two."

Lieutenant Cho and I walked over to the jeep with the .50 caliber. Two agents were standing in the back seat, huddled close to the machine gun; the senior agent stood against the right rear fender with a submachine gun.

We climbed into our seat, Lieutenant Cho at the wheel. The senior agent handed over to me the submachine gun he had been holding in his hands. "It's loaded and ready to go, sir." He took another one from the back seat. I put the submachine gun on my lap; it felt heavy.

Lieutenant Cho whispered to me, "Everything is going to turn out all right, sir."

I had to nod my head.

We waited.

Lights shone suddenly beyond a cluster of low trees and a dark clump of shrubbery on the dirt road leading to the western entrance to the airstrip. They came fast. The light beams shot out straight, then swiveled to our direction, then swiveled back to a straight line, jerking up and down. It was a sedan — General Mah's black, armor-plated Plymouth.

"Look! There's another car behind it!" whispered Lieutenant Cho.

Before I could make out the shape of the car behind the Plymouth, light beams flashed out from the sedan, lighting up the rear of the Plymouth. I heard the senior agent mutter behind me, "I didn't know about that car." The car was long and low, obviously an American make.

They were now driving into the entrance, their lights galloping, tires squealing. They stopped just inside the entrance. Their headlights bounced wildly up and down, then they came slowly toward us. They picked up speed and, suddenly, they both swerved to the left as though going back toward the entrance. The two agents manning the .50-caliber machine gun behind me sprang to their feet, pulling the long barrel up.

"Hold it!" hissed the senior agent stepping up.

The cars stopped, skidding and shrieking, then instantly began backing up toward us. The other car was a convertible.

"Cadillac!" whispered the senior agent. "When did he get that?"

Colonel Min was standing erect, his back fully illuminated by the lights from our jeep. Colonel Son stood about ten paces apart from Colonel Min to the right, illuminated by the lights from the other jeep. Colonel Son's own jeep had the lights off. I picked up the submachine gun from my lap. The stubby barrel and the long magazine felt cold. Lieutenant Cho had already picked up his and had rested the barrel over the folded-down windshield. The cars had now come to a complete stop. They turned off the lights. Their red taillights glowed in our lights. Colonel Son took a step forward.

"Now!" whispered the senior agent to me.

I slid out of the seat. My submachine gun clattered against my knee. I stood beside the senior agent. "Take care, sir!"

I watched Colonel Son. He took another step. I went forward slowly, as quietly as I could. I held the submachine gun in my right hand, holding it behind my right leg, pointing it downward. "That's good!" I heard the senior agent whisper behind me. Colonel Son was moving toward the cars. I quickened my pace, trying to stay in the shadow cast by Colonel Son. There was no sign of activity in the cars. No one came out. No sound came from them. I walked past Colonel Min, about fifteen paces to his right. Suddenly I thought I heard the faint humming of the L-17 over my head. I was now about five paces behind Colonel Son. Still there was no sound from the cars. No one opened the doors. We were now about twenty, twenty-five paces from the Plymouth. The rear window of the Plymouth gleamed. I was now directly behind Colonel Son. Still — no one came out of the cars. Not a sound came from inside the cars. We moved on slowly. Ten paces from the Plymouth. Colonel Son stopped. I stopped. Colonel Son looked back toward Colonel Min. Then, looking at the Plymouth — its windows were all closed tight and I could see a dark figure in the right front seat, not looking at us but facing toward the western end of the runway — Colonel Son said aloud, "General!"

There was no response from either of the cars, which were side by side about five paces apart from each other.

Colonel Son called again, "General!"

Instantly, the right front door of the Plymouth swung open. General Mah stood on the concrete runway, his left hand holding onto the door.

Colonel Son said, "General!"

I stepped back a pace from Colonel Son, whipping out the submachine gun from behind me. I had the muzzle jammed into Colonel Son's back. Colonel Son jerked slightly. "General," he said, "as you see, sir, I am at gunpoint."

General Mah took a step forward, fully coming into the light. He was of medium height, of an ordinary build; a common, ordinary face; a double-breasted brown suit, baggy pants, a black bow tie; long, thick hair, pomaded, parted in the middle; shiny black shoes. He stood there silently for a few moments, his eyes darting from here to there to Colonel Min. He left the door open and took another step. I stepped aside, behind Colonel Son; I could cover the side of the car, I thought.

General Mah said to me, "Put that thing down." It was not a command or an angry voice. "You won't need it," he said. He turned to Colonel Son. "What's Colonel Min doing, standing there like an idiot. Tell him to come close over here."

Colonel Son said with his clipped accent, "I regret to report, sir, that General Ham is not here at the moment."

"Oh, I knew that," said General Mah matter-of-factly.

"I beg your pardon, General?" said Colonel Son. I thought his voice sounded genuinely surprised. "Then why did you send me out here, sir? Why didn't you tell me before?"

"Since when do I have to explain everything?" he said. "I am sorry you had to go through this."

Colonel Son looked at me and then toward Colonel Min. He turned to General Mah. He said angrily, "They could have shot me, General! Was that part of your plan, too, sir?"

General Mah ignored that. He spoke to me. "You must be Major Lee, aren't you?"

I did not reply. I had the submachine gun pointed at him.

"You are Major Lee, General Ahn's assistant, aren't you? I am General Mah."

I ignored that.

General Mah said, "Well, if Colonel Min isn't going to come closer, then we will have to go to him." Before I could say a word, General Mah took a step toward Colonel Min, then turned back to Colonel Son. "Well, come along! Colonel Min is waiting."

I did not know whether to follow behind them or stay there and cover the cars. There was no one in the back seat of the Plymouth; only the driver in the front seat. From where I stood I could not tell who was in the Cadillac convertible or how many there were. I hesitated for a moment. I stepped back, slowly, pointing the submachine gun at the Plymouth. When I was certain that it could be covered by the special agents in one of our jeeps, I turned around and followed behind the two. Colonel Min was coming toward them. The glaring headlights from the jeep blinded me for a moment. Colonel Min stopped. General Mah and Colonel Son stood three paces from Colonel Min. I went to their left, to Colonel Min's right, and held the submachine gun level, pointing it at the two of them.

"Colonel Min," said General Mah. "How are you?"

"General," said Colonel Min quietly.

"I hope you are treating General Ham well?"

Colonel Min said, "I am sure he is enjoying a quiet vacation. Thank you for your concern."

General Mah laughed. "I knew he wouldn't be here."

Colonel Min said, "I knew that you knew that, General."

"Then we can talk."

"I am listening, General."

"I've come in good faith and spirit, Colonel. How about you?"

"Same here, General."

"Well, aren't you surprised that I came in spite of what I knew I was getting into?"

"You are a very clever man, General," said Colonel Min, "and a very dangerous one."

General Mah laughed. "It depends on which side I am on, doesn't it?"

"I never thought you were on anyone's side, General."

"True, true!" He laughed again.

"General, what do you have on your mind?" said Colonel Min; his voice was now cold.

"I trust General Ahn has told you what I have in mind?"

"Yes, he has."

"Well, so here I am. I am ready to negotiate if you are."

"If I am not ready to negotiate, General, then what?"

"I am sure you are smarter than that."

"I can be quite dumb sometimes, General, and deaf, too, perhaps."

General Mah gazed at Colonel Min, squinting his small eyes. He was standing there facing the glaring lights. Colonel Son watched General Mah's face. "If you are not ready to negotiate, Colonel Min, I can always make you ready."

"That was in old days, General, when I was under your command."

General Mah was silent for a moment.

I felt awkward and out of place, holding the submachine gun up.

General Mah said at last, "All right, Colonel Min. Let's talk straight, then. As I said, I am here to negotiate with you. But let me tell you a few things first."

"Go ahead," said Colonel Min, "General."

"To begin with, I know all I need to know about you and your Command Group. Colonel Song, Colonel Kim, Colonel Park, Colonel Moon, and, well, shall I go on?"

"And General Ahn, too, General."

He laughed. "Oh, yes! General Ahn, too, though I wouldn't know how long he will be with you."

"You see, General, I am not surprised that you know about us."

"It's a formidable organization you've got, Colonel. The cream of the Army. I envy you. I could never persuade those men to work for me."

"They do not work for me, General. We work together."

"What's the difference? Anyway, as I said before, I am here in good faith."

"Your fake assassination attempt — was that done in good faith, General!" I said.

"As I always say, it all depends on which side you are on, Major Lee," said General Mah. "In any case, you did manage to touch a sore spot in me."

Colonel Min said, "What do you have in mind, General?"

Colonel Son said, "General Mah, I don't know what you are up to, but I do not like what you are doing, what you seem to be thinking of doing. You have known of their coup plans and you have kept it to yourself. And now — are you defecting to them!"

General Mah scrutinized Colonel Son's face. He turned to Colonel Min. "Don't worry about Colonel Son. He will do what I tell him. For his own sake. Colonel Son, I am trying to do you a favor. You may not believe me, but it will be in your own interest — to save your neck, to put it bluntly — that you do what I tell you to do."

Colonel Son did not speak.

General Mah said, "Colonel Min, you know the terms of my deal. What are yours?"

"There are no terms, General." His voice sounded weary.

"What do you mean by that?"

"There is no deal."

General Mah glared at him. "Then there is no negotiation?"

"Precisely."

"You are not playing it smart, Colonel. You don't know what you are saying."

"No deal, General."

"Suppose I still want to negotiate with you in spite of what you just said. What will you do with me?"

"You will come with us."

"And then?"

"When our coup is completed, you will stand trial. We will guarantee that the trial will be strictly impartial and you will have ample opportunity to defend yourself in court."

"You don't seriously think I would go through all this trouble of coming out here like this just to get that sort of promise from you, or do you?"

"General, you know better than anyone else that you are in a very dangerous position. You are about to be sacked from your position, as you well know. There are many people who will try to kill you before you get sacked, as you well know. Your beloved President himself will be more than glad to put you away quietly before you make trouble for him — as you well know. And who knows? Perhaps the Americans may do just that — as you suspect. General, we don't need to make a deal with you, to tell you the truth. You are no longer a threat to our cause. We don't have to kill you, do you understand? Others will be glad to kill you and you know that better than anyone else. General Mah, you are in trouble."

"You really don't know me, do you, Colonel?"

"I know you only too well," Colonel Min said bluffly.

"In that case, let me assure you that my offer for a mutually satisfactory deal was and still is quite genuine. I have not discussed this in any depth with Colonel Son here, but I have assumed and I am still assuming that Colonel Son and I shall be acting together.

If we make a deal with each other, Colonel Son will be part of the deal."

Colonel Son stared at him. "Are you suggesting that I defect to them — with you?"

"Well, why not? But wait till I am finished. Colonel Min, let me tell you what I had and still have in mind. I came out here in good faith. I've said that before, haven't I? Anyway, I came with my bags packed and ready. I am willing to disappear, do you understand? I shall go wherever you want me to go — for the time being. You are right. I am beset with troubles at the moment and I am getting tired of those who want to get rid of me. Make no mistake. I can take care of them if I want to. Anytime. But I am tired. Let me tell you this. If I had really wanted to solve all those troubles and let them have it, if you know what I mean, all I would have needed was to smash up your coup plans and have you all shot. I could have done that."

"No bluffing, please, General," said Colonel Min. "I am getting tired, too, General. Getting tired of too many people bluffing."

"This is no bluff, Colonel," he said; his voice was suddenly edgy. "Ah, why argue at a time like this. Let me go on. So — I could quietly disappear from Seoul for a while."

"Then what, General?" said Colonel Son.

"Then you, as my deputy, will remain in Seoul and take full charge of our operations. You will have a perfect, legitimate excuse and reason for launching a search and investigation. I am sure Colonel Min and his group have a lot of generals and colonels in and near Seoul whom they would rather not have to deal with at the time of their coup. Later, perhaps. Do you follow my reasoning, Colonel Min? Colonel Son will then have those undesirable characters quietly called into our headquarters — let's say — for a quiet talk. In short, Colonel Son here can quietly have them locked up until your coup is over. And that can be done and will be done with the full consent and advice of our dear President. After all, there was someone who tried to kill me and, now, I have vanished! If anyone can do that to me, well, it can happen to the President now that I am gone. Do you understand?"

"Yes."

"Good! Now, as you can see, that is why Colonel Son comes into our deal and I am sure Colonel Son would not object to being part of our cooperative venture."

"I am listening, General," said Colonel Son.

"Therefore, my proposal is this. I want Colonel Son to remain in Seoul, looking after your interests as well as mine. If we come to an agreement on our deal, I shall be in daily contact with Colonel Son. Should anything happen to me — you might want to kill me, you know — then Colonel Son, knowing that you might want to kill him, too, will take proper action against you. Then, there's always the question of the hostages as you know. Anything can happen to them, if you know what I mean. You see, even now, if either of us does not return to headquarters by one o'clock, my men have my instructions to shoot some of those who are related to your people."

"You see, General," said Colonel Min, "I know you only too well."

"So much the better for all of us."

"Your scheme, General, as I see it, will depend entirely on Colonel Son, won't it, General?"

General Mah looked at Colonel Son and tapped him on the shoulder. "You can always count on Colonel Son."

I thought Colonel Min smiled.

"If I still say," said Colonel Min, "that there will be no deal?"

"No deal but I should come obediently with you and wait for my trial which no doubt will find me guilty of all those horrible things you would say I've done and hang me?"

Colonel Min's shadowy eyes narrowed. "Yes."

"Then I will say you are out of your mind," he said matter-of-factly. "If that is the case, then Colonel Son and I will simply have to arrest you all and have you shot. We will take our chances from there. Does that sound agreeable to you?"

"Yes."

General Mah screwed up his eyes, frowning. "You are so cock-sure of everything, aren't you? You always have been."

"You know me only too well, General."

"Shall we then consider that our little chat has come to an end?" General Mah was grinning. "Eh?"

"If you like, General. But you will have to come with us, whether you like it or not, to put it bluntly to you."

General Mah gazed at Colonel Min for a long moment. "What a pity!" he said. He turned to Colonel Son. "All right. We have no other choice. Give the signal. What a pity, Colonel Min! We could have gained so much from each other! Put that thing away, Major Lee! You are all under arrest."

"Try it, General," said Colonel Min wearily.

"Don't put up a fight now. I wouldn't if I were you. You may kill me but you will be shot and the hostages, too. Think about it." He nodded to Colonel Son. "Go ahead now."

I found myself beside General Mah in one big stride and had the submachine gun leveled at him. He ignored me.

Colonel Son looked toward the bushes. "Colonel Jung!" he called out. "You may come out now!"

Colonel Min stepped back a few paces.

Colonel Jung came toward us slowly, as if measuring each step. He carried a submachine gun in his right hand and a flashlight in the other. He came closer and into the bright light.

General Mah screwed up his face. "What are you doing here!"

Colonel Jung said, with a nod, "General!"

General Mah whipped around to Colonel Son. "What is this man doing here!"

Colonel Son ignored him. "Colonel Jung, have your men come out."

Colonel Jung raised his flashlight. He blinked it twice. Then he shouted into the dark hills. "Lights on!"

Instantly, two powerful beams from searchlights, one from the west and the other from beyond the bushes, lit up the runway, one focusing on the two cars, the other on us. The blinding, white-hot lights, while they lit up the runway brilliantly like a stage with blinding footlights, rendered the surrounding darkness much darker. The silent hills swiftly blended into the murky backdrop of night air. I could not help feeling that we were all there sealed in on the runway by impenetrable, black, heavy curtains. The foggy night air was suddenly throbbing with sounds and noises — boots sliding down the hills, weapons clattering and clanking, boots crunching on gravel and squishing on muddy dirt. Then, as suddenly, all was quiet. The shadowy figures of Colonel Jung's men silently emerged onto the fringes of the runway, fanning out, weapons ready. In a moment they surrounded us.

General Mah stood still, blinking his eyes at the glaring white of the searchlights.

I saw his driver step out of the Plymouth. He was not armed. There was no sign of life in the other car.

The men were now hushed, lined up in a semicircle. I saw three light machine guns set up on the runway, manned by soldiers flat on the ground.

Colonel Jung turned around. "Colonel Min, we are at your disposal, sir."

General Mah looked at Colonel Son, then at Colonel Min.

Colonel Min came up to General Mah.

Colonel Son went closer to them.

My submachine gun was pointing downward; I felt all my strength was now draining away from me.

Somber and austere, Colonel Min said quietly, "General Mah, meet Colonel Son, my good friend and member of our Command Group."

General Mah said, "And a very good actor, too, I must say!" There was neither anger nor sarcasm in the tone of his voice; he sounded more amused than anything else. "Ah — we are wasting our precious time, don't you think, Colonel Min?" He quickly looked back toward the Plymouth. I saw his driver slide into the car.

"General Mah," said Colonel Min, "you will come with us."

"Not so fast, not so fast," he said. "Patience, Colonel! We still have a few things we haven't settled yet."

"General, I am in no mood for any further talk."

"You don't have to talk, because I will be doing the talking from this point on."

"We are wasting time, General, as you put it."

We all heard the L-17, heard its engine sputtering and crackling, as it came swooping down from the west; its green and red lights flashing, it came diving down toward the runway, its engine now spurting. It buzzed the runway with a deafening roar and sharply pulled up, banking away to the north, whipping us with a gust of wind in its wake.

"What is this!" said General Mah.

We ignored him.

We were watching the lights of the L-17. In a moment it buzzed us again, then flew off into the dark toward the east.

Colonel Jung strode up to Colonel Min. "Do you want me to redeploy my men, sir?"

"Hold it for a moment," said Colonel Min. His voice was unruffled.

The senior agent came running toward us. "What's our move, Colonel?" he said.

"You stay here and cover him," said Colonel Min, pointing at General Mah.

"Well! How clever, how clever!" said General Mah. "I'll be damned! Who would have thought of that! A reconnaissance plane!"

I saw him smile.

The senior agent slapped his left palm against his glistening submachine gun. "Will you shut up, General!"

Someone from the line of Colonel Jung's men came running toward us. It was a young lieutenant. "Colonel Jung," he said panting, "the third platoon reports a column of vehicles heading this way, sir. Wants your instructions."

Colonel Jung looked at Colonel Min.

General Mah said, "I am afraid we are going to have a little duel, Colonel Min. You didn't expect that, did you? I told you you are too damn cocksure."

Colonel Min said to Colonel Son, "I suppose we will have to get it over with."

Colonel Son nodded. "I want you to get out of here. With him. Take your men. I will stay here and see this through. What do you say, Colonel Jung?"

"I am ready. Anytime. Just give me the word. I can have the platoon out there ambush them."

"Let them come in here," said Colonel Son. "We'll trap them right in here."

"You are the one being trapped, Colonel Son," said General Mah. "There's no way out."

He was ignored by all.

"All right," said Colonel Min, pulling himself up. "Let's get moving. Colonel Jung, redeploy your men as before. Turn off the searchlights."

The young lieutenant ran back to the men.

"Wait!" said Colonel Min. "Colonel Jung, don't turn them off. Have one of them light up the road out there. I want that road covered."

The lieutenant came back to us. "Sir, there's another column coming in from the eastern approach. Four trucks there."

"What about the western approach?" said Colonel Jung.

"Five there, sir. Four trucks and a jeep."

"Troops?"

"Loaded, sir."

"All right. Let's have it out!" said Colonel Jung. "Colonel Min, you'd better take off with him. And you, too, sir, Colonel Son!"

"I am staying," said Colonel Son.

"You are all staying here!" said General Mah who was holding his arms crossed over his chest. 'Don't you want to see your rat?"

No one paid any attention to him.

Colonel Jung was giving his instructions to the lieutenant.

The lieutenant ran back to the troops.

Colonel Son ran to his jeep, came back with a carbine.

The troops withdrew from the runway, melting back into the dark.

I saw the special agents on the jeep swivel the .50 caliber aiming at the cars.

"Colonel Min, you'd better hurry," said Colonel Jung.

The senior agent went behind General Mah, his submachine gun at the general's back.

Colonel Min stood silent, his shadowy face lowered and his hands on his hips.

The searchlight on the west, halfway up the hill, swung its beam out of the runway and focused on the dirt road leading up to the western entrance; it began sweeping the road. The Plymouth and the Cadillac were now lit up by the headlights from our jeeps.

Colonel Son said to Colonel Jung, "Whoever may be in those cars, you'd better have them come out."

Colonel Jung nodded. He called out to his men. "Sergeant Bang, bring your squad out here!"

"No need for that!" said General Mah, grinning. "I was going to have them come out, but you weren't listening! Well, Colonel Min, I told you I've brought you the rat you wanted."

"What?" said Colonel Son.

"I said I've brought you my fox which you would want to call your rat. Well, you wanted to know if I had brought the rat, didn't you? Now, you can have it. I don't want it."

"What are you talking about?" said Colonel Son again.

Colonel Min said calmly, "He is talking about General Ahn."

"What!" Both Colonel Son and I exclaimed at the same time.

"General Ahn," said Colonel Min. "Our rat."

"And my fox." General Mah laughed.

A squad of troopers, all with submachine guns, came out of the dark into the runway.

Colonel Jung told the sergeant to have his men cover the cars.

General Mah said, "Let me show you a nice, little, new gadget I have on my new car." He laughed. Then he shouted out, "Driver! Let General Ahn out!"

The Cadillac started its engine and backed up toward us. It stopped about a car's length behind the Plymouth.

The lieutenant was coming out again, carrying a walkie-talkie. "Colonel Jung, the columns stopped, sir."

"How far are they away from here?"

"Not very far, sir. The troops got off the trucks and they are coming this way."

"How many of them?"

"About four platoons, sir. Two on each side."

"We can handle that! You stay here with me."

"Yes, sir."

Colonel Min and Colonel Son stood side by side a few paces to the right of General Mah, who was facing the cars. "Now watch this!" he said. "Clever, those Americans!"

The top of the Cadillac was rising up and up and the trunk lid was rising up, too; the top was now folding itself, whining and creaking, and now it was coming down and down . . .

"Look out!" shouted the senior agent, jamming the muzzle of his submachine gun at General Mah's side, at the same time, pulling him roughly by the arm closer toward Colonel Min and Colonel Son. I leaped to the right and forward, beside them, raising my submachine gun. Colonel Son, too, had pointed his carbine at the Cadillac.

There was a .30-caliber machine gun manned by two men set up in the back seat of the Cadillac. It was pointing at us.

General Ahn, in the right front seat, opened the door and got out. He stood there.

The top of the Cadillac had by this point disappeared into the trunk; the trunk lid slid forward and down and shut.

"Well, well, there's your rat," said General Mah. "I am not going with you but you can take him and do whatever you want to do with him. Ah! I forgot that you weren't going anywhere!"

General Ahn, in khaki uniform, limped his way, leaning on his silver-topped cane, slowly toward us.

Colonel Jung, behind me now, was saying to the lieutenant, "Get back to the line. Have the searchlights begin sweeping the area. Tell the third platoon to close in on them from behind. Hold fire until I give the word, is that clear!"

The lieutenant ran back.

General Ahn stopped. He was about ten paces from us. His face was lit up in the searchlight's beam and the jeeps' headlights.

General Mah said, "Well, aren't you going to shoot him?"

No one spoke. No one stirred.

Suddenly, we heard the unmistakable sounds of the whirring of a helicopter to the east.

"Major Lee!" said Colonel Min.

"Yes!"

Colonel Min did not stir; his eyes were fixed on General Ahn. He did not look at me when he said, "Will you take care of that helicopter?"

"Yes!"

He said almost in a whisper, "I think we have a visitor."

General Mah was craning his neck upward, squinting into the dark sky.

The moon had disappeared altogether. The rain clouds had plastered most of the sky. I saw the lights, blinking green and red lights, on the helicopter. It came swishing in, whirring, whipping up a whirling gust, then hovering above the eastern entrance to the runway, swaying to and fro, up and down, roaring and roaring.

I left them. I ran toward the helicopter. Lieutenant Cho leaped out of the jeep and joined me. Together we ran. The helicopter touched down on the end of the runway. It cut off its engine after spurting out an ear-shattering, final roar. The searchlight had swung its beam around and focused on the helicopter. The glassy cockpit of the copter glistened, reflecting the light. Someone got out of the cockpit. He stood still on the runway. We went toward him.

It was Colonel McKay.

His hands clasped behind his back, he moved slowly into the shadow of the helicopter. He turned around and waited for us.

We made a dash. "Colonel McKay!" I could not help exclaiming. "What are you doing here!" He was in fatigues, unarmed.

"Colonel Min all right?"

"Yes. What are you doing here!"

"Look, Major Lee, you know troops are coming this way?"

"Yes!"

"Nothing to worry about. They are friendly. Our men."

"I don't follow you!"

"The L-17 warned you?"

"You knew that?"

"I've been in touch with Colonel Kim and Colonel Park. You'd better go and tell Colonel Min the troops are our men."

"Your men?"

"Yes. Our own Commandos — all Koreans, of course. I had them stop out there now but I'll radio them to close in when you give me a go signal. You'd better make sure Colonel Jung's men don't go haywire and trigger-happy. You do that, will you? I don't want our men to get all shot up. Just wave your arm to me and I'll have Major Yoon come in. He'll drive in in his jeep, so don't shoot him up."

"Major Yoon? General Mah's man?"

"Too bad we had to blow him, but it couldn't be helped. He had some quick thinking to do and he did well."

"He is your man?" I said. "He is your man!"

"Sorry about that. Is General Ahn here?"

I nodded.

"That's fine! What's the matter?"

I confessed. "I am terribly confused. I can't make head or tail of anything!"

"Well, cheer up, Major. Everything's going to be all right."

I found myself shaking my head. "I feel lost, to tell you the truth."

"Well, don't! You won't get anything done that way. Look! General Mah thought he had one more trick up his sleeve, see what I mean? He had ordered Major Yoon to bring out that bunch of goons — his private army if you know what I mean. Colonel Son didn't know about that, of course. Major Yoon was in a spot, so he got in touch with our people in Seoul, who got in touch with me."

"So?"

"Well, we gave Major Yoon our men instead. So there they are, out there now. Your people didn't know about it, so the L-17 did what it was supposed to do. Damn lucky I got hold of Colonel Kim and Colonel Park just in time. We could have had a bloody mess. You'd better get going now. I'll see you later. How are you, Lieutenant Cho? Doing all right?"

"O.K., Colonel McKay."

"Fine! Go now! And better keep it quiet among yourselves, all right?"

We ran back. I told Lieutenant Cho what had happened.

"Whew!" he said.

When we got back to the group, I had Lieutenant Cho cover General Ahn. Colonel Min and Colonel Son came over to me.

"Colonel Jung," I said, panting, to my annoyance for I had to whisper. "You, too." I told them about Colonel McKay's move.

"Good, good!" said Colonel Son.

Colonel Min merely nodded.

Colonel Jung quietly walked away from us and went back to his men.

Colonel Min said to me, "Give him the signal."

I turned around. I waved my arm to Colonel McKay. I could not see him too clearly. He was still standing in the shadow.

"All right," said Colonel Min. "Let's get it over with!"

"Well, are you all properly warned?" said General Mah. His face twisted into a bland smile. "It won't do you any good."

General Ahn was still standing quiet and immobile, leaning on his cane. The scar on his face looked longer and deeper in the bright light.

The searchlight moved its beam away from the helicopter and began sweeping the area near the eastern entrance to the airstrip. The other searchlight was sweeping the road, up and down, near the western entrance.

A jeep came into sight, lit up by the searchlight, on the dirt road. It stopped. The searchlight's beam focused on it for a second, then let it go. The jeep started again. It came toward the western entrance.

"Now!" said General Mah. "Now!"

"We'll see, General," said Colonel Min. His face revealed nothing more than a stony impassivity. "We'll see."

The jeep drove in onto the runway. It came straight to us. It stopped alongside the Cadillac to its left. The open jeep had two men in the back seat. Major Yoon leaped out of it. The two men in fatigues stood up in the back seat; they both had submachine guns. The driver came out; he went around the back of the jeep; he stood behind General Mah's driver, who was standing between the Plymouth and the Cadillac. The driver, too, was armed with a submachine gun.

Then — no one spoke, no one stirred.

Colonel Jung was coming back to us, his shoes clicking on the runway. "The troops are closing in," he said quietly to no one in particular.

"Well, now, shall we shoot it out or shall we resume our chat?" said General Mah. He laughed. "What a pity! If we have to shoot it out, eh? We will all die here — and so will those hostages in Seoul." He cluck-clucked. "What a pity!" He looked at his wristwatch, which flashed in the light. "If my men don't hear from me soon," he said, looking up, "the hostages will be all shot!"

Major Yoon, who was standing a few paces behind General Ahn, in his shadow, shook his head, slowly, imperceptibly, to the left and to the right; he was looking at Colonel Min.

Suddenly, the searchlights, on both sides of the airstrip, whipped their beams away from where they had been sweeping before and focused fully on the runway itself. Then we heard the footsteps of the troops, in the dark, near both entrances. They came quietly, in formation, it seemed. At the same time, Colonel Jung's men emerged from the surrounding darkness again, one by one, here and there, all over the runway. Major Yoon's troops — Colonel Mc-Kay's Commandos — they, too, broke their formation, and began filing onto the runway, from the east and from the west, swiftly fanning out, linking up with Colonel Jung's men. In a moment, they stood surrounding us all on three sides of the runway, in a circle that was open only on the southern side. The glaring beams from the searchlights were now sweeping to the left and to the right, behind the line of the silent troopers. A wide, jagged, black path of shadows of the soldiers stretched in front of them.

General Mah's eyes were darting about to and fro, squinting and peering at the shadowy figures of the troopers.

The searchlights went off. A blinding darkness engulfed the troopers.

Colonel Min said quietly, "Lieutenant Cho, escort General Ahn to the jeep, will you?"

Lieutenant Cho held the submachine gun in his right hand and stepped up to General Ahn. "Come with me, General," he said with an undisguised contempt in his voice.

General Ahn silently took a few steps, limping, past General Mah. His black cane tap-tapped on the wet concrete. He was perhaps five, six paces from General Mah, to our left, when he stopped and slowly turned around. He glared at General Mah. "Don't you see he's framing me!" he said in a hoarse voice. "Can't you see he's trying to split us?"

Colonel Min did not stir.

Colonel Son flicked his thumb to Lieutenant Cho. "Take him away!"

General Ahn brushed off Lieutenant Cho's hand. "You are finished, General Mah. You are finished!"

General Mah was not looking at him. He had his small eyes glued to Colonel Min's face.

Colonel Min looked toward Major Yoon and nodded his head once.

Major Yoon looked back to his men and nodded his head. The two men in the back seat of the jeep jumped out. Major Yoon's driver stepped up and held General Mah's driver. The driver of the Cadillac and the two men who manned the light machine gun in its back seat climbed out. One of Major Yoon's men covered them with his submachine gun. The other man hopped into the back seat of the Cadillac and dismantled the machine gun.

Major Yoon turned to Colonel Min. "All yours, sir!"

Colonel Min nodded. "General Mah, now you will come with us."

General Mah did not stir.

"If you are pinning your hope on the hostages," said Major Yoon to General Mah, "you'd better forget that. I've taken care of that."

General Mah did not look back at Major Yoon. "You, too, eh?"

Colonel Min said, "We will leave now, General."

"And what will you do with me?" said General Mah. "Kill me?"

"We could kill you," said Colonel Min. His voice was heavy and weary. "But we won't. My promise still stands. You will be given a fair trial."

General Mah snickered. "When? After your coup is successful? And may I ask what if your coup flops? Then what?"

Colonel Min said simply, "We will have to shoot you."

"I am sure you will," said General Mah, suddenly serious. "I would, too, if I were in your shoes. I can understand that. We are birds of a feather, Colonel Min, you and me, wouldn't you know?"

Abruptly, Colonel Min turned on his heels and made as if to go. "Take care of him!" he shouted in a furious whisper to Colonel Son.

"Wait!" hissed General Mah. "You haven't heard me out yet!"

Colonel Min turned around. His dark face was cold. "Yes?"

General Mah said, "I know I am beaten, Colonel Min. You won.

And I admire you for that. It takes someone like you, someone like me, well, someone better than I am, to finish me up. All right. I will just have to take my chances with you, so I will come. But I have something to tell you too, all of you." He looked at me. "Is that Colonel McKay over there?"

I ignored him.

"Ah — it does not matter. I know it's him," he said.

To my left, General Ahn shifted his weight — or so I thought; I heard the tip of his cane scrape at the concrete runway. He was staring at General Mah.

General Mah said, "I've brought you a present, Colonel Min. That fox there who ratted on you. That's how I've learned all about your coup plans. He wanted me to kill you all off. Can you imagine that! A real crook — worse than I am!" He tut-tutted. "But there's more to him than that. He is our common enemy! Do you know that?" His finger wagged, pointing to General Ahn. "Colonel Min, my intention of negotiating with you was and is quite genuine. You'd better believe that. I wanted to bargain with you. You may ask then why I bothered to have Major Yoon bring out these men although he turned sour on me. Well, I just wanted to drive a hard bargain, that's all. A simple matter of precaution, just as you have taken care of that yourself. So! Now, you won't buy my deal and I have nothing else to sell. Except that rat there!"

"He's desperate to save his own neck, don't you see that!" shouted General Ahn. He tapped his cane hard on the concrete in a theatrical gesture of impatience and frustration. "Look at him!"

Our eyes were focused on General Mah.

"Take a good look at that evil face! Look at him!" General Ahn screamed out.

It suddenly occurred to me how strange and incongruous General Mah looked among us, in mufti — a double-breasted brown suit, baggy pants, a black bow tie — surrounded by men, us, in combat fatigues, armed to the teeth. Except for General Ahn — in neatly pressed, starchy khaki uniform, a big silver star shining on each tip of his collar, his tilted head wearing a khaki, general officer's cap with a gold-braided band. General Mah's slick, pomaded hair gleamed in the light. There were beads of sweat on his forehead where a strand of his black hair fell like a deep scar.

His face squeezed out a contemptuous smile. "Listen to that dirty son of a bitch barking, eh!"

Out of the corner of my eye, I saw General Ahn's hand clasp and unclasp the silver top of his cane.

General Mah raised his arm; his index finger shot out of his clenched fist and pointed at General Ahn. He spat out, "Do you know who he really is! Do you realize who that bastard really is!" His face was triumphant as he looked at Colonel Min. "Let me tell you! That son of a bitch there —" He swung his face over to General Ahn.

And General Ahn was raising his cane, first slowly, then swiftly, as if to ward off General Mah's wagging finger, and it was then that, suddenly, it struck me — like a flash in the dark — the cane, the cane —

I made a flying leap at General Ahn. I was too late.

His black cane hissed out — whish-whish — a split second before I knocked him down with my submachine gun. The cane flew out of his hand and fell on the concrete with a metallic clang.

He had shot two long, needle-sharp, gleaming darts at General Mah, who stood for a moment with his eyes open wide and bulging and his mouth gaping — one dart stuck in his throat through the black bow tie, the other dart tore into his face on the left cheek.

As though paralyzed, no one moved, no one stirred, no one uttered a word, no one made any sound.

General Ahn was at my feet, down on his side, one knee drawn up.

General Mah staggered, his gaping mouth gasping out and sucking in hoarse, crackling air and dribbling blood. His baggy pants swayed and bent. His bloody chubby hands were clutching his throat. His body, first slowly, then abruptly, collapsed on the concrete, face down, with a thud, his black, greasy hair glistening in the light.

Colonel Min swooped down to the body and Colonel Son, too, and they were turning the body over —

General Ahn sprang up and dashed to the edge of the runway, and I ran after him and he was running down the slope beyond the runway, running and leaping and rolling down and I bounded after him and fell. He was running fast in spite of his limping leg and down the slope it was a muddy and watery rice paddy, and he was hopping, falling, running, and leaping, and I got up shouting "Stop! Stop!" and ran after him gasping. The searchlights came on and their fiery beams were burning down on the black muddy water and slushy dirt, and the beams caught him as if in a cross fire but he kept on running and running, stumbling, falling, and running, and leaping. And I shouted after him "Stop! Stop!" but he kept on running, slogging and squishing muddy water, and I was sinking in the soft, stinking muddy earth to my knees and muddy water splashed against my face, against my body, and there he was leap-frogging away from me and from the lights. The beams caught him again, pinning him down just as he was crawling up a grassy dike and he was pulling and pushing himself up the dike but then he stood still in the glaring, searing, white light. I shouted, gasping and panting, again and again "Stop! Stop!" and he was standing still with his back to me, and his khaki was stained dark with mud and water. He turned around in the crossed beams of the light as I slogged, sloshed my way toward him, and he was slowly raising his arms, oddly looking like a man hung on a cross — no! — like a scarecrow. I heard someone behind me on the runway shouting "Hold fire!" though I didn't think I heard any shooting. I looked back toward the runway for a second and saw the shadowy, dark figures clustered around and someone was running toward me and I turned around and saw him — saw his raised arm pointing toward me — then I saw a red flash and heard a muffled clap, then a loud bang and I knew he was shooting at me. Then — I killed him. A long, fast, clattering burst from my wildly jerking, rebounding sub-machine gun mowed him down flat on the brightly lit dike until its magazine went empty. I sank down deep into the slimy, stinking mud, on my knees. I heard sloshing and splashing of water and mud behind me. Someone came beside me. He gripped my arm.

"Get up!" he said in a whisper. It was Colonel Min.

I looked up at him, at his shadowy face as he stood, his back to the blazing light. He was smeared with mud and soaked with muddy water, sunk up to his knees into the slimy, stinking mud.

"Come on!" he whispered again. "Here — hold onto my hand!"

I reached out for his hand.

He pulled me up out of the mud. "Are you all right?"

I nodded. I tried to look back to the dike, where I had killed General Ahn, when Colonel Min, putting his arm around my shoulder, said in the gentlest voice I had ever heard from him:

"You didn't kill him."

I stared at him.

"I shot him in the leg," he said quietly. "He isn't dead."

Only then did I see that he had a carbine in his hand.

"Come!" he said in a firm voice. "We have work to do."

I *Chapter 13*

n the chaotic aftermath of the fateful rendezvous with General Mah and the frantic rush to get myself ready for the trip to Japan, it had occurred to neither me nor Colonel Min to go over the details of my trip or, for that matter, what precisely I was expected to accomplish once I was in Japan with Colonel McKay's people. Colonel McKay had already had an L-19 waiting for me at the Corps airstrip, so that when we returned to the headquarters there was barely enough time for me to change into clean uniform and dash out to the airstrip. It had begun raining again — a misty drizzling rain. It was a little after two o'clock in the morning.

"Take care of yourself," said Colonel Min just before Lieutenant Cho was to drive me down to the airstrip.

"You, too," I said. "Is everything going to be under control here?"

"Don't worry about a thing," he said. "Everything will be all right here."

It was then that it dawned on me to ask, "What exactly is the nature of my mission?" I thought I saw a faint smile on his shadowy face. "I haven't the slightest idea what I am supposed to do in Japan. With Colonel McKay's people, I mean."

He peered into my face. "Colonel McKay will take care of you. So — don't worry."

"It is all rather vague," I confessed.

He said quickly, "You just be my spokesman, all right?"

"Do I speak for you?"

"Yes." Then he added, "You always have."

I did not respond.

"You'd better hurry," he said. "I am sure everything will turn out fine. Colonel McKay has everything arranged for you, all right?"

"When do I come back?"

He withdrew his face from under the cover of the jeep and straightened up. "Whenever you think you are ready. Now, get going. Good luck. Take good care of yourself." Lieutenant Cho started up the engine. Colonel Min tapped me lightly on the shoulder. "And get some rest, too, while you are there, will you?"

The jeep began moving. I said, "Hold it a second, Lieutenant."

Colonel Min came up to me. "What is it?"

I said, "Thanks."

"For what?"

"You know — General Ahn, I mean, if it hadn't been for you, you know, do you understand?"

In the misty, pale light of the jeep, I saw his dark face stiffen. His voice was mercilessly brutal. "I didn't exactly spare his life for your sake, Major Lee!"

I felt my face flush. I could not help stammering out, "I didn't mean it quite that way."

He stood silently for a long moment; then, abruptly, he turned his back to me and strode away into the rainy darkness.

When our L-19 touched down on a runway at an American air base near Pusan, Captain Brooke, the young pilot, said, "This is as far as I come, Major Lee. There will be someone waiting for you. You're going to have to change planes here."

It was raining lightly. Captain Brooke did not taxi the L-19 down the runway to the air terminal. He wheeled the plane around at the end of the runway and cut off the engine.

"We'll wait here," he said.

The air base was dark and quiet as though deserted. In the fine, thin misty rain, the lights on the control tower dimly illuminated the buildings around it.

"Very quiet here," I said.

"This area here is reserved for light aircraft," he said. "The main base is back there behind us."

I looked back, but I could not see much except the hazy glow of lights hovering above the ground.

"There it is," he said.

A car with dimmed headlights was coming toward us. It pulled up close to the L-19. A man, an American, a civilian, got out of the black sedan.

"So long, Major Lee," said Captain Brooke. "See you around."

I climbed out of the L-19.

The American, in short-sleeved sport shirt and tan slacks, held an umbrella for me. "Major Lee?"

"Yes. Who are you?"

"Your plane is waiting for you. This way."

We got into his sedan. The air was stale with cigar smoke inside the car. It was humid and, for the first time since I had left the Corps headquarters, I felt the dampness from my khaki shirt that clung to my back.

The American was small and thin. He did not speak to me while he drove down the runway. We left the area behind us and drove into the main base. It was better lighted there. We slowly drove by rows of fighters and light bombers and went all the way to the other side of the main base. He swerved the car to the left and drove down a runway, at the end of which a transport plane of DC-6 type was parked in the dark. He said, "Sorry, Major, but that's the best thing I could get for you."

I managed to say, "Quite all right."

"The weather in Japan is clear," he said. "So, it will be all right."

He stopped the car almost under the tip of the left wing of the transport. "Wait here," he said and got out. Someone was standing near the wing and they were talking. In the headlights of the car, I saw that the other man was also a civilian. He was tall and I could see his face dimly through the wet windshield as he looked toward the car. Then the driver of the car motioned to me to get out of the car.

"He's your pilot," he said. "He'll take care of you from this point on, O.K.?"

We shook hands. His big, sweaty hand squeezed mine hard. "Glad to have you aboard, Major," he said in a booming voice. "I am ready anytime you are."

"I am ready," I said.

"O.K.," he said. "Let's go."

The driver of the car went back to the car and came back with a large, bulky manila envelope, which he handed over to the pilot who took it with a slight nod of his head. His hair was cut short and he wore a tan windbreaker and dark slacks. We climbed into the plane. I was the only passenger. The car drove off. He closed the hatch. He led me down the short aisle to a front seat to the right of the door to the pilot's compartment. "A little more leg room, see what I mean?" he said, smiling.

I nodded.

"The lavatory is in the back. I guess you know that."

I nodded again. "What is our destination? Tokyo?"

"Not quite," he said. "Almost there, though. Don't worry. Someone will pick you up when we get there. You'll have a car. Want something to drink?"

"No, thank you."

Just then, a younger man came out of the pilot's compartment. He nodded to me. He was of medium height, slightly built. He had long, dark, wavy hair. "My traveling companion," said the pilot.

We shook hands. I was already seated, so that the young man had to bend over. "Welcome aboard," he said with a soft twang in his quiet voice. "Need anything, just holler."

"If you get lonesome back here, just come on up," said the pilot.

"See you later." They both disappeared into the pilot's compartment. Before the door was closed, the young copilot stuck his head out. "No smoking until we're in the air, Major. And you'd better buckle up. It's going to be a little rough over the Straits."

"All right."

"See you."

So we left Korea behind us. As the plane soared above the twinkling lights of the harbor and the city of Pusan into the dark, raining, turbulent sky over the Korea Straits, a thought flashed across my tired, dazed mind with an uncontrollable, shocking jolt that benumbed me in the seat as I sat upright, rigid and cold: What if — what if our coup were to be foiled by some unforeseen turn of fortune — I should never be able to return to my homeland, and who, indeed, who would then save the suffering country and her suffering people!

T

Chapter 14

he weather in Japan was not clear. It was raining. I could see the thin, fine rain falling on the plane's wing through the wet window. To my surprise, I had slept through the entire flight; when I came to, the transport plane had already landed — somewhere in Japan near Tokyo for all I knew — and I found myself alone in the plane. The sky was dark. I sat straight up in my seat. My face was puffed and eyes swollen. I felt as though I had been drugged. I felt numb and aching. I could not shake myself completely out of the dull feeling of inertia — as though I had been stricken with paralysis. It was hushed there. The very shadowy quietness of the plane's interior and the gray rainy morning outside did not help me much in trying to come to my senses.

I heard whispering voices behind me. I stood bolt upright in the seat — fast, as though I had felt someone was going to shoot me in the back.

"Good morning, Major," a shadowy figure said in the back of the plane. It was the young copilot. The big, burly pilot was standing next to him. It took me a moment to distinguish them as they stood in the near darkness of the tail section.

"Morning," said the pilot.

"Good morning," I said. "How long have we been landed?"

The pilot said, "Oh, not so long. You were so sound asleep we thought we'd let you sleep as long as you could. Feel O.K.?"

"Fine, thank you. We are in Japan?"

He said, "We're in Japan all right. Would you like some coffee to wake you up?"

"Yes, please."

"Come on over," he said.

I straightened up my uniform and went to them.

The young copilot handed me a mug. "It's instant coffee, O.K. with you?"

I nodded. There was a tiny kitchenette of a sort in the back. My watch had stopped. "What time is it?"

The pilot said, "A little after seven. Someone's going to come pick you up pretty soon."

"If you want to freshen up," said the young copilot, thumbing toward the lavatory.

It occurred to me that, in the rush, I had not brought my traveling bag. I went to the lavatory, washed my face, rinsed my mouth, and came out.

We heard a car outside. The pilot looked out a small window on his side. "There he is," he said. "Right on time."

I swallowed down the coffee.

"Take your time, Major," said the copilot. "No hurry."

The car pulled up near the hatch and blew its horn twice.

The pilot got up and went to open the hatch door.

I stood up. A cool air rushed in. It was raining harder outside than I had thought.

A young Oriental in a tan raincoat came aboard. He was short, deeply tanned; short hair, a big nose, about thirty-five. He had to look up when he talked with the pilot.

"Major Lee," said the pilot, coming toward me with the Oriental behind him, "he's going to take care of you from this end on."

We shook hands.

"Call me George, Major," he said in English, taking off his raincoat. He wore a dark gray suit with a blue tie.

I nodded. I saw he had a large suitcase with him.

He turned to the pilot and the copilot. "O.K. You can take off now and thanks a lot."

I shook hands with the pilot and the copilot. They both nodded to me and left the plane.

"O.K., Major. Let's get to the business," said the Oriental. His English was fluent — as far as I knew. "First, you're going to have to change clothes. I can't have you walking around downtown Tokyo in your ROK Army combat fatigues." He grinned. "See what I mean?"

"Are you a Japanese?"

"Wondered when you'd ask that," he said. "I am what they call back in the States a Nisei, except that I am a Korean-American. Do you know what I mean?"

"I see," I said. "Are you in the military?"

"Can't tell you that."

"I understand."

He went over to a rear seat with his suitcase. I followed behind him. He opened the suitcase, saying, "Do you speak Japanese?"

"Yes."

"Fluent?" He snapped open the inside pockets of the suitcase.

"Fair enough."

"As good as your English?" He was taking out ties, a pair of dark brown shoes, shirts, handkerchiefs — spreading them over the seat like a peddler showing off his wares.

"My English is better," I said.

He looked up, giving me a big smile. "I guess your Japanese is good enough. That's handy." He took out underwear, socks, a light tan raincoat, and a dark blue suit. He looked up at me again. "You need a shave." He pulled out a small brown leather bag from the bottom of the suitcase and handed it to me. "Go ahead," he said.

George had everything spread out neatly on the seat when I came out of the lavatory. "Help yourself. I want you to change everything, down to your socks. I'll wait for you in the car outside."

"What do I do with my things?"

"Oh, yes. Here." He took out a large plastic bag from the pocket of his raincoat. "Just put them in here and bring it to the car with you. And the suitcase, too, of course."

He put the raincoat on, and checked his wristwatch. "Take your time. There's no hurry." He got off the plane.

Until I began taking off my uniform it had not occurred to me to wonder if any of those clothes George had brought would fit me; but they did perfectly. They were all American made, down to socks as George had put it. At least, the label on each item was American. I folded my uniform and underwear and put them in the plastic bag; I put my shoes and everything else in, too.

I got out of the plane into the rain. George's car was a compact sedan of Japanese make. George saw me coming out of the plane and stepped out of the car. There was someone sitting in the back seat but I could not see in well through the wet rear window. George closed the hatch door of the plane. He opened the front door of the car and put the suitcase and the plastic bag in. Then he opened the back door. The passenger in the back seat was a young girl — an American.

She slid over to the corner of the back seat, saying, "Hi!"

I said, "Hello." I got inside and sat down.

"Did you have a good trip?" said the girl. She looked barely twenty. A light blue raincoat with a belt and the collar up. Dark brown hair pulled straight back into a bun. Brown eyes. "Tired?" she said, smiling.

"No. I slept through."

"That's good." When she smiled she had small dimples in her cheeks. "Hungry?"

I shook my head. "I had breakfast with the pilots."

"It couldn't have been much of a breakfast," she said.

George looked back, leaning over the back of his seat. "Major Lee," he said, "this is Jeanne."

"Hello," I said.

"Hello there again," she said, smiling. "Glad to meet you, Major Lee." She said to George, "Would you hand me the briefcase, please?"

George picked up a black attaché case from the front seat and gave it to her. She put it over her lap and snapped it open. "Now," she said, her voice suddenly crisp. "Here's your passport, all in order."

It was an American passport — all in order, my picture, an American address, stamped — I looked at her.

She held out a ballpoint pen. "Would you sign here please."

I signed my name in English. "But this is an American passport."

"It's more convenient that way," she said matter-of-factly. "It's not a fake one, if you are wondering. It's quite genuine as far as we are concerned. Now, here's your wallet, containing your driver's license, California. Do you drive?"

"Yes."

"Of course. And this is your American Express card and et cetera. And two hundred fifty dollars in fifties and tens, and twenty thousand Japanese yen in five hundreds and hundreds. Would you mind counting these and signing this slip please?"

I did. "But what am I to do with all this money?"

She gave me a puzzled look.

George said, "Spend it."

"I wouldn't know how," I said. "Am I expected to stay here long? I wasn't expecting to stay here more than a day. I must return to Korea as soon as I can. Do you understand?"

She said, "That we don't know, if you know what I mean."

I said, "What then do you know? About me, that is. Rather, what is your assignment with me?"

George said, "We pick you up at the plane, drive you into Tokyo, deposit you at the Tokyo-Hilton Hotel where you have a room reserved and paid for you, then wait for further instructions."

"From whom?"

"We can't tell you that, Major," she said.

"I understand," I said. "Where does Colonel McKay come in?"

They exchanged a quick look. She said, "This is all arranged by Colonel McKay, so you don't have to worry about anything, all right?"

"Am I expected to meet with anyone, other than you?"

"We wouldn't know that," said George.

"All right," I said.

She smiled. "Let me finish then," she said. "As you can see in your passport, you have just arrived in Japan this morning from Los Angeles on a Pan American flight. Here is your ticket. You have baggage already deposited in your room at the Tokyo-Hilton, all right? Some clothes and odds and ends."

"What am I supposed to be, an American citizen?"

"Yes. A Korean Nisei, all right?"

I frowned. "A Nisei is a Japanese. I am a Korean."

She looked puzzled again.

George said quickly, "I understand, Major."

She said, "Oh, I see."

"All right," I said. "Go on."

She said, "Your occupation: a schoolteacher on vacation. Is that all right with you?"

I nodded. "I was a university instructor before the war."

She said, "We knew that, so we thought of sending you back to your old job. You are going to be in Tokyo for an indefinite period of time, then perhaps move on to Hong Kong and so on. Your travel plans don't have to be definite. And, by the way, you teach Far Eastern history at — what's the name of the school? I wrote it down somewhere . . . Here it is. I think that'll do, don't you? O.K., now." She was checking off a list in her small notebook. "A

Tokyo telephone number — I have that in your wallet. That's our number in case you need us."

I said, "I want to get it over with as quickly as I can or your people can. I must return to Korea fast, do you understand? There's no time to lose."

She said demurely, "I guess I've covered just about all you need to know. Any questions?"

I said, "No."

George started up the car.

She settled herself down on the seat. She said, "I'm hungry."

George said, driving the car out down the runway, "Me too."

"How about you?" she said to me. "Would you join us?"

"Yes."

"A nice Japanese breakfast," she said, peering up at me. "Would you mind?"

"Fine."

"We could go to a Korean restaurant in Tokyo, you know," said George, looking back.

"Anything she wants," I said.

"Aren't you nice," she said. "Just imagine! Here I am riding with a man who is about to overthrow his government!" She tut-tutted.

I could not resist saying, "And here I am riding with a young girl who is helping that very man."

"Hey, that's good, that's pretty good, Major," said George.

She laughed, tossing her head back, turning to me. "Wait till I tell my folks about it when it's over!"

"Yes," I said, "when it is over."

The car was going fast on an American-style express highway. The rain had become heavy. There were few cars on the road. I tried to look out ahead of us through the windshield. George turned on the radio, which blared out American-style rock and roll music; the voices with the loud music could have been either Japanese or English. Was I really in Japan?

I settled back, leaning my head against the seat. I closed my eyes for a moment, feeling weary. The last few scenes of the rendez-vous with General Mah the night before flashed through my mind. I shook my head and opened my eyes.

The car was speeding along fast on the deserted highway. A road sign I caught a glimpse of through the windshield said in English: Tokyo-25 miles. So I was in Japan — after all.

They took me up to the room they had reserved for me in the Tokyo-Hilton Hotel. It was on the seventh floor at the end of a long, dark, and hushed hallway.

"How do you like it?" she said, pulling the drapes open on the windows. The hotel was on a hill and would have had a wide view of Tokyo had it not been raining and cloudy. The sky was dark and the air hazy with rain and mist.

"Fine," I said. A single bed, a couch, a table and chairs, a telephone on a bedside night table, and a television set on a swivel stand."

She was looking into the bathroom and closet.

George put the suitcase on the bed and picked up the hotel direc-tory from the top of the dresser with a round mirror. "If you want anything, call the room service and have it brought up."

I nodded.

"You have that telephone number I gave you?" she said.

"Yes."

"O.K., George. I guess we should go now," she said, looking at her watch. She turned to me. "Why don't you get some rest? Take a good, long bath and take a nap, maybe. We'll be in touch with you a little later on, all right?"

"Yes."

"What do you say," said George, looking at us, "if we drive out to the Hakone tonight?"

"That's a wonderful idea," she said, beaming at me.

"You don't think anything will come up during the day?" I said.

"Tomorrow afternoon, Major," said George. "Someone will see you tomorrow afternoon."

"So there's no reason you have to sit around here and do nothing, right?" she said.

"All right, then," I said.

"We'll pick you up here, all right?" she said.

"That will be fine. What time shall I expect you?"

"Oh — around six? That all right?" she said.

"Fine."

"O.K. See you later," said George, walking toward the door.

She gave me a wink. "Get some sleep. You look as if you are going to need a long one."

"Yes. I think I will take a nap."

"Good. You do that," she said. "See you later."

George looked back. "Oh — don't worry about your uniform and your things. She will take good care of them, won't you?"

"Sure thing," Jeanne said. "Night!"

I had been to the Hakone before when I had stayed in Japan briefly on my way back to Korea from Europe; a friend of mine who was then a junior miltary attaché at our embassy in Tokyo had made a reservation for me at one of the mountaintop resort hotels in the Hakone and had come out with me. But we had taken a different road to the Hakone from the one we were now driving on, so that the terrain I saw in the graying mist of the twilight did not seem familiar to me. It did not really matter, because the general feature of the Hakone region was very much the same whichever direction you came from — lovely lush, green mountains and hills, through which meandering mountain roads climbed up higher and higher, those exhilarating mountain roads that went up and up through hairpin curves, under innumerable cliffs, over roaring brooks, quaint bridges and waterfalls, several thousand feet high with a breathtaking view of an infinite expanse of emerald-green mountain ranges in

232 / *The Innocent*

all directions, high above giddy precipices, deep ravines and gorges. The Hakone was what the Diamond Mountain region on the eastern coast of northern Korea was like, though I would have preferred the latter for its far more dramatic flair. An American friend of mine had once said that the Hakone was like the Catskill Mountain region in New York State, but I had never been to the Catskills while I was in the States so that I would never have known their similarities or differences. The Hakone was the place to go in this part of Japan — for the rich, who had their cottages and summer houses there, and the poor who would manage to come for a day on trains and buses — to escape from the hustle and bustle and the stifling heat and humidity of the cities — far, far from the maddening crowd . . . The air was getting cooler as George's blue Porsche roared up the ever-ascending road.

We were now on a mist-shrouded paved road on the summit of a mountain. Soon we were driving downhill on the road that sliced through a dark, silent, brooding forest of tall trees. George slowed the car down and took a sharp right turn, coming out onto a narrow, unpaved, uphill road. A thick, misty dusk had fallen and the sky looked darker than ever with the slowly spreading black rain clouds. He switched on the headlights.

"May I ask where we are going?"

"You'll see in a minute," said Jeanne.

A minute turned into five minutes. There was a bend ahead on the road. George downshifted the car and charged it plunging into the forest on a narrow dirt road just before we reached the bend. The dirt road, a minute later, merged into a graveled driveway which went upward for some twenty yards, then became level.

"Here we are," he said, slowing down the car.

The driveway went straight through a garden of pine trees and flowering shrubs, then turned to the right going by a rock-studded, large pond with a wooden footbridge across it. He stopped the car at the entrance to the footbridge. He pressed the horn twice, then got out of the car.

"Help me put the top up, will you?" he said. "I think it's going to rain, don't you?"

The pond lit up. There were four stone lanterns in the pond, two on each side of the footbridge; a soft, misty light glowed through the panes of frosted glass that shielded the lamps inside the lanterns. Beyond the footbridge, surrounded by soaring, gigantic pine trees with low branches which, spreading like enormous umbrellas, nearly touched the lawn, there was a large two-storied house. Light came on within the house downstairs.

"Someone in there?"

"Yes. I guess that'll do," he said, closing the doors of the car. "Come on. Let's go."

I followed behind them over the footbridge. Her shoes clicked on the wooden boards. She leaped off the bridge at the other end and turned around, facing me. "Welcome to Colonel McKay's mountain hideaway!" she said. "His castle to get away from it all!"

"He owns this?"

"Well, not exactly. He rents it from a Japanese friend of his who is a professor of American literature at Tokyo University and who is in the States right now for a year. Like it?"

"Very nice."

The front of the wooden house was quite modest, I thought, in the style of most Japanese houses, with wooden walls on the outside and a small, narrow front entrance with a sliding door. We approached the door which was open, then I saw in the dim glow of an overhead paper lantern within the door a Japanese woman of about forty, in her native costume of multicolored flowery designs, quietly standing, her head slightly bowed.

Jeanne spoke to her in Japanese. Was the guest room ready?

The woman bowed again, saying that all was ready.

The woman neither spoke nor smiled her welcome. She merely bent her waist and gave me a deep bow. Her black hair was neatly combed and pulled tight at the back of her neck in a small bun. Jeanne said in fast English, "She's marvelous. She lives in during the summer and the fall when we have the house open. She cooks, she shops for us, and she does everything."

"You mentioned the guest room," I said to Jeanne. "Are we staying here overnight?"

"Why not?" George said. "But we don't have to decide on that now. I want you to go ahead and take a bath, then we'll have dinner and a drink. Then we'll see, all right?"

There was a paper screen door just beyond the main door. The maid slid the screen door open, stepped aside, bowing again; she then came on tiptoe, noiselessly, and stood behind us. We took off our shoes, which the maid promptly picked up and disappeared with down the wooden hallway. We went into the house through the open paper screen door. Another wooden hallway of dark, polished teak ran all the way along the U-shaped house. Along the hallway downstairs were matted rooms of Japanese style with paper screen sliding windows which were open. There were six rooms altogether on the first floor, and a paper lantern was on in each room. A balcony ran the length of the hallway upstairs. In the middle of the U-shape was a small pond, or a swimming pool for all I knew, and an open hexagonal, wooden arbor with a bamboo thatched roof sat on a large flat rock in the center of the pond; three wooden boardwalks connected the arbor with the house. In the arbor, the floor was matted and had a low table and cushions, and two candles glowed inside orange-colored frosted-glass cylinders on the table.

"Like it?" said Jeanne.

I nodded. "Very nice."

"Come on," she said, walking down the hallway to the right.

George and I followed her.

At the end of the hallway, she stopped and turned on a light switch on a pillar. Light came on and brightly lit up a graveled path beyond the pond and rows of flower beds. A low stone wall ran from one end of the house to the other; the floodlights were mounted on the stone steps down from the pond to the garden. She said, "You can't see it now, but beyond the stone wall out there is a cliff and you can see miles and miles of deep, green, mountain forests all around. Listen!" She gave out a loud "Hello, there!" The sound came alive in deep, throaty echoes in the dark forest. "See?"

The mountain air was chilly. She was breathing it in deeply, indulging in a luxuriant "Uhuhmm!"

"Come on," said George.

The maid was waiting for us.

"You go and take a bath, all right? I'll, too, and I'll meet you out there," George said, thumbing at the arbor.

I followed the maid down the hallway and went into a large room at the end of it on the left side of the house. The bath was beyond the room through a paper screen door. The maid had already placed towels and a neatly folded, dark blue and white checkered Japanese kimono — a *yukata* — out by the door. She opened the sliding door and bowed to me, then withdrew from the room.

The bathroom was softly lit by two oval-shaped overhead paper lanterns. The large, square tub was sunken in the floor of green and white tiles. The water, steaming, looked green. I went in, flinching at first in the hot water, then giving in to the luxurious warmth and buoyancy of the scented water. Stretching out in the tub, I let my body sink deep up to my chin, then with a slight push of my fingers on the bottom, float up and down. What was I doing here — immersed deeply in the perfumed water, in a Japanese mountain retreat, in Colonel McKay's "castle to get away from it all," in the heart of the Hakone, waited on by a Japanese maidservant, while back in the dark, muddy, slushy, stench-filled battlefront of Korea's rocky, rugged, barren hills my comrades in life and death were desperately diagnosing the grave ills of the crippled nation and her stricken people, dreaming of the salvation of the motherland and her suffering people, irrevocably committing themselves to the new destiny and the new future of the country and her people, and? . . .

A thin shadow crept up on the paper screen of the bathroom door. "How's the water? Having a good bath?" said Jeanne's laughing voice. Her bare feet pitter-pattered away, dragging the thin shadow behind them. She was whistling a tune from an American musical. I remembered the French female voice that had twanged out a chanson in that dreadful tearoom in that primitive town of Chunchun — ". . . my little heart flutters like a little dove . . ." I closed my eyes, sniffing in the fragrant steam of the perfumed water, and, my fingertips feeling the smoothness of the polished tiles of the bottom of the tub, I, with a sigh, abandoned myself to a drowsy, dreamy, soft sensation of my weightless body drowning and floating in the warm, velvety, all-embracing, supple, scented water . . .

After the bath, I joined Jeanne and George in the arbor in the middle of the small pond. The dinner was to be served there. The maid came with a large tray laden with covered lacquered bowls, plates of fried shrimp, vegetables, and sukiyaki; and also cooked rice, soup of red bean paste with diced bean curd, pickled radish and such. It was a fairly typical Japanese dinner. Perhaps I was too tired from the trip — I did not have much appetite.

George poured warm sake into our tiny cups.

Jeanne raised her cup. *"Skoal!"*

George said, also raising his cup, "Here's to your health and success."

I returned the toast.

George poured another round of sake. "Here's to Colonel Min!"

"To Colonel Min!" joined Jeanne.

"To Colonel Min," I said, "and my comrades!"

"To the success of your coup!" said George.

We drained our cups. George started pouring more into them.

"Speaking of your coup," said Jeanne, "you know . . ."

"Yes?" I said.

She looked into her cup which she was balancing on her palm. "Oh, nothing, really. I was just thinking aloud."

"Go ahead," I said.

She looked up at me. "Oh, I was just thinking about you and Colonel Min and your coup," she said. "You know."

"Well?"

"I mean — aren't you worried about it?"

"No."

"You think the coup will be successful," said George.

"Yes."

"There's going to be a lot of shooting and all that," said Jeanne.

"No."

"No! How can you say that so calmly! Of course there's going to be a lot of shooting, which means a lot of people are going to get hurt . . . killed, I mean."

"It will be a bloodless coup," I said firmly. "I assure you."

"Let's hope so," said George, "but is it up to you to say that?"

Jeanne was dishing out the sizzling sukiyaki on our plates.

I said, "As long as there are people like Colonel Min and . . ."

"And like you," said Jeanne.

"Yes. As long as we have voices in our policy-making, it will be and it is our policy, our strong conviction, that our coup will be bloodless. There will be no shooting unless absolutely necessary, I mean, shooting to kill. No! Not that!"

"But that's exactly what I mean," said George. "Is it up to you and Colonel Min and others to lay down that rule? What if the opposition people, your enemies, start fighting back, and you know they will?"

"We will be strong enough to make them realize that it is useless to resist. They will be smart enough to know that when it comes."

"I wouldn't count on that, if I were you," said George.

I said, "You — and your people — are worried about it?"

"Of course we are!" said Jeanne.

"You don't have to worry," I said. "I assure you. The coup will be quick and peaceful and over in a matter of hours. You shall see. I have worked on our plans very hard to make sure of that."

"Well, I sure hope so," said George. "But I won't bet on that, you know, a bloodless coup as you put it. Ah — come on. Let's have the dinner. I am sure you have the coup on your mind too much already."

I nodded. I felt gloomy, suddenly.

She said, "Come on, you all. Don't look so glum. Everything will turn out all right."

Halfway through the dinner, which we ate without much talking, George said, quite abruptly, "I hope you don't mind my saying this, but, you know, although I am a Korean-American and all that, I don't really understand much about the way things are in Korea. For example, do you believe that a military coup d'état will really solve the problems in your country?"

I tried my best to appear unruffled. "Problems in *my* country?"

"Well, you know," he said, with a smile, "is your coup the only way to solve the problems in the country?"

I said, "If *your* country had not been convinced that our coup was the only way to deal with the problems in my country, George, *you* wouldn't be here with me right this moment, if you understand what I mean. In any case, since you posed that question to me, let me tell you something. The intellectuals in a country like yours may not understand our problems. For one thing, in our country the intellectuals and even the liberal intellectuals in the true sense of the term are to be found in the military. When you consider the peculiar nature of the division of the country which caused a mass exodus of the intellectuals and the liberals from the Communist-dominated North to the South, you can understand that better. What I mean is that of those intellectuals and liberals who fled the Communist North — such as Colonel Min, and many others like him — many found themselves in the military, primarily because they perhaps thought, having been persecuted by the brute force of the Communists in the North, that there was no other better way to resist the Communists than by force, in short, by serving in the military; and those intellectuals and university-educated liberals, many of them educated in Japan, had been forced by the Japanese into their military services; consequently, when the country became independent and free, they were the only ones who had had some sort of military background and experience — again, like Colonel Min; and, of course, they were badly needed. Needless to say, there were many others who were simply professional soldiers, whether they had gone to the Japanese military schools and had had actual combat experiences or had been engaged in the military resistance against the Japanese in China and elsewhere. Then came the war, which found many university people, like myself, and the students who joined the military and who later decided to stay on, in the military services. What emerges from this observation is that our military establishment is unlike any other in the world, we think. Certainly not like yours. A quite unique phenomenon is that we have an officer corps which is composed of many officers who are nonprofessional professional soldiers, if you know what I mean."

"Like you and Colonel Min," said George.

"And many others, too." He smiled. I went on. "On the other hand, we have not yet seen the emergence of a new breed of politicians and statesmen, at the same time this totally new national institution, the military, was not only emerging from scratch, organized and staffed and commanded by those people I have just described to you, but also developing, learning, and training the young. The military has been able to send its young officers and men to America and a few European countries to be trained not only in military matters but in the most modern technological and scientific skills and knowledge and, above all, ways and means of dealing with organizational problems, in short, developing managerial talents; but more than that, these young people have returned to the country having been exposed to, if not already in the country while working with the Americans, a new way of life and a new way of thinking, indeed, a wholly new outlook on the world — and, most important of all, they have had an opportunity to view and evaluate objectively the conditions of the country, an invaluable experience which has been unavailable to the young of the nation — injecting a drop of dispassionate, rational objectivity into the bloodstream of their emotional, insular, hypersensitive national consciousness. Meanwhile, the political stage has been dominated by homemade politicians of the old school, of tired blood and of worn-out energy, or by those from abroad whose only credential for being in the government and in politics was that they had been political exiles when the country was under the Japanese. And they had only one thing in sight — power and wealth, an instant wealth, and they have been carrying on nothing but a dog-eat-dog power struggle, assassinating each other, destroying each other, slowly corroding the spirit of the people and squandering the resources of the nation. The government was a plaything, a ball to be kicked around, a feast to gorge themselves on, a gold mine to exploit. Who cared about the people! And there was this intolerable inefficiency, this idiotic, impotent, incompetent administration of day-to-day affairs of the government. You see, George, we lack a trained and experienced class of civil servants and technicians and scientists. But what did those politicians care about that problem? Nothing, nothing whatsoever! And that is not all! We have fought a bloody war against the Communists in the North, and they are still there, guns pointing at us a scant thirty miles from our capital. We have fought the war in the name of liberty and democracy and justice, but what do we have now in the country? Injustice, dictatorship, tyranny, and corruption everywhere. The country could go down the drain, as you would say, if someone did not take a drastic measure to dam up the sweeping tide of stupidity, evil, corruption, injustice, and flunkyism, a blind, subservient, material and spiritual dependence on the American aid. Like a surgeon who must wield his knife to cut open a deadly sore, we had to act. We have waited and waited for someone in the nation to stand up and shout for reforms and revolutions — to sweep out the ancient, the antiquated, the anachronistic, the corrupted. But no one came, do you understand? Do you understand that, George? No one! There was no one with enough strength and courage and conviction to stand up. So we had to act! It was an agonizing, painful task we have assumed for ourselves, but there was no other choice!"

George nodded, saying, "I guess you really had no other choice."

"Yes. We had no other choice," I said firmly, imbuing my voice with all the strength of conviction that I could muster. "Yes. We had no other choice!"

After the dinner, the maid came with a bottle of Courvoisier and three snifters, and cleared the table.

We sipped the cognac in silence for a while. It was quiet in the forest. The night air of the mountains felt hushed and chilly. The sky was black. A cool breeze drifted in over the water of the pond.

"Tell me about your family," said Jeanne, rather halfheartedly, I thought.

"Don't you know about my family already?" I said.

George said quickly, "We don't know much about you or about Colonel Min, as far as your families are concerned, you know. We don't go into that. We know, of course, about your service records, what you have done and where you have been. You know, like you were in Political Intelligence when you were stationed in Pyungyang, and your military attaché assignments in Europe and so on."

"My parents are dead," I said.

"Oh, I am sorry," she said, with a slight frown on her face.

"My folks, as you would say, died during the war, I think."

"You think!" she said.

"I never found their bodies. We lived in Seoul and when I came back to Seoul after the Inchon landing, the house was gone and so were they. Bombs."

"If you never found their bodies," said George.

I shook my head. "The neighbors who had survived told me they were dead. A bomb hit the house directly."

"Oh, how horrible!" Jeanne said.

"It happened to many people," I said. "At least it was a quick death."

"Oh, I am sorry," she said.

"It was a long time ago."

242 / The Innocent

She took my snifter out of my hand and poured the golden liquid in; she swished the cognac in the snifter and handed it to me. "Why didn't you go back to your teaching job after the war?" she said quietly. "I know you told us the reasons why you decided to stay in the Army. But, I guess what I really meant was, don't you ever regret your decision?"

"No."

"Are you sure?"

"Yes. I am quite sure."

"How can you be so sure, though?" said George. "I had a talk with Colonel Min once — this was back in the States some time ago — and he said you were more of a scholarly type than he ever was and you really should be in an academic world rather than in the Army. I think so, too, from what I know about you. You strike me as more of an academic person than a soldier. Let me ask you this. When you are finished with the coup, I mean after it is carried out successfully, would you go back to teaching? Eventually, I mean. I know you will be busy in the government. Running the country and all. But you can't always be a caretaker of your country, you know what I mean? Either you will have to stay in the government for good or let someone else get on with the job of looking after it, I mean, once you accomplish the goals of your coup. And I think once you have the satisfaction of knowing that your country is cleaned up and is on a right track, you would want to do something else."

"Like what?"

"Oh, I don't know. Not back in the Army for sure. Well, like developing your career in an academic field, maybe."

"I have not had the time or the peace of mind to think that far ahead. But I expect that I will be in politics for some time. In any case, this is not the time to think about what I am going to do after the coup, which calls for all the sacrifice and effort from me."

"Oh, but Colonel Min seems to know what he wants to do after the coup."

"We have never discussed it between us."

"Well, he wants to retire to a farm somewhere and be a farmer."
I smiled. "I can't quite imagine him as a farmer, can you?"

"Oh, I can."

"You are not serious?" said Jeanne.

"Oh, I don't really know. But if that's what he wants to do, then that's up to him," said George.

"I don't know what I want to do in the future," I said, "but I know what I wanted to do in the past."

"And what did you want to do?" said Jeanne.

"I was in a university, as you know, teaching. History. There was a time when I thought I would go to the States to study. At places like Princeton, Yale, Harvard, or perhaps at universities in Europe."

"I am sure you would have made a good scholar," she said.

"Perhaps. I was dreaming of becoming a professor someday, a full-fledged professor as you would say, devoting his life to the study of history and the teaching of young minds. I don't deny that I used to dream of the academic, intellectual life of a professor, with his study lined with books and books, his desk always cluttered with his notes and manuscripts. And good music, a companionship with the best, original minds of the country, and a quiet, meditative, tranquil world of academic, philosophical atmosphere. Respected by his colleagues and venerated by his students . . . you know, that sort of thing."

"And a nice family of your own?" she said.

"Yes, why not? Of course!" said George.

"A quiet, loving wife, a gracious hostess who serves sherry when you have your colleagues and students over to your house," she said smiling.

I laughed. "Ah — we would have served corn whisky!"

She laughed. "If you get everyone drunk, how can you have a serious philosophical discussion!"

"So you see," I said. "I wouldn't have made a good professor."

"Oh, I wouldn't be so sure. I think you would make a good professor," she said.

"If not a good farmer!" said George, laughing.

The bamboo roof crackled just then. Big drops of rain showered down as a chilly wind blew in from the dark forests below.

"Brr!" Jeanne said, her arms crossed, hugging her shoulders. "Come on. Let's go ashore before we get drenched and drowned out here. Naomi-san!"

The maid appeared in the hallway.

The rain came down hard, rippling the water in the pond.

"Come on," said George, "let's make a dash." He blew the candles out.

She stepped a foot out onto the boardwalk, saying, "Don't you push me, George!" She did not run. She edged on slowly and she was drenched instantly. She stopped in the middle of the boardwalk, letting the rain soak her, raising her arms, balancing herself on the walk. Her kimono clung to her, making her look thin and tall. For a moment, I had an absurd impression that she looked like a Japanese version of the Statue of Liberty . . . the image of General Ahn as I saw him last flashed before my eyes just as a blinding flash of lightning lit up, for a split second, the house, the pond, and the black sky. A rolling thunder drummed in the distance.

She ran and leaped into the house. The maid had come out with towels for us. Jeanne took a towel from the maid and, drying her hair with it, disappeared down the hallway.

I stood immobile in the dark arbor as though the lightning and the thunder and the cold, heavy rain had petrified me. I felt dizzy and a little unsteady. I sat down, shivering. My head and face were hot and burning. I felt wobbly. I heard myself muttering something unintelligible even to me. What was I doing here in the dark?

"Are you all right?" said George, bending down toward me.

The rain came pouring down, splashing and clapping on the water and the boardwalks.

"Do you feel all right?" he said.

It was as though I had been stricken by the freezing wind from the dark, black, deep forests.

"I am all right," I said.

"Are you sure? Something wrong?"

"Tell me," I said. "What am I doing here?"

He did not reply.

"What am I really doing here — here in Japan, in the Hakone, in Colonel McKay's hideaway, his castle to get away from it all, with you and her? What am I doing here?"

He was quiet for a while. "That's not what's really bothering you, is it?" he said. He sat down next to me at the table.

I smelled the pungent odor of the smoke from the candles. "No," I confessed. "No, you are right."

"You don't have to tell me, you know," he said. "You don't have to, you know, because I think I know."

"What do you know?"

"Last night. General Ahn. You almost killed him," he said. "But you couldn't kill him, could you?"

In the shadowy darkness, I shook my head. "No."

He said, "No."

I stared at his dark face. "If it hadn't been for Colonel Min, I would have killed him."

"No, you wouldn't have. You couldn't bring yourself to kill him."

I kept silent.

"Come on, Major," he said. "Let's go back into the house."

I stood up. I felt a little sick.

Without a word, he led me across the boardwalk into the house. We were drenched in the rain.

"Are we going to stay here tonight?" I said.

"Unless you want to go back to Tokyo."

I shook my head. "No."

"All right, then. Come on. I'll take you to your room."

My room was upstairs at the end of the left-hand balcony. It was a

Japanese-style room, with a matted floor and paper screen windows. The maid had already rolled out the bedding.

"Don't think about the generals and the colonels and all those big problems. Not tonight. You'll have a good night's sleep and when you wake up tomorrow morning you'll feel all rested and ready to tackle the big problems and everything will go all right." He said good-night and left me alone.

I changed into a silk kimono the maid had left on the bedroll which was spread out on the floor. The deep purple silk of the kimono felt smooth and cool on my skin. I opened the paper screen door and stepped out onto the balcony. I stood there alone for a while, breathing in the chilly air, listening to the rain, staring hard into the black forests and the mountains below. Holding on to the rail of the balcony, looking out over the dark, waving top of the deep forests, I felt, for a moment, as though I were on a ship drifting in an undulating, dark ocean. I withdrew to the room and crept into the bed, but I could not sleep.

I was still awake when, a little after two in the morning, I heard the faint ringing of a telephone somewhere down the hallway. It was raining. I had been listening to the dreary pitter-pattering of the cold rain falling on the roof and the water in the pond. The ringing stopped. The dim light in the hallway which had not been turned off filtered into the room through the paper screen sliding door, creeping up on the matted floor to the bottom of my bedroll. It was quiet once again, except for the stirrings and rustlings of the paper screen door that opened to the balcony when a whip of chilly breeze rushed up from the forest. I strained my ears but I could not hear any sound. I wanted to sleep and hoped the dull pitter-pattering of the rain would lull me asleep. But I was wide awake.

I heard a slow creak, then a tiny, metallic click of a doorknob, and a squeak. I raised myself on my side on an elbow and listened. I heard footsteps slithering down the hallway toward my room. They stopped, and started again, coming closer, more slowly and quietly.

Then I saw a shadow creeping into the frame of the paper screen door. It was George. His shadow now stood full, thin and long.

His voice whispered, "Are you awake?"

I held my breath.

As in a shadow pantomime, his hand and arm silently slid out of the sleeve of his kimono and touched the door. The door inched open. A shaft of hazy light slanted into the room. Noiselessly, I lay flat on my back in the bed, swallowing my breath, my half-open eyes watching his shadowy figure slip into the room. He took a few steps toward me on tiptoe. I could hear the creaking of the mat under his weight. I lay immobile. He came now at the foot of my bed, standing still, the silhouette of his body blurred against the dim light in the hallway.

I felt him bending down. "Are you sleeping?"

I did not stir.

I heard him sigh, then shift his body on the mat. He slowly backed away toward the door, where he paused for a second before he squeezed his body out into the hallway. Then I saw another shadow appearing outside the door. It was Jeanne. He quietly slid the door shut. She whispered, "Sound asleep?" He whispered back, "Like a log." She said, "It can wait. Let him sleep." "Sure," he said. Their footsteps were quick and loud as they went away from my room.

The rain was still pitter-pattering. I turned over in the bed and felt a sudden, irresistible onrush of sweet drowsiness. In minutes, I was falling asleep, dreamily listening to the hypnotic, soft, pitter-pattering of the gentle rain. I slept soundly. Now — there was nothing else I could do.

Chapter 15

The next morning, after I came out of the bath, the maid showed me into what she called the western room. There was no one in the room. The maid left me there alone, saying that George-san would join me shortly and that she would bring our breakfast to the room. I asked her about Jeanne. "She left for Tokyo early this morning," she said, bowing out of the room.

The western room was the study of the owner of the house, the Japanese professor who was away in America. There was a big, dark brown mahogany desk with neat piles of notebooks, literary journals both in Japanese and in English, a desk calendar, a Leatherette box with pencils and pens, a letter tray with a Harvard emblem. A black straight-back chair with a golden Harvard emblem sat between the side drawers of the desk. A gray steel filing cabinet stood next to the desk, behind which, flanking the desk, stood large, tall, glass-encased bookcases against the knotted pine-paneled walls. Between the bookcases, a bulky, open dictionary lay on a bookstand beside a steel typing table with an old portable Smith-Corona. A large oil painting of a landscape hung above the mantelpiece. Two deep red leather armchairs faced the fireplace. There were more books, in English, lined on the mantelpieces, held by mahogany bookends with brass emblems of Harvard. A round table between the chairs had a small reading lamp and was piled with literary quarterlies in English.

There was a fire going in the red brick fireplace. With my back to the fire, I looked out the French windows. It had not stopped raining. The thin, slanting rain quietly came down from the dark gray sky. The forests and the mountains down below the cliff were misty and silent in the rain. The door opened and George came in. "Good morning, Major Lee."

"Good morning," I said. "The maid told me Jeanne has gone to Tokyo early this morning."

He came over to the fireplace and stood beside me. He nodded. "Yes, she has. She may be back here this afternoon."

"Do you mean to tell me that we are going to be here till then? Aren't we going back to Tokyo? You said yesterday that someone would see me this afternoon."

"Yes. Someone will see you this afternoon," he said. "Here."

"Here?"

"Yes," he said, bending down to stoke the fire with an iron poker. He stood up.

The maid came in with a tray laden with a bottle and two glasses. She put the bottle and the glasses on a small table between the two armchairs. It was a champagne bottle.

George thanked the maid, who withdrew from the room without a word.

He opened the champagne bottle, which gave out a muffled pop, and filled the glasses with the bubbling liquid. He handed me one.

I took the glass silently, watching him raise his glass.

He said, "Last night, this morning rather, there was a coup d'état in your country."

I managed to say, "When!"

"Two o'clock this morning. We had a call from our Tokyo office last night and I was going to tell you about it but you were sleeping so soundly I didn't want to wake you up. Besides, it could wait."

He was gazing out toward the forests. "We had another call this morning around six o'clock and that's why Jeanne had to leave. They wanted her down in Tokyo."

"Is Colonel Min all right?"

"He is in Seoul."

"Where in Seoul! It is important!"

"He's taken over the Army GHQ. Don't worry about him. He is in full charge."

"Yes. I am sure."

"The coup is over," he said, looking at me closely. "It is a complete success as far as we know. Are you glad?"

I nodded. I felt a little weak. "Of course!"

He said, "Congratulations."

I felt neither elated nor remorseful.

He raised his glass again. "Let's toast!" he said cheerfully. "What shall we toast?"

I raised my glass. "To the success of the coup!"

"To you and Colonel Min and everyone!"

"To the new destiny and the future of Korea!"

"Hear, hear!" he said, laughing, pouring more champagne into my glass.

I stared out the window, and saw the hazy, foggy silhouette of the deep, dark forests and the mountains. Everything went blurred and misty. Suddenly, I felt alone and lonely . . . and I found myself laughing. "Come on!" I was saying to him. "Let's celebrate!"

"Well, what do you think we are doing? We are celebrating!"

I drained my glass in one, big swallow.

He quickly filled my glass with more champagne.

The chilled drink tingled my throat.

"Well, now that the coup is over and done with," he was saying, "what will you be doing? Will you be in charge of the foreign ministry?"

"I don't think any one of us will be in charge of anything exclusively. There will be a revolutionary council, which will oversee the operations of all the government ministries and agencies."

"Of course," he said, sitting down in an armchair. "It must be quite exciting for you."

I did not respond.

"You know," he said, shaking his head, "running a country . . . I wouldn't know where to begin or how. How do you feel about it, now that your coup is successfully carried out?"

I said, "Our plan calls for the participation in the council of the chiefs of all the branches of the services. It will also include key commanders of both frontline and rear commands. Of course, the nucleus of the council will be composed of those members of our Command Group and the delegates from the subcommand groups composed of the representatives of the other branches, you know, the Navy, the Air Force, and the Marines. That was the original plan, anyway. And, after a due course of time, the council will recruit and incorporate civilian representatives of our choice."

He listened to me quietly, without stirring.

"Well, all this is still in the planning stage. It will all depend on the final outcome of the coup."

"When you left Korea," he said, "did you know that Colonel Min would launch the coup last night?"

I drained my glass. "Didn't you know?" I smiled at him.

He shook his head slowly. "No. We didn't know the precise date and the time of the launching. Oh, we knew it would come soon. Colonel Min would never divulge that part of the plan. You knew *that!*"

"Of course."

"He sure pulled a fast one on us. It was a surprise."

"You do understand that we couldn't take a chance, don't you?"

"You mean — Colonel McKay might have betrayed you? How can you say that?"

"One never knows. I do not mean to insult you or Colonel McKay, but, surely, you understand that anything could have happened."

"Sure. Anything could have happened and — anything still can happen."

"What do you mean?"

"Well, for example, the final outcome of the coup is by no means certain. I mean — the coup's success has not been really guaranteed. You know that."

I nodded.

"Tell me," he said. "You didn't really know that Colonel Min would launch the coup?"

"I never said that I didn't know that."

"Did you know?"

"What do you think?"

"I don't think anything. I want you to tell me."

I did not know what to tell him. I took my time. "I knew."

I thought he glowered at me. "And you still came here."

"It was my duty. I obeyed Colonel Min's instructions."

"So did I," he said.

I frowned. "What?"

He shook his head. "What I meant was — I did what Colonel Min and Colonel McKay told me to do."

"And may I ask what was it that they wanted you to do?"

"Nothing really. Nothing of importance."

"Perhaps it may be of importance to me?"

He looked at me. "It doesn't matter now, does it?"

I sipped on the champagne for a moment. "Perhaps it does not matter any more as you said. You did know that Colonel Min would launch the coup last night, didn't you?"

He took his time. He nodded. "We did."

"Good."

He said, "You didn't, did you?"

I did not reply.

"Listen," he said. His voice was impatient and insistent. "Between us, I mean, between you and me and Colonel Min . . ."

I cut in, "And your Colonel McKay?"

"All right. Between us, then, it doesn't matter any more, does it? I mean — who knew what when, you know what I mean?"

"Perhaps."

"We knew the coup would be launched last night," he said, "while you were here."

I kept silent.

"Did you know that?"

I shook my head.

"No, you didn't know that. And I'll tell you a truth. Neither did we, until the last moment. Would you believe me?"

"Colonel Min did not tell Colonel McKay?"

"Not until the last minute. After you left Korea. Do you understand that?"

I said, "No."

"When Colonel McKay got in touch with us here and told us that you were coming, we assumed, at first, that the coup wouldn't be launched immediately, I mean, at least not until you finished your mission here and returned to Colonel Min. Understand?"

I nodded.

"You did have a mission, you know."

I stared at him. "And now I don't have a mission?"

"Your mission has been accomplished, Major Lee," he said. "Now we both know what your mission was."

I pretended not to have grasped his words. "And what was my mission?"

"To keep us in your company!"

"To keep me in your company, rather," I said. "Yes, it has been a delightful mission."

"Why are you bitter about it?"

"I am not bitter. Did I sound bitter?"

"You certainly did. Listen! Your coming here, yourself not knowing that Colonel Min would launch the coup in your absence, completely fooled us, until the last minute. *That* was your mission, do you understand that? And you carried out your mission marvelously."

I did not reply.

"And, as far as I am concerned . . ." He peered up into my face. "Oh, come on! Don't look glum. Don't sulk! Listen! Would you please listen?"

"Yes. I am listening."

He was smiling. "As far as I am concerned, I didn't and I don't give a damn what your mission was, do you understand me? And I am glad *you* didn't know about the timing of the coup, because . . ."

"Yes?"

"Because, you know, you weren't deliberately fooling us. How could you have? You didn't know it yourself."

"Were you supposed to have found it out from me?"

He pursed his lips, his eyes giving me a wink. "Ah-ha."

"I see."

"What do you mean — I see?"

"You were to spy on me, weren't you?"

"That is not true!" he laughed.

"Isn't it?" I shouted.

"Oh! How can I make you understand? Listen to me now, Major. It is this way. When we met you at the air base, yes, that was what we were going to do. But, what difference does it make? Colonel McKay's people weren't going to change their mind about your coup or anything like that. All they wanted was to be prepared."

"To be prepared for what?"

"So they could quietly pass the word around to the units not to interfere with your coup. What did you think? They would have gone to your President and spilled everything? Your Excellency, we have been secretly aiding a group of idealistic, patriotic, conscientious officers who are planning a coup against you, but, your Highness, we've changed our mind about them, so your Majesty may roll out your goons and crush them before they crush you, hee, hee! Good heavens!"

I could not help laughing. I sat down in an armchair next to him.

"Well, Colonel Min didn't trust us enough," he said.

"You can't really blame him, can you?" I said.

"And you can't really blame him for not having let you in on his plan, can you?"

I closed my eyes for a moment. "He told me to get a good rest while I am here."

"That has been our mission! And I am thoroughly enjoying it. I hope you are, aren't you?"

We laughed. We had more champagne.

"Seriously now," he said, stretching out in the chair. "Don't you want to know how the coup is going?"

I stood up from the chair and went to the fireplace. I stirred up the fire with an iron poker. "I've been waiting for you to give me the briefing."

I felt his eyes boring into my back. I turned around. "After all, here I am without my own sources of intelligence, so that I'll have to rely on yours entirely. How is the coup going?"

"Badly," he snapped.

"I don't believe it!"

"Oh, I didn't mean to sound pessimistic."

"It is a success, isn't it?"

"Oh, it is! What I meant was — "

"Yes?"

"It's a bloody mess. I am sorry."

I kept silent.

"You expected that, didn't you?" he said. "I know you said it would be a bloodless coup, but surely, you didn't expect it would turn out all neat and clean, did you?"

I could not lie. "Yes."

"I knew that."

"How bad is it?"

"It isn't all that bad as I might have sounded, really."

"Any shooting?"

"Lots of shooting."

"Any casualties?"

"Lots."

"On both sides?"

"Yes, of course!"

"I see."

He stood and drew up to me. "How can you be so calm about it! I've been dying to tell you and you weren't asking me and I didn't want to gab about it. I don't understand you! You seemed so worried that the coup might be bloody and you were bravely insisting that it would be bloodless and so on, and now you seem not to really care! I mean, it's as if you knew and expected it would be bloody with lots of shooting and people getting killed and you don't seem to think it could have been otherwise."

"In any case, no matter what you think is my attitude, I couldn't have done anything to change what happened. How could I have? I was here! I assure you that if I had been there when the coup was launched, I would have done my best to avoid bloodshed. Do you understand me? Do you believe me? I have consistently opposed those members of the Command Group, including Colonel Min, who advocated violence, who insisted on violent means to achieve the success of our coup. I am the minority in the Group, believe me; I didn't get too far with the majority. And that's why I have worked so hard on the details of our plans. I wanted to make sure every single detail of our operations plans would be perfect and I made sure to the best of my ability and knowledge. The plan I worked on, concerning our operations, the final stage of them, in Seoul, was perfect. It couldn't go wrong. I wanted to see that our operations and movements in Seoul, that is, when we were to move into and take Seoul, would work like clockwork, perfect, so perfect that the other side wouldn't even have a chance to counter us with any kind of organized resistance. Do you understand me? The plans for our operations in Seoul, which I was responsible for, could not have been better conceived insofar as my desire to avoid bloodshed was concerned. I don't mind telling you, George, that the plans were absolutely perfect! I had every corner of every building in

Seoul which we were to occupy surveyed and sketched and memorized by those who would move in and carry out their parts in the operation. My aim was to have our movement go so swiftly that we wouldn't even have to fire a single shot."

"I know you are a brilliant tactician; everybody knows that. Colonel McKay is almost awed by your skills and brains. I mean it! He told me once how you were at the top of your class at the Command and General Staff College, in spite of your having to compete with the American officers and the other foreign officers. I know. Colonel McKay said you are absolutely a genius when it comes to organizing and drawing up operations plans and figuring out tactical problems. The best brain in the ROK Army, that's what he used to say. So I know your plans were perfect. But something can always go wrong, you know, and something did go wrong. There was a mutiny."

"A mutiny? Against which side?"

"Your side. Just when the troops on your side were coming into Seoul, you know, to join with those units already in Seoul, there was a desertion of a sort. A mutiny, I would say. A battalion of Paratroopers . . ."

I said, "Colonel Hwang!"

"I don't know who he is. Anyway, a battalion of Paratroopers defected from your side and put up a fight. And that, of course, gave time for the other side to get organized. Is it Colonel Hwang who could have led the Paratroopers?"

"Lieutenant Colonel Hwang. The Airborne Brigade. He was in charge of my operations while I was out of Seoul."

"So there was bloody street fighting. For a couple of hours. Colonel Min's Marines and the units from the Presidential Brigade had to storm the Army GHQ and the Metropolitan Police Headquarters."

"The Presidential residence?"

"That was taken easily. The President is still in there under guard."

"What else?"

"We don't know too much yet. The Prime Minister was shot and a few other cabinet members, I don't know who."

"Did they put up a fight?"

"I wouldn't know the details. Everything seems to have gotten out of hand. Oh, the Army Chief of Staff is dead, too, among several other generals at the GHQ."

"Any casualties on our side?"

"There must be, because the fighting lasted until about eight this morning. Seoul is now taken and Colonel Min is in complete control of the situation. He's already issued the proclamation, which has been broadcast, and also announced the formation of the Revolutionary Council and martial law throughout the country. Of course, it was all done in your general's name, you know what I mean?"

I nodded.

"As far as the world is concerned, no one knows about Colonel Min's real position."

"What about the Paratroopers?"

"They have been crushed. I think this colonel has been arrested. Will he be shot?"

I did not reply.

"It's a bloody mess."

I straightened up. "George, you must make an arrangement immediately for my transportation. I must fly back home as soon as it is possible for you to get me a plane."

Without a word, he shook his head.

"What do you mean by that!" I went up to him. "I must go back immediately. Colonel Min needs me in Seoul! I must be there to stop any more of this bloody mess! Do you understand!"

"You are not going back," he said quietly.

"What?"

"I said you are *not* going back now. At least not for a while. At least not until we get a word to let you go back."

"What is this! You get a word from whom!"

"Oh, listen! I hate to do this to you, believe me! But I can't let you go now! The coup isn't over yet, really, and anything can happen! Don't you understand? I am to keep you here until everything is more certain and settled."

"Who gave you that order! Who is giving you that order!"

"Colonel Min," he said, abruptly turning away from me. "And Colonel McKay, too."

"Why!" I tried my best to shout as though in suppressed fury. "Am I a prisoner here! I happen to be a member of the Command Group! And of the Revolutionary Council! I am the one who planned the final stage of our operations. And what am I doing here at a time like this! What do you mean by saying that Colonel Min wants you to keep me here!"

He faced me. "He doesn't want you to come home! Not now anyway. There may still be a lot of shooting, you know, and anything can happen. And he doesn't want you to come home right now."

"Why? Why!"

"I don't know. How would I ever know what makes him tick? Colonel McKay is doing what Colonel Min wants him to do, that's all. So we are going to keep you here and *I* want you to be here now."

"What does Colonel Min want to do with me! What is this! Is he trying to keep me out of the country!"

"Oh, I am sure it's nothing like that! How can you say such a thing! He is your best friend!"

"What is he trying to do with me? Keep me away so that they could go ahead and turn everything into a bloody mess! The Prime Minister, the cabinet ministers, and the Chief of Staff — they didn't have to be shot!"

"How can we know that? I wasn't there and you weren't there either!"

"They didn't have to be shot and that's that! There was to be no killing, you understand!"

"I told you. Everything seemed to have gone haywire and you can't ever predict that everything, your perfect plan, would go like clockwork. Anything could have gone wrong."

"He knew I would oppose it!"

"Oppose what?"

"Shooting! Turning the country into a bloody civil war! That was not part of our plan, at least, not my plan!"

"No one is going to have a civil war on his hands."

"What is he trying to do with me? I know! He and the others didn't want me around because they knew I would oppose their policy. I opposed killing General Mah, too."

"Well, you didn't kill him!"

"Or is he trying to drop me from the Group?"

He flared up. He looked furious and his voice was sharp. "You are being very silly, Major! You know him better than that! Even I know him better than that! Listen! Doesn't this possibility ever occur to you, that he might have wanted to send you away here because he wanted to protect you?"

"Protect me from what!"

"Maybe he knew there would be a bloody shooting and he couldn't afford losing you, you know what I mean. Anything could happen. You could get killed. Someone died, one of the Command Group."

"Who?"

"I don't know."

"Colonel Park?"

"I said I don't know. Anyway, do you see what I mean? You could have gotten killed. It could have happened. He couldn't risk that chance. He needs you. He would need you more than ever after the coup. You are his brains. You are needed to work on the plans and organizations, you know, the actual business of looking after the administration of policies and so on. So, maybe, he wanted to keep you safe here. Look! Suppose the coup failed? Then what! Somebody has to carry on the work somewhere, somehow; and maybe he had that already on his mind. If anything went wrong, you could still be here and carry on his work. Don't you see that? And if all went well as it seems it will as of now, then you can come back and take it over from there. Oh, I don't know what's what, really. How would I ever know what's ticking in his brains? Anyway, *I* am glad you are here right now, because not only Colonel Min and your friends but the country is going to need people like you once the coup is over and done with. And *I* am glad I am playing a small part in making sure that a treasure like you is well protected!" He smiled, "For the sake of my ancestor's motherland!"

"A treasure like me!" I burst out. "A priceless museum piece! A precious antique!"

The maid came in with our breakfast.

I shut up.

Although George had said that Jeanne would be back in the afternoon, she did not return from Tokyo. I had tried to persuade him to drive us back to Tokyo, but he had insisted that someone would come out from Tokyo to see me, though he would not tell me who I was to meet. The thin, misty rain of the morning had turned into a torrential downpour shortly after one o'clock in the afternoon. A little after three o'clock, George left the house, saying that he would drive down to a resort hotel nearby to see if he could get hold of newspapers, which he thought might have something to report on the coup d'état.

He came back within half an hour, drenched from top to bottom. He brought back a Japanese newspaper, which had come out as an extra edition by two o'clock. The extra edition was devoted entirely to the coup in Korea, with interviews of both Japanese politicians and Korean residents supplementing a long report by a Japanese correspondent stationed in Seoul. The report was accompanied by two photographs.

One Wirephoto was a blurry picture of a column of Patton tanks lined along the wide avenue leading to the Central Governmental

Building. I could vaguely make out machine-gun emplacements here and there manned by the Marines. Another photo, apparently taken with a telephoto-lensed camera, showed two Sherman tanks firing at a building which I recognized as the headquarters of the Metropolitan Police; the heavy machine guns on the tanks' turrets were also firing, and troopers with automatic rifles were crouching behind the tanks. It had rained there. The troopers were wearing ponchos.

A lightning, predawn military coup that began at two o'clock this morning toppled the Korean regime following savage street fighting that lasted for more than three hours. The casualty figure is estimated to be high, running into the hundreds on both sides. The fierce fighting between the rebel troops and the loyal government troops appears to have been most intense in and out of the Army GHQ, the Metropolitan Police Headquarters, and the Presidential residence; less intense fighting also raged near the National Assembly Building and City Hall as well as at the crucial Han River bridge. The government forces fought against the rebel attack in an ill-organized and poorly coordinated resistance offered by the Presidential Security units, several units of the Presidential Brigade and two battalions of Paratroopers, in addition to the National Police. There was no question that the rebel forces overpowered the government forces not only by the number of troops they had thrown into Seoul but also by superior firepower and armor. As of this moment, there is little organized resistance from the government troops except for sporadic sniper actions; the Paratroopers were the last ones to be routed and taken prisoners by the victorious rebel forces. The Prime Minister, several cabinet members including the Defense Minister, and the Army Chief of Staff as well as the Joint Chief of Staff are believed to be among those high-ranking government officials who were killed in the bloody struggle for power. The photos above show the American-made Sherman and Patton tanks of the elite Presidential Brigade, the bulk of which sided with the rebel forces and spearheaded the early-morning attack. Two regiments of the 1st Korean Marine Brigade stormed across the Han River bridge into Seoul, while a regiment of the 17th Infantry Division and another regiment of the 5th Infantry Division swooped down to the capital from the western front along the DMZ line near Panmunjom. The main forces of two divisions are believed to have taken up positions on the western outskirts of Seoul in an apparent effort to defend the capital in the event of any possible countercoup attacks from frontline combat units. A regiment of the Army's 22nd Infantry Division on the east-central front has been airlifted into the eastern outskirts of Seoul. The Armored and Mechanized Units of the Presidential Brigade and the units of the Army Commandos occupied major governmental offices, communications centers, radio and television stations, supported by at least five artillery and anti-aircraft battalions the rebels had brought into Seoul. The fighting in the capital was savage. Tanks and armored cars rumbled down the streets and avenues of Seoul at full speed, cannonading and machine-gunning buildings held by the loyal troops. Machine-gun fire clattered throughout the rain-drenched city suddenly plunged into a bloody coup and countercoup battle. Rocket launchers and recoilless rifles and even flame throwers were used by both sides. The rebel Commando units stormed into the Presidential residence, battling against the desperate resistance of the heavily barricaded Presidential Security troops which were crushed by the rebel tanks and artillery which at times had to fire at point-blank range. The fighting is also reported to have been fierce at the Army GHQ. It was surrounded by two battalions of the rebel artillery and a company of the Marine tanks supporting the rebel infantry units from the 17th and the 5th Divisions. The Army GHQ had been taken over by the rebel forces' Command Group, which is directing the operations from the headquarters a short distance from the compound of the U.S. Command. At times, there was a fear of possible air attack by the rebel forces' jet fighters which have been constantly in the air since early morning, but so far there has been no sign that the American-made Super-Sabers have been used against the government forces. The coup had been carefully and painstakingly planned, with a widespread support from the various branches of the services; it is now confirmed that the Air Force units had successfully airlifted a full combat regiment from the south to Suwon air base, in addition to the one already airlifted from the east central front. Although the details of the coup are still uncertain, it is believed that the majority of the armed forces are in full support of the coup and that factor seems to have contributed to a swift and apparently bloodless seizure by the rebel forces of most of the major cities in the country. There is a general calm among the population, though there have been reports that spontaneous demonstrations supporting the coup have been staged in several cities. The nation appears to welcome the coup, though there is clear evidence that at least the sophisticated citizenry of Seoul with their traditional cynicism and customary skepticism seem to show an attitude of wait and see. A Korean hotel clerk this reporter talked to had only this to say: "Those who want to run the country are all alike." A middle-aged Korean businessman said, "I always thought the ousted regime was the worst in the world, so how can anything new be worse than that!" There seems to be a consensus of opinion here that a coup had to come sooner or later. A suave Korean gentleman who recognized this reporter as a foreign correspondent of this paper stopped me in the hotel lobby and said, "You Japanese ought to know what it is like to live under a totalitarian dictatorship, what with your emperor and the fascist military in the old days. The coup d'état was expected by everyone who had any insight into the nature of the power structure of the crushed regime. I am not surprised. I only hope those who led the coup won't turn out to be as corrupt and evil as those they are replacing now." The coup leadership is believed to be composed of young, frontline officers, generally pro-Western and pro-American, all trained and educated in the West. A Korean reporter has remarked, "These officers represent a new breed of Korean officers in the military," emphasizing that it was time for most of the generals in the armed forces to be retired or fired outright. The precise composition of the coup leadership is not yet known and there is clear evidence that the planners of the coup — the prime movers as another Korean reporter put it — are scrupulously guarding the identities of the top planners, who apparently command the real power behind the coup. A martial law was proclaimed by the rebel forces' Revolutionary Council, which also suspended the Constitution. A policy statement believed to be upholding this nation's traditionally staunch anti-Communist stand and friendly relations with the U.S. and the nations of the Free World is expected to be issued soon. However, the U.S. officials and the U.S. commanders here have been silent on the coup, though they have scrupulously maintained a position of neutrality, which is interpreted here by well-informed Koreans as a tacit U.S. endorsement of the coup. It has been commonly known here for some time that the U.S., which has poured in billions of dollars of aid, both military and economic, in the past, has not held the ousted regime in high regard. The coup is believed to be a colonels' revolt, although the formal leadership of the coup is said to be composed of a small group of relatively unknown general officers headed by Lieutenant General S. K. Hyun, the commanding general of the frontline 7th Army Corps. There is an unconfirmed report that certain high-ranking frontline commanders have not yet made their positions publicly known, and, so far, no word has been heard from Lieutenant General C. M. Ham, the commanding general of the powerful 4th Field Army with headquarters in the central front, commanding nearly a quarter of a million troops. Tension and ambiguity are felt here in the capital as to who among the better known and powerful field commanders and the rear-echelon commanders are in support of the coup and who have not yet come out one way or the other. Seoul has become an armed camp, ringed by rebel troops of nearly three full divisions and barricaded by the Armored and Mechanized Units of the elite Presidential Brigade and the units of the tough, U.S.-style Korean Marines in full battle gear. Tanks and armored cars are ceaselessly patrolling the streets accompanied by detachments of rebel soldiers with bayoneted rifles and automatic weapons. Machine-gun emplacements are at every corner of the streets and on rooftops, and several artillery battalions have been deployed throughout the city, especially on the Nam San — the South Hill — within the city's residential area — thus commanding all the major approaches to the capital. As of now, the rebel forces are in complete control of the capital and the major cities, and the declarations of support have been pouring in from the local commanders in the south, the rear. Yet, it is unmistakably clear that, in spite of the initial success and the support it has gained from the majority of the armed forces and the population, the coup leadership is preparing for a major showdown with the frontline commanders in case any of the more ambitious and politically motivated generals decide to launch a countercoup. The Military Police, which has now gone over to the rebels, is patrolling the city and maintaining order in place of the National Police, which was swiftly subdued by the combat-experienced and hardened veterans of the Korean War. All international flights in and out of Korea have been canceled, except for those of the U.N. Command. Steel-helmeted and fully armed rebel soldiers are seen everywhere as they man communications centers, radio and television stations, newspaper offices, power plants, and all government office buildings. Schools have been closed until further notice. There is an as yet unconfirmed report that several hundred — possibly a few thousand throughout the nation — political leaders, National Assemblymen and the officials of the ousted regime, as well as those belonging to Korea's innumerable political factions and splinter parties, have been arrested and taken to detention camps. A Korean career diplomat in Seoul, home from his European post, remarked that the coup did not seem to be aimed exclusively against the ousted regime: "The coup seems to be politically neutral," he said calmly as tanks were cannonading the nearby National Assembly Building. "It appears to have been launched not so much as a bid for political power as a moral movement to clean up the nation's soul. Their impartial arrest of all the corrupt politicians both of the old regime and of its opposition parties seems to bear out my sentiment." This reporter asked him if he feared a possible establishment of a totalitarian regime headed by the military. "I know the people who had planned and who are now involved in the coup. There is not the slightest chance of their establishing a totalitarian regime after this. You may rest assured that there will be a new era of democracy in this country from this point on in our political life, although there will be a period of adjustment and transition which I am sure the foreign presses, both of the Free World and of the Communist Camp, will brand as harsh and dictatorial." This reporter pressed him for the identities of the "prime movers" of the coup, only to be met with his enigmatic smile. The fate of the ousted President is uncertain as he is now reported to be under guard in the rebel forces' custody in the Presidential residence. Although the coup was bloody, most foreign observers here seem to agree that the plan for occupying the capital was a model of military precision and a marvel of brilliant tactics and foresight. Every major building, every room in those buildings, every strategic and tactical position, every key area throughout the capital seemed to have been surveyed and covered in the coup plan with a meticulous care and astounding precision. The rebel troops' movement and deployment in the capital had been planned and executed with such a brilliant clockwork efficiency and swiftness that an American correspondent here was led to remark, albeit begrudgingly, that whoever had planned the rebels' operations in Seoul must have been highly sophisticated and efficient staff officers thoroughly familiar with the counterinsurgency tactics as they are being developed in the U.S. "I've seen coups in Latin America and in the Middle East, but I have never seen anything like this. This tops them all in conception and execution." Whoever the planners may be, there is no doubt that the plan of operations had been conceived down to every minute detail. Had it not been for the apparently unexpected and fierce resistance of the Paratroopers, the coup might have been a bloodless one. There is a speculation here that the Airborne Brigade had not been known to be particularly pro-government in the recent past; now stationed outside Seoul, it had been scheduled to be moved to somewhere in the east by the ousted regime. Therefore, the unexpected support of the government by the units of the Paratroopers seems to have aroused a considerable amount of curiosity and bewilderment among the knowledgeable Koreans here. In connection with this is a hitherto unconfirmed rumor that General Mah, the wily and dreaded chief of the Secret Police, has been missing since immediately prior to the launching of the coup. Any chance of General Mah being one of the planners of the coup is dismissed by nearly all Koreans as being fantastic and unthinkable. Only a short time before his mysterious disappearance from Seoul, he had barely escaped a bloody assassination attempt on his life. There seems to be a certain amount of mystery concerning the fates of several general officers, such as that of the commander of the Army Commandos which participated in the coup, Brigadier General Y. U. Ahn, who is not reported to have been seen in Seoul directing the Commandos' operation. In any case, as the situation now stands here in the turbulent capital of this troubled nation, the coup d'état is now a *fait accompli,* and for better or

worse the nation now has a new regime, though its immediate survival may depend on its ability to rally and secure the support and
loyalty of key field commanders, some of whom are reported to be
conferring with their American advisers. An urgent and frightening
issue before the nation shrouded with uncertainty and fear is whether
the country at large, both the civilian and the military elements of
the society, will come to accept the new order imposed on it by the
leaders of this coup d'état or whether it will be plunged into a tragic,
bloody, civil war. As this reporter watches the nation's capital from
the rooftop of the Bando Hotel in the heart of the city, cannon fires
and machine-gun fires are still echoing in the rain-drenched streets
and the alleys; smoke is rising here and there and the Super-Sabers
are making sporadic low passes over the roofs of this historic Oriental
city, where the ancient and the modern, the East and the West
mingle, often incongruously and haphazardly; a battery of 105-mm.
howitzers is now rolling down the wide avenue past the City Hall
toward the South Gate and the Seoul Railway Station, where the
frontline troops of the rebels' 17th and 5th Divisions have been un-
loaded from trains in the early morning; there is a remnant of a
Sherman tank, charred black and its turret hatch open, its long,
sleek cannon now bent, abandoned at the crossroad near the elegant
Chosun Hotel. Jeeps with loudspeakers are prowling in the streets
below, broadcasting the latest developments, not for the citizenry
but for the rebel troops; an olive-green military ambulance with a
red cross painted on its side is parked in front of the City Hall steps;
the rebel troopers are wearing white armbands now, replacing the
blue armbands they wore an hour before; beside this reporter has
gathered a small group of foreign tourists, in bright sport shirts,
awkwardly mixing with the combat-ready rebel troopers who are
manning heavy machine guns and recoilless rifles here on the rooftop
balcony; a young American woman is snapping pictures of the stolid-
faced soldiers with her Polaroid camera under the umbrella held by
a hotel bellboy. Life goes on. But what future shape life will take
for the 27 millions of South Koreans in this hard, embittered nation,
not yet fully recovered from the ravages and the harsh experiences of
the Korean War, is at this moment uncertain. In this raining, misty
city, surrounded by a landscape as harsh as the nation's past, teeming

with restless, poverty-stricken masses, the people are now silently watching the power struggle, as a coup d'état is being carried out in their names and for their salvation. Whether or not an ominous cloud of civil war is looming beyond the dark, craggy range of the Bukhan Mountain to the north and beyond the ancient gates of the East, the West, and the South — heaven only knows. So far, no one here, Koreans or foreigners, is prepared to predict the course of events within the next twenty-four hours . . .

When I finished reading the article, George said, "Congratulations!"

"For what?"

"Here," he said, pointing at the report, reading, ". . . 'the plan for occupying the capital was a model of military precision and a marvel of brilliant tactics and foresight,' et cetera, et cetera. My compliments, too."

"Well, thank you, George," I said. "I did the best I could. As a matter of fact, it wasn't all that difficult really. You see, this is what I had my men do. First of all . . ."

There was a knock on the door.

George said, "Who is it?"

"The maid?" I said. "Is Jeanne back, perhaps?"

He got up from his chair and walked over to the door.

Before he reached the door, it was opened from outside the room and someone stepped in.

It was Colonel McKay. "Hello there," he said, "Major Lee!"

Chapter 16

Colonel McKay, in a dark gray suit, stood at the threshold for a moment before he briskly marched into the room. "Major Lee."

We shook hands.

"That plan of yours," he said. "It was splendid! Beautiful! Saved lots of trouble and lots of lives, too. My congratulations!" He took off his jacket and loosened his tie. "Colonel Min sends you his regards."

"Does he?"

He did not look at me. "He's doing real fine."

"George told me one of us in the Command Group was killed," I said. "Who?"

"No, that isn't true. It's Colonel Jung of the Presidential Brigade Armor. The Paratroopers got his command tank with a rocket. I am sorry. He was one of your former students, was he not?"

"Yes."

"He was a very promising fellow. Brilliant. I am sorry." He sat down in the armchair opposite from me. "Well, Major, now that it's all out between us, I can tell you this, but when Colonel Min first brought this up, you know, sending you here with this arrangement which he asked me to make, I wasn't too sure just how you would take it."

"What do you mean, Colonel?"

"You know, it was a bit too touchy for me to handle. I didn't want to see you and Colonel Min fall out, if you know what I mean. You might have misunderstood him and me too."

"What could I have misunderstood?"

"Oh, you might have thought that Colonel Min was trying to exile you . . ."

"Exile me?"

"Or something along that line. The point is he wanted to keep you safe and alive, see? And that's where we came in. Of course, Colonel Min had a trick up his sleeve by sending you here. You see, the original plan was to have you meet with some of our people in Tokyo and I had suggested that myself. Only, at the last minute, Colonel Min dropped that and asked me to make this arrangement. I couldn't possibly refuse him, could I? Anyway, it's over now."

"Is it?"

His blue eyes stared into mine. "I want you back in Seoul."

I did my best not to show my surprise. "Do you really?"

"Yes."

"I am not to return to Korea until Colonel Min gives the word," I said. "Isn't that the arrangement?"

"Is that so?"

I raised my voice a little. "You know *that*, don't you, Colonel?"

"Well, I suppose, yes. But look, Major. I am going to need your help and that's why I am here."

"You are going to need my help? That," I said, "is a surprise, Colonel."

He gave me a quick grin. "Yes, isn't it?"

"It is, indeed."

"I suppose you know how the coup went?"

"Yes," I said. I picked up the Japanese paper from the floor. "I have just read all about it in the paper."

His eyes narrowed for a second. "I see."

"Yes. It was remarkably comprehensive reporting."

"I am sure it was," he said, lighting up his pipe. "Then you know about the Paratroopers."

"Yes. I can't tell you enough how mortified I am about that. After all, I am the one responsible for having recruited Lieutenant Colonel Hwang who came over to us with his Paratroopers. I did have a talk with Colonel Min about him."

"Anything specific?" said Colonel McKay, rolling up the sleeves of his white shirt. "Did Colonel Min suspect him?"

"We didn't go into that. He merely questioned me about Colonel Hwang's ability to take charge of what I had left behind me in Seoul."

"Well, don't blame yourself too much, Major Lee. It's over."

"What do you have on him? Is he dead?"

"No, he is alive. He's been taken prisoner. Everything went like clockwork. Your plan worked beautifully down to every detail. You've really covered everything, Major, and the coordination between all the participating units was simply fantastic. It couldn't have been better. My congratulations. Anyway, this is what happened. The Commandos were taken over by your people after what had happened to General Ahn, as you know. So there was no problem there. It is a little hard to believe but General Ahn had not been able to infiltrate the Commandos with his own men."

"What do you mean by that?"

"Well, Colonel Min had ordered a quiet investigation of some of the officers in the Commando units, but nothing conclusive has turned up yet. You see, he wanted to make sure that General Ahn had not planted his men inside the Commandos. I had my own people work on that, too, and so far it appears that the loyalty of the Commando officers is genuine and can be trusted."

"I am not sure if I grasp the situation. You just mentioned the loyalty of the Commando officers. Am I to understand that Colonel Min and you have suspected that there was a subversive element in the Commando units?"

"Right."

"Communists?"

"Precisely."

"General Ahn is a Communist?"

"I was going to break it gently to you, but you don't seem to be too surprised."

"I had a hunch, I must admit. Colonel Min must have told you about General Ahn. In connection with a certain North Korean colonel?"

"Yes. That's where I came in originally into this. Let me see if I can brief you on General Ahn more or less in chronological order. First of all, we have been suspecting him for a long time. Oh, maybe for a year or so. What triggered our suspicion, which was initially a mild curiosity, was this. I hope you don't mind my saying all this about him, who is still one of your generals, although as a Communist agent he no longer is entitled to a — well, you know what I mean."

"I think we can do away with niceties, Colonel. So go ahead."

"It all started rather accidentally. Some of our people were trying to update the biographies and service records of your generals and one man happened to remark, more or less as a joke, I suppose, that he had spotted a candidate for a Korean counterpart of Superman. He was talking about General Ahn of course. Are you familiar with this Superman stuff?"

"The comic-strip character in your country?"

"Right. What he meant was that the service records of General Ahn were simply too fantastic. They were too good to be true, superhuman, you know. Victory here and victory there. All over in North Korea. Never had a defeat, that sort of thing. Some of our people have a tendency, as you surely know, to downgrade the extent and degree of some of your generals' battle reports on such matters as enemy dead and friendly casualty counts and so on."

"The sentiment is mutual, Colonel. We don't mind."

"Right. We know where we stand. General Ahn's reports on his illustrious battle results were a bit too much. So we began a quiet investigation, you know, just to double-check for the sake of credibility and future reference."

"So you contacted your agents in North Korea."

"Exactly."

"And they reported discrepancies."

"Right. That really got us going. We thought we had something big on our hands, especially considering his personality and the way he has successfully wormed his way up in both military and political circles. You must grant that General Ahn has been very popular with many generals and politicians. He was a darling young man of your President."

"Yes."

"Then we latched on to something that we felt was quite serious and which more or less confirmed our suspicion. We discovered that General Mah was also investigating General Ahn. Not in his usual way, you know, just to blackmail him as he has done many others by digging up all the sordid scandals and so on. No, it was something else. Quite serious. As a matter of fact, it was General Mah who first dropped a hint or two to us that he was on to something big. 'I am about to catch a big Red fox whose skin will keep me warm when I catch cold.' I think that's the way he said it. He wouldn't give us the name, though. You know how he was. We worked on our end and dug up what General Mah was working on at his end."

"This North Korean colonel?"

He nodded. "Right. We've had that story before, you see, but we had dismissed it as a case of simple brutality. General Ahn had a reputation, you know, as a tough, brutal man who showed no mercy to captured Communists. But we thought about the relative high rank of the North Korean and the fact that the incident had occurred where it was unlikely to find high-ranking Communist officers. The point is that this North Korean colonel was captured by General Ahn's Commandos in an area which had been clearly abandoned by the Communists. Do you know what I mean? We thought perhaps there was a slim chance, a very slim chance, that the North Korean might have wanted to defect or surrender. He should have been escorted back to the Intelligence authorities in any case, either to yours or ours. We hadn't captured that many high-ranking Communist officers in the war and anyone of that rank could have been and should have been extremely valuable to us. Well, as you know, General Ahn, who was a lieutenant colonel then, well, he simply shot him. Just like that. We dug into this case, of course, and quietly interrogated some of the men who were in the Commandos at that time, and what we came up with was that the North Korean had indeed wanted to surrender. As a matter of fact, he hadn't even been captured; he had surrendered voluntarily."

"Then he asked to be referred to Colonel Min, who was a major then."

"We didn't know that until Colonel Min told us about it. General Ahn made a slip of the tongue as you know, a fatal one, no doubt about that. Flattery will get you nowhere — that's it. Colonel Min was suspicious of General Ahn's story and when he told me about it, we had something concrete to go on with. And at about the same time, only a few days ago really, we got the word that General Mah, too, seemed to have come up with something tangible. General Mah, of course, kept it all very quiet and that's why Colonel Son knew nothing about it. General Mah had something up his sleeve; he was, I am sure, going to use General Ahn for a political purpose."

"As a pawn? To bring him as a sacrificial offering to us?"

"And we mustn't discount the possibility that General Mah might have crossed the border to the North if things got really bad for him."

"Possible but improbable. The Communists would simply have shot him."

Colonel McKay scrutinized me for a moment. "Well, now that we know General Ahn is a Communist agent, would you have him shot? Supposing that he may want to defect to us now and cooperate with us in matters of high level intelligence?"

"He should be tried as an enemy espionage agent first."

"That will tell the North Koreans that we have uncovered one of their biggest Intelligence agents. General Ahn has been planted for a long time, Major. For nearly twenty years. He came to the South posing as an anti-Communist refugee and immediately joined the South Korean Army, which was then called the Constabulary, and steadily rose in rank, just waiting for the day when he would be big enough to command a corps, a field army, or even become the Chief of Staff. Heavens! It gives me the creeps just to think of what could have happened. A cold-blooded scheme, too. During the war, the North Koreans would deliberately sabotage their own troops so their superagent, General Ahn, could massacre them with the South Korean Commandos, just to make it look all real and bloody enough. Argh, it's an ugly business. There was, for example, a coastal gun battery position on the west coast which the South Korean Navy and our navy couldn't quite knock out, in spite of our air attack in addition to the naval guns. So General Ahn was ordered to go in and knock it out with his Commandos. So what does he do? He gets in touch with his courier, who sends the message to the North Koreans that General Ahn and his Commandos are going to be dropped from the air and attack the coastal gun battery position. The North Koreans would then quietly evacuate the key officers of the battery and replace them with what they would call incompetent and politically unreliable officers, who, of course, are sabotaged and then are massacred by General Ahn's Commandos. Things like that happened in Europe, too, mind you, during the Second World War. It is not unknown. Anyway, General Mah could have thought of sparing the life of General Ahn as a big favor, in return for which he would ask the North Koreans for a chance to defect and be promised a clandestine position in the service of their Intelligence. It has been done and can be done, though how he would have done it is too complicated to unravel at this time. Well, we got on to *that!* With the details we got from Colonel Min on the identity of the North Korean colonel, who Colonel Min thought was dead, we contacted our agents in Pyungyang. What we learned from them was simply fantastic. You know what happened to Colonel Min and this North Korean colonel in Colonel Min's hometown. Now, Colonel Min thought the North Korean killed himself after they escaped from the Russian garrison. Well, he wasn't dead. Not dead, that is, when the Russians and the local Communist police found him where Colonel Min had left him thinking he was dead. Can't blame Colonel Min for not having made sure of that. He had to get away quickly. The North Korean wasn't dead and when he came to he found himself in a hospital, a Russian hospital with Russian doctors and nurses and so on. He was panicky, naturally, thinking that the Russians found out what had truly happened. Now, this is an authentic story because he had contacted our agents shortly before he was to surrender to General Ahn's Commandos; it's a pity that our agents didn't have a chance to contact us on this. So, he thought he was going to be shot eventually, but then he noticed that the Russians were quite friendly and treated him well. Then the local Korean Communist police chief came to see him in the hospital and he was very sympathetic and expressed his regret that the villain — Colonel Min, that is — had managed to slip out of their hands and apparently escaped to the South and so on. It was then that he caught on to what was really going on. The Russians had obviously assumed that it was all Colonel Min's doing — the garrison commander, the Russian lieutenant, and the two guards who were all dead; of course, they thought Colonel Min had kidnapped this North Korean at gunpoint and then shot him before he escaped. Well, he finally grasped that, luckily before he was well enough to undergo the Russians' interrogation. So that's the story he gave them and apparently he was believed. The rest of the story is simple enough. The Russians returned him to the North Koreans with a letter of commendation — God knows for what! — and wanted the matter hush-hushed. The only theory we can come up with is that the Russians didn't want to divulge the fact that the garrison commander indulged in torturing Koreans; apparently, the Russian major had been known to the local Korean Communists as a sadist of a sort and the Koreans had reported to the Communist Party in Pyungyang about him. It was around the time when the Chinese Communists were vying with the Russians there, so the Russians decided to turn this incident into some sort of a political gesture; they even gave this North Korean a medal! That assured him a favorable treatment from his superiors, and from then on he knew just where he stood. Having killed the Russians didn't seem to have bothered him as much as the fact that he had consented to come to the South with Colonel Min and then tried to shoot himself. He was a nationalist first and a Communist second, you see; so he stuck around as long as he could, until he couldn't go along with the Communist regime any longer, but then the war was on. And the war seemed to have clinched the matter for him; after all, he was one of the high-level operations staff in their High Command and he *knew* about the invasion and the war plans. That did it for him; he couldn't go along with a military venture which he knew would plunge the whole of Korea into a bloody war. He was too much of a nationalist to endorse *that*. So, then, we know the rest. It's a great pity that he hadn't gotten in touch with us sooner. It's your country's loss, Major Lee. He was caught in a dilemma which he could not solve himself, like a butterfly caught in a spider's web."

"The history, past and present, of our country is just that, Colonel, the story of a butterfly caught in a spider's web as you put it. Consider this from his point of view. So he escapes from one spider's web only to be caught and swallowed up in another spider's web. He couldn't have known about General Ahn, so that when he was about to be shot, I can imagine what must have passed through his mind. It is a dirty, stinking world, Colonel, where the strong kicks the weak around like a battered ball."

"I appreciate your sentiment, Major Lee. Believe me I do. But you mustn't be too bitter in this case. It was General Ahn, the Communist agent, who shot him. Of course, it didn't make any difference to him when he was shot; he didn't know the truth and he thought he was being shot by a cold-blooded, brutal, South Korean officer. I am sorry. He must have had an agonizing sense of betrayal from all sides."

"We are used to *that*, Colonel."

"I have read the preamble you wrote for the policy statement of the Revolutionary Council, Major Lee. So I know how you feel and where you stand. Colonel Min approved the preamble, so I suppose I know where he stands, too. I think you expressed your views admirably in the preamble and I hope the new order will be able to guide the nation in a new direction toward a new and different destiny. Incidentally, the version of the policy statement I read was translated by one of our interpreters and I am not sure he translated it well. I have his translation with me and I wonder if you wouldn't mind going through it later to clarify some part in your preamble."

I nodded.

"After all, you wrote it, so I thought you should be the first person to come to in order to check out the accuracy of the English translation. But that can wait for now. Let me get back to where we began from. The Paratroopers. Lieutenant Colonel Hwang. Now, as far as I know, there was no indication whatsoever before the coup was launched that the Paratroopers would come out against your side. Colonel Hwang was in charge in Seoul, as you know, and he made sure everything went according to your plan. When the coup began, 0200 hour sharp, he was with his Paratroopers, ready to strike, not against you but for you."

"I don't understand this. When did he change his mind?"

"We have a few theories on that. Someone thought that he had been an opportunist all along and at the last minute he decided that the coup didn't have a chance of success and so he changed his mind and tipped the government on the coup. But I am inclined to go along with Colonel Min's theory that he was General Ahn's man. Colonel Min's reasoning is this. Colonel Hwang had not been told about General Ahn, who was taken to Seoul by Colonel Son and kept in General Mah's headquarters; of course, Colonel Son was now in charge there. Colonel Hwang knew Colonel Son was on your side, as you know, but, for whatever reason, he was not informed of the arrest of General Ahn and the death of General Mah. Only at the last minute was he informed of the whereabouts and why of General Ahn, because someone now had to take charge of the Commando units and your Command Group wanted to make sure Colonel Hwang knew about *that*. Colonel Min's theory is that Colonel Hwang then changed his mind with *that* information which told him that General Ahn had been exposed as a Communist agent and was now in Colonel Son's custody. Nevertheless, Colonel Hwang rolled out his Paratroopers just as your plan prescribed as if he were still on your side. He deployed his Paratroopers while he was getting in touch with the Prime Minister and the Chief of Staff, telling them about the coup. The government knew then that it could not rely on the Presidential Brigade, so they appointed Colonel Son as the commander of all the government forces in Seoul and ordered him to have his Paratroopers provide protection for the Prime Minister and his cabinet members and also for the Army GHQ. For some reason, the government decided not to trust the National Police. The defense of the Presidential residence was left up to the Presidential Security troops and the President's bodyguards, and there weren't enough military police around to properly defend the Army GHQ and the Joint Chiefs of Staff Headquarters. So, the Paratroopers provided the bulk of the defense forces. In the meantime, the Marines were closing in from the south and the regiments of the 17th and the 5th were rolling down to Seoul from the north. A regiment from General Yoon's Division was being airlifted to the eastern outskirts."

"Exactly when was it discovered that the Paratroopers had gone over to the other side?"

"A little too late, unfortunately. When the Marines approached the Han River bridge, which was defended by the Paratroopers and a company of Military Police, they assumed that the passage was safe, since the Paratroopers gave them a signal which you had worked on in your plan. An entire advance company of the Marines was knocked out there at the bridge and that's when your Command Group knew something had gone wrong. From that point on, everything went wild. The signals and passwords had to be revised instantly and communications procedures had to be changed. But — it all came out all right in the end, except that there are a few things that will have to be cleared up."

"Yes?"

"The Paratroopers attacked Colonel Son's headquarters, apparently trying to free General Ahn, but Colonel Son had quickly removed him elsewhere and called for Colonel Jung's help. Damn lucky you had the Presidential Brigade all sewed up. Colonel Jung had by then taken over the overall command of the Presidential Brigade and dispatched a company of tanks to Colonel Son's headquarters. Just in time, too. I am sorry about Colonel Jung. As I told you before, his command tank was knocked out by the Paratroopers' rocket and flame thrower. So I was told. He didn't have to risk his own life out there but he did. Now, this attack on Colonel Son's headquarters. As far as Colonel Min is concerned, he sees only one explanation for that attack there. To free General Ahn. So, he concluded that Colonel Hwang is General Ahn's man, which, of course, implies that he, too, is a Communist agent."

"Is there any evidence that the killing of the Prime Minister and . . ."

Colonel McKay did not let me finish. "I knew you would see that point instantly. Precisely that is the question. It was *not* in *your* plan to shoot anyone if at all possible and it wasn't in anyone's plan to do *that*. Now this bloody mess you have on your hands . . . So far, no one is absolutely certain as to just who shot these people at whose orders. Colonel Min was terribly upset about this and ordered an immediate investigation into this. The battle was so intense and the situation was so confusing at times that it will take a while to check out all the participating units as well as those taken prisoners. Colonel Hwang was taken alive but he wouldn't talk. He is kept with General Ahn now and I suggested to Colonel Min to have them bugged. There hadn't been anything significant on this bloody incident until I left for Tokyo but I am sure we'll find out soon just who did all this killing. I am inclined to think, and I am sure you are too, that there seems to be a pattern emerging somewhere in this. It was as though Colonel Hwang was trying to kill almost everyone of any importance, on both sides if you know what I mean. He must have been quite desperate to do that. He could still have done that, if that's what he wanted to do, by siding with your coup, but I suppose he knew he too had been exposed along with General Ahn and decided to take his chance with the government side. He would kill off the big wheels on the government side in the confusion and if the coup failed, then he's got it made, see what I mean?"

"And if the coup succeeded as it has?"

"Oh, he had an escape plan all worked out. He had an aircraft waiting on the airstrip in his headquarters."

"The air base of his Brigade headquarters?"

"Yes. And that's where General Yoon's regiment came in and they had to slug it out with the Paratroopers to take the air base. Bloody mess there, too."

"So we now have General Ahn and Colonel Hwang as our prisoners, the confirmed Communist agents."

"Well, we don't know for sure just what Colonel Hwang is, but I suppose we can reasonably assume that he is. Now, I have to tell you bad news. And that's why I am really here."

"You want me to go back to Seoul, Colonel. This bad news — does it have something to do with your wanting me to be back there?"

"I haven't talked this over with Colonel Min, to tell you the truth," said Colonel McKay, getting up. He went over to the fireplace and emptied his pipe, tapping it against the firewall. "I'll have to take the full responsibility, but I think it is important enough that you should be back there *now*."

I did not speak out.

"The frontline generals . . . that's why I am here and that's why I think you should go back to Seoul with me."

"You are afraid of a civil war?" I said.

"I am afraid yes."

"Why?" I tried to appear as nonchalant as I could.

"General Ham has escaped, you see," he said quietly.

His words threw me off my guard. To my regret, I could not help exclaiming, "When?"

"While the coup was going on. It's my responsibility really."

"I don't understand! He was to be released after the coup, I knew that. But what do you mean? Your responsibility? I can make neither head nor tail of anything any longer!"

"Ah, you've said that to me before, Major Lee. But we've got to pull ourselves together."

"If General Ham has escaped . . . escaped from General Yoon's Division, then what happened to General Yoon? You aren't going to tell me that General Yoon has defected from us?"

"Oh, no! Not that. General Yoon has been taken prisoner by General Ham."

"What?"

"Exactly what I said."

"Where?"

"At his own headquarters. The 22nd Division."

"I think you'd better spell this all out for me, Colonel."

"This is what happened. General Yoon had sent one of his regiments to Chunchun air base, where it was later airlifted to Seoul. Then he stayed put in his headquarters. Colonel Min wanted him there taking charge of the reserve forces. Meanwhile, General Ham had somehow managed to bribe one of the officers who were guarding him and had him contact a certain Lieutenant Hinckley who was an adviser to the Division's Civil Affairs Section. That's where my responsibility comes in. He — this lieutenant — hadn't been briefed by the Division's senior American adviser on the coup. It burns me up like hell, let me tell you! It now turns out that all the advisers assigned to combat and supporting units had been briefed but this man had not been told. Something about his not having had a security clearance and so on. I'll have to check on that later. Anyway, this Lieutenant Hinckley is supposed to have met General Ham before on civil affairs problems and to have known the general well. So, General Ham sent a secret message through him to his people in the neighboring division which belonged to another corps. Heaven knows how he persuaded the lieutenant or why the damn lieutenant didn't go directly to the senior adviser. When it all began, General Yoon, having dispatched his reserve regiment to Seoul, was in the process of mobilizing another regiment which he intended to bring to the Division headquarters area. What I mean is that the Division headquarters were not sufficiently defended when the troops from the neighboring division started rolling in. I think it is the 34th Division commanded by Colonel somebody. I forgot his name."

"Colonel Shin. General Ham's nephew. That's why he was given a division command though there were generals available."

"I see. We weren't aware of *that*. So Colonel Shin mobilized his division and sent an armored battalion and a whole regiment which surrounded the 22nd Division headquarters. It was a fast movement and I hope all the divisions can move that fast in time of war. General Ham was freed and joined the troops which by then had taken the division headquarters and General Yoon."

"General Yoon didn't resist?"

"He didn't have a chance. Besides, Colonel Shin threatened to massacre everyone if he resisted. So, he had to give up. Meanwhile, Colonel Shin had sent a message to General Ham's men at General Ham's own headquarters, which had been already taken over by your people though General Ham's people hadn't known that General Ham had been in General Yoon's custody. Well, General Ham's men then quickly organized a countercoup move there and seized the headquarters and sent word to Colonel Shin that General Ham could return to the headquarters."

"Did he return?"

"Yes, he did. He left Colonel Shin in charge of both divisions, the 34th and the 22nd. He went back to his headquarters and alerted the entire Field Army."

"Not the entire Field Army. At least two thirds of it was on our side."

"Well, it did turn out that way, but he still had the support and loyalty from one third of it anyway. About three divisions and an armored brigade and so on. Of course, the units under General Hyun's 7th Army Corps are solidly behind the coup. So, they are at bay with one another, here and there, and the situation out there is not only touchy but very confusing. What with communications and supply routes all mixed up and getting in each other's way."

"What happened to General Yoon and his staff? And what about our people at General Ham's headquarters?"

"They are all taken to General Ham's headquarters as hostages. And wouldn't you know! General Ham packed all the American advisers off to Seoul, including this idiot, Hinckley. I am going to see to it that he gets sacked."

"How much of this is known to the country at large?"

"Not any of it. Now that's where you and I come in. General Ham has made no move whatsoever up to this moment."

"You mean — he hasn't made any threat of a countercoup move?"

"Nothing whatsoever. He is staying put where he is."

"Any word from him to Colonel Min?"

"Not a word, though of course he knows that Colonel Min knows what happened."

"He wants to make a deal."

"Exactly the point, Major."

"He wanted to make a deal with General Mah, too, as you know."

"Yes."

"When Colonel Min, General Yoon, and I saw him last, he let us know quite explicitly that he wanted to head the coup."

"Yes," he sighed. "He can be very stupid sometimes."

"Now he thinks he can wreck the coup but he is a coward enough not to take the initiative."

"I think you are right, Major."

"Colonel Park has a theory on General Ham which I agree with, Colonel. General Ham is too ambitious to risk everything he has. He will never take an either-or chance."

"You are absolutely right."

"This does not rule out the possibility that he might do something quite stupid and reckless, if he thinks he has a good chance of winning."

"Right."

"It seems to me, Colonel, that he can't possibly move his troops to Seoul without taking an enormous chance. To begin with, the defense of Seoul is solid, wouldn't you agree?"

"Yes. And you have the Air Force on your side."

"He will have to mobilize his divisions and transport them and there aren't too many routes available to him to do that without having his flanks exposed to the units on our side, to say nothing of his chance of being assaulted from the rear once he moved his troops out toward Seoul."

"Right." Colonel McKay was gazing at me as though he had thought about this already but was willing to let me go on.

"What I am trying to point out, Colonel, is that he will not and he will not be able to move his troops. We have an upper hand as far as the number of troops and tactical choices are concerned. We have a definite tactical advantage on him."

"That doesn't mean he can't make a hell of a lot of trouble."

"No. But I doubt he will take that chance. We can crush him easily."

"Hypothetically speaking, yes."

"Then you rule out that possibility?"

"A civil war? No, we can't have *that!*"

"No. Where does Colonel Min stand on this?"

"I would rather hear what you have to say."

"What difference would that make to you or to Colonel Min?"

"It would make a difference to me."

"Why?"

"If your position on this problem of dealing with General Ham is what I think it is, then I can count on you to do something which might avoid bloodshed."

"What makes you think that I am averse to bloodshed, Colonel?"

"I know you, Major. So does everyone in your Command Group. Especially Colonel Min."

"What about Colonel Min?"

"All right. I wasn't going to tell you this, but there's no time to play a game now. The real reason Colonel Min wanted you to be out of the country when the coup was launched, as much as I could fathom his inscrutable mind, was that he was afraid of you. What do you say to *that?* Colonel Min, I think, was afraid of having you near him when the coup was on."

"Did he tell you that?" I said.

"No. But I think I knew."

"What do you think you knew, Colonel?"

"You seem to have a certain amount of influence over him and I don't think he wanted you to exert *that* influence on him when the time for a showdown came. I am sure you know what I am talking about, don't you?"

"I would like to hear your explanation, Colonel."

"To tell you the truth, I can't explain it really. It is just my hunch. I know there's a sore spot in him somewhere and you are the man, it seems to me, who keeps reminding him of *that* sore spot. He is very fond of you. I know that and everyone knows that. He respects your intelligence and your talents as a brilliant planner and organizer. You are the theoretician of the coup, if I may say so, as evidenced by your preamble which Colonel Min wholeheartedly approves of and supports. Now, I am sure he wanted to send you here to protect you because he didn't want anything to happen to you and he needed you very badly after the coup. But I also think that he wanted you to be at a distance from him when he — well, how shall I put it? — when he had to take an enormous risk, an either-or chance as you put it, a dangerous risk so great that nothing personal should interfere with his command and decision-making. Do you follow me?"

I did not reply.

"I am sure you do," he went on. "I do not want to get involved in any kind of personal problems he might or might not have. I want to make that very clear, Major. But, as I said, this is no time to play a game. So, let me spill this out. I think you have a certain influence over him which he finds painful at times."

"I am not aware of that!"

"I hadn't realized this, Major, until he let it drop from him just as you were leaving. 'Major Lee has been digging into my past like a detective,' he said to me. I didn't think too much of it then. I thought it was just a friendly joke he was making on you. You know, perhaps you have been teasing him about his wild days before the war."

"His wild days?"

"You don't know?"

I shook my head. "We never discussed it."

"He was a wild young man about town before the war. Wine and song and women. That sort of thing. Good heavens! You mean to tell me that you didn't know *that?*"

"No. I didn't know."

"Well, in any case, that's what I thought he was referring to, so I said to him, rather stupidly I admit, now that I look back on it, 'So Major Lee's been digging into your scandalous past?' 'Yes, my sordid past, like a prosecutor, like a judge.' I laughed then, but it dawned on me later that he was very serious when he said that to me. He wasn't joking."

I kept silent. The fire in the fireplace was going out. The embers glowed red-hot, quietly sizzling. I could feel the colonel's eyes watching me.

He said, "Now that it is all over, let me tell you this, Major. Do you recall the meeting of your Command Group the night before you left Korea?"

I nodded. "About General Mah."

"The majority decision was to kill him, was it not?"

"Yes."

"Would you like to know how that majority decision came to be reversed?"

I neither spoke nor looked at him.

"Well, it happened this way, Major. Colonel Min and I had a talk after that meeting. You know that. What he asked me to do for him was that I go to see General Hyun. Colonel Min had to tell General Hyun about the Command Group's decision on General Mah, and he wanted me to persuade General Hyun to make a motion to reverse the decision. I asked why. Why did he have to go through this? You know as well as I do that General Hyun would do anything Colonel Min asks him to do. I wouldn't go as far as saying that General Hyun would do whatever Colonel Min tells him to do, but you know the situation. What Colonel Min said to me was this. He wanted the decision reversed and he wanted to have a word from the general as a legitimate excuse to bring the matter up again with the Command Group. 'You could simply put it to the Group and they would listen to you, wouldn't they?' That's what I said to him. He agreed with me on that. The Group would listen to him and accept his opinion without too much difficulty as you surely know. Colonel Min said this: 'If I don't bring this up again with the Group as an advice and a motion from the general, they are going to think that I am doing it for Major Lee's sake and the motion would be defeated. If on the other hand I present this as coming from you and the general, they would think it is in fact coming from me and would go along with the motion. Do you understand?' Well, Major, so that's how it was. Do you understand that now? He did it for you — in spite of himself."

"And for himself, too, Colonel!" I said. "You don't understand that part of the story, do you?"

"I am not interested in that, Major, to tell you the truth. I am more interested in what you can do with Colonel Min. Or, to be more precise, I am interested in that you seem to be able to trigger him to do certain things which he would not do if he were left alone to make his own decision. Do you follow me?"

"It is all rather esoteric, Colonel."

"Well, there, you said it all. You and Colonel Min are really inscrutable, you know. It's taken me a long time to have a glimpse of what makes you two tick."

I stared at him. "What do you want me to do once I am back in Seoul?"

"Ah, now we are getting somewhere. Look, Major, this is my estimation of the situation as I left Korea. I am afraid Colonel Min and the Command Group have decided to fight it out with General Ham. A showdown, if you know what I mean. I think any sort of compromise with General Ham has been ruled out absolutely."

"That is absurd!" I said. "We can plunge the whole nation into a bloody civil war. We will win against General Ham. There is no question about that, but the price we will have to pay in terms of human lives, on both sides, will not justify that absurd decision."

"Well, you've got to see it this way, Major. The coup is a success for the moment. The country has been taken, more or less. You now have a chance to carry out your policies and, if I may say so, your dreams. It is the country or else now, Major. Do you see that? Colonel Min and the Command Group are now in Seoul. The old regime is out. Colonel Min and the Command Group are the regime in the country, do you understand? Colonel Min has the support of the majority of the armed forces and the nation at large as things stand now. What prevents him from making the coup a complete, total success is General Ham. You have to be in Colonel Min's shoes, in Seoul, in the capital, Major. His viewpoint now must be based on the totality of the nation, and his perspective is *from* Seoul, *from* your capital. There is a new phase in his coup movement, do you see that? The old perspective from the top of the hills and mountains of your central front has been transformed into a new perspective from the top of the dome of your Capitol Building. Now do you see what I mean? Although the dream of your coup has been for the nation as a whole, so far, until this morning, the focus of your vision, the target of your immediate concern, has been on the old regime. Now, Colonel Min is in Seoul. The coup is over. There is a new regime in the nation and as the peculiar political nature of any coup dictates Colonel Min *is* the nation, if I may say so without offending your sensibility. I am simply speaking about it figuratively. Don't misunderstand me. I am not suggesting or implying that Colonel Min is or will become a totalitarian dictator. We know him better, don't we, Major?"

"Yes."

"So then, we understand that Colonel Min and the Command Group have to think and make decisions as representing the nation as a whole. The time has come, I am afraid, for them to think either-or, as we said before. Either lose the nation or win it and carry out the dreams and hopes."

"I am also part of that Command Group, Colonel. And I cannot and I refuse to think in such a simple term as either-or."

"Well, I am an outsider, Major, so I can't think of the destiny of your country in an either-or term myself."

"I am not an outsider, Colonel! I am part of that destiny and part of the spirit of the coup that intends to guide that destiny."

"Of course, of course! But first you've got to have a nation in order to worry about its destiny or do something about it. That's where I come in. That's where we Americans come in. We do not want to see a bloody civil war. Period!"

"Neither do I, Colonel! And I am sure neither does Colonel Min! Or any of my comrades!"

"You are wrong on that, Major. You have to understand the profound change in their state of mind and perspective brought about by their experiences and actions in the last twelve hours. Don't forget, Major. *They are in Seoul!*"

I did not know how to reply. I sank down into the chair.

292 / The Innocent

"They are in the capital of the nation, Major!"

I heard myself whispering, perhaps to myself alone, "Yes — and here I am!"

"Ah, that's why I want you to be *there* now," exclaimed Colonel McKay.

"Do you think I will be able to change their minds?"

"I am not worried about your being able to change their minds. I want you to change Colonel Min's mind is all. As I said, I think he's coming to a decisive decision on General Ham. And I am afraid it will come to this. Colonel Min is going to slap General Ham with an ultimatum. He might have done that already for all I know. I have our people in Tokyo monitoring the reports from our people in Seoul, so we should be able to find out soon."

"And if General Ham does not accept Colonel Min's ultimatum?"

"Heaven only knows what will happen next!"

"An attack on General Ham?"

"I suppose."

"It will be bloody. Isn't there anything you can do?"

"We are working on it, Major. Like mad! We are working on the possibility of a compromise. Some sort of compromise. I haven't got the slightest notion what compromise and how much compromise can be reached."

"And you still think Colonel Min would go ahead with his ultimatum and all?" I said.

"Exactly! That's why I want you to go back with me," said Colonel McKay. He stirred up the dying fire.

"But if he refuses to listen to me? Then what, Colonel?"

"We will have to figure something out. Look, Major. I wouldn't go through all this trouble if I hadn't thought there might be a chance, a good chance really, of getting us all somewhere. You see, General Ham has sent his word to us that he would be willing to talk with Colonel Min to reach some sort of a compromise. Just what he has in mind is not known. He hasn't said a thing about that. But he is willing to talk. So it is now up to Colonel Min, do you see that?"

I stood up from the chair, and went to him at the fireplace. "When can we leave, Colonel?"

He looked straight into my eyes with his icy blue, unblinking eyes. He looked at his watch, which was strapped onto his wrist with a wide, black leather band.

"As soon as I can arrange a flight for us," said Colonel McKay. "In an hour. I will send for a chopper to take us to the base."

"All right," I said. I turned to George. "You will take care of my things at the hotel? And my uniform?"

"I'll call Tokyo. Don't worry," said George. "Someone will meet you at the base, O.K.?"

"Fine," said Colonel McKay. "Oh, this, Major." He handed me a white envelope. "The policy statement. Do you mind? Just the preamble will do. We can go over the rest later. George, when Major Lee is finished with it, would you have it Xeroxed when you go back to Tokyo? A copy goes to the general, and the rest you know where."

"Yes, sir."

"Fine. Let's get busy now. I am going to radio the office from my car." He left the room. George trotted after him.

It was still raining outside, coming down harder than before.

So — I was going back to Korea — after all. A strange, undefinable mood seized me suddenly. To my annoyance, I felt tears welling up in my eyes — neither for joy nor for regret, but for the soft nostalgia that smothered my heart. I had to shake myself out of the mood. There was work to do.

I went over to the Japanese professor's desk and read the English translation of the policy statement of the Revolutionary Council of the Armed Forces. It was a poor translation, inaccurate and inarticulate. I began revising it.

I
Chapter 17

t was twenty minutes past six when we
landed at the American section of the
Kimpo air base. It was not raining. The sky was plastered with
heavy black rain clouds. The air was humid and damp. I could
smell the rain in the air. It was dark, too, as if the dusk had already
fallen.

We were met at the plane by a middle-aged American in a gray
business suit with a red bow tie. Colonel McKay had changed into
his fatigues on the plane, as I had into mine. The American with
stooped shoulders peered at me through his rimless thick glasses.
We shook hands. We were not introduced. He had a light blue
Chevrolet sedan waiting for us. I got into the back seat. Colonel
McKay and the American were exchanging a whispered conversation outside the car, still standing under the wingtip of the plane.
The American got in behind the wheel. Colonel McKay sat with me
in the back.

"Bad news, Major," said Colonel McKay when we were driving
out of the base entrance, waved on by the American Air Policemen.
"I am afraid we are a bit too late."

The American was driving fast; the car sped along on the Seoul-

Inchun Highway, continuously hopping and jolting over innumerable bumps and holes on the road.

As though he had not really expected any reaction from me, Colonel McKay went on calmly, "Colonel Min has already sent his ultimatum to General Ham."

There was no other car on the road. A formation of four jet fighters roared over us toward Seoul. "What are the terms of his ultimatum?"

"Very simple," said Colonel McKay, taking out his pipe from his breast pocket. "He is being summoned to Seoul immediately. He is to present himself to the Revolutionary Council."

"Then what?"

"God knows!"

"Was there any deadline to Colonel Min's ultimatum?"

"It's past the deadline already. The ultimatum was sent to General Ham at 1600. He was to reply by 1800." He checked his watch.

"He hasn't replied yet?"

He shook his head. "No. Not to Colonel Min. He has been in touch with us, though."

"Yes?"

"He is willing to come to Seoul."

I could not help snorting. "He is out of his mind!"

"Why do you say that?"

"He will be arrested!"

"Naturally. But then, General Ham isn't that stupid. He would come to Seoul on condition that we guarantee his safety."

"He has asked for a safe-conduct from the U.N. Command?"

"Not exactly. He wouldn't deal with the U.N. Command. He is smart enough to know that we would not involve ourselves on his behalf as an agency of the United Nations Command. No. He wants the American protection."

"Will you give it to him?"

"We are willing, Major," he said, glancing at the back of the

American driver, "provided Colonel Min would promise to honor our pledge to General Ham for his safety."

"I am sure that can be worked out."

"I wouldn't be too sure of that, Major, if I were you. You don't know just what sort of atmosphere and state of tension Colonel Min and the others are in now. It is very touchy."

"Has General Ham said anything about what he wants? If he wants to make a deal with us, that is?"

"He wants the job of the Army Chief of Staff," he said, shaking his head, "*and* the post of Defense Minister."

"That is out of the question!"

The American driver turned his head slightly to the side, looking at us from the corner of his eye. "That's what we had to tell him, Major. We had to tell him that was simply stoking the fire. Provocation, simply speaking."

Colonel McKay said, "We told General Ham that the best he could do at this time was to come to Seoul and sit down with the leaders of the coup and talk. Just talk, understand? We don't care how long the talk might last. We want them to have a talk. Once he is in Seoul, we think General Ham would be able to sniff the air and realize that his cause is a lost cause. Back where he is, surrounded by his own men armed to their teeth, commanding as he is all those troops, he might be more susceptible to a dangerous delusion of self-grandeur. He does not yet understand the nature of political power, I am afraid. So we want him to come to Seoul, to give him a chance to go through some sort of psychological shock treatment, figuratively speaking."

"I wouldn't count on that too much, if I were you," said the driver. "Sorry to say this, Major, but he is a stupid ass."

"I am sure Major Lee doesn't need our estimate of General Ham," said Colonel McKay. "He knows that already."

"Have you any news of General Yoon and our people General Ham is holding as hostages?" I said. "What about them? Will General Ham consent to release them when he comes to Seoul?"

"Not a chance! He wouldn't do that."

"In that case, we will have to allow him to return to his head-quarters. We can't take a chance on the lives of our people he is holding."

"If Colonel Min honors our safe-conduct for General Ham, yes, he would have to let him go. But, as a matter of fact, Major, the hostages there aren't all that important. What I mean is, General Ham seems to think this way. By coming to Seoul with our safe-conduct, he believes and rightly so that Colonel Min would not dare shoot him, to put it bluntly. The worst that could happen to him would be to be placed under guard, imprisoned, that is. He knows that Colonel Min cannot, at this time, jeopardize his relationship with us, if you know what I mean. Supposing then that he might be detained in Seoul under arrest, and Colonel Min could do just that without really putting us in a spot, General Ham still has the hostages to exploit. Besides his people with all those troops could still make a hell of a lot of trouble. Do you know what I mean?"

"Yes. Arresting him is not going to solve the problem."

"No. I am afraid not."

"Then what? What is the alternative?"

"I don't know," he said. "Can you think of any?"

"There is no question that General Ham will have to be removed from his command. Retire him from the Army for good."

"I will go along with that," said Colonel McKay.

"This is purely a hypothetical speculation on my part, Colonel. The only alternative tactic we have, although it would not be used, would be this, from my point of view. Strictly hypothetical, Colonel."

"I understand that."

"We would demand that when you guarantee him your safe-conduct you insist that General Ham release our people in return for your favor. Otherwise, we would not agree to honor your safe-conduct."

"Go on."

"Suppose he agrees to that condition. You would convince him that he still has the troops under his command and that even if he

298 / *The Innocent*

were in Seoul his men could still make a hell of a lot of trouble as
you put it."

"Right."

"Suppose he would agree to all that and come to Seoul."

"Then what?"

"We would simply arrest him."

"And not honor our safe-conduct?"

"Precisely, Colonel. Hypothetically speaking."

"Hum. Then what would you do with his men and all their
troops?"

"We would bluff them, Colonel. We would bluff an all-out attack."

"And if your bluff didn't work?"

"It may work or it may not work. But I am tempted to think that
it would work."

"Why?"

"I am counting on General Ham's men. I know them. The kind
of men General Ham has surrounded himself with cannot be counted
on in time of crisis. We would bluff them, I think, and they would
buy our bluff. We would threaten them with an all-out attack as I
said, and they would give up once they knew that General Ham was
finished and that they could not depend on your help."

"Well, still, suppose the bluff does not work?"

"Then we would have no other choice. We would have to attack
them and blast them off."

"It's a bloody scheme, Major, if I may say so."

"I said it was purely hypothetical."

"All right. Let me tell you this. General Ham has agreed to release
the hostages."

"How did you manage that?"

"Doing exactly what you've just suggested," he said.

"He is very stupid."

"Ah, not quite. He would release them but not General Yoon
and his staff."

"I see."

"Better than nothing, but there's a problem right there."

"And you couldn't persuade him to release General Yoon and his staff, too?"

"Not a chance."

"Then there is no other choice. We would have to do this. We would insist that you tell him this. Either he releases General Yoon and his staff or no safe-conduct. If he refuses, then he should be made to agree to release them once a compromise has been reached between us."

"And if no compromise is reached?"

"Then we would have to shoot him."

"Would you?"

"Hypothetically speaking, Colonel, yes. It is either him or General Yoon and his staff. And I am sure General Ham values his life more than theirs."

"And then what happens to our safe-conduct?"

"We would simply disregard it, Colonel."

"You won't honor your promise. Cheating us, that is?"

"I suppose so, Colonel. We would withdraw our promise in view of the changing circumstances. That is what we would have to say."

"Suppose we withdraw our support from you?"

I said flatly, "You can't, Colonel, and you know *that*."

He gave me a small grin. "We shall see about that."

"If you decide to — how shall I say? — defect from us or crush our coup by exerting your influence on certain Korean generals and have them defect from us, you would not only fail in your venture but also very likely have a bloody civil war on your hands and in that case, you would have gone back to where we began, one way or the other. Besides, the power structure at this stage is such that the troops on our side are not really commanded by their generals. Surely you must know that, too, Colonel, don't you?"

He gave me another small grin, wiggling his moustache. "We are of one mind, Major. Brilliant! All right. This is what's happening now, Major. General Ham has already released your people, with the exception of General Yoon and his staff. He is coming to Seoul. He is to land at the Paratroopers' air base, which is now held by General Yoon's regiment, ironically enough. Colonel Min and the Command Group would meet with him there."

"Is that all?"

"Is that all, you say! Major! Do you realize what it took us to accomplish that!"

"I know that, Colonel. What I mean is, what if there is no compromise? Would you return him to his headquarters?"

"Yes. We would have to."

"Then nothing would have been achieved."

"We will have to begin all over again somewhere."

Suddenly, the American driver slowed the car down. "A roadblock, gentlemen!"

There were three jeeps, one with a machine gun mounted on it, forming a roadblock. Steel-helmeted troopers of the Presidential Brigade with automatic rifles lined up on the road. A lieutenant with a submachine gun was coming toward our car.

Colonel McKay said to the American, "Watch your language, now. They are awfully touchy."

The young lieutenant gave us a salute when he came close to us. "Major Lee, sir?"

"Yes."

He glanced at Colonel McKay. "Is he Colonel McKay, sir?"

"Yes," said Colonel McKay in Korean, smiling.

The lieutenant grinned. "I am your escort, Major. We will lead your way."

"Who sent you?"

He did not reply.

Colonel McKay said to the American driver, "How the hell did they know we were here?"

"Who sent you, Lieutenant?" I asked again.

"The Revolutionary Council Headquarters, Major. That's all I know. I am to escort you to Seoul." He started back to his men, when we all saw a jeep coming toward us. I got out of the car.

"Lieutenant, who gave you the orders?"

"I don't know, sir. I am here at my commanding officer's orders. I wouldn't know who ordered him."

"Do you know who I am?"

"I don't know what you mean, sir."

"I am a member of the Revolutionary Council."

"Oh, I know that, sir."

"Are you Colonel Jung's men?"

"Yes, sir. I mean, we were, sir. He was killed in action."

"I know that."

The jeep came at full speed. It stopped behind the Presidential Brigade jeeps. Someone in green fatigues leaped out. He came running toward us. It was Lieutenant Cho, with a revolver in a shoulder holster.

"Welcome back, Major Lee!"

"What are you doing here?" We shook hands. Lieutenant Cho peeked into the car. "Hello, Colonel McKay!" he said in English.

"How're you doing, Lieutenant?" He said in Korean.

"Fine, Colonel. Just fine," said Lieutenant Cho in Korean.

"Well, what is all this?" I said, pointing at the troopers.

"Colonel Min's orders, Major. Your escort."

"What's the matter? Is it unsafe on the road?"

"No, sir."

"Then why all this? Am I under arrest?"

He sighed. "I wish you'd quit talking like that, Major. Colonel Min just wanted to welcome you back, that's all, sir."

"Then he knows I am back."

"Of course, sir."

"I was not to return until he gave his word, you know."

"I wouldn't know anything about that, Major. I just do what he tells me to do."

"All right. Let's go then."

"Yes, sir. May I ride with you?"

"Why?"

"I have a couple of things I have to tell you."

I asked Colonel McKay if it was all right with him if Lieutenant Cho rode with us.

"Sure," he said, getting out of the car. He got into the front seat.

Lieutenant Cho went back to his jeep and told the driver to follow us. The Presidential Brigade troopers climbed into their jeeps. One jeep went ahead of us, with the lieutenant in it. The other jeeps would follow us.

We got into the car.

Lieutenant Cho took off his helmet. His hair was wet and stuck close to his big skull.

Colonel McKay wanted to know if there was anything new about General Ham. "My Korean isn't good enough," he added.

"So, General Ham is coming to Seoul," I said. "What more do you know about him?"

"He is coming all right, Major. But he's still got General Yoon and you know how Colonel Min feels about General Yoon."

I nodded.

"Has the Command Group decided what to do with him when he gets here?"

"That I don't know, sir. Colonel Min's been thinking. Oh, he's been thinking, Major! He's been alone for several hours."

"Where is he now?"

"I left him at the GHQ. But I think he is on his way out to the Paratroopers' base. General Ham is coming in there."

"I know that. What about the rest of the Command Group?"

"They are going out there, too."

I looked at him hard. "Am I expected to go there?"

He shook his head. "No, Major."

"What do you mean by that!"

"I don't know how to tell you, Major, but Colonel Min doesn't want you there. I am to take you to the Bando Hotel. We have a room there for you."

"Then I am under arrest!"

"What's the matter?" said Colonel McKay.

I ignored him. "You'd better tell me, Lieutenant. What is going on?"

"I don't know, sir. All I know is I am to take you to your room at the Bando, then call Colonel Min. He wants to speak to you when you get there."

"Is he angry that I came back?"

"Not that I know of, sir. No, I don't think so. You know, sir, he was worried if anything might happen to you. That's why he wanted you to go to Japan for a while."

"Everyone tells me that!"

"What was it like in Japan, Major?"

"Look! I am in no mood to talk about that now. What is Colonel Min going to do with General Ham? You'd better tell me."

"I wish I knew, sir." He gave a quick glance at Colonel McKay. "Sir?"

"Yes?"

"You'd better not tell this to our foreign friends here."

I stared at him. I spoke fast. "If it's confidential, you'd better speak fast. He understands Korean."

Lieutenant Cho spoke fast in a Northern dialect. "Colonel Min has ringed the air base with tanks. There's going to be a shooting out there, I think, sir. Please don't tell them this."

"Did Colonel Min ask you to tell me this?"

He shook his head. "No, sir. It's all done quietly, if you know what I mean, Major. Only the Command Group knows about it."

"Well, I am in the Command Group. Does this mean that they have made a decision on General Ham? Any plan what to do with General Yoon and his staff?"

"General Yoon, did you say?" said Colonel McKay, without looking back at us.

"He is still being held at General Ham's headquarters," I said.

"Oh."

"What more do you know?" I said to Lieutenant Cho.

"The Command Group has alerted the Commandos and the Para-troopers. I don't know why, sir. And Colonel Min's been going over something with our Air Force people."

"An attack plan on General Ham's headquarters?"

"I wouldn't know, sir. All I know is that this alert went out after Colonel Min and the Group had a long talk with Major General Chang from Taegue."

"General Chang. Of the 2nd Army?"

"Yes, sir."

"Is he going to take over from General Ham?"

"I don't know that, sir."

"I think they have decided on a showdown."

"Well, goddamn it, it's about time, sir!"

"You don't know what you are saying! Do you realize how bloody it is going to be!"

"It can't be helped, sir! It's General Ham's fault!"

I did not speak.

Colonel McKay said, "Have you learned anything new?"

"No," I said. "Except that I am to go to the Bando Hotel and get in touch with Colonel Min from there."

"Where is he now?"

"On his way out to the air base."

"I see."

We did not speak after that for a while.

We were driving through the muddy, potholed street of Yong-dongpo. The street was deserted. As we approached the entrance to the Han River bridge, we saw two medium tanks of the Ma-rines; the Marines, with bayoneted rifles, manned sandbagged ma-chine-gun emplacements and the roadblocks. Lieutenant Cho pro-duced a handful of armbands — blue, white, orange, and black. "These are for you, sir," he said; he was wearing a blue armband.

"Better wear the blue one for now, Major. Then, the white one after the curfew starts at eight o'clock. Change to the black one at midnight. Change again to the orange one tomorrow morning. It will be all changed tomorrow. Just to be on the safe side, sir."

I put the blue one on.

He pinned it for me on my sleeve. He reached into his breast pocket, and took out a small brown leather wallet. "This is yours, sir. Your identification card as a member of the Command Group and the Revolutionary Council, telephone numbers you need to know, communications procedures and codes, and so on. They are all in there."

It was getting darker outside. I could not see beyond the Han River too clearly. At the entrance to the bridge, we had to stop at a checkpoint manned by the Army Military Police. There were two more tanks on both sides of the entrance. Battle-ready Marines on jeeps and three-quarter-ton trucks lined the road. Jet fighters were circling over our heads. We drove onto the bridge.

"It was pretty bad here, sir," said Lieutenant Cho. "See that, sir?" He was pointing at the tangled mess of steel cables and beams, bent and twisted, dangling from the top of the bridge. We were driving behind a Marine armored personnel carrier on half-tracks, which went fast, clattering on the bridge. The water in the river was full and roaring against the bridge. The damage to the bridge was not as heavy as I had expected. At the other end of the bridge, there were two more Marine tanks, Shermans, their cannons pointing at the dark sky. We picked up speed and drove fast on the quiet, deserted street. Only when we came near the Seoul Railway Station did we begin to see passers-by and a few civilian vehicles, buses and taxicabs. In the plaza of the railway station, heavy trucks with troops of the 17th Division on them lined up in a row. Tents had been set up there. I could see an ambulance parked in front of a tent with a Red Cross sign. Two 105-mm. howitzers, both pointing toward the north, stood in the middle of a ring of sandbagged machine-gun emplacements. Troopers were everywhere in the plaza, which served as a staging area. I could hear trains huffing and clanking in the yard. The South Gate was intact. On the wide avenue leading toward City Hall there was a medium tank, scorched and its turret blown apart, halfway onto the sidewalk; its cannon was stuck into the shopwindow of a shoe store it had crashed into. City Hall loomed ahead. The steps of City Hall were swarming with troopers. Sandbagged machine-gun emplacements ringed the front of City Hall. There was a Sherman tank on its right, dominating the crossroad there. Another Sherman tank of the Presidential Brigade was on its left, its cannon pointing toward the National Assembly Building across the street. There were trucks and jeeps, all loaded with the soldiers, near the Assembly Building. Troopers with automatic rifles lined both sides of the wide avenue which led to the Capitol Building. There were no civilians in sight in this section of the city; only the soldiers wearing blue armbands, fully armed, on foot and in vehicles, near the tanks and some on top of the tanks. At the intersection, we turned to the right, coming into the driveway of the Bando Hotel. The Presidential Brigade lieutenant jumped out of his jeep. He came to us. Across the street from the Bando, a long line of American sedans was parked in front of the American Embassy. The Korean Marines lined up along the sidewalk near the embassy, facing the hotel. Jeeps and jeeps everywhere near the hotel. Down the block to the east, there were two tanks, facing each other across the street, at the intersection there. A convoy of trucks was just passing by, going toward the Chongno to the north. A Military Police jeep sped alongside the trucks, shrieking its siren.

All the entrances to the hotel were guarded by the heavily armed troopers of the Presidential Brigade Infantry.

We got out of the car. The American driver stayed in it.

Lieutenant Cho ran to his jeep. He came back with a .45 automatic pistol in a holster on a belt with cartridges. "Yours, Major."

I strapped it on. "All right," I said. "Show me in."

"I would like to stay with you if you don't mind," said Colonel McKay.

"I don't mind."

The troopers saluted us. Their submachine guns clanked and clattered as we passed them. We walked into the dim lobby. The coffee shop was brightly lit. I could see few people in it. The small lobby was crowded with Marines and MP's. Boots squishing, rifles and submachine guns rattling, and telephones ringing at the front desk manned by the MP's — the stifling air of the lobby buzzed and bustled. A Marine lieutenant was coming out of the coffee shop, trailed by a Marine corporal with a radio set on his back. All the Marines were wearing camouflaged battle dress and steel helmets. A Military Police sergeant came over to us from behind the front desk. "Major Lee, sir?"

"Yes, Sergeant," said Lieutenant Cho. "Room 1007."

"All right, Lieutenant. It's on the tenth floor."

We took the elevator. The Marine lieutenant was talking on the radio. The door slowly closed shut.

"Hot!" said Colonel McKay. Beads of sweat were dribbling down his cheeks.

Lieutenant Cho said, still in his Northern dialect, "You know the Prime Minister and the Chief of Staff got shot, don't you, sir?"

"The Joint Chiefs of Staff, too."

"Yes, sir."

"Did we do it?"

"We captured Lieutenant Colonel Hwang, did you know that, sir?"

I nodded.

"He did it," he whispered, maintaining a casual air, glancing at Colonel McKay who was wiping the inside of his cap with a handkerchief.

"Did he confess?"

"We beat it out of him, sir. He did it. We've checked all our units and we know we didn't do it."

I remained silent.

"He is going to be shot," he hissed quietly, flashing his enormous, bloodshot eyes. "And General Ahn, too!"

"What!"

"They are both Reds, sir. They have been Reds all these years!"

"I know that!"

"They were going to kill us all!"

"We can't just shoot them!"

"Serve them right, Major!"

The elevator stopped at the third floor. The door slid open. A Marine private with a carbine said, "Going down, sir?"

"We're going up," said Lieutenant Cho.

"Oh, excuse me, sir. Sorry."

The door closed.

"Has the Command Group decided on that?" I said.

"On what, sir?"

"On General Ahn and Colonel Hwang. To shoot them, I mean."

"Oh, that, sir. Yes, sir. Unanimous."

"*I* haven't voted on *that!*"

Colonel McKay gazed at me.

Lieutenant Cho looked down at the floor.

"Has Colonel Min approved the decision?"

"Yes, sir. He brought it up himself, as a matter of fact." He looked at me defiantly. "They are traitors, sir. Reds! They almost wrecked our coup! Besides, they are both responsible for the murders of the Prime Minister and . . ."

I cut him short. "We can't just murder the murderers!"

"It's a just execution, sir!"

"What's the difference! It mustn't be done! We can't just kill them off!"

"What are you two arguing about?" said Colonel McKay grinning.

I ignored him and his silly grin. .

"They killed lots of our men, sir!" said Lieutenant Cho in a furious whisper. "Sometimes, I really don't understand you, Major!"

The elevator stopped again at the sixth floor. A foreign woman of about thirty in a pink and green dress and a long white necklace stood alone, clutching a green leather handbag. "Going up?"

"Right," said Colonel McKay. "Step in."

She came in. She stood next to the colonel, away from us. She had her blond hair short and curled. She smelled strongly of perfume and powder. She was openly scrutinizing Colonel McKay, who said, "Are you an American?"

"When is the execution set?" I said to Lieutenant Cho.

"Yes. I'm from Darien, Connecticut. You?"

"Tonight, sir."

"Michigan, originally. On vacation?"

"When tonight?"

She was dabbing her small forehead with a silky, pink handkerchief.

"I don't know, sir."

"I was going to go to Hong Kong and then on to Bangkok, you know, from Japan."

"We can't kill them until they are tried!"

"But I stopped here for a few days and then got trapped here by the coup."

"There's no time for that, Major!"

"I am flying out tomorrow, though."

"Is that so?"

"Besides, sir, what difference would that make? They'll be executed anyway."

"Yes! They said the international flights were going out by tomorrow afternoon." She peered at me, shrugging her shoulders.

"I see. Well, that's good news."

"Anyway, I am glad you told me about it, Lieutenant."

"I sure hope they keep their word, though. You never know these people."

Lieutenant Cho shook his head. "I really can't figure you out, Major. Excuse me for saying that, sir."

The elevator stopped once more at the eighth floor. A stocky Marine captain stomped in. His .45 automatic was bulging out of its shoulder holster. His camouflaged steel helmet bobbed as he nodded to me. He turned around and stood in front of us; the back of his camouflaged jacket was darkly stained with sweat.

The American woman said in a whisper, "Colonel, are we for them or against them? Do you know what I mean?"

A small, mischievous grin flickered on his ruddy face. "Why don't you ask the major here? He'll tell you."

"Oh?" She looked at me past the colonel, slightly leaning forward. "You speak English?"

Colonel McKay was looking up at the elevator's ceiling.

"We are not against you, miss," I said, "if that's what you are interested to know."

She gave the colonel a quick glance, then looked at me. She shrugged her shoulders. "I guess we are for you, then. What do you know!" She smiled, looking at Colonel McKay. She raised her penciled eyebrows, crinkling her big nose. Her pink lips pouted. She said, "Boy! What a story I am gonna have for my friends! I got some nice pictures of these people in action, too."

"That's fine, miss," said Colonel McKay.

The elevator stopped at the tenth floor. We trooped out. The Marine captain remained with the woman.

"Well, take care now, Colonel. Nice meeting you," she said.

"Have a good trip home," said the colonel through the closing doors. "And behave yourself now!"

She giggled. "Oh, you naughty!"

A Marine in combat gear with a submachine gun stood up behind a desk with a telephone on it at the corner. Another Marine was down at the other end of the thickly carpeted, hushed, long corridor. "The seventh room to your right, sir," the Marine sentry said. "The bellboy will be up in a minute," he said to Lieutenant Cho.

We went to the room. It was a large room with twin beds, a sofa, a few chairs and tables. The room looked out through the windows to the dark back garden of the Chosun Hotel.

Lieutenant Cho turned the air-conditioner on. "Will this room do, Major?"

I nodded.

He said, "Would you like something to eat or drink, sir?" He said to Colonel McKay in English, "A drink, Colonel McKay?"

"Yes. Something cool would be nice."

Lieutenant Cho said to me, "A nice bathroom there, sir. Would you like to take a bath?"

I snapped, "There's no time for that! I want to speak to Colonel Min!"

"Yes, sir. Excuse me, sir. I'll be right back." He hurried out of the room.

Colonel McKay watched the door shut with a click. "Major Lee," he said, adjusting the dial on the air-conditioner. He stood in front of the air-conditioner with his back to it. "I think you and Lieutenant Cho were talking about General Ahn and Colonel Hwang, weren't you?"

I did not speak.

"Is something up?"

I kept silent.

"You don't have to tell me, Major, if it is confidential. But you know I'll find out sooner or later."

I went to him. "General Ahn and Colonel Hwang are going to be executed. The Command Group has acted on it unanimously, with one member not voting. Me!"

He did not speak for a moment. He crossed his arms over his chest, staring at me. "When are they to be executed?"

"Tonight. Sometime tonight."

He shook his head. "That won't do! We can't let them be shot! This is ridiculous!"

I gazed at him. "Why?"

"Why! It's sheer idiocy to execute them at this time!" He was agitated. He nearly shouted at me. He quickly composed himself. He said in a calm voice, "We can't let that happen, Major."

"Are you including me? Or are you talking about you and your people?"

"Everyone! We are all involved in this. Look, Major. This is complete nonsense. Do you realize who they are? General Ahn and Colonel Hwang, I mean. They are the biggest catches we've ever made here. They are the biggest Communist agents we've bagged so far in this part of the world. Not just Korea! Good God! Colonel Min must be out of his mind! They must have all gone berserk!"

"Berserk?"

"You know — gone wild!" he said, slapping his head.

"You are thinking of General Ahn and Colonel Hwang from the point of view of your Intelligence organization, aren't you?"

"Damn right, Major! Do you realize how valuable . . ."

"Yes, I do realize that, Colonel. All right. You have your interest in these two men and I have my interest in them."

"What do you mean?"

"You want them kept alive because you think they are valuable properties from the point of view of your Intelligence organization. Well, Colonel, we do have our own Intelligence service, which will find them very valuable indeed."

"Right."

"In addition to that, I do not want to see a kangaroo court and a firing squad marring the spirit of our revolution, Colonel. Do you understand me?"

"Of course I do. Don't think for a moment that I don't. You have my fullest sympathy. As a matter of fact, I've always told Colonel Min . . ."

"Yes. So then, there must be something you and I can do."

"Yes. Let me hear what you have to say."

"We can't just execute them now. Not just like that!"

"No."

"They must be tried, first, as Communist agents, and, second, as those responsible for the murders of the Prime Minister and the Chief of Staff and . . ."

"Has Colonel Hwang confessed to that?"

"You are not really surprised, are you, Colonel?"

"No. I can't say I am."

"You see, Colonel, we didn't kill those people!"

"Well, they are all dead."

"We have to try those two to show the nation that we were not responsible for the murders, that we had not planned to kill them. Do you understand that, Colonel?"

He did not respond.

"Well, don't you, Colonel?"

"I do, I do, but, Major, look, we can't have a trial."

I stared at him.

"I've told you before, Major. We can't have a trial, not an open trial which you'll have to have to let the nation know who is responsible for what and so on. No, we can't have that."

"I know your reasoning, Colonel. You want to keep it all secret. You don't want the North Koreans to know about it."

"Right."

"Perhaps they already know about it."

"I doubt it, Major. They know nothing about General Ahn's arrest. Besides, even if they did, it doesn't really matter."

"Why not?"

"Oh, I don't want to go into that now, Major. Now, about Colonel Hwang. Well, you can always announce that he was killed in action. And the North Koreans can write him off. At any rate, we can soon find out if the North Koreans know about General Ahn's arrest and anything else that goes with it."

"All right, Colonel. We have then a common interest, although from different points of view."

"Right. I want to see Colonel Min about this right away. This is absolutely idiotic!"

"I do understand Colonel Min's motive, Colonel."

"Oh, I do too, Major! He has my fullest sympathy and understanding. But he is not doing the right thing. He can't let his personal emotion and revenge interfere with a matter of this magnitude which is really a matter of the state. You see that, don't you, Major?"

"From a different point of view, Colonel."

"Ah, what's the difference! It all comes out the same way. You are supposed to get in touch with Colonel Min, are you not?"

"Yes."

"Well, let's get busy. I want to see him."

"So do I, Colonel."

"Is Lieutenant Cho getting in touch with him now?"

"I don't know. I suppose yes."

"All right. I will be right back. Try not to leave here without me."

I did not answer.

He drew himself up to me. "Major, if you want to avoid bloodshed, if you want to prevent Colonel Min from killing General Ham and General Ahn *and* Colonel Hwang, you'd better stick with me. Do you understand that!"

I remained silent.

"Well, I am sure you do. I will come right back." He trotted out of the room in a hurry.

The sky outside was dark. There were few people in the back garden of the Chosun Hotel, only a handful of Marines with bayoneted rifles near the small pagoda in the middle of the garden. A searing pain seized me in the head. I went into the bathroom to get a drink of water. I washed my face with the cold water. I put my head under the faucet, letting the water chill my burning head. I heard the telephone ring in the room.

The telephone was on a small desk near the window. I picked up the receiver. "Yes?"

A voice said, "Major Lee, sir?"

"Yes. This is Major Lee."

"Room 1007, sir?"

"Yes. Who is it?"

"One moment, sir. Colonel Min would like to speak with you."

At the other end of the line, I could hear telephones ringing and voices speaking and papers crackling and shuffling.

Colonel Min came on the line. "How are you?"

"Fine."

"Did you get some rest in Japan?"

"Yes. Thanks to you."

He paused for a moment. "I didn't want you to be back here." His voice was flat and without a trace of emotion.

"I know that."

"I suppose Colonel McKay persuaded you to come back with him?"

"Not exactly."

"It doesn't matter now. You are here. Are you prepared to see me?"

"What do you mean?"

He was silent for a moment. "Let me put it to you bluntly, Major Lee. Are you ready to rejoin us?"

I did not reply.

He said coldly, "Rejoin us and carry on your task?"

"Am I being judged?" I said, suppressing my fury.

"Yes. You were judged by us and you are being judged right now."

The brutal candidness of his statement took me aback. "Are you judging me?"

"Yes."

"Why? About what?"

"I am judging your capacity to shoulder the heavy burden of saving the nation and carrying on the task of running the nation without succumbing to your sentimentality. Does that make it clear to you?"

"It is not sentimentality!"

"Nonsense!"

"It is my capacity to distinguish good and evil!"

"That's a sheer rationalization, Major."

"It is not a rationalization! I am trying to be a decent human being from the point of view of my conviction and belief in my understanding of humanistic philosophy!"

A moment of silence and he said wearily, "Look, Major Lee. I

316 / *The Innocent*

didn't let you return or call you up to carry on a pseudo-intellectual conversation. The question simply is this: Do you wish to join me and the others again and get on with the job?"

I kept quiet.

"Let me ask you this," he said, his voice a little louder. "We are fighting for our lives now. Do you understand me?"

"Yes."

"Good! We are also fighting for our chance —and we now have a very good chance — for our chance of saving the country and helping the people. Do you understand that?"

"Yes!"

"Well, good! Now then, Major Lee, would you agree that our aims and ideals in launching this coup have always been based on what you call humanistic philosophy?"

"Yes, but our ideals have been steadily degenerating! We are becoming more and more like the ones we have replaced!"

"Absolutely nonsensical! You do not have to jump into an either-or conclusion, Major! Everything takes time! Trial and error, Major! We can't afford now to lose our chance and lose the nation! If we lose this chance, we will never find out whether we are decent human beings or simply diabolical monsters. Ah, but this is nonsense! We are wasting our time. Look, we have to win the country first to find out whether we are just like the ones we have replaced, as you said. Don't you agree?"

I did not speak.

"Let me ask you one more question. Are you prepared to shoot our enemies?" It was a quiet voice but I knew he spoke the words without a flicker of emotion on his taut, austere face, with his tight lips barely moving. "Are you?"

"Are you implying General Ahn and Colonel Hwang? And General Ham, too?"

"So you know."

"Yes."

"Yes. They are our enemies, among others. They are, and there may be many more. Are you prepared to shoot them?"

I could not reply to his cold-blooded question.

"What's the matter?"

"I am prepared, Colonel Min, to approve their execution depending on the circumstances in which they are judged guilty and sentenced to death."

"You do not approve of the circumstances?"

"No. You know *that!*"

"I *knew* that."

"And that's why you sent me away."

"You knew *that,* didn't you?"

I kept quiet.

"Well, don't talk about that now," he said. "Let me, then, ask you a final question. Do you want to contribute yourself to the rebuilding of our nation and helping our people?"

"Yes, of course!"

"Well, then! Here's what we can do, Major. We can either welcome you back or send you away."

"You mean — *you* can."

He was silent for a while. "This is not the time to wallow in a private sentimentality, Major. We have the nation to think about. Do you want us to welcome you back or do you want us to send you away?"

"Welcome me back and expect me to participate in your crimes?"

"You are judging us, Major. You have no right to do that! Not yet! Someday — someday, when it is all over, then you will have all the rights and time needed to judge me. But not until then. Do you understand!"

I did not know what to say.

I heard him sigh. His voice spoke rapidly, impatiently, and with a touch of resignation. "All right, Major, welcome back! I need you more than ever. There are many things we have to do together, do you understand? I suppose I can afford to have one prosecutor and one judge all put together in you?"

"I am not your prosecutor and your judge!"

"Ah, but you are, yes, you are!"

"I have never judged you!"

"Yes, you have, don't you know? And you are judging me, now."

"And you are judging me, too!"

"How fortunate you are to be judged as you are! Listen, I asked you once if you'd judge me, and you said you'd never judge me. Remember?"

"Yes. You said that to me. At the front."

"Yes. Remember this? I said, 'You'll judge me.' "

"Yes."

"I say this to you now. You will not only judge me but you will have to judge me. Do you understand me? You will have to judge me someday. If not for me, then for your own sake. For your own sanity!"

"I don't know what you are saying!"

"Ah, but you will understand me later. Someday. Let us hope so. You must judge me in cold blood, not for me, but for you. Listen, stay where you are! Will you promise?"

"Where are you now?"

"I will see you soon. And when I see you, I don't want to hear anything more about this. Do you understand? Is Colonel McKay with you?"

"Yes. He is downstairs right now but he'll be up shortly."

"Good. I want to see him. Will you tell him that?"

"He wants to see you, too."

"I know he does. I should think he would want to see me. Is it about General Ahn?"

"And Colonel Hwang. Did you know?"

"Know what?"

"That Colonel McKay will try to stop the execution?"

"Of course! But if he thinks he is running this country, he is quite mistaken. He has a surprise coming to him. I know why he wants to meddle in this but he is *not* one of us. His view is from Washington, not from Seoul. Will you keep him there?"

"Yes." I heard a knock on the door. Colonel McKay came in, followed by a bellboy with a trayful of bottles and glasses.

"Good. I'll see you soon."

"General Ham is flying in?"

"Yes. We have enough time. Stay where you are."

"Colonel McKay is here now. I will tell him."

The bellboy left the room. Colonel McKay was pouring beer into the glasses.

"And, Major Lee."

"Yes?"

"When we are all together, I don't want you to bring up any matters which do not concern Colonel McKay as a professional representative of his organization. Understood?"

"Yes, Colonel Min."

I saw Colonel McKay raise his eyebrows, nodding to me.

We hung up. "That was Colonel Min," I said, taking a glass of beer from him. "Thank you. He wants to see you."

"Well, about time he did," he said, refilling his glass with the beer. "Where is he now?"

"He didn't say." I sat down on the edge of the bed. I faced him on the sofa. "I told him you wanted to see him."

"Fine! Is he coming here?"

"Yes."

A few minutes later, there was a knock on the door.

"Who is it?" I said.

"Lieutenant Cho, sir."

"Oh! Well, come on in."

The door opened. Colonel Min walked in, followed by Lieutenant Cho. There were three young lieutenants of the Presidential Brigade Armor outside in the corridor. They were all armed with submachine guns, in fatigues but not wearing steel helmets. They took positions outside the door.

Colonel Min was also in fatigues, wearing combat boots, a small revolver in a shoulder holster, and dark sunglasses.

Colonel McKay gave him a salute. "Colonel Min."

We shook hands and sat down. Colonel Min took a seat on the armchair facing the sofa where Colonel McKay and I sat. Lieutenant

Cho poured the beer into a glass and handed it to Colonel Min. Colonel McKay and I already had our glasses filled with beer. Colonel Min reached for another glass. He filled it with beer. He gave it to the lieutenant, who took it from him with an awkward bow, standing up. We raised our glasses.

"To the success of your coup!" said Colonel McKay.

Colonel Min took off his sunglasses; his eyes were bloodshot; there were dark, shadowy hollows about them. He said quietly, "To the dead, gentlemen. To Colonel Jung and to all the dead, friends and foes."

We drained our glasses in silence.

Lieutenant Cho filled the glasses again.

"All right, Lieutenant Cho," said Colonel Min, "will you excuse us now."

Lieutenant Cho gave us a quick bow and withdrew from the room. As the door was opened, I could see the three lieutenants with their submachine guns slung on their shoulders standing against the wall in the corridor. The door closed.

"You were in the hotel somewhere?" I said to Colonel Min.

"No. I was at a meeting over at the Chosun Hotel."

"I see."

He looked at us. "Well, here we are," he said, putting his glass down on the table.

"Here we are," said Colonel McKay.

Colonel Min said, "Now, I am ready to hear what you have on your mind, Colonel McKay." He looked at his wristwatch which was fastened on his lapel through a buttonhole. "We have one hour. General Ham has just left his headquarters for the airfield."

It was eight o'clock sharp.

Chapter 18

Colonel McKay said, "I think you know what I have on my mind, Colonel Min."

Colonel Min said, "I do."

"We don't approve of your decision to execute General Ahn and Colonel Kim."

"I see."

"You must have known that we wouldn't."

"Should we have known that, Colonel McKay?"

Colonel McKay smiled. "Oh, I wouldn't put it that way. But, surely you understand our position."

"Perhaps and perhaps not. We have been very busy."

"I understand, of course. We have been very busy, too, Colonel Min."

"Yes. Negotiating with General Ham and guaranteeing him your safe-conduct and so on. Yes, you have been very busy, too."

Colonel McKay gave me a quick glance. "We have your interests in mind, Colonel. You can't afford a bloody civil war at this stage of your coup. You do know that we are not particularly fond of or protective about General Ham and his gang."

Colonel Min switched off the small lamp on the table. The light from the floor lamp on Colonel McKay's side of the sofa did not quite reach Colonel McKay. He said, "We have your interests in mind, too, as well as ours. You do know that we are not especially fond of Communist agents operating against us in our own Army. And, you are not particularly fond of Communists either, Colonel."

"Do you resent, by any chance, that we have offered safe-conduct to General Ham?"

"Resent? Of course not, Colonel McKay. What gave you that silly idea! You are doing what you think is the best for your interests and we are doing what we think is the best for our own interests. It is very simple. What is not simple is that we may not see eye to eye on occasions. You do understand that?"

"Yes, I understand that perfectly. Naturally, what we think is the best for you may not turn out to be the best for you at all. Sometimes."

"And what we think is the best for you may not turn out to be the best for you. That is quite possible."

"Yes, it is possible. And I think we are of one mind on that, then."

"Precisely so, Colonel McKay."

"You are going to go through with this execution?"

"Of course."

"We can stop it, you know, Colonel, if we really want to."

"Of course. You do have all those troops and more in Japan and so on," said Colonel Min, picking up his glass from the table. "But then, we, too, have troops here, you know. And when your troops and our troops meet, well, it may be interesting to see just what will happen."

Colonel McKay fixed his eyes on Colonel Min but did not reply.

Colonel Min said, "Ah, but it won't look good, will it? Oh, I am not worrying about public opinion in your country and in the world. World opinion is a very whimsical thing, Colonel. You can always change it, although you may end up losing many of your friends in the meantime."

Colonel McKay grinned. "We have a word to describe what you

are saying right now, but I won't use it if that's all right with you."

Colonel Min smiled. "If you think I am blackmailing you, you are quite wrong. I am merely stating a fact. You are an intelligent Intelligence officer, Colonel McKay, and a good friend of mine, so you should be able to understand the situation."

"Yes, I do. And you, too, Colonel, should be able to understand it. Oh, I would say we both understand each other quite well, wouldn't you?"

Colonel Min nodded. "Yes," he said leaning slightly forward. "You know you can't stop the execution."

"And you know you can't do what you want to do with General Ham as long as we guarantee his safety and mean to stick by our word."

"Well, we understand each other perfectly."

"Right, Colonel Min."

"Well, then, shall we get down to business, as you Americans say?"

"Yes, I think we should." He looked at me. "If you don't mind, Major Lee, I would like to have a talk with Colonel Min alone."

Colonel Min said, "He can stay, Colonel. We ought to have a witness, after all. Besides, I want Major Lee here for educational purposes."

I stood up from the sofa. "I would like to be excused, gentlemen, if you don't mind. I think I know what you two are up to and I would rather not take part in it."

Colonel Min said sharply, "Sit down."

"Really, Colonel Min, I would rather we were left alone," said Colonel McKay.

"Sit down, Major," said Colonel Min again. "I did not ask you to take part. I merely want you here as an observer."

I had no other choice. I sat down. "You are going to make some sort of deal with each other and I do not like the smell of it, if you will allow me to say so. Colonel Min, are you going to trade General Ahn and Colonel Hwang for General Ham?"

He did not reply.

"Bargaining with human lives!" I said, raising my voice, unable to restrain my anger. "This is beastly, gentlemen!"

"Enough!" said Colonel Min. "Sit down and just listen!"

"Is this your personal dealing, Colonel Min," I said, my heart pounding with rage, "or has the Command Group agreed on this? If the Command Group has not decided on this deal you are about to make, I would like to protest this and put the matter before the Group!"

"I said that's enough!"

"Now, now, let's all calm down, shall we?" said Colonel McKay. "I know we are all touchy and quite jumpy but we can settle this peacefully, I am sure."

"Peacefully!" I said. "How can you sit there calmly and say that, Colonel!"

"Well, Major, otherwise we won't get anything accomplished! What do you want? Would you rather have General Ahn and Colonel Hwang shot?"

Colonel Min stared at me.

"Of course not," I said, pleading, "but there must be some other more decent way . . ."

"We are not dealing with decent people, Major," said Colonel Min. "When will you ever understand that?"

"I beg your pardon, Colonel Min?" said Colonel McKay.

"I meant General Ahn and the others. No offense meant to you and your people. Certainly not."

Colonel McKay shook his head slightly, grinning. "Certainly not!"

"All right. That's enough," said Colonel Min. "Time is running out fast, gentlemen. Let's get this over with. First of all, Colonel McKay, you've had two companies of your Military Police dispatched to the Paratroopers' air base. With armored cars and so on. Why?"

"Well, Colonel Min, you've had the base swarming with tanks and troops. Why?"

"I have been expecting to see your troops out there. It was simply a matter of precaution and prudence."

"We have been expecting you would do just that. So, it is also a matter of prudence on our part. We are both very prudent people."

"That means you intend to protect General Ham."

"And your move implies that you do not intend to allow us to offer our protection to General Ham according to the terms of our safe-conduct agreement."

"It all depends, Colonel."

"Naturally."

"You want General Ahn and Colonel Hwang."

"Do you think we should want them?"

"Yes, I think you should."

"Don't you want them?"

"Not as badly as you do, Colonel. Oh, we do want them to carry out our execution orders, but then you don't want dead bodies."

"And you don't want to see General Ham back safely at his headquarters in good health, do you?"

"Depends, Colonel."

"I see."

I could not help speaking out. "This sounds like a slave market, gentlemen! I can smell the flesh and blood and hear the crack of a whip and the voices bidding the prices."

They ignored me completely.

"Yes. We want those two men very badly, I admit, Colonel Min."

"And we want our freedom to deal with General Ham, Colonel McKay."

"Right."

"Very well."

"There's one thing more, Colonel Min. We do not want a civil war, which will inevitably involve all of us in a very tricky situation. You do understand that."

"There will be no civil war, I assure you, once you stop playing the role of a brother's keeper. We have a plan. It will work."

"We don't want to know your plan."

"I didn't think you would want to know."

"Right."

"So we won't tell you about our plan. When it is all over, you knew nothing about it. Understood?"

Colonel McKay nodded, lighting up his pipe. "Very considerate of you."

"You are welcome, Colonel. We know each other well by now, I trust. Everything is going to be all right, as you Americans keep saying."

"Fine!" Colonel McKay grinned, standing up.

"All right," said Colonel Min. "I think you have gained more than we have, don't you?"

Colonel McKay squinted at him, sucking on his pipe, holding a lighted match over the bowl. "Well, I won't try to be picayune about it."

Colonel Min stood up. They shook hands.

"When shall I see you again?" said Colonel McKay.

"Tonight. Midnight. Is that too late for you?"

"Not at all. Where?"

"At Colonel Son's headquarters."

"Fine. I will be there."

"I will be expecting you."

"Well, good luck, Colonel Min, and you, too, Major Lee."

Colonel Min nodded. "All right, let's get this over with. Come along, Major Lee. We have a lot of work to do."

I stood up.

Colonel McKay offered his hand to me. "Take care now," he said.

I did not take his hand. "I don't know what to make of all this, Colonel. I no longer know what to trust, whom to believe in!"

"Well!" he said, taking his pipe out of his mouth. "Start trusting yourself, then."

"He will have to know first what he really wants," said Colonel Min, striding toward the door. "Come along!"

Colonel McKay said with an unexpected gentleness in his voice, "Major, we are not playing a game, you know. Certainly not a neat little intellectual game. The fortune of your country is at stake, Major. And the stakes are too high to let yourself be bogged down by private misgivings, et cetera. All the ideals and hopes you expressed in your preamble to the policy statement — well, don't you expect to see them realized?"

I did not speak.

He tapped me on the shoulder lightly. "I'll see you around." He went out of the room, exchanged a few whispered words with Colonel Min, and disappeared down the hallway.

Colonel Min stood outside the open door, flanked by the three lieutenants and Lieutenant Cho. He was waiting for me. He did not look my way. In the dim light his face was shadowy and dark. I held myself in check.

"Let's go!" said Colonel Min to the lieutenants. He took a step.

I hurried out of the room. I felt like a helpless prisoner. I followed him. Lieutenant Cho and one of the lieutenants silently flanked me as though I were now in their protective custody.

The lobby was dim and quiet. Apparently, the combat-ready Marines and the troopers of the Presidential Brigade had been relieved by the Army Military Police. There were a few armed MP's at the front desk and the entrances. I did not see any of the Marines and the troopers I had seen before. The sky was dark. The air was heavy and humid. In the brightly lit driveway of the hotel, three jeeps, one with its top up, waited for us. Across the street, the windows of the American Embassy building were dark; only the main entrance of the embassy and three windows directly above the entrance shone with light. Two U.S. Marines stood at the entrance, joined on their sides by a small detachment of the Korean Marines. The street was quiet. There was not one civilian in sight, nor a civilian vehicle, except for the three American sedans with small American flags on their front bumpers parked across the street in front of the embassy.

Colonel Min got into the jeep in the middle, with the top up. Two lieutenants of the Presidential Brigade jumped into the back of Colonel Min's jeep. The other lieutenant went into the rear jeep. It was twenty minutes after eight. We left the hotel and turned toward the City Hall plaza. The tanks were still there, near the steps of the dark, massive building. The tanks' hatches were open and helmeted crew members leaned out of the tanks. The .50-caliber heavy machine guns on the tanks pointed at the dark sky. The plaza was filled with heavy trucks, loaded with helmeted troops. The floodlights from the top of the City Hall building lit up the plaza down below, illuminating the trucks and jeeps and armored personnel carriers, and several anti-aircraft guns on half-tracks. A convoy of trucks was moving up the wide avenue across from the plaza, passing by the dark National Assembly Building, heading toward the Capitol Building. A Military Police jeep, with its long radio antenna swaying, escorted the convoy, flashing its red revolving light. We stopped in front of the steps to the main entrance of the City Hall building. Steel-helmeted troopers of the 5th Division manned the sandbagged machine-gun emplacements on both sides of the steps. A makeshift command post had been set up there, to the left of the steps in a small tent. Telephones were ringing, voices were shouting, and radios were beeping. Someone came bounding down the steps and saluted us. A young lieutenant colonel, armed with grenades and submachine gun, peered into the jeep. He wore a white armband on his left sleeve; his sleeves were rolled up over his elbows.

"Hello, Colonel Min!" he said. "I still have most of my regiment here, Colonel. We can move out anytime, though. Just give me the word."

Colonel Min said, "Good. Who is going to relieve you?"

"The Marines. At midnight. But if we have to move out before midnight, the reserve battalion from the 17th Division can relieve us anytime."

Colonel Min glanced at the trucks. "The trucks," he said to the colonel. "They have canvas tops? It might rain."

"They do, but it was too damn hot, Colonel. We won't get wet."

"Supplies all right? Have they eaten?"

"Yes, sir. We are fine. Don't worry about us, sir."

"All right. Keep in touch with the headquarters."

"Yes, sir."

"All right. Thank the men for me, will you?"

"Yes, sir."

Someone came running out of the command post tent. A tall warrant officer came to us and spoke to the lieutenant colonel. "Sir, a call from the Division headquarters."

The young regimental commander excused himself and dashed back into the tent.

Just then the radio on our jeep crackled. Lieutenant Cho picked up the receiver. Colonel Min was wanted on the radio. Colonel Min took the receiver. "Yes?"

The Revolutionary Council Command Headquarters had been trying to reach Colonel Min at the Bando Hotel. A certain Colonel Chang would meet us where we were.

The regimental commander came back to us. "I have just been alerted, Colonel Min. Something's up! I am to wait here for further instructions."

Colonel Min nodded. We got out of the jeep. I shook hands with the young colonel. The black sky over the Nam San hill was flashing, like lightning, with crisscrossing searchlights. Across from the plaza, the Duksoo Palace was quiet and dark. Another convoy of trucks, with their headlights fully blazing, came toward the plaza from the direction of the South Gate and the Seoul Railway Station. "The Marines," said the young colonel. "From the First Brigade." The Marines on the open trucks started singing their battle song when they came in sight of the colonel's men. The Marines stood up on the trucks, waving their arms, calling out, cheering. The Army troopers returned the cheer and started singing their own battle song. The young colonel kept on grinning happily, looking at one of the Sherman tanks which was swinging its long, sleek cannon up and down.

Lieutenant Cho reminded us that we should wear our white arm-bands. It was past the curfew.

A jeep was coming toward us from the street by the Chosun Hotel, flashing a red light.

"That must be it, sir," said Lieutenant Cho.

The young regimental commander called for a certain captain, who emerged from the tent. They excused themselves from us, when the jeep came to a halt next to ours. A young lieutenant colonel leaped out of the open jeep and saluted Colonel Min.

"Colonel Chang," said Colonel Min. "What's up?"

I knew him. He was an operations officer from the Presidential Brigade Infantry. We exchanged a nod.

"Colonel Min, this is confidential, " he said.

Colonel Min indicated that Lieutenant Cho and the driver wait for us in the jeep. We moved a few steps away from the jeeps.

"Well?" said Colonel Min. "What is it?"

"Bad news, Colonel. I am sorry I am the one who has to tell you this," he said in a whisper. "There was a mutiny at General Ham's headquarters."

"What? A mutiny?"

"Apparently General Ham's men were split over what their stand ought to be. It now appears that there was a faction which wanted to come over to our side."

Colonel Min said, "Well, we knew *that*."

"Yes, sir. Anyway, after General Ham had left his headquarters, this faction decided to strike against the others who have been urging General Ham to launch a countercoup attack. The opposition group apparently decided that they could not persuade the others and that their best chance was to free the hostages and take over the headquarters."

"Go on."

"So they struck, sir, but the other side struck back and crushed the group."

"The hostages!" I exclaimed. "What happened to them!"

"Colonel Min, I am sorry to report this. General Yoon is dead and so are his staff. The opposition group, too, sir. They are all shot!"

I could not restrain myself. "This means a war!"

Colonel Min, with his arms crossed over his chest, did not speak. His dark face did not stir.

"I'm sorry, sir. I know how you must feel," said Colonel Chang. "General Yoon — I knew him well, too, sir, and this — "

"That's enough," said Colonel Min quietly. "Anything else?"

"We got this information from someone who escaped from General Ham's headquarters. One of the opposition group. He managed to get away and joined up with a neighboring regiment on our side. The regimental commander relayed this to us. He wants to attack General Ham's headquarters!"

"No, no!" said Colonel Min impatiently. "Not yet!"

"We told him to wait for your instructions, Colonel. Are we going to attack?"

Colonel Min did not reply.

Colonel Chang went on, "Colonel Shin, the 34th Division, General Ham's nephew."

"Yes?"

"He's taken over General Ham's headquarters. He wants to fight us."

"I know he does."

"Apparently he had the headquarters surrounded with his troops and has taken over the command there. He had the hostages shot, Colonel! That little bastard had the nerve to do it!"

"Does General Ham know about it?"

"We don't know, Colonel. He is still on his way. Of course, I can't be too sure whether or not he does know what happened at his headquarters. I am inclined to believe that he does."

"It does not really matter," said Colonel Min quietly. "Not now."

"I see what you mean, sir."

"Where is he now?" said Colonel Min. "General Ham, I mean."

"He flew out to one of his divisions first. He changed planes there, and as far as we know, he is on his way to Seoul. He should be arriving soon." He checked his watch.

Colonel Min nodded.

"I am truly sorry about General Yoon, sir."

I said, "I am sorry!"

Colonel Min looked up. His dark, hollow eyes stared at me. He said in a whisper, "Now, Major Lee, you tell me what I should do. Can you tell me what you would do if you were in my place?"

I stood between them feeling bewildered and helpless. "We must do something!" I muttered. "Something!"

Colonel Min pulled himself up. He stood straight. His voice was calm. "We will do something."

"You're damn right, sir!" exclaimed Colonel Chang. "We will do something!"

Colonel Min nodded. His arms now on his hips and his head lowered, he remained silent for a long moment. His face was in the dark shadow of his cap. I could not tell if his eyes were open. At last, he said in a deathly quiet whisper, "Why! Why! Why is it always this way!"

"Sir?" said Colonel Chang.

Colonel Min looked up. His shadowy face was twitching. "This is it!" he said.

"Yes, sir! This is it!" Colonel Chang said.

Colonel Min said, "Go back to the headquarters, Colonel. I want the general alert out. Do it quietly. Did you see Colonel Park there?"

"Yes, sir!"

"I know he is there. I told him to stay put. Tell him this. I want the contingency plan number four put into effect immediately."

Colonel Chang's face brightened up with a grin. "Goddamn, it's about time, sir!"

"You will stay with Colonel Park and see this through," said Colonel Min. "I want the general alert to go out to the Air Force, too. Keep it quiet from the Americans, understand? Are the Commandos and the Paratroopers ready?"

"Yes, sir. They are all assembled and ready to fly out anytime."

"All right." He checked the watch on his lapel.

"Are you going to launch an attack?" I said, alarmed.

He ignored me. "Colonel Chang, tell Colonel Park the Commandos and the Paratroopers can start at nine o'clock sharp. Let's synchronize our watches." They did.

"Nine o'clock sharp!" said Colonel Chang.

Colonel Min said, "I am going out to the airfield now. Keep me informed. Have someone tell General Hyun about General Yoon and his staff. Don't tell him about the contingency plan four, is that clear?"

Colonel Chang smiled. "Yes, sir! I understand!"

"I will tell him about that myself. Later. Get hold of Colonel Mc-Kay and tell him to get in touch with me as soon as possible. All right. Let's go."

"Good luck, Colonel! Take care of yourself."

Colonel Min was already striding toward his jeep.

Colonel Chang turned to me. "Good luck, Major Lee! Take good care of him, will you! Goddamn! I know how close he was to General Yoon!"

"Yes."

"It must be tearing him apart inside though he doesn't show it!"

"Yes. I know."

"Well, this is it!"

"What is the contingency plan four? I was in Japan on a mission, so I don't know about *this* one."

"I know. The plan was drawn up by Colonel Min himself after we learned about General Ham's escape and the subsequent developments. It is an all-out attack plan on his headquarters and on all the headquarters of his cohorts. The first stage calls for an advance warning from us. We opposed this part of the plan but Colonel Min insisted on it. The Air Force will take part in this. If the advance warning and our ultimatum to surrender don't work, then we will send the jets and the bombers in to blast them out. Then the Commandos and the Paratroopers will be airdropped right on top of them in coordination with an assault from our own units out there. It may turn out to be bloody but, goddamn it, it is going to work!" He gripped my arm. "Don't worry. It will work! You just take good care of Colonel Min!" He ran back to his jeep and roared off. I dashed to the jeep. I climbed into the back. The jeep started, when the young regimental commander came running to us. "Good luck, Colonel Min!"

"Good luck," said Colonel Min. "Be sure to give my thanks to your men, will you?"

"Yes, sir!"

Colonel Min held the colonel's outstretched hand. "Thanks, Colonel! The defense of Seoul depends on you and your men! I depend on you, too."

"You can count on us, Colonel Min. Don't worry about a thing!"

"Good! All right! Let's go!"

The jeeps swung out of the plaza, heading for the Capitol Building. The dome of the building was glowing with pale floodlights. We passed by the dark and silent National Assembly Building and the tanks and the troopers in front of it. The tree-lined wide avenue was full of trucks, jeeps, and the troops of the 5th Division. MP's with flashlights were directing the traffic. Three tanks were rumbling down the avenue, clanking and clattering, their massive bodies swarming with troopers in steel helmets and with bayoneted rifles. At the intersection, we turned right onto Chongno Street, going at full speed toward the East Gate. The street was dark. Here and there, in the dark shadows of the trees, soldiers stood silently, their bayonets gleaming. Military Police jeeps with machine guns were prowling in and out of the black alleys. There were two tanks at the intersection and the rotary near Hwashin Department Store, facing each other, crouched in the shadows of the tall office buildings. A convoy of trucks was moving on the street a few blocks north of the main street. I thought I heard a faint screaming of a siren somewhere behind us beyond the Capitol Building. An MP jeep, with its red revolving light flashing, whipped past us at full speed, swishing down the street toward Midopa Department Store and the South Gate beyond it.

I began awkwardly, "Colonel Min, I know how you feel about this. About General Yoon and all. I do." My voice shook. I went on as calmly as I could. "I feel the same way, too."

"Do you?"

"Yes! General Yoon! We didn't always agree with each other but I was fond of him, too! But you can't take this chance! You simply can't!"

"Why not?" His voice was cold.

"The fate of the nation hangs on this!"

"Precisely the reason why I am taking this chance."

"No, no! You can't do this merely because you are . . ."

"Enough!"

We were driving around and past the dark, brooding, ponderous East Gate. Colonel Min did not look back at me; he did not stir. "Major Lee, I want you to remember this," he said quietly, matter-of-factly. "I do not want to hear any more from you on this matter. Is that clearly understood?"

I felt defeated, I felt crushed, and I felt betrayed. In despair and helplessness, I said, "Yes." I had done my best; I did not know what more I could do to prevent the impending bloodshed; now, it was all out of my hands, beyond my power, beyond my hope.

Suddenly, Colonel Min sat up straight in his seat and exclaimed, "You — you always tell me what I can't do, what I mustn't do! Why? Why can't you tell me what I can do, what I must do? Do you understand that?" He turned his shadowy face with its shadowy eyes. I saw the glimmer in his hollow eyes. "If I always listened to your voice, Major, I would never, never get anything done in this maddening world! This world, do you understand, this world full of idiots like me in flesh and blood — not pale, lifeless saints like you!"

Somewhere, a machine gun was crackling away in the dark hill that rose above the shacks and huts of the dark slum. A formation of jet fighters, invisible in the black sky, roared over us, swishing toward the mountains of the eastern front.

Colonel Min stretched his hand toward me. He gripped my arm. "No matter!" he whispered. "No matter! It is too late, don't you see?"

Bewildered and confused, I could only mutter a banality of banalities. "Nothing is too late!"

"It is too late," he said quietly, "for me." He added, quickly, "But not for you." I thought he smiled then.

Chapter 19

The Paratroopers' airfield, still under construction, was nothing more than a series of runways large enough to handle transport planes. Three miles to the north of the base camp of the Airborne Brigade, it was not meant to be a fully equipped and operational airfield. The runways themselves were completed but other facilities such as a control tower and hangars and storages had not been finished by the engineers who had been working on it for the past few months. The airfield was now secured by one of General Yoon's regiments. The bulk of the Paratroopers had been stationed in Seoul; and, from what I could gather, they were now aboard transport planes somewhere, either at Kimpo or Suwon air bases, and so were the Commandos.

General Ham had already arrived at the airfield, ahead of schedule. It was ten minutes after nine when we drove into the airfield and approached the northernmost runway, where, at the other end of it, an L-17 and a small transport plane were parked, their landing lights on and their engines roaring. Colonel Min ordered the driver to stop our jeep, while the lead jeep slowly proceeded down the runway toward the center. We remained at the entrance of the runway. The Presidential Brigade lieutenant who had been riding in the jeep behind us came up, accompanied by a sergeant; they stood quietly on both sides of our jeep, clutching their submachine guns.

On the left of the runway, I saw a row of jeeps and armored cars of the American Military Police, their headlights on shining across the width of the concrete runway, illuminating, at the right of the runway, the troopers of General Yoon's 22nd Division who were lined, with their weapons at ready, in between half a dozen tanks, whose cannons pointed directly at the Americans. The lights of the tanks were fully on. A few tanks had searchlights mounted on their turrets. All the .50-caliber heavy machine guns on the tanks were manned by helmeted tank crews. There were seven tanks. There were two more tanks, apart from the other tanks, with their lights off, one at the far end of the runway and the other close to where we now were. The Americans were on the vehicles, on the jeeps with machine guns and recoilless rifles, and on the armored cars. Each side was zeroing in on the other side at point-blank range. The night air shone harshly in the lights from the tanks and the jeeps and the armored cars and the planes. The air was damp and a little chilly. The sky was black, looking blacker with all the lights glaring on the runway. A small group of people was standing in the center of the runway, not moving, looking like a cluster of floodlighted statuettes in the blinding lights shining directly from the American armored cars and the tanks of the Presidential Brigade. The Presidential Brigade lieutenant who stood beside the front fender of our jeep clicked the safety off his submachine gun. The sergeant did so, too.

"All right," said Colonel Min to the driver, "let's go."

Colonel Min had the jeep stopped about a third of the way down the runway. We got out. We walked slowly toward the group. Someone came away from the group. It was Colonel Kim.

We stopped. We waited for him. The lieutenant and the sergeant stood slightly apart from us, facing the Americans. Lieutenant Cho and I stood behind Colonel Min.

General Ham was flanked by three officers, combat ready with submachine guns and steel helmets. There were five or six more officers and men behind them, also armed with submachine guns. They were General Ham's men. Facing them, Colonel Moon, Colonel Song, Colonel Son, a Marine brigadier general and an Air Force colonel stood in a semicircle. Between them, closer to General Ham and his men, stood two American officers, one with an MP armband on. Colonel Kim was armed with only a .45 automatic. He gave me a nod. Colonel Min and he were standing a few feet apart from us. They slowly moved toward the group, whispering to each other. Lieutenant Cho and I followed behind them, flanked slightly ahead of us by the lieutenant and the sergeant.

There was a Communications van behind two tanks to the right of the group. Someone from the van came running toward Colonel Min and Colonel Kim. A young captain joined them. He was reporting to them in a whisper. I caught a few words — radio broadcasting — ultimatum — jet fighter-bombers — the Commandos and the Paratroopers — Colonel McKay. Colonel Min was nodding his head.

It was seventeen minutes after nine. The Commandos and the Paratroopers had been in the air, somewhere, since nine.

Colonels Song, Moon, Son, the Marine general — the commanding general of the 3rd Marine Task Force — and the Air Force colonel — the commanding officer of the Air Force 7th Fighter-Bomber Wing — broke the semicircle and let Colonel Min and Colonel Kim in. Lieutenant Cho joined the Presidential Brigade lieutenant and the sergeant. I stood directly behind Colonel Min.

Colonel Min saluted General Ham, who did not return the salute.

General Ham, in fatigues, wearing a small automatic in a shoulder holster, stood still, facing Colonel Min, squinting his eyes in the glaring light. "We meet again, Colonel Min," he said. His voice was hoarse. His men — two lieutenant colonels and a captain — edged forward, flanking General Ham; their submachine guns were pointing at us. "So — we meet again," he said, crossing his arms over his chest. The three silver stars on his cap glinted in the light. Stocky and short, he stood between the tall colonels, now his hands on his hips, thrusting his chest forward. The silver disk — a commander's badge — on his breast pocket gleamed.

The other American between us was the man who had met me and Colonel McKay at the Kimpo air base, now in the uniform of a major, surveying us through his thick, rimless glasses. The American Military Police officer was a lieutenant colonel, unarmed, with a small toothbrush moustache, tall and heavy-shouldered.

Colonel Min did not speak.

General Ham said, partly to Colonel Min and partly to the American major, "Where is Colonel McKay?"

No one answered him.

I heard Colonel Kim whispering to the others on our side, "The contingency plan four is on the way." The others nodded their heads, looking at Colonel Min, who took a step closer to General Ham.

General Ham said, clearing his throat, "Colonel Min, speak up now. I don't have much time."

"Neither do I, General," said Colonel Min. I thought his voice, though quiet, was a little shaky. "You wanted to come here to speak to us, General. So, go ahead."

"You wanted me to come, Colonel."

"You refused to come when we asked you, General," said Colonel Min, raising his voice. "What's the matter, General? Do you always have to have Americans to protect you?"

"I am not here to be insulted, Colonel."

Colonel Min took another step. We edged forward with him.

Colonel Min said, "General Ham, we are here to ask you to resign from the Army."

General Ham did not reply.

"Your command will be taken over by General Chang of the Second Army. He is on his way to your headquarters, General Ham," said Colonel Min. His voice was now steady and businesslike. "We are here, General, as the representatives of the Revolutionary

Council, to accept your resignation. We are authorized and em-
powered to assure you of your safety as soon as your resignation
goes into effect."

General Ham looked at the American major. "Where is Colonel
McKay!" he said in English.

"I don't know, General Ham," said the American. "I wasn't expecting to see him here, General."

General Ham twisted his neck toward his men, whispering.

"General Ham," said Colonel Min. "We do not have much time
for talking now. We would like to get this thing over with. We
would accept your resignation here and escort you to General Hyun
and the members of the Revolutionary Council. Your men may
either return to their posts or may also submit their resignations."

General Ham said, "You are out of your mind, Colonel. All of
you! Do you think we came here to resign? Nonsense! Remember, Colonel, your coup is far from being completed successfully. I
am here at the request of the Americans, who have pledged their
support for my cause in the interest of the unity and political in-
dependence of the armed forces and also in the larger interest of
our alliance. Your coup is in a tenuous position, Colonel, and you
should be the first person to know that you have now lost the support of the Americans. I have their support, Colonel, and don't
forget that your coup will not succeed without their support!"

"You are a disgrace to the nation!" snapped Colonel Min.
"Americans, Americans! You are always crying for their help!
Can't you ever think of anything without running over to the
Americans? You are a disgrace, General Ham, a disgusting example
of the gutless, subservient, slavish lost souls among our generals!"

"I am not here to be insulted by you, Colonel!" shouted General
Ham. "What is this! I didn't have to come here to take this from
you and you and you! Traitors! Murderers!"

Colonel Min said coldly, "One more word out of you about our
being murderers, General, and I will have you shot."

General Ham looked around at his men.

Colonel Min went on. As General Ham had noted a moment be-

fore, Colonel Min was deliberately provoking him. I had never
seen him speak the way he was now, savagely, furiously, and cold-
bloodedly needling the megalomaniac general's vain sense of self-
grandeur. "Ah, General Ham, look at yourself! Take a good look
at yourself and your idiots around you! What do you see! What
do you see, ah! A fat little idiot who wormed his way up in the
Japanese Army, fawning, like a soulless clown, buttering them up,
like a gutless slave, a stinking example of a spineless flatterer and
a subservient fox, changing his color and smell as the wind blows.
A blind worshiper of anything foreign, anything powerful, anything
that will give him a little money and a little power, so he can parade
around like a tin soldier! Argh! General Ham, you are disgusting!
You are utterly worthless! You tyrannize your men, you indulge
in the most shameless conduct unbecoming a general, whoring,
drinking, beating your men, stealing their pay, selling their rations, war-profiteering, bribing the politicians, stashing your hoard
in Japan while the nation is starving, and what are you but a little
mongrel, a son of a bitch, a stinking, rotten bastard trotting around
all important and pompous. You are nothing but a pompous ass,
General, sir, and you know it! And you!" Colonel Min pointed
his finger at one of the lieutenant colonels. "You! What the hell
do you think you are? You, who filched rice and money from your
battalion, selling the gasoline and rations, taking the kickback from
the merchants, and now, you — you with the little brain of a black-
marketeer and with the bloodsucking cunning of a leech, a para-
site! You! You who murdered your officers who had the courage
to testify against you in court! You little nincompoop! And you!
Colonel Nam! You who massacred the prisoners! You who supplied whores to your American advisers! A regular pimp! You
who beats our patriots to death as a Japanese lackey! You are all
a disgrace! You are nothing but a bunch of the worst men in the
Army, the worst in the nation! And you, Captain, whatever your
name is! I know you! You who flunked the Academy, bribed
General Ham to let you off the hook! You, and your war-profit-

eering father! What is this! A rogues' gallery we have here! Criminals! Crooks!"

General Ham's eyes narrowed and he kept on squinting at Colonel Min, who stood immobile, his shadowy face drawn tight and taut.

Colonel Min said, "General Ham, we don't really care whether you submit your resignation or not. I will tell you why. It is too late, General. Too late for you and for me. At this moment, our Commandos and Paratroopers are flying over your headquarters, General. Your men have been given our ultimatum to surrender."

"And what if they do not surrender!"

Colonel Min stepped up to the general. "We have our fighter-bombers out there, General, and we shall blast your men and your headquarters."

"The Americans would let you do that, eh? You are stark raving mad! You are drunk, Colonel! You don't know what you are saying!"

Colonel Min mocked him. "Americans, Americans! Sir, you make me sick!"

General Ham whipped around to one of his men and snatched the submachine gun from him and pointed it at Colonel Min.

The Presidential Brigade lieutenant and Lieutenant Cho dashed forward, their submachine guns ready. Colonel Min stood still, I could see his cheeks twitching. He said, "Go ahead, General. A toy soldier, a tin soldier you are! What do you think I am! A tin can that you can shoot at! Try it, General, and see what will happen."

General Ham was sweating; his round face was glistening with beads of sweat and fat.

An American MP, a corporal, ran over to us and said to the American major, "You are wanted on the radio, sir."

The major ran to the line of jeeps and armored cars with the corporal.

General Ham gave the submachine gun back to his colonel. "Come on!" he said to his men. "We are going back!"

"No, you are not, General," said Colonel Kim.

"Try and stop me!"

The Marine brigadier general said, "Don't try it, General Ham. We are not buying your bluff!"

The same corporal came running back. He whispered something to the American MP colonel. They went away from us to their line.

Suddenly, I became aware of the roaring engines of the planes down the runway and the engines of the American jeeps and the armored cars. The tanks with the searchlights began sweeping the runway, slowly, lighting up blindingly the line of American vehicles and the planes.

In a moment, the Americans climbed into their vehicles. The armored cars and the jeeps began backing away from the runway, swinging around, forming a double line. They were moving out of the runway and out of the airfield.

General Ham looked at the withdrawing American vehicles. He looked at us. He looked back at his men.

Colonel Min said to him, "Make up your mind, General. We are giving you a chance to surrender, General. You can either order your men to surrender or fight."

General Ham did not speak. He was breathing heavily, staring at us.

Colonel Min said, "Or else, we shall proceed with our plan and begin bombing your headquarters and the headquarters of your men. You have five minutes, General."

The American major, alone, drove his jeep over to us. He got out. He came to Colonel Min. Silently, they shook hands. The major looked at us briefly and nodded to me. He went back to his jeep. He drove away, following behind an armored car, the last of the American column.

"General Ham," said Colonel Min. "Make up your mind!"

General Ham shouted back. "So you made a deal with the

Americans! All right! But I still have the power, enough power to crush you, to destroy you all!"

"I am getting tired of your babbling, General!" snapped Colonel Min.

General Ham and his men, in a tight group, edged backward toward their plane, pointing the submachine guns at us.

"Let them have it!" said Colonel Kim to Colonel Min.

"Are we going to let them get away!" said the Marine brigadier general. "Let's stop them now!"

Colonel Min was not stirring; he was quietly gazing at the group slowly retreating toward the planes.

"Colonel Min!" said Colonel Kim.

The young captain from the Communications van came over. He said to us all, "Our fighter-bombers are at their destinations. They want your instructions."

The Air Force colonel said, "Colonel Min, let's have it out. It's either now or never!"

I edged forward next to Colonel Min. "Let them go! You can't shoot them down like dogs!" I found myself shaking. I heard my voice hissing. "You can't do this!"

Colonel Min did not look at me.

"General Ham!" he said, raising his voice. "I warn you!"

General Ham stopped. "It is either you or me, Colonel! It is too late, as you said, too late for me and for you, too!"

The Americans were still at the entrance to the runway.

General Ham said, "I will crush you!" His face, sweaty and oily, forced a grin. "I have all the power I need to resist you!"

I gripped Colonel Min's arm. "Let them go! You can't kill them in cold blood! Let them go!"

He did not look at me, though I stood only inches from him. I heard him mumble, "He is a murderer. He murdered General Yoon. He murdered them all."

Then he looked at me straight in my face and my eyes. "You!" he whispered. "You again!"

"Colonel Min!" said Colonel Kim. "What now!"

General Ham was now almost trotting toward the planes, his back turned to us. His men, facing us, backed away from us.

Colonel Min turned around, looking at us. His dark face was like a mask, a hard, iron mask, devoid of flesh and blood, impersonal, cold, and impenetrable.

"Let them go!" I shouted at the group. "You can't just murder them like dogs!" Only a second later did it occur to me that, even if we had let them go, they would not have been able to return to their headquarters, which would soon come under the attack of our fighter-bombers.

Colonel Min turned around and shouted after General Ham. "General Ham!"

General Ham stopped. He craned his neck. He looked back at Colonel Min.

Colonel Min said in a clipped, booming voice, "General Ham, I've warned you! You still have a chance to stay alive!" He was slowly walking toward General Ham and his men. Lieutenant Cho and the Presidential Brigade lieutenant followed him on the sides. I followed him, too. "General Ham," he said, "I have the power to crush you, to destroy you all!"

His words slashed at me savagely. I stopped. I stared at Colonel Min's back. He was now standing still, with his hands on his hips. "I have the power to crush you, General Ham." I thought his voice was cruel and triumphant. Harshly lit up by the lights from the planes and the tanks, he stood tall and imperious. His thin, long shadow stretched behind him. Without turning his head, he said, "Colonel Kim, go ahead!"

Colonel Kim walked briskly over toward the tanks and the Communications van. I looked behind me. The others stood quietly, not looking at me as I retraced my steps toward them. The American column of jeeps and the armored cars had moved out of the runway completely. In a moment, they disappeared out of the airfield.

Colonel Kim was giving orders to two officers, standing with them between the tanks. Colonel Min turned around and came back to us. His face was expressionless. He said, "This is it!"

They walked out of the runway to the side near the tanks. The troopers were clicking and bolting their rifles. I went to them. "Colonel Min!" I said. "What are you going to do now?"

He ignored me. I looked toward the planes. General Ham and his men had climbed into the planes. The planes began roaring their engines, their wings vibrating.

Colonel Kim said, "You'd better come behind here!"

We all moved behind the tanks. The troopers stayed close to the tanks. Suddenly, a tank at the entrance of the runway began to move, its searchlight coming on and focusing on the front of the planes, which began moving down the runway. Another tank, at the other end of the runway, started up, cluttering and clanking, swiveling around on its treads. Its cannon was rising, then, abruptly, taking me by surprise, it roared down the runway from behind the planes. The other tank jolted up and, creaking and groaning, it, too, swiveled around on its treads, its flank shining in the planes' lights. It then backed down a little, facing squarely toward the planes, which now did not move.

Colonel Kim said, "Colonel Min, just give us the word!"

A tank officer, a major, was standing next to him, holding a gun, a flare gun, in his hand.

The Marine brigadier general said, "He's so stupid. Do you think he will come out?"

The young captain from the Communications van came and stood beside Colonel Min.

The planes roared louder and started as if they would try to run down the runway. Then they stopped again.

I said, "Give him a chance! I think he will come out! He knows he can't take off! Give him time!"

Colonel Min looked at the watch on his lapel. I looked at mine on my wrist. It was two minutes to ten.

Colonel Min tapped the Communications officer on the shoulder. "Send the message: Procced!"

"You can't do this!" I said, drawing up close to Colonel Min.

No one paid any attention to me. Colonel Min looked away.
The planes started up again and raced their engines at full speed.
It was ten o'clock.

Colonel Min said to no one in particular, "I take the full responsibility." His voice was deadly quiet.

In desperation and panic, I thrust my face up to his. "You are a murderer!" I heard myself whispering to him. "You are a cold-blooded murderer!"

The planes' engines sputtered. They moved down the runway. It was madness! It was nightmare! Everyone was out of his mind! All gone berserk — as Colonel McKay would have said. Colonel McKay! The double-dealer! It was a maddening world we were caught in! A maddening world? Colonel Min's words slashed at me in my mind: " — this maddening world full of idiots like me in flesh and blood — not pale, lifeless saints like you!" Idiots in flesh and blood! Like you, like you! I found myself whispering to myself and to Colonel Min. "Idiots like you, idiots in flesh and blood like you!" Then — what was I? What was I, then and there! A pale, lifeless saint?

The planes were racing down the runway — a maddening world full of idiots! Colonel Min said, "Now!" The tank officer fired his flare gun. Even before the flare burst in the black night sky, the tanks opened up their cannons and their machine guns at the planes from a point-blank range. The tank at the entrance to the runway slammed at the L-17 with a rapid fire from its fire-breathing cannon, clanking forward as though it were going to crush the little plane. The other tank from the rear also was advancing toward the potbellied transport plane, raking it with its machine-gun fire. The troopers remained still and not firing in the shadows of the tanks, which, shuddering, bombarded the planes. The planes crumbled and crumpled down on the runway, staggering and wheeling and then, suddenly, they burst into flames with deafening booms and crackling and roaring, shooting up into the black sky, spattering and showering fires and flames on the runway, the balls of fire whooshing and swishing, sucking up the air and spitting out darting flames. Then all was quiet, only the fires slowly crackling and flames licking at the carcasses of the planes. The tanks wheeled around and clanked out of the runway, joining on each side the other tanks.

The planes kept on burning on the deserted runway, now and then exploding debris into the sky.

I was gasping, gripping the arm of Colonel Min. "You had the power to crush them!" I was whispering to him. "Yes — *you* had the power to destroy them! You — you are a murderer! Do you hear me! You are a murderer as cold-blooded as he ever was! You are a cold-blooded murderer just like him and worse!"

Colonel Min shook himself violently out of my grip. "Shut up!" he whispered. "I don't want to hear your voice!" He grabbed my shoulders and shook me in rage. "Not one more word from you! Not another word! I can't stand your tear-jerking, mushy, holier-than-thou self-righteousness and melodrama! Do you understand me? Get away from me! You and your bleeding, loving heart! Go away! Leave me alone! You and your pure heart, you and your clean conscience, you and your innocence! Leave me alone! I have work to do! I have lots of work to do in this maddening world! Go away!"

I stood speechless and dumbfounded, my mind dizzy with his out-raged words and with his savage tirade and my heart bleeding with the wounds slashed open by his denunciation and by his ferocious judgment of me. At last, when I found my faltering, trembling voice, I said in a whisper, with all my compassion and understand-ing and pity:

"I am sorry for you!"

With a jerk, he let go of my shoulders which ached with the pain from his grip. He strode away from me and from the others. I ran after him. He flung himself into his jeep. I stood by him.

I looked back toward the runway. The wreckage of the planes was still burning, hissing and crackling. The tanks started up with beastly roars. They began clanking out of their positions. The troopers assembled behind the tanks and began to march out of the airfield.

Colonel Kim came running to us from the Communications van, shouting, "Colonel Min, the reports are coming in!"

Colonel Min leaped out of the jeep.

Colonel Kim stood beside him, panting from his running. "This is it, Colonel Min! We've made it!" He was pumping Colonel Min on the shoulder. "It worked! They've just surrendered, Colonel! Your plans worked!"

Colonel Min was nodding his head. "Were they bombed?"

Colonel Kim shook his head. "The surrender message came just before that. The Commandos and the Paratroopers have been air-dropped. They are now holding the headquarters. Our units are moving in, too."

"Any casualties?" said Colonel Min.

"None! Declarations of support and loyalty are pouring in from the commanders. We've made it!"

Colonel Min gripped Colonel Kim's hand. "It worked!"

"It worked!" said Colonel Kim, slamming his fist into his palm. "The Commandos are on their way back to Seoul with the prisoners. Goddamn, it worked!"

"Yes, it worked," said Colonel Min quietly.

"Yes, sir!" said Colonel Kim. "My congratulations, sir!"

The others came. Colonel Son, Colonel Song, Colonel Moon, the Marine general, and the Air Force colonel. They ringed Colonel Min. They were shaking hands with Colonel Min. As I stood behind them in their shadows, I could not see Colonel Min's face. They were congratulating him for the success of his daring plans and his daring decision to carry them out.

I remained alone in the dark.

They were now slowly walking away from me. Colonel Min's jeep followed them. The Presidential Brigade lieutenants joined the group. Lieutenant Cho came running from the Communications van. He ran past me without a glance to me and caught up with them. They were talking and laughing. Lieutenant Cho was speaking to Colonel Min. There was a moment of silence.

They stopped. They turned around.

I did not stir.

They turned around. They began walking away. Jeeps drove past me slowly, following the group.

Behind them, on the runway, the ruins of the planes and the bodies of General Ham and his men were still burning like bonfires.

The Presidential Brigade lieutenants left the group. They came back to me.

They saluted me. Their submachine guns glinted in the flickering light and shadows from the fires of the runway. One of them said, "Colonel Min's orders, Major. Come with us, please."

"Am I under arrest?"

They did not reply.

A jeep came backing toward us.

I got in. The lieutenants climbed into the back.

"Where are you taking me?"

No one spoke to me.

Colonel Min and the others were getting into their jeeps.

Our jeep followed behind them.

It was only when we were on the main road toward the capital that I realized I was now the first innocent victim of their coup d'état.

Chapter 20

I had expected that the Presidential Brigade lieutenants would take me to a prison, either to the West Gate Prison which was known to have political prisoners behind bars or to the Army Prison near the Han River bridge, but, to my surprise, they took me directly back to my room at the Bando Hotel. "We'll be outside the room, sir, if you need anything," one of them said when we walked into the room. "May we have your pistol, sir?" Without a word, I surrendered it to them. Then they left me alone.

It was five minutes past eleven o'clock.

I was calm and composed — and relieved that the coup was over, all over, for me, at last. Now there was not much more I could do but to make the most of the situation I was in. I took a shower. I shaved. I even asked the lieutenants to have some beer brought up to the room. In a moment, a hotel bellboy brought me three bottles of cold beer and a glass. I drank slowly, savoring the tingling coolness of the beer soothing my burning throat, feeling suddenly very tired and weary. I needed sleep, a night of good sleep. I finished the last bottle of beer quickly, and lay down on the bed, marveling, for a fleeting moment, at the serenity of my mind. But I could not sleep.

I was still awake when, shortly after midnight, I heard shrieking sounds of jet planes, close overhead as though the jets were diving out of the black sky and plunging into the hotel. In a few seconds, I heard a series of explosions some distance away to the north. The jets were once again roaring over the hotel toward the south. Suddenly, machine guns were bursting away nearby as though from the rooftop of the hotel, then the cannons and the heavy machine guns of the tanks near City Hall were booming and crackling.

One of the lieutenants stepped into the room, leaving the door open behind him.

"What is going on?" I said. I was standing at the window near the bed, trying to open it; the window would not open. I became aware of the insistent humming of the air-conditioner at the other window, which faced out toward the City Hall plaza. I shut it off.

The lieutenant turned off all the lamps. I had left them on. The room was now dim with the only light from the corridor. He came and stood next to me. "We're trying to find out, sir. Sounded like bombs," he said quietly.

We looked out the windows. The searchlights on the South Hill were wildly jerking, crisscrossing the black sky. Bombs were going off with muffled booms toward the Han River bridge. The machine guns on the rooftop of the hotel were silent now and the tanks' cannons were quiet, too. Then we heard the whines and screams of the jets again diving in very low from the south toward us, though we could not see them and, in a moment, the jets were over us and anti-aircraft guns were hammering away all over and around us, and the tanks' heavy machine guns were blasting away, their tracer bullets shooting up into the black sky like streams of blazing sparks, then long bursts of machine-gun fire were coming from the direction of the Capitol Building.

The other lieutenant walked into the room, clutching his submachine gun.

"Well?" I said. "What is all this?"

"I guess we are being attacked, Major."

There was a moment of quiet outside.

"I know we are being attacked! Who is attacking?"

"We'll find that out in a minute, sir." With that, he stalked out of the room.

Machine guns were firing again, not near the hotel, but several blocks away toward the South Gate. Tanks were clanking up near City Hall, then clattering down the street by the Changduk Palace toward the South Gate. The trucks and armored personnel carriers of the units of the 5th Division were moving out of the City Hall plaza, without lights on. It was only then that I noticed that the floodlights on the top of City Hall had been blacked out.

The other lieutenant came back into the room. "Two fighter-bombers," he said.

"Well?"

"They tried to bomb the Presidential residence, sir," he said, "and the Army Headquarters. Bombs missed but there are some casualties. They were trying to get away to North Korea but couldn't make it. One was shot down by our anti-aircraft guns and the other was shot down by American jets, both of them near the DMZ line."

Someone marched in. It was Lieutenant Cho. The Presidential Brigade lieutenants stepped forward and met him at the door. They talked in whispers. The lieutenants went out of the room.

Lieutenant Cho came to me. "Are you all right, sir?"

"Yes."

He turned on the lamp near the couch. "There's a mutiny," he said. "Two companies of the Commandos broke out of their compound and started shooting, sir. One company tried to charge into the Army Headquarters and the other company shot their way into the Railway Station." He, too, had a submachine gun with him. "It's nothing to worry about, sir. They are trapped inside the Railway Station anyway. The Marines are taking care of them now. We also have some Infantry units inside the Station."

"I heard the 5th Division units moving out of the City Hall plaza."

"They are heading for the Army Headquarters. There's nothing to worry about, sir."

"The Presidential residence was bombed?"

Three bombs there. No damage, sir. Everyone is all right."

"The President, you mean?"

"Oh, I meant — Colonel Min and the others, sir. They were on their way to the Presidential residence when all this started. Colonel Min is all right, sir."

"What are you doing here?" I said, sitting down on the edge of the bed. "Why aren't you with him?"

"Colonel Min wanted me to go to your quarters, sir, and get a few things which you might like to have. I thought I would ask you first what you would like me to bring back here."

"I don't need anything," I said, a little impatiently. "Why all this?"

He shook his head. "I wouldn't know, sir. But I can go and get you some clothes or anything you want."

"Am I supposed to be staying in this hotel for long?"

"I don't know that, sir."

"Well, just what do you know?"

"Nothing, Major. All I know is I am to go to your quarters and get things you might need."

"Need for what?"

"I don't know, sir."

"Do whatever you want, then. No one tells me anything! No one tells me what I am supposed to be doing here. No one knows what I am supposed to be doing or where I am supposed to be tomorrow. No one knows anything! What is this? Am I a tourist in a hotel?"

He smiled — but I thought it was a sad smile. "I am sorry, sir," he said, now with a sullen look. "I am sorry it had to happen this way between you and Colonel Min. I don't understand why it had to happen this way, sir, between you two, of all people."

I lay down on the bed. "There are certain things which you simply wouldn't understand."

"Oh, I know that, sir. I know that! But — why, Major?"

"There was no other way, no other choice. Someday, Lieutenant, you may understand."

"Are you angry with Colonel Min? Are you still angry with him, sir?"

"No, I am not angry with him," I said, getting up. "I am sorry for him. You don't understand that, do you?"

"No, I don't, sir. But that's not right, sir, if you don't mind my saying so. He needs help, all the help he can get, right now, sir, but not anyone's pity."

I stared at him.

His big, bloodshot eyes, unflinching, challenged mine.

"To call him a bloody murderer, sir," he said quietly. "That was going a little too far, don't you think so, sir? That was not very kind of you, Major Lee. After all, you are his best friend. You are supposed to be his best friend and everyone knows that, sir." He took a few steps closer to me. His submachine gun brushed against a chair. It made a dull thudding noise. I could not help frowning. He went on, "Anyway, sir, you made Colonel Kim so mad he was going to shoot you down right there out at the Paratroopers' airfield. Did you know that, sir?"

"No, I didn't! Perhaps he should have!"

"That's being silly, sir, and you know it. If it hadn't been for Colonel Min, sir . . ."

"Well?"

"Nothing, sir."

"Colonel Kim would have shot me?"

"He would have, sir."

"What about you? Would you have shot me, too?"

He did not reply.

"I suppose you were and you still are angry with me?"

"I am not saying anything, sir. I just do what Colonel Min wants me to do."

"And he wants you to go over to my quarters and get a few things I might need."

The Innocent / 357

"That's right, sir."

"Well, then, go and do it, Lieutenant. I do need some clean clothes."

"Anything else, sir?"

"Tell me, Lieutenant. What is Colonel Min up to? Is he going to lock me up in prison? Is he so afraid of me that he is going to lock me up?"

"No, sir, and I don't think he is afraid of you, sir."

"Well, then?"

"I wouldn't know his mind, sir." He looked at me steadily — rather mournfully, I thought. "But I do know that he had a talk with Colonel McKay about you."

"About what?"

"I don't know, Major," he said, shaking his head. "My English isn't good enough."

"Speaking of Colonel McKay, what happened to General Ahn and Colonel Hwang of the Airborne?"

"General Ahn is wounded, as you know."

"I know that!"

"They are in Colonel McKay's custody now, sir. They have been taken over by his people. Colonel McKay's people took them away somewhere, but I don't know exactly where. Probably to Japan, I understand, sir."

I stood up from the bed and faced him. "Tell me, Lieutenant. Has Colonel Min said anything about sending me away? Sending me out of the country?"

He stared at me in silence.

"Tell me, Lieutenant! He is sending me out of the country, isn't he? He's told you to get me ready to be shipped out, hasn't he? And that's why you are going to get my things?"

Without a second of hesitation, as though he had been anticipating that moment, he said straightaway, "Yes, Major. He is going to let you leave the country."

"Let me leave the country, indeed!" I could not help crying out. "He is sending me away, don't you understand?"

"It doesn't make that much difference, sir, really. He wants you to be away from the country for a while. That's all, sir. Yes, sir, he wanted me to help you get ready."

"Very thoughtful of you two."

He looked away.

"Well, cheer up, Lieutenant," I said, forcing myself to smile. "When do I leave?"

"Immediately, sir."

"Immediately?"

"As soon as possible, I meant, sir."

"I see. As soon as Colonel McKay can make the arrangements, isn't that right?"

"Yes, sir," he mumbled, looking down.

"I see."

He looked up. "I am going to go over to your quarters now, Major. What would you like me to bring back?"

"I suppose I am not allowed to go and get things myself?"

He shook his head firmly. "No, sir."

"Why not? Are you afraid I might run away from you?"

"No, sir. It's simply that we are concerned about the mutineers, those Commandos who we are convinced are all North Korean Reds. They may get out of our traps and infiltrate the city and start making trouble. Like snipers and such, sir. It's too dangerous outside just now, sir."

"You are not afraid of the danger?"

He gave me a big grin, "I am not indispensable, sir. No, I am not afraid. I guess the shooting is still going on."

We could still hear machine guns and, at irregular intervals, tank cannons, mingled with the thudding and thumping of mortar shells.

"Nothing to worry about, Major. I'll be back soon. Try to get some sleep."

"Yes. I don't seem to have any other choice, do I?"

"Get some rest, sir. Colonel Min may come to see you sometime. Probably — in the morning."

"Yes." I was tired and weary. "Yes." I lay down on the bed. "Be careful now, Lieutenant. Take care of yourself, will you?"

He smiled. "I will, sir. Nothing to worry about. I'll see you again soon."

"Yes."

He went out of the room slowly. I could see the dark shadows of the Presidential Brigade lieutenants on the white wall outside the room. The door closed quickly behind Lieutenant Cho — and I was alone once again. The shooting near the Railway Station beyond the South Gate seemed to be subsiding a little, but there were still machine-gun bursts and rifle shots occasionally accompanied by a series of artillery bombardment.

There was nothing to worry about — as Lieutenant Cho had said — nothing to worry about. My fate had been decided on, without my consent and without my refusal either, for that matter; I felt like a powerless dummy at the whim of a heartless bully. Yet — I could not help feeling relieved, indescribably relieved, now that I was to go on the path of an exile. I looked about me — a strange room in a strange hotel.

I turned off the light. In the darkness, the gunfire and bombardment sounded louder and fiercer, but so did the pounding of my heart that was riddled with unfathomable sorrow and grief.

I Chapter 21

It was four o'clock in the morning.

Machine guns, tanks, cannons, and mortars had stopped firing altogether shortly after three o'clock. Although scattered shots had been coming from here and there, it was quiet now. It had begun to rain outside. The rainwater dripped down the windowpanes quietly and monotonously. The sky was black. Outside the dark room, there were no sounds of footsteps or of voices. I lay awake, fully clothed, straining my ears to catch some sign of life, but the hotel, the streets, the entire city were as silent as a deserted graveyard, except for the steady falling of the rain.

Twenty minutes past four o'clock.

I was dozing off — feeling numb — when I heard footsteps and muted voices outside the room. There was a moment of hush, then the door of my room opened. I raised myself on the bed. Someone stood at the threshold silently. The light from the corridor cast a thin, long shadow of the man into the room. I stood up and saw that it was Colonel Min.

Outside the room, the Presidential Brigade lieutenants stood at attention, their gleaming submachine guns in their hands.

Colonel Min closed the door behind me. The room was dark again. He came toward me.

I turned on the lamp beside the couch.

He stopped in the middle of the room. He was unarmed, still in fatigues that were wet from the rain. Drops of water dribbled down from his cap. "Turn off the light," he said quickly.

I did. The room seemed darker. I heard a door being opened with a key in the room adjoining mine.

Colonel Min stood there for a moment. "I didn't mean to snap at you, Major, but we have some snipers to deal with." He took a few steps closer to me and sat down on the couch. "Sit down," he said.

I sat down on the edge of the bed. "Snipers?"

"Yes. The mutineers, the Reds, slipped out of the Railway Station. Not too many of them, but enough to make some trouble."

"Who are they? Who is behind them?"

"We don't know yet."

"Lieutenant Cho said they are North Korean Reds."

"Perhaps. They were General Ahn's handpicked men, if that's what Lieutenant Cho meant. We will find out soon. Did you get some sleep?"

I nodded, though I realized that he would not be able to see me in the dark. "Yes."

"Good. I suppose Lieutenant Cho has told you that we would like you to leave the country."

"Yes. He has told me that you, Colonel, you would like me to leave the country. I think his exact words were that you would let me leave the country."

"No time to quibble about words. Yes. I would like you to leave the country."

"Do I have any other choice?"

"No, you don't."

I took my time. "Why?"

He did not speak for a while.

"Why?" I said. "Why?"

"I have told Colonel McKay to make the necessary arrangements for your travel," he said matter-of-factly. "You will be flying out from Kimpo this afternoon, at three o'clock. You will proceed to Tokyo, where you will be met by George, whom you have met before, and also by one of our people there, who will give you further instructions and assistance. Is that understood?"

"Where do I go from there?"

"You will proceed to America and Colonel McKay will see to it that you need not worry about anything. You will go to New York, where you will be met by someone from our embassy who will give you any assistance you need from there on."

"And after that?"

"Go anywhere you like and do anything you like. You will find yourself more at home in Europe, perhaps? In any case, you are not to return to the country until further notice and you are to report your address regularly to our embassies or consulates, whichever may be the case. That is all you will be required to do and that is for your own benefit. Will you remember that?"

"Why?"

"You are going to need money. It is as simple as that. I have made sure that you are not to be short of funds, and that's why I want you to report your address regularly."

I tried to laugh. "Is this an offer of bribery?"

"It is a reward, Major. The country and I owe you much for the success of our coup d'état. It is simply a token of our appreciation for the contribution you have made to the launching of a new destiny of our nation. You deserve it, so don't think too much about it."

"And you will say that I am not in a position to refuse it?"

"Yes, and you know you can't refuse it."

I fell silent.

He stood up from the couch. "I am a little tired and I am going to sleep for a while in the next room. So you will have to excuse me now. Is there anything else you want to know? Anything you would like to ask me?"

I stood up, too. "Yes."

"Well, let's hear it."

"Why all this?"

"What?"

I edged closer to him, groping my way in the humid, suffocating darkness. "Lieutenant Cho told me that Colonel Kim almost shot me down at the Paratroopers' airfield."

"Yes. He almost did."

"You stopped him?"

"Yes."

"Why?"

"Why?" I thought his voice sounded amused.

"Yes. Why?" I cried out in whispers.

"I don't have any reason or excuse for destroying a man like you." His voice was unruffled. "You were not a threat to our cause then and you are not now."

"I called you a bloody murderer, Colonel! I judged you! I still say you are a cold-blooded murderer!"

"Well, you did what I have asked you to do," he said simply. His voice was without any hint of anger.

"What?"

"I asked you to judge me someday. So you did."

"And you are sending me out of the country for that!"

He was silent for a long while, then his quiet voice began wafting toward me through the dark space between us. "It is for your own good, Major. You may not understand this now, but you will someday. Let us hope so. I want you to go out of the country now — but to come back someday. You need to be alone for a while. You need to be away from this land for a while. You have lived for other people for too long, Major. For this country and for these people. Do you understand me? You have lived your life always for others. For this suffering country and for that suffering people. You have lived your life for too long for the people, for the world, for humanity that suffer from miseries and injustices, and evils. You have lived your life for so many others that you have not lived a life that you can call truly your own. You have gained humanity, Major, whatever that may be, only to lose a man and to lose your capacity to see a single human being — you, yourself. I want you to be alone with yourself for a while now. It is time, I think, that you lived your own life, with your own miseries, with your own injustices, and with your own evils. You have dedicated yourself and your life to matters of cosmic, universal significance and importance, Major. You see — your evil, your idea of evil is universal, abstract, so that when you are thrust against the ugly face of an evil that you can see, smell, and touch, you are paralyzed and you are impotent. How ironic, Major! But evil is not abstract, Major Lee. Its manifestations are concrete, tangible, and particular, and, therefore, they can be destroyed one at a time, one by one. I don't know how to tackle such a problem as your idea of evil — a vast, universal, intangible, abstract evil. And goodness, too, Major. For me, goodness is tangible, concrete, and particular. I can see it, smell it, and touch it — and cherish it. I don't see a universal, cosmic goodness and love that a man only has to open his eyes to see and believe in. You are a decent, good man, Major Lee, but good, decent men don't destroy evil." He stopped, and slowly walked toward the window that faced the City Hall plaza. There he stood, looking out into the sky of early dawn, the faint light of which made the room dim. I could vaguely see the dark profile of his face. In the silence, I edged toward him, feeling very small, suddenly overwhelmed by my memories of him, long ago, at our university — of him quietly facing the students, of him enthralling them with his passionate yet lucid discourse on philosophies of history. For a moment, watching him relieved against the window as he stood looking out, I could not help feeling as if the plaza down below were filled with those students, hushed, waiting for his words. And he began, without turning around to me, standing fixed, with his hands on the windowsill. "No — decent, good men do not destroy evil, Major. They can only see it and cry out that there is evil. Yes — you are a decent, good man, Major, and I understand — yes — I understand how agonizing, how painful, and how unbearable it must have been and it must be for you to try to be a decent, good human being, a mortal man without God and without superhuman laws, desperately trying to arm yourself with human decency and pity for fellow mortal men, eternally confronted by the insufferable presence of what you call universal evil. You cry out, 'Look! Look! There! There! Can't you see? Don't you see? There! The Evil!' But it seems to you as though your voice is lost in the din and dust and the sounds and the furies of this mad, maddening world — and the evil triumphs, so it seems to you, and you are helpless and powerless, and you are left with nothing but a withering sense of futility. So — you hate. Yes — you hate — oh — how you hate! You hate this misery, that injustice, you hate this and that suffering of mankind. You hate evil men doing evil things. You hate this, and you hate that — all in the name of your universal justice, goodness, and love. You love goodness and justice and love so much that you hate evil so much, too, Major. But when your hatred of evil paralyzes you, rendering you helpless and powerless and impotent, you pity it. You are sorry. You lavish your pity and your understanding and your kindness, not knowing and not caring that your hatred is becoming more intense and more fierce, until, someday, you will either cynically renounce the world or embark on destroying everything that does not measure up to your holy vision of universal goodness, justice, and love. You are a decent, good man, Major Lee — and I have needed a man like you with me, but I don't need you any longer." He paused, turning around. He left the window and came back into the middle of the room. "Why?" he said. "Because, you see, I have at last come to terms with myself, because I have at last seen the face of peace, my peace. It is done, it is finished, you know. It is almost like the end of a bloody battle, which empties me hollow inside so that something new has to fill me again. And you have done that service for me, Major, and so it is time for you to begin to look after yourself."

I stared hard at his dark face etched against the pale, white wall

366 / The Innocent

of the room that began to emerge from the rainy darkness of the night. I whispered to him. "Why? Why do you say you have needed me?"

He was silent.

"What have I done for you?" I said. "What have I done to you? All I have done, all I could do for you, was to judge you and condemn you — a cold-blooded murderer."

Once again, he turned his face toward the window. "I must thank you for that, Major. Don't you see? Yes — the world needs a man like me. Someone to destroy evil men. Someone to get things done. Someone to move the world. Someone to come to the help of people like you. But what am I? What have I been all my life? I will tell you, Major. I am a man condemned to a life of battling evils for my survival — which ought to be your task. But you — men like you are helpless and powerless, for fear that if you carried through with your task the consequences of your battle with evil men might contaminate you and corrupt you with the sweat, blood, and stench of the evil you would like to see wiped from the face of the earth. That's where I come in. That is why you need a man like me. Do you understand that?" He was at the window again, looking out. "But I, too, need a man like you. I have needed a man like you all my life. To help me answer my own question, my bloody question — what am I to myself? What I really am to myself in the dreadful, dark moment of utter solitude. Am I a gallant knight? Am I a hero, as the people of my hometown thought and adored me? Am I a brave soldier charging up to the aid of goodness and justice? Is what I am compelled to do an act of noble justice and admirable heroism? No, no, Major. You have judged me right. I am a murderer and my acts are bloody and sordid. Someone like you ought to see that truth. Like a beast, you said. Yes — like a beast devouring other beasts. How I envy you, Major! How I have envied a man like you all my life! Why? Because when a man is called on to sacrifice himself for others, to give up his body and soul for others, for his despairing, weak, mortal, fellow human beings,

that is when a man like you can become a saint. But what else is
there in the world that is easier for a man to do than to sacrifice
himself for others? By sacrificing your own life for others, you
become a saint and a martyr — and the world applauds you. Yes —
the world is full of people willing to sacrifice themselves for others,
for this cause and for that cause and for this and that ideal. The
world, Major Lee, is full, too full, of instant saints and instant martyrs — don't you see? — self-styled holy little men intent on saving
fellow human beings from this and from that. Yes, Major Lee, we
live in an age in this world crowded with an army of saints and martyrs who are so obsessed with their desire to help others, to save
others, that they do not know how to help themselves — how to
save themselves.

"But, you see, Major, by destroying others for others, you become a murderer, a beast. The world needs you, you see; it needs
saints and martyrs — and it needs me, too; it needs murderers, too,
Major. Why murderers? Why am I a murderer as you have rightly
judged me and condemned me?"

He stirred himself and came toward me. "There is nothing out
there in the heavens, Major. Remember? We have only ourselves.
Remember?"

In a whisper, I echoed his words. "Yes, we have only ourselves."

"There! There!" His eyes glinted in the gray air.

"What? What?"

"Don't you know? Major, when we have only ourselves, where —
tell me — where do we go to hear the final verdict on our deeds,
on our acts? Where do we go? Where can we go?"

"To ourselves, Colonel Min," I said, in sudden, ponderous awe.
"To ourselves!"

"Yes — I, to myself. You, to yourself."

"Yes?"

"That's why I have needed you, Major. All my life, all my bloody
life, I have closed my eyes to what I really was, to what I really am,
to myself. All my life, I have resisted, delayed, and avoided going to

myself, do you understand? Going to myself for my final verdict. All in the holy name of battles against evil men, against injustices, against miseries of life, against the oppressors, and for the oppressed. You see — that's why I have needed you — you, my judge and my prosecutor. You — someone who had to give me one last push to face what I am. And I cannot plead, my good friend, that I am something other than what I am. I am a murderer like any other criminal, for in whose name, behind whose divine commandment, can I defend myself and insist that I am any better? Am I any better than common criminals and common murderers because I destroy in the name of justice and love and the new destiny of the nation? In this frightening moment, in this terrifying moment in a chilling, absolute vacuum when our coup d'état is at last triumphant, no, there is nothing behind which I can hide, Major. And that is what you have done for me — to give me one, final reminder that a man like me, a man without God, a mortal man without immutable, inviolable, inexorable, and transcendental laws, a mortal man like me is a simple murderer and must not be called by any other name. You have helped me, Major, helped me gain my sanity, indeed, to regain my sanity and to save myself from the intoxicating temptation of a self-styled godlike lawgiver, from the tantalizing delusion and illusion of omnipotence — in this mad, maddening world, to know and to accept my own verdict."

"What have I done!" I could not restrain myself from crying out. "What have I done to you? And — and to myself!"

"Sanity, Major, and the truth without illusions and delusions. I am not bitter, Major Lee. I am not defeated. To be what I am has been my fate and I must accept this without bitterness, without disillusionment, and without the sense of having been betrayed or having been cheated out of something — a beautiful life that is filled with nothing but love and goodness — a life which may not exist. But I have lived my bloody life with hope, Major, trying — trying so hard — to catch a glimpse of hope here and there, to see a glimmer, however faint, of goodness and love here and there, in

this man and in that man, in this corner of the world and in that
nook of the earth. You have said to me once that the world is not
absurd but that it is in an absurd state. Perhaps and perhaps not.
But, call it what you may, Major — absurdity, paradox, riddle —
the fate of this mortal world is that it needs men like me — and men
like you, too, to tell the world that it is so."

He reached out and gripped my arm. "Listen! I have told you
that you would judge me someday and that you would have to judge
me, if not for me, then for your sanity. Do you remember?"

"Yes." It was now light enough in the room so that I could see his
dark, brooding face clearly. "Yes."

"Did you understand me, then? Do you understand, now, that
you have to look deep into your own troubled soul in order to judge
me and finally condemn me? And you have judged me right, and
that is the only way for a man like you to hang on to your sanity,
to live through your life and live with this maddening, mortal
world."

I, too, reached out and held his arm. But I could not find words —
words to confess, words to denounce myself in his presence.

"I must leave you now," he said, letting my arm go. "I must sleep.
You, too."

I held on to his arm as he turned to go. "You are not a criminal,
Colonel Min. You are not a murderer like other common criminals
and murderers. You have work to do. You have a task to fulfill.
You have a destiny to live with, Colonel. You have a higher purpose in your life and in this world, this maddening world as you say.
There is a difference, there is a world of difference, Colonel, between
you and the . . ."

"Don't! Don't make *that* distinction, Major!" he said, pulling
himself up straight. "Others may keep on making *that* distinction
so that they may go on believing that they are special, unique, and
superior! But not you, Major Lee. Not you! Don't you realize
that I had to come this far in my life to renounce at last *that* godlike power and right which makes *that* distinction?" His voice

softened in a moment and he said quietly, "No matter. It is too late now."

I held my breath, in awe and in shame, waiting for his words.

He said, so quietly that I could hardly hear, "My good friend, don't you see? I am only an instrument of evil that knows when to destroy itself, because, you see, that is the only way a man like me may regain his innocence and gain his salvation."

Then he was gone.

Chapter 22

The rain must have stopped sometime early in the morning. When I woke up, the room was bright and filled with dazzling sunshine, but it was hot and humid in the room with all the windows closed tight. The sky was clear and blue with white, fluffy clouds placidly floating over the Capitol. I turned on the air-conditioner and went to the bathroom to take a shower. When I was finished with the shower and was dressed, the telephone on the desk rang. It was Lieutenant Cho, who said that he had just been told that I was awake. "I hope you slept well, sir," he said.

"Yes. Did you get some sleep at all?"

"I am afraid not, sir. We've had a pretty hectic night, and the damned snipers have been keeping us busy all morning. I am afraid Colonel Min didn't get more than an hour of sleep. He's been out all morning, sir, what with so many meetings here and there. There was a big meeting with the American commanders, then one with the American Ambassador, who is upset over our coup, for no good reason, if you know what I mean, sir. Anyway, the reason I am calling you is — Colonel Min would like to have lunch with you, sir."

I looked at my watch. It was nearly twelve o'clock.

"And he has asked Chaplain Koh to join you and him," Lieutenant Cho was saying. "Colonel Min is with General Hyun right
now, but he will meet you in about half an hour in front of the Capitol Building. I've had a jeep sent around for you at the hotel and it
should be there waiting for you in ten minutes. All right, sir?"

"Yes, that'll be fine."

"Then, we will meet you in half an hour."

"What about Chaplain Koh?"

"He will be waiting for us, sir. I am sorry I can't tell you where
over the telephone, if you know what I mean, sir."

"Is the situation under control?"

"Yes, sir. The mutineers, well, most of them anyway, have been
crushed. Some got away but we will catch up with them soon
enough. There's nothing to worry about."

"All right, Lieutenant."

The jeep was from the Presidential Brigade headquarters, driven
by a young sergeant, steel-helmeted and armed with a .45 automatic,
wearing dark sunglasses. He was putting the jeep's top down when
I walked out of the hotel.

He saluted me. "Major Lee, sir?"

"Yes."

"Give me a few seconds to put this thing down, sir. It's too hot
today, for a change."

The air was heavy and humid. The sun was hot. The street in
front of the hotel was quiet, almost hushed, with few cars, military
or civilian. The Marines, the Paratroopers, the Presidential Brigade
troopers, and the Military Policemen who had crowded the hotel
the night before had all gone; now, there was only a handful of
policemen with carbines idly pacing around. There were two dark
blue sedans parked across the street in front of the dirty gray
building of the American Embassy. The detachment of the Korean
Marines had disappeared and the main entrance of the embassy
was guarded by four American Marines in khakis with carbines and

shotguns and two Korean policemen armed with submachine guns.

We drove away from the hotel toward City Hall. The trucks, armored personnel carriers, and jeeps of the 5th Division were gone from the plaza, but two tanks — Patton tanks — were still there in front of City Hall. There were two more tanks and three armored cars across from City Hall, lined along the wide avenue near the National Assembly Building and the Duksoo Palace. We drove down the avenue, past the National Assembly and Seoul Fire Station toward the Capitol Building. At the intersection of Tae-Pyung-no Street and Chongno Street, there was a Marine tank, a Sherman, off the street, near the gray concrete building of the Ministry of Finance, pointing its long cannon toward the hazy blue sky. The sun over our heads in the now cloudless sky sizzled the air. The mountains looming behind the dome of the Capitol Building were blurred in the blinding haze. We drove up to the front gate of the Capitol Building that was guarded by a platoon of the Marines, backed up by two Sherman tanks outside and another two inside the walled compound. I had the sergeant stop the jeep outside the main gate under the thin shade of a tree. The Marines in full battle gear had set up barricades on both sides of the gate, manning heavy machine guns. Military Police jeeps with mounted machine guns were cruising up and down the streets. To the east, toward the Changduk Palace, a convoy of six Army trucks was pulling up. A squad of troopers got out of a truck and, quickly fanning out, took up positions along the street, their bayonets fixed on their rifles flashing in the sun. The trucks moved on. An armored car came down the street from the west; it drove by us quietly; a crewman, leaning out of the open hatch, waved at the Marines as the olive-green armored car, picking up speed, whished down the avenue toward the National Assembly Building.

A Marine sergeant came to me, carrying an M-1 rifle. "May I see your identification papers, sir?"

I showed him the card which identified me as a member of the Command Group and of the Supreme Revolutionary Council.

He saluted me and walked back to the barricades.
I waited.

A jeep with its top up drove down toward us from the west at high speed, followed by another jeep with two helmeted troopers in the back. The first jeep stopped directly across the street from us. The second jeep stopped behind it. The troopers leaped out, brandishing their submachine guns, and took up positions, one in front of the first jeep and the other directly behind it. Lieutenant Cho, who was at the wheel of the first jeep, jumped out of the covered jeep and came to me. I got out of the jeep.

"Come with us, Major Lee," he said. He told the Presidential Brigade sergeant to go back to the Bando Hotel.

We walked across the street, side by side. The broiling asphalt pavement felt soft and sticky like clay.

Colonel Min, wearing dark sunglasses, looked my way but did not speak. I nodded to him and climbed into the back. The troopers, who were Presidential Brigade lieutenants, ran back into their jeep. We started and drove down the wide avenue toward the direction of the Changduk Palace. We drove by the Army troopers who lined the avenue by the Palace, turned left at an intersection, went for several more blocks, turned right at a rotary, and sped down the wide, deserted street that went by the buildings of the Seoul National University.

I broke the silence. "Lieutenant Cho told me the situation is now under control."

Colonel Min nodded, without turning around to me. "But we've lost over forty of our own men."

"Who were those Commandos?" I said, leaning slightly forward so that I would not have to speak too loudly. "You said they were men handpicked by General Ahn."

"They are Communists," said Colonel Min, "sent down from North Korea years ago. They tried to break into the Army Headquarters, apparently thinking that's where we were. In the meantime, another company of them tried to take the Railway Station, as you know."

"Why? Why the Railway Station?"

"It now seems that they wanted to take over a train and run it up north as far as they could go, then go into the mountains near the front and cross the DMZ line. It might have worked out for them, for a while anyway, except that we had had a battalion of the 17th Division right inside the Station yard as a reserve force, and the Reds hadn't known about that. But it was a messy fight, what with all those trains and freight cars in there. The battalion commander, who was supported by the Marines, said it was worse than house-to-house street fighting."

We were now driving by the buildings of the College of Arts and Science of the Seoul National University.

Colonel Min was saying, "Otherwise, everything is well under control now. It is quiet on the front line, and that makes it easier for us to get on with our work here. We have been able to persuade the President to stay on the job for the time being, for a week or so anyway, and it helps to have him there — for the Americans anyway."

He turned around to me for the first time and took off his sunglasses. "Have you eaten anything yet?"

I shook my head. "No. I woke up only a short while ago."

"You must be starving."

"Lieutenant Cho said you didn't get any sleep at all."

"Lieutenant Cho here is a bigmouthed mother hen, you know." He laughed, patting the lieutenant on the shoulder. "Well, Major Lee, you won't be having home-cooked Korean meals for a while, but I suppose you are used to Western meals."

"I don't think I can ever get used to them though."

"I couldn't. When I was in America, a group of us went to New York and the first thing we did was to find and go to a Korean restaurant and stuff ourselves. Our American host simply couldn't understand that, you know. I remember he kept saying — with all the

fine French restaurants in the city, why do you have to have a
Korean meal and so on. Anyway, I never took his advice, you
know, and when I was in West Berlin, I did just the same thing. I
had to go to the Korean restaurant there. Imagine, though, when
I learned that there was one right in West Berlin, of all places."

Lieutenant Cho spoke up. "The only American food I like is hot
dogs. They are easy to eat, you know, sir, without forks and knives
and all that."

We laughed.

I said, "Speaking of American hot dogs, what's the negotiation
with the Americans like? Is it going all right?"

Colonel Min said, "It is a matter of formality at this stage." He
sat up straight on the seat. "But we must make sure that they understand this. That if they genuinely wish to cooperate with us,
then they will have to realize that they no longer have a bunch of
idiotic yes-men in Seoul. I am going to propose that we get together
and make the United Nations Command truly what it is supposed
to be rather than a cover-up for what really amounts to an American Command. In short, I want to put some of our men right in
there. Do you know what I mean? The Americans are always saying we are their staunchest ally and so on but they don't really
trust us enough and if they don't, then we can't trust them completely either. It is time, I think, that they stopped acting as though
they were here as an occupation army and that they got rid of their
condescension. We all have to realize, we and the Americans, that
we are working with and working for new generations . . ."

Suddenly, the jeep behind us blew its horns. I looked back.

The Presidential Brigade lieutenants were half standing up, clutching their submachine guns. Their driver was waving his hand to us
as though telling us to hurry. I saw a small black sedan behind us.

Colonel Min said, looking straight ahead, "What is it?"

I saw the black sedan swerving out from behind the jeep and
roaring down the street to our left as though it were trying to pass
us — and I was shouting to Lieutenant Cho, "Speed up! Speed up!"

Lieutenant Cho charged our jeep and the jeep went lurching forward and shrieking down the street, when I saw a flash and heard the bursts of submachine-gun fire all at the same time coming from the black sedan as it passed the jeep behind ours, and I saw the Presidential Brigade lieutenants fly into the blinding air, toppling down out of their jeep, their submachine guns glazing in the glaring sunshine — then their jeep careened off the street — and the black sedan, barreling down, came behind our jeep, and a man with sunglasses, leaning out of the rolled-down window, was firing at us with a submachine gun. I was screaming to Lieutenant Cho to speed up, speed up! — and frantically yelling to Colonel Min to get down, get down! Bullets were ripping through the canvas top over our heads and tearing into the back of the jeep. Colonel Min, crouching down, was reaching into the back and it was only then that I saw a submachine gun at my feet, and Colonel Min was firing the submachine gun through the canvas cover at the black sedan. Lieutenant Cho was roaring in anger, whipping the jeep, zigzagging it down the empty street, then screaming to me, "Grenades! Grenades! In the toolbox! Grenades!" I tore into the toolbox and there were hand grenades, four of them, wrapped in a greasy cloth, and I took them out of the rag, grabbed one and pulled off the safety pin, not really knowing what I would do, what I could do with the grenade at that second, when I heard the black sedan zooming out from behind us, and Colonel Min, pushing me down flat in the back, rammed the submachine gun between me and Lieutenant Cho, blasting away. And I saw Lieutenant Cho jerk up, then crumple down on the steering wheel, and the jeep ran wildly to the right and to the left, and Lieutenant Cho pulled himself up and he swung the jeep to the right toward the side of the street, braking it hard, when the black sedan, pulling ahead of us, let loose a long burst of submachine-gun fire — there were two guns, two men firing — and it stopped about twenty-five, thirty yards from us, spewing out black smoke and billowing clouds of dust. Our jeep came to a crashing halt on the sidewalk that was fenced by a long, low wall of stones. Colonel Min leaped out, pulling my arm behind him and I was screaming, "Lieutenant Cho! Get out! Get out!" And Colonel Min cried, "He's dead!" We got down on the ground, flat against the right front fender of the riddled jeep and I was still gripping the hand grenade and I saw three men in dark green Army fatigues, all wearing sunglasses, running out of the black sedan, and Colonel Min was firing short bursts from his submachine gun. I crawled back into the jeep, on top of Lieutenant Cho's bloody, limp body — his face was shot out — and bullets were crashing into the windshield and I grabbed two hand grenades in my left hand, and Colonel Min was calmly whispering to me to get another magazine for the submachine gun from the back seat and I crawled back out of the jeep, having tossed a magazine to Colonel Min, who was now firing his revolver. The three men were firing at us from behind the black sedan and I threw the hand grenade I had been gripping but it overshot and burst into the air behind them, but it gave Colonel Min a second to reload his submachine gun, which he began firing away again, and it was then that I saw he had been hit and his left shoulder was bleeding, a dark, wet stain of blood drenching his jacket, and he was also bleeding in the right side. I threw another grenade and it hit the black sedan and blew it up and I threw another one and it landed just behind the black sedan and the black sedan jerked up and I saw one of them rolling out from behind the blown-up sedan. Colonel Min was standing up then, firing short, quick bursts and I saw another one of them — a body, which had stepped out from behind the sedan — lurch forward, then tumble backward, mowed down by Colonel Min's submachine gun. Colonel Min was stepping forward, and I flung myself into the jeep and grabbed the last of the hand grenades. I was standing up, too, pulling off the safety pin of the grenade, when the last of them, screaming and howling like a beast, ran out from behind the sedan, running toward us, firing a hand gun. Colonel Min was looking back at me for a split second, then he was raising the submachine gun as if ready to shoot the man down, then he suddenly dropped the submachine gun and it fell to the ground, clanging — and the man was still shooting and Colonel Min was just standing there, then he fell down on the street sideways, and the man, still howling and hissing like a crazed beast, pointed the gun toward me but I did not hear it go off and, in that split second, he looked at his gun and at me, and when he whipped around to run away, I dashed and bounded after him, screaming and howling and roaring like a beast, and I hit him with the hand grenade, flinging myself down flat on the hot, scalding, asphalt pavement and I heard the grenade's explosion and the whipping and whining of its fragments cutting and spinning through the sizzling air. The man was blown up to pieces, riddled and chopped by steel shrapnels from the grenade, his back torn off and hacked — dead, looking like a dirty, bloody pile of rotten meat. I staggered back to where Colonel Min lay bleeding and I collapsed beside him on my knees, my eyes blinded by the broiling, flashing sun and my stinging sweat.

Colonel Min was dead.

Chapter 23

The American driver, a short little man with dark sunglasses perched on his ruddy nose, parked the black Chevrolet sedan at the end of a runway in the American section of Kimpo air base. "We will wait here for a while, Major Lee." He shut off the engine, got out of the sedan, and opened the door for us. Chaplain Koh and I stepped out.

It was twenty minutes to three in the afternoon.

The sky was clear and azure blue without a trace of clouds in the distant sky over Seoul. A cool breeze drifted toward us from the waters of the Yellow Sea, soothing our faces glowing in the hot sun. Behind us, there were rows and rows of American jet fighters and bombers, their silvery bodies gleaming in the sunshine. Two jet fighters were circling overhead, gradually blending into the blue sky, then they disappeared toward the Capitol. At the other end of the long, straight runway, a medium-sized transport plane was being loaded with cargo.

Chaplain Koh, in khaki uniform, stood beside me on the grass along the runway, folding his arms across his chest. He was looking up at the wondrously serene sky. "Must you go?" he said quietly without looking at me.

I nodded.

He turned to me and gazed at me for a moment. "It is a strange fate," he said, "that, years ago, on the Tent Island in Pusan, I shared with you the memories of our mutual friend, and now, here, we share once again the memories of another friend."

"Yes. They are all dead."

"And here we are," he said, bowing his head. He looked up. "Must you really go? The others want you to stay, you know. Colonel Park, Colonel Son, Colonel Moon — and Colonel Kim, too. They all want you to stay and work with them. Work with me, Major. We must carry on, you know. We must carry on the task which men like Mr. Shin and Colonel Min have left behind."

I did not speak.

"You mustn't let yourself be overcome by your private grief, Major. Not at a time like this. We have work to do. Lots of work to do for our people and we will do it."

"I will come back, Chaplain," I said; I did not know what else I could tell him at that moment.

"Of course, you will come back," he said.

"This is what Colonel Min wanted me to do."

The chaplain looked at me. "Yes, I know."

"Then you do understand me, don't you, Chaplain," I said, "that I have to be alone with myself for a while?"

Without a word, he nodded.

"Before I can live and work for others," I was saying, "before I can die for others . . ."

"You must learn to live with yourself," he said quickly, placing his hand on my shoulder. "Yes, I know, I know. I can understand that. I, too, had to learn that. Many times in my life."

And I was muttering, "There is a riddle, Chaplain, a great riddle that Colonel Min has left behind for me. I have to learn to live with that, too."

Chaplain Koh frowned slightly, squinting his eyes in the sun. "Listen, Major. I don't really know what you mean by those words. Perhaps you are wondering why a man like Colonel Min — a good, courageous, just and honorable man like Colonel Min — had to meet with his death so absurdly."

His hand gripped my shoulder. "So absurdly!" he said. "At the moment when our coup was successful and our dreams and hopes became a reality, at the moment when there was so much a man like him could have accomplished for this country, he is killed by some bloody thugs sent by the loathsome, fanatical murderers and you live, and perhaps you are wondering why — why!"

I kept silent, looking at his old, wrinkled, tired face.

He went on. "I wish I could tell you and make you believe that God's will works in a mysterious way that we, mortals, shall never comprehend, Major. But you must believe that Colonel Min did not die in vain. Whether or not he ever knew, he was an instrument of God's justice, Major, and as such . . ."

"Please, Chaplain," I begged him. "Please, no more."

He dropped his hand and closed his eyes for a moment. "I understand, Major. I understand how you feel."

I faced him. "If you must know, Chaplain, I am not overcome by my private grief and sorrow. Do you know that? It is more than that, you see. Much more than that."

"Yes?"

"My nostalgia — you know. It is my nostalgia for something that I had once — or I had thought I had. You see, Chaplain? Something lost."

"Listen, Major, you must . . ."

I had not wanted to speak; I had not wanted to give in to my sentiment; and I had fought to control myself. But I could not restrain myself any longer; I had to pour out my words; I had to confess. I was blurting out, "A man can't go on living with his nostalgia alone, can he, Chaplain? Or — for his nostalgia alone? No, no, Chaplain! That would be like living with a shadow, a ghost. I must live with this world and for this world. Not for a world that I had once dreamed could get along without a man like Colonel Min. Don't you see, Chaplain? The world of mortal men like us

needs a man like Colonel Min, don't you see?" I stopped, turning
my face away from him. Had I been alone, I would have wept. A
man like Colonel Min — that terrifying and tragic reality in this
mad, maddening world — I had to accept that reality and learn to
live with it — to know that there was no room in this world for easy
despair — or easy denunciation. I turned around and looked at the
chaplain.

He was shaking his head. "You speak in riddles, Major."

I said — and I was smiling, my mind suddenly calm and peaceful, "Yes, Chaplain, but I have said enough."

He smiled, too. "Well, Major, whatever may be on your mind and
wherever you may be, I'll be praying for you."

I nodded.

"Remember this, Major, that God does not grant His blessing to
those who have not wrestled with their souls. So — may God bless
you, and we will meet again someday."

"Yes, Chaplain. We will meet again someday."

At the other end of the shimmering runway, the transport plane
began sputtering its engines. A small group of people were lined
up at the foot of a ladder, going aboard the plane.

The American driver, who had been sitting in the sedan smoking
a cigar, came toward us. "Guess they are ready to take off, Major
Lee."

We got into the sedan, and the American drove slowly down the
runway toward the transport plane.

Colonel McKay, in a light tan suit, was waiting for me. "Ready
to go, Major?"

"Yes. You are coming, too? I wasn't expecting you."

"I am coming along, Major. After all, I've promised Colonel Min
to look after you." He smiled, nodding to Chaplain Koh. "Well, we
are ready to take off anytime you are."

"I am ready," I said.

"All right. Let's go then." He waved to Chaplain Koh and started
up the ladder and disappeared into the plane.

An American Air Force corporal took my suitcase into the plane. The plane's engines were roaring now, coughing out black and white smoke.

I turned to Chaplain Koh. "Good-bye, Chaplain."

Without a word, he held my hands. His hands, holding mine gently, were old, wrinkled, and gnarled. His eyes were welling with tears. "May God bless you," he muttered.

I nodded and turned away and walked into the plane.

The plane was now circling over the sprawling city of Seoul, the capital, with its rocky, majestic mountains in the north and its dark green, meandering river in the south. Under the glowing afternoon sun, the city — with its millions of people, rich and poor, good and bad, happy and miserable, just and unjust — the city lay quiet and peaceful and dear to me.

Colonel McKay, who sat beside me looking out the window, said, slowly shaking his head, "It's a godforsaken crazy place but I love it, don't you?" There was gentleness and warmth in his voice that I had never sensed in him before.

And — perhaps — it was the way he had said his words; perhaps it was the way the city became smaller and smaller as the plane lumbered up in the blue sky toward the south. I turned my eyes away from the window, my heart pounding and aching — and I, in deep shame and sorrow, buried my face in my hands, offering my silent dirge for the dead — and for my nostalgia.

But — all this, too, is by the way.

I was still very young when I left the country.

THE INNOCENT